SPECIAL MESSAGE TO READERS

Anne Perry is a *New York Times* bestselling author noted for her memorable characters, historical accuracy and exploration of social and ethical issues. Her two series, one featuring Inspector Thomas Pitt and one featuring Inspector William Monk, have been published in multiple languages. She has also published a successful series based around World War One and the Reavley family. Anne Perry was selected by *The Times* as one of the twentieth century's '100 Masters of Crime'.

You can discover more about the author at www.anneperry.co.uk

TWENTY-ONE DAYS

1910: Sir Thomas Pitt's son Daniel is in the middle of his first case as a barrister when he is summoned to the Old Bailey for an important trial. Renowned biographer Russell Graves is charged with the brutal murder of his wife, and Daniel must assist in his defence. When the jury finds the accused guilty, Graves insists he has been framed. He is writing a shocking exposé of a powerful figure, revealing state secrets so damning that someone might well have wanted to silence him. And so, with the help of some eccentric new acquaintances who don't mind bending the rules, and the reputations of those closest to him at stake, Daniel has twenty-one days to uncover the truth and ensure that an innocent man isn't sent to the gallows . . .

ANNE PERRY

TWENTY-ONE DAYS

Complete and Unabridged

CHARNWOOD
Leicester

First published in Great Britain in 2017 by
Headline Publishing Group
London

First Charnwood Edition
published 2019
by arrangement with
Headline Publishing Group
An Hachette UK Company
London

The moral right of the author has been asserted

All characters in this publication — other than the obvious historical figures — are fictitious and any resemblance to real persons, living or dead, is purely coincidental.

A catalogue record for this book is available from the British Library.

ISBN 978–1–4448–4286–9

Published by
F. A. Thorpe (Publishing)
Anstey, Leicestershire

Set by Words & Graphics Ltd.
Anstey, Leicestershire
Printed and bound in Great Britain by
T. J. International Ltd., Padstow, Cornwall

This book is printed on acid-free paper

To Aviva Layton, in friendship

List of Characters

Daniel Pitt, a recently qualified barrister
Roman Blackwell, a private enquiry agent and
    ex-policeman
Sir Thomas Pitt, Daniel's father, head of Special
    Branch
Charlotte, Lady Pitt, Daniel's mother
Jemima, Daniel's sister, a mother of two girls
    who now lives in New York
Douglas Sefton, an experienced barrister
Oscar Park, the main witness against Roman
    Blackwell
Mercedes Blackwell, Roman Blackwell's mother
Marcus fford Croft, head of fford Croft and
    Gibson
Miriam fford Croft, his daughter
Apperly, a clerk at fford Croft and Gibson
Dunham, a junior barrister at fford Croft and
    Gibson, injured in a motor accident
Toby Kitteridge, a senior barrister at fford Croft
    and Gibson
Mrs Portiscale, Daniel's landlady
Dr Octavius Ottershaw, a fingerprint expert
Major Lydden, a prosecution witness
Russell Graves, a biographer, charged with kill-
    ing his wife
Ebony Graves, his dead wife
Sarah Graves, his daughter
Arthur Graves, his son

Alister Tranmere, King's Counsel, prosecuting the
    Graves case
Impney, chief clerk at fford Croft and Gibson
Falthorne, Graves' butler
Mrs Warlaby, Graves' housekeeper
Mrs Hanslope, Graves' cook
Salcombe, an elderly gardener at Graves' house
Miss Purbright, Ebony's lady's maid
Joe, the bootboy at Graves' house
Bessie, kitchen maid at Graves' house
Maisie, housemaid at Graves' house
Yeats, the Pitts' manservant
Membury, the fford Crofts' butler
Winifred Graves, Russell Graves' first wife
Mrs Wilson, a trusted ally of Ebony's
Grisewood, a barrister
Dr French, a police surgeon

1

They were alone in the small room where the accused was allowed to be visited by his lawyer.

'They'll hang me, won't they?' Roman Blackwell's soft voice was almost steady, but Daniel could see the fear in his eyes. What should he say? He had been dreading this moment all day. The trial was going badly and Daniel was hardly a year qualified to practise at the bar, let alone to defend a man on trial for his life.

But how could he have refused? Daniel's father, Sir Thomas Pitt, had asked the head of the law firm if he would allow Daniel to take the case. Blackwell was a private enquiry agent and something of an adventurer. Perhaps some of his cases were dubious, his clients not always the obviously innocent.

Blackwell had been a policeman at the time when Pitt was at Bow Street, long before he had joined Special Branch. He had liked Blackwell, understood not only his sense of humour, but his individual morality. Pitt had saved Blackwell more than once from the consequences of his more quixotic and irregular actions. Blackwell had, on occasion, saved Pitt, too. But the time finally came when Pitt begged Blackwell to leave the police before he made a mistake from which he could not escape. Reluctantly, Blackwell had taken his advice.

Pitt had never forgotten their friendship, and

now that Blackwell had fallen seriously afoul of the law, the best Pitt could do for him was to ask Daniel to represent him in court.

Daniel could not refuse. He, too, liked Blackwell, probably for all the same reasons that his father did: his wry humour, his optimism and his imagination.

Daniel frankly found the law far more tedious than he had expected to. The study of it had been interesting at university, but the actuality involved mountains of detailed paperwork. There was nothing glamorous in it, none of the crusading activity he had hoped for.

He was a novice, feeling his inexperience with some pain. He was up against Douglas Sefton, who was skilled, articulate and determined at this, his fifth attempt, finally to convict Roman Blackwell for something, this time for murder.

Blackwell was watching Daniel, waiting for him to answer. He would recognise a lie if he heard one. And what was the use of Daniel lying anyway? Blackwell would only resent it.

'Yes,' Daniel replied very quietly. 'Which is why we have to prove you did not kill John Hinton.'

'Reasonable doubt?' Blackwell tried to put hope in his voice, but for once the charm and the music in it did not work.

'We're beyond reasonable,' Daniel answered as gently as he could. 'They'll need very strong doubt indeed, and someone the jury can believe is guilty, if you aren't.'

'I'm not!' Blackwell's voice cracked. The desperation was there for only an instant, but it was unmistakable. 'I never even touched the gun!'

'Neither did anyone else, according to the fingerprints — '

'What fingerprints?' Blackwell heatedly demanded. 'There were none!'

'Somebody fired it,' Daniel pointed out.

'Gloves on?' Blackwell asked with sudden light in his face. 'That means somebody who knew about fingerprints, and that everyone's are different!'

'The Chinese have known about them for centuries,' Daniel told him. It was a piece of information he found particularly interesting. It was just five years ago — actually, in 1905 — that fingerprints had first been used to identify two murderers and convict them in a British court.

'If you didn't kill him, someone else did. There's no question Hinton was shot — deliberately. And unfortunately, there is no doubt that you knew him well, and quarrelled over a debt . . . '

'Only a few pounds!' Blackwell said indignantly. 'I'm not going to kill a man over a few quid!'

'Park says it was four hundred,' Daniel pointed out. 'That's a lot of money.'

'So it is,' Blackwell agreed. 'And I'm going to lend that much to a chancer like Hinton? I'm not a complete fool!'

Daniel smiled bleakly. 'You're generous occasionally, Roman. And — '

'Not that generous!' Blackwell said incredulously.

' — and known to drink a little too freely, and then forget what you've done?' Daniel finished.

'I never forget money,' Blackwell said fiercely. 'Not that much!'

'Not even when you are . . . ' he hesitated, then went on, ' . . . thoroughly drunk?'

'I couldn't even if I wished to,' Blackwell shook his head. 'I haven't got that much . . . at least I hadn't then.'

'Can you prove that?' Daniel knew he couldn't. There was no way he could do so.

'I didn't kill him,' Blackwell repeated desperately. His face puckered at the unreasonableness of it. 'Why would I lend that kind of money to a useless article like Hinton? It makes no sense.'

'They'll say you were drunk at the time,' Daniel replied reasonably. 'Look, Roman, there's no point in arguing something we can't prove.' He leaned forward a little over the table between them. 'The only way to change the jury's minds is to make them seriously consider somebody else. If Hinton were not as useless as the prosecution say, he will have had other enemies. Think carefully. Who were they, and why? Think of people he cheated, lied to, or lied about. People he got into trouble. People he could have been a witness against.'

Blackwell thought hard. He was a big man, not tall, but broad and strong, with a shock of jet-black hair. Only lately, he seemed to have shrunk into himself, as if he would retreat without actually moving from the hard wooden chair.

Daniel searched for something to encourage

Blackwell with, not only for kindness' sake, but because Blackwell was the only source of any information that could implicate anyone else, or at least provide Daniel with another course to follow.

Blackwell looked up hopelessly.

Oscar Park was the main witness against Blackwell, and Daniel had not made a dent in his testimony yet. He felt he was clutching at straws. 'Well then, what can we find out about Park to make the jury doubt him? Hinton owed you money; he's no use to you dead.'

'He's no use alive, either,' Blackwell said with a wry smile. 'Do you think that counts?'

Daniel was too desperate to return the smile. 'If Park is lying on the witness stand, why? It's a big risk he's taking. There must be a reason, and we've got to find it.'

'I don't know,' Blackwell said wearily. 'I never did him any harm.'

Daniel leaned forward a little. 'It doesn't have to be as direct as that. Come on! You've got enough imagination to see the oblique. What do we know as fact? You didn't lend Hinton four hundred pounds, whether he paid it back or not. How would Park know, anyway? That's the price of a small house. Did he owe it to Park?'

'Maybe. Park was tight,' Blackwell responded. 'I once lent him fifty pounds, and he never paid me back.'

'That could be something. I wonder if he owed anyone else? Who else can I call? I've got to have something to build on!' He heard the sharpness in his own voice. He must control it.

Blackwell said nothing.

Daniel racked his mind for anything that made sense. 'Then revenge? Does Park hate you? Have you done something to him?'

'No, but I'd like to,' Blackwell replied with feeling. 'The bastard. After the money I've lent him.' His expression was screwed up with the injustice of it.

But Daniel was concentrating on the evidence. He reached across the table and gripped Blackwell's wrist. 'He owes you money and he's repaying you like this? It's more than ingratitude, Roman.'

'It wasn't only the money,' Blackwell said quickly, shaking his head a little.

'But it was something. You said, 'It wasn't only the money,' ' Daniel insisted.

'You can't mention it in court,' Blackwell said with a flash of self-mockery. 'It was just a little against the law. Fine line, but the wrong side of it — definitely. If it comes out they'll can me for that, too, while they've got the chance.'

Daniel wondered for a moment if he should press the issue further.

'Don't,' Blackwell said, reading his mind. 'You don't want to know. Just a little document with a . . . questionable signature.'

'Does Park know of this?' Daniel said quickly. When Blackwell looked chagrined, Daniel realised it was Park for whom he'd forged a document. 'So that might give him a reason to damage you,' Daniel said eagerly. At last he might be on to something.

Blackwell's eyebrows rose high. 'I did him a favour.'

6

'He incurred a debt. He either can't pay it, or doesn't want to.'

'How old are you?'

'Twenty-five.'

'And so cynical!' Blackwell sighed.

'It comes from being a lawyer. What was the favour?'

Blackwell was silent for several moments.

Daniel tightened his grip on Blackwell's wrist 'Roman — we haven't got time to spare. They'll be coming for us any moment now. What did you do for Park that he can't afford to repay you?'

'I told you — I've got no proof!' Blackwell repeated.

'He doesn't know that. Come on!' Daniel said sharply 'Details . . . '

Blackwell remained silent.

'You asked me if they would hang you,' Daniel said between his teeth, hating the sound of his voice. 'Yes, they will! And once the verdict is in, it's hell's own job to change it!'

'All right! I wrote up some documents for him . . . once. And a letter to recommend him. It was — inventive.' Blackwell wrinkled his nose. 'Do I need to spell it out for you?'

'Why was that so bad? What did you say that wasn't true?' Daniel asked.

'That he was honest, and had a position of trust in a company doing business abroad.'

'And he hadn't?'

'No such company. I signed a dead man's name.'

Blackwell looked rueful. 'Does he still have the position?'

7

'Yes. On the strength of that letter.'

'And has he abused that position?' Daniel already knew the answer. It was written on Blackwell's face, the pride and shame at the same time.

'But the owners don't know yet, and if I speak now, somebody else will get the blame,' he answered.

'And if I don't call him into question, somebody else will get the blame for killing Hinton: you will!'

Before Blackwell could reply, the door swung open. A remarkably handsome woman stood on the threshold. She was of less than average height, and time had added to her magnificent bosom and a certain amount to her hips. Her black hair was wound thickly at the back of her head, made the more striking by a streak of white at the front. Her olive skin was flushed with exertion, and probably temper, and her eyes flashed black fire.

She ignored Blackwell and looked straight at Daniel.

'You'd better do something, young man! I'm not paying you to be charming. If charm would work, I could do it myself!'

Daniel rose to his feet. 'Mrs Blackwell . . . ' he began.

'Call me Mercy.'

'Mercy.' It was not a plea for clemency, it was an abbreviation of her name, Mercedes. She was Blackwell's mother, and it was she who had engaged Daniel's services, to the very mixed feelings of Mr fford Croft, head of the firm fford Croft and Gibson.

8

She closed the door behind her and came over to stand next to the table. Roman rose also, but she did not accept the chair offered to her. She was not going to accept courtesy or excuses.

'Well? What are you going to do? How are you going to attack these miserable creatures?' She did not need to explain herself. The brief adjournment for luncheon had come during the testimony of Park.

Before Blackwell could answer, and express his desperation, Daniel spoke.

'We are going to attack, Mrs Blackwell . . . '

'Good.' she said. 'Who?'

'The man whose evidence is the most important, and who has every reason to lie,' Daniel replied, trying to sound confident.

She gave a little grunt of agreement, but her eyes were cautious. She was going to need proof before she dared to hope.

Daniel knew what she was waiting for. He took a deep breath. 'Park. He's vulnerable, and now I know how,' he answered.

She nodded slowly. Had they been alone, he was sure she would have demanded to know the details, but one quick glance at Roman told her how desperate he was, and how close to despair. Daniel knew that she would not have spared him anything. He was used to their banter, and he saw, beneath the mock fights, and the fierce arguments, that her long and deep loyalty was unquestioning and unshakeable. She would criticise her son in all sorts of ways, even slap him if tried sorely enough, but let anyone else find fault with him, and they would rue the day.

Before Daniel could explain himself any further, he was saved by the warder returning and telling him the luncheon adjournment was over. He was taking Roman back to the dock, where the accused sat throughout the trial. Daniel would go to the place in the courtroom he thought of as the arena. Mercedes Blackwell would go to sit in the public gallery.

As soon as Roman and the warder were gone, she turned to Daniel, her black eyes relentless.

'Have you really got a plan, young man?' she said. Her eyes seemed to burn a hole through his head, as if she could read his mind.

He thought it was her way of hiding how afraid she was. He had a mother, too, one who could be formidable if she wished to be. He had worked at least twenty of his twenty-five years at standing up to her. He also had an elder sister, Jemima, who had given as good as she got throughout their childhoods. So he was well accustomed to fierce women.

'Yes, I think Park may well have killed Hinton himself. I intend to make the jury very well aware of why he would do that and then try to see Roman suffer for it. In fact, the more I think of it, the more it seems a reasonable alternative. That's all we need: someone else to be believed guilty.' He spoke with a confidence he did not feel, but he would make himself feel it by the time he stood up in front of the jury.

He smiled, and offered her his arm.

She hesitated for a long moment, then she took it. Her acceptance of him was conditional upon his success, he knew that. But for the moment, she was giving him her trust.

He could not afford to think of failing. He forced the possibility of it out of his mind and walked into the hallway, across the paved floor, and into the court exactly as if he knew he was going to win. He must conduct himself so that Park knew that, too.

Oscar Park stood in the witness box, well above the other people in the court. He was a tall man, smartly dressed. The height of the box above the floor, up its own set of steps, made him even more imposing. Daniel preferred to use, in his own mind, the word *exposed*. Perhaps *vulnerable* would be too much?

'Mr Park,' he began, 'you say that the accused, Mr Blackwell, lent the victim, Mr Hinton, a very large sum of money.'

Park nodded. 'Yes. On the surface, it looked generous — even extravagant.' He was very calm. He looked down on Daniel benignly. Did he know how young he was? How very inexperienced?

'Did it surprise you?' Daniel asked. He must establish a trust with Park, if possible. Certainly, he must with the jury. They were the ones who mattered.

'Yes. Frankly, it did,' Park answered. 'I didn't take Blackwell for such a fool.'

'You knew Hinton well enough to distrust him?' Daniel asked innocently.

Park tried to look modest, and failed. 'I'm a pretty good judge of a man, if I say so as shouldn't.' He smirked very slightly.

'You were right about Hinton? That he was a

small-time moneylender who took too many chances?'

'Yes. Facts have proved me so,' Park agreed.

'But wrong about Blackwell?'

Park looked irritated and it showed in two pink spots on his cheeks.

Daniel saw a flicker of amusement on the faces of two of the jurors.

'He seems to have lost his grip,' Park said tartly, putting one of his hands on the railing of the witness box.

'Agreed,' Daniel nodded and smiled. 'Losing your temper and shooting a man is no way to get your money back. It will go to his heirs now, won't it? When probate is granted of the estate, of course. However long that takes.' Daniel kept his face as sober as he could. 'I suppose Blackwell didn't take that into account.'

Park was irritated. 'He just made a bad judgement about Hinton.'

'And about shooting him, too?' Daniel observed wryly.

Mr Sefton, the prosecutor, rose to his feet wearily. 'My lord, the witness has already said he did not see that the accused was so dangerous. My *learned* — ' he gave the word a sarcastic edge — 'friend . . . is missing the point.'

'Yes, yes.' The judge raised his hand in an elegant gesture of dismissal. 'Mr Pitt, you appear to be questioning your own conclusions. Would you like to begin that train of thought again, with rather more guidance as to its destination?'

Daniel liked this judge, but he was wary of the edge of his tongue. 'Thank you, my lord,' he answered. His mind was racing. He was trying to establish Park's own debt to Blackwell, but he had to do it obliquely. 'Thank you,' he repeated.

He faced Park again. 'Would it be true to say you did not warn John Hinton of any danger from Mr Blackwell because you had no cause to believe there was any?'

'I thought I already said that,' Park replied, raising his eyebrows.

'Yes, you did,' Daniel smiled back at him. 'Even though Mr Hinton was deep in debt and had no way of repaying such an enormous sum.'

'I have said so,' Park shook his head.

'No danger, because Mr Blackwell was a man of considerable means, or so you believed, and great generosity.'

Sefton stood up again. 'My lord, the court grants that this witness did not judge Mr Blackwell's nature accurately. Mr Pitt is labouring the point to no purpose. I am sure Mr Park regrets that he did not warn Mr Hinton, but he is not at fault. The accused had given him no cause to think he would react violently, and self-destructively, towards him.' He looked as if his patience was worn thin by such time-wasting.

The judge looked mildly at Daniel. 'Mr Pitt, have you a point?'

'Yes, my lord,' Daniel said quickly. He had made the opening, now he must get this exactly right. 'I quite believe that Mr Park did not foresee such an extreme departure from Mr Blackwell's usual behaviour . . . '

'Then why belabour the point, sir?' Sefton demanded.

The judge stiffened. 'Mr Sefton, I will tell Mr Pitt what he may do. It is not your position.'

Sefton looked annoyed, but he apologised. He had no option.

'Thank you, my lord,' Daniel murmured. Then, before the judge lost patience completely, he continued, addressing Park, 'You had reason for your judgement, did you not?'

Park blinked. Then slowly, his expression changed as he realised he was caught in something of a dilemma.

'Sir . . . ?' Daniel did not let him have time to find a way out. 'You did not warn John Hinton of Mr Blackwell's temper, specifically in repayment of debt, because you yourself owed Mr Blackwell a considerable amount. Indeed, you still do! And yet you have not been shot — '

'That's a private matter between him and me!' Park said, swivelling to look at the judge, and then at Sefton. 'And it wasn't that much. If my debt to Blackwell added to his . . . his violence . . . I'm sorry. But how could I know?'

'Convenient, though, isn't it?' Daniel observed. 'If they hang him for killing Hinton, he can't come and collect from you.'

There was an uproar in the court. Now Park was leaning over the railing of the witness stand, face red with fury.

The jurors were looking at each other. One looked as if he were about to cheer.

Sefton was on his feet protesting.

Those in the public gallery were divided between outrage and hilarity.

The judge was demanding order in the court.

14

Daniel was very afraid he had gone too far.

It was at this point that he felt the tug on his sleeve, and he turned round and saw Apperly almost at his elbow. He was one of the clerks at fford Croft and Gibson, a man of indeterminate age and a sharper wit than most people gave him credit for. He looked untidy and out of breath as well, his frizzy hair all over the place. Right at this moment, he appeared profoundly unhappy. 'I'm sorry — ' he began.

Daniel cut him off. 'What? I'm in a mess, I know, but I'll resolve it. I had to — '

'You can't,' Apperly shook his head. 'Dunham has had a motor accident. He's rather badly hurt. Kitteridge is on a big case . . . '

Daniel was instantly sorry. 'Poor devil. How is he? Is he going to be all right?'

'Yes, yes, in time. A few weeks, or so. But he can't assist Mr Kitteridge now. And it is a very serious case . . . '

'I know,' Daniel agreed. 'Graves, or something like that. Murdered his wife.'

'Yes,' Apperly agreed. 'It's at the Old Bailey, and it's going badly.' He looked flushed and thoroughly miserable.

'Well, I'm sorry, but there's nothing I can do. If anybody can pull it off, it's Kitteridge.' That was true. He was the most gifted advocate in the firm, as he well knew and more than once had reminded Daniel. 'As you can see, my case is . . . on the brink of disaster.'

'All the same,' Apperly insisted. 'You've got to close it tonight, and then tomorrow go to the Old Bailey and take Dunham's place. Mr fford

Croft insists. I don't know why, but this case matters to him deeply.'

'Anyone could help Kitteridge,' Daniel whispered. 'He'll do it all himself anyway. Poor Dunham just sits there and looks obedient.'

Apperly shook his head. 'Mr fford Croft's orders. Be there tomorrow morning.'

'No.' Daniel heard his own voice and scarcely believed it. You did not defy Marcus fford Croft — well, not twice, anyway. 'I must finish this case . . . '

'Blackwell's a chancer,' Apperly said firmly. 'He couldn't get away with it for ever. It's not worth wrecking your career over.'

'I don't believe he's guilty,' Daniel insisted, aware that both Sefton and the judge were staring at him. 'But even if he is, he deserves a decent defence . . . and I gave my word. I'll come to the Old Bailey and fetch and carry for Kitteridge as soon as this case is closed.' He felt his chest so tight he could hardly breathe, and the sweat stood out on his skin. Was he throwing everything away? His father would not forgive him. No — that was not true. He would be disappointed, profoundly, but even more so if he walked away. His father had taken many risks himself and understood the value of a man's word.

The court was regaining order.

The judge was looking at Daniel with concern. 'Are you ready to proceed, Mr Pitt?'

'Yes, my lord. My company's legal clerk has just — '

Apperly stepped forward. 'Forgive me, my

lord.' He bowed his head, almost as if he were before royalty. 'One of our barristers has had a serious traffic accident, and Mr Pitt is required to take his place.'

'Now?' the judge said with heavy disapproval.

'No, my lord, tomorrow, early. I am informing him so that he can spend the night studying to catch up. I'm sorry, my lord. I did not realise I was interrupting.'

'You are not, Mr Apperly,' the judge said rather drily. 'The interruption preceded you by several minutes. And now that order is restored, with your permission, we will continue the case of the Crown versus Roman Blackwell, in the matter of the unfortunate shooting of John Hinton. You may continue, Mr Pitt. You have about half an hour before we adjourn for the day. Make the best use of it you can.'

Daniel gulped. 'Thank you, my lord. I would respectfully remind the court that the witness has admitted himself to having a considerable debt to Mr Blackwell, which he has not repaid; nor, as far as I know, is he in any position to do so. Therefore, I now suggest to the court that he is far from being as impartial in the matter as he has represented himself to be. I would like to exercise that doubt, my lord.'

The jury were all staring at him. They scented a fight at last.

2

Daniel spent the last moments of the afternoon eliciting the details of Park's debt. It was a frail thread to hang onto, but it was all he had.

He left the court with his mind in a whirl. The thought of assisting Toby Kitteridge, even if in name only, was both daunting and exciting. He did not like Kitteridge, who was approximately ten years older than Daniel and immeasurably more experienced. Kitteridge himself had made that advantage unpleasantly clear.

But it was an opportunity come far sooner than Daniel had expected. He might do nothing but run errands; however, he would sit beside Kitteridge in the Old Bailey, the central criminal court in London. Some of the most important cases in history had been decided there, beginning in 1585 with the medieval court.

He was so consumed in the thought he walked straight past his bus stop. He had to retrace his steps and wait for the next omnibus from Greenwich to his lodgings in James Street. It was not so very far away, but too far to travel on foot at the end of the day. He must find a way to help Roman Blackwell tomorrow morning. He had promised he would, and that was enough to hold him to the task. But he also knew no one else could do it this late in the trial. It was almost lost.

If only he could magnify the chink in Park's

armour and hope to raise some reasonable doubt. The more he thought about it, the more likely it seemed that Park himself, the chief witness against Blackwell, was the killer. But Daniel needed more than a slight possibility. Outwardly at least, Park was a respectable man.

So far, no question had been raised as to his honesty. It would be hard to introduce, unless he could be led into contradicting himself. The more he talked, the better chance Daniel would have of doing that.

He reached the bus stop again, and now the queue was lengthy! Three men were at the back of the line, two of them carrying briefcases, like himself, only theirs were not as new, nor as fine quality leather. Daniel's was his father's gift on gaining his degree, and carrying it still gave him pleasure, not only for itself, but remembering the look of pride in his father's face. He wanted very much to live up to that. The fact that his father said nothing to push him increased the unspoken hope all the more.

The men in front of him shifted their weight impatiently. One changed his briefcase from his left hand to his right, as if it were heavy.

Wasn't the bus ever coming? Had he just missed one?

He looked around the crowded street full of both motor vehicles and horse-drawn ones. He could not afford to make a habit of riding around in cabs. Very junior barristers, newly qualified, like himself, were paid little, and he refused to take an allowance from his father. He felt such a thing would place him under a moral obligation, not that his father would ever say so. There was a lot to be said for financial security, but just now there was even more to be said for freedom. It was a fine line.

He had half a day left in which to trip Park on his own words, and save Blackwell. It must be enough to turn the balance entirely the other way, against Park. What mattered to him? First of all, his own safety; second, money. It was money that had got him into this mess in the first place. And lies, of course.

Perhaps Daniel should ask a few more questions about who else owed money, and to whom? Among the men in the case, money seemed to form the basis of all the relationships. Daniel would go over all the papers he had and see what alternative ways there were to interpret them.

The bus finally came and he climbed on board. There was standing room only, but the passengers were wedged in too firmly to fall down, however much the bus lurched as they proceeded up Gray's Inn Road.

He got off at the other end of his journey, walked the few hundred yards and turned the corner into James Street where he had rooms. It was quiet and very clean. Most of the time, it was also warm. Mrs Portiscale, his landlady, fussed over him a bit. At times it was annoying, but on the whole, he appreciated it. Having grown up in a family, albeit a small one, he was used to company. Then he had gone up to university in Cambridge where there was always company, whether he wished it or not. But most of the time, he was glad of it.

He had imagined he would welcome the independence of his own lodgings, no one interrupting him to know this or that, and to ask his opinion about something. But occasionally it was lonely, and he would have welcomed the awareness of other people around him. Most of the men at his law firm were considerably older than he, and he was careful not to be seen to be closer to any particular one rather than another. There were undercurrents of alliances and rivalries, and Daniel knew that he could make serious errors with a single misjudgement.

It was warm inside the hallway and smelled pleasantly of lavender furniture polish.

'That you, Mr Pitt?' Mrs Portiscale's voice came from the kitchen at the far end of the passage. 'Like a cup of tea, dear? It'll be an hour before supper's ready.'

'Yes, please, Mrs Portiscale,' he called back. He never refused, because if he did she might stop asking. Besides, it was nice having someone welcome you back and take that little bit of care.

He sat in the front room, where residents met their visitors. Mrs Portiscale was very strict about not having young ladies go up into gentlemen's apartments. 'Of course, I trust you, dear,' she had said when he first moved in, 'but one rule for all, you know? That's fair.'

'How's your case going, dear?' she asked as she brought a small tray with a cup of piping hot tea and a couple of crisp biscuits. She knew he did not take sugar in his tea. In exchange for her extra attention, Daniel regaled her with accounts

21

of his cases, although only sharing those elements in the public domain. He had told her about odd witnesses, and jurors, without ever mentioning names. He was surprised how astute she was at seeing through pretence. She often made guesses that seemed at first to him preposterous, but that turned out to be accurate.

She stood there now in her dark skirt and plain white blouse, hands on her hips, ready for a conversation.

'Got to finish it up early as I can tomorrow,' he said with a smile. It was not that he felt cheerful about it, but he had learned he could get away with almost anything if he said it with a smile. He had a feeling that Mrs Portiscale saw through that, but she was almost his mother's age, though she had no sons of her own. 'Thank you for the tea, Mrs Portiscale.'

'You're welcome,' she said. 'Don't you stop up too late over your books, young man. You've got to get your sleep. Supper will be shepherd's pie, and will be served in about an hour.'

He gave her another smile, and sat back to think.

What was the evidence against Blackwell? He should divide it between the arguable and the unarguable. There was no time to waste on the latter.

Unarguably, Hinton had been shot sometime between nine and midnight five weeks ago. It had been with his own gun, and at his lodgings just off the Pentonville Road. The gun had no fingerprints on it.

Roman Blackwell was a student of life and

especially of its quirks. Unarguable was the fact that he had lent Hinton a very large sum of money and that Hinton had not repaid it, and indeed had not even paid interest on it.

Blackwell could not account for where he had been at the time of Hinton's death. His claim was that he had been hired, in his capacity as private enquiry agent, to follow a man suspected of extortion, but since he had taken some trouble to wear a disguise, no one could swear to having seen him.

Daniel finished his tea and carried his tray back to the kitchen, then went upstairs to reread all he had on the Blackwell case. He stopped for dinner, and resumed again.

At midnight, he was still reading, without finding anything useful. Finally, he put the last piece of paper back on the table. He hated letting Blackwell down, the more so because Blackwell had trusted him, even though Daniel had never before tried a case for anything bigger than petty theft. He was aware that Blackwell might know perfectly well how Daniel felt about being trusted, and used those emotions to make him take the case. He didn't believe Blackwell would manipulate him like that, but it had occurred to him. Blackwell was a master at reading people, and using them if he wanted to. His history was full of such incidents.

But there was no pretence in Blackwell's fear. His hanging, if it happened — and it would, if Daniel could not save him — would be very real indeed. Daniel felt ice cold at the thought of it, even in this warm room with its fireplace, bookcases, and polished wooden desk. One gaslight burned softly, shedding a yellow light. It was an old house. Generations of people had been comfortable here. The pictures on the wall were old, but pleasant. One day he must get around to bringing some of his own, something he really liked — beautiful, not just pretty. Bare trees in winter, perhaps? A ragged sky, wind-driven clouds — something that held his mind and stirred it, not merely was agreeable to the eye.

Think! No time to sleep.

He imagined Blackwell taking the gun and loading it. He went through the motions of it in his mind, opening the breach, picking up the shell, carefully placing it, then closing the chamber, and then wiping it clean to take off the marks of his fingers. You couldn't load a gun with gloves on: too clumsy, Perhaps you'd use a cotton cloth; better still, a leather chamois.

He froze. Had the killer remembered to wipe the cartridge case too? His fingermarks would be on that!

Ottershaw! The fingerprint expert who had examined the gun. Nice man. Clever. Surely, he had thought of that? Or had he even been given the shell casing? At the scene, the police had collected the evidence tied to the crime. Had they even thought of looking for the casing?

Daniel stood up. It was after midnight, but time was too short to wait until tomorrow. He put on his coat and went to the door. He must leave quietly, and not disturb the whole household, certainly not Mrs Portiscale. She would come down to enquire.

It took him nearly half an hour to get to Ottershaw's house, even though there was very little traffic on the road. And then he had to ring the bell three times before the door finally opened to show Ottershaw himself, in a dressing robe, blinking in the hall light, his hair standing in all directions.

'I'm sorry, Dr Ottershaw,' Daniel said, stepping inside and apologising again. 'I do know what time it is — but I have an idea, and Roman Blackwell's life might rest on it.'

'Really?' Ottershaw looked at him doubtfully. He was a tall, thin man, almost as tall as Daniel, and was wearing pyjamas and one slipper.

Daniel realised how foolish he would look if Ottershaw had thought of testing the shell casing. He was an expert, so probably he would have. Daniel had woken him at one o'clock in the morning for nothing.

'Well, what is it?' Ottershaw asked.

'I was thinking about loading a gun,' Daniel said, closing the front door behind him.

Ottershaw's eyebrows shot up. 'My dear boy, please . . . '

'No.' Daniel blushed at his clumsiness. 'I mean, what would you touch?'

'The butt, probably the trigger guard, probably the barrel. But there were no prints on any of them.'

'And the shell casing?'

'Ah! They only brought me the shell casing afterwards. Different young constable. I see what you mean.' His face was suddenly filled with enthusiasm. 'Quite possibly, the casing — in fact, for certain. If he did not wear gloves to handle the gun itself, then he would not to handle the shell. Awkward things, gloves, for fine work. I cannot even write my name legibly with gloves on.' He looked rueful. 'Or without, for that matter,' he added, backing into the hall and towards the stairs. 'Let me get dressed, and we will have a look. I work in my cellar, you know. I had it converted into my laboratory. Wonderful places, cellars. Nobody bothers you. Would offer you a cup of tea, but we must get to work, dear boy. Wouldn't actually know how to make one, and I'm not wakening the butler. Lives on the top floor, and sleeps like the dead. Just give me a few minutes.'

Actually, it took him ten minutes and he found Daniel still standing in the hall when he returned.

'Oh dear. Should have asked you to wait in the sitting room,' he said. 'But the fire is out anyway. Not really comfortable. Now come with me, and we'll see what we can find.'

He led the way to a cellar door, switched on an electric light, and led the way down the fairly steep steps.

Daniel followed, and was immediately in a different world. There were glass jars, tubes, and retorts everywhere. All kinds of instruments were laid out in cases. Bottles with carefully labelled substances made it for the moment look like a sweet shop. There were various pieces of equipment, most of which Daniel could not name. And in a wide space by itself, at the far end, a wood-burning, round-bellied stove. It still retained some heat and, although below ground, the room was neither chilly nor damp.

Ottershaw noticed Daniel's surprise. 'Ah!' he said with satisfaction. 'You took me for an eccentric, didn't you? Not at all. Most practical man. Science doesn't lie, we merely misunderstand her sometimes. We find what we expect to find, or worse still, what we want to.'

He led the way over to a filing cabinet, produced keys from his pocket, and opened the locked section. He withdrew a file, and from the bottom of the drawer a gun wrapped in muslin. 'See!' he said, like a conjurer about to begin a trick. 'We shall now examine the shell casing very carefully, and see what we have.' With that, he pulled on cotton gloves, removed the gun from its wrapping, along with the separately wrapped shell casing.

'What is the file?' Daniel asked.

'Why, a picture of the prints we took of Mr Blackwell, so we might compare them with the ones we were hoping to find on the gun, of course.'

'But we didn't find any,' Daniel pointed out.

Ottershaw gave a sharp, wry look. 'No, dear boy, and this is only of use to us if we find on the casing some that are not Mr Blackwell's. If, after all, we find some that are, it's a very different matter indeed. Now, are you sure you wish me to look?'

Daniel thought only for a moment. His decision would be irreversible, and he was gambling with Blackwell's life. If he was innocent, it was his only chance. If he was guilty, he was lost. If Daniel did nothing, it was time that he faced the fact that he could not save Blackwell. 'Yes,' he said. 'Better be damned for action than inaction.'

Ottershaw gave him a brief, tight smile, his face dramatically lit and appearing out of proportion in the fixed lamplight of the laboratory. Then he turned and began to work in absolute silence, except for the faint click of the metal, as he picked up the casing on a stick and wedged the end of the stick into a vice.

Daniel stared in fascination as Ottershaw opened a box of powder, dipped a brush into it, and then lightly dusted the shell casing, leaving a residue on it. He moved closer and drew in his breath sharply. There were tiny lines forming patterns on the surface of the metal.

Ottershaw breathed out slowly. It was only a faint sigh, but he was clearly on the brink of discovery. 'Not yet!' he warned. 'There are fingerprints, but whose?'

Daniel nearly answered, then realised that Ottershaw was talking to himself. The man's face was alive with the intensity of exploration. This was his art, his miracle.

Ottershaw ignored Daniel entirely now, absorbed in study through a magnifying glass.

Daniel held his breath.

'Possible . . . ' Ottershaw said at last. 'They are like Blackwell's, but there are differences. Yes, definite differences. See — here.' He moved back from the table, gesturing towards both the photographs of Blackwell's prints and the print on the casing. 'Look — there are whorls . . . ' He pointed with the tip of a small, sharp instrument. 'Look.'

Daniel peered at it and saw fine lines in almost a circle.

'See?' Ottershaw urged.

'Yes.'

'And those are Blackwell's that we took before. See where the thumbs are almost the same?'

'Yes . . .'

'Now look at these.' Ottershaw pointed to the casing and a break in the lines below the whorl. Only a print of a thumb was there, but the lines were at a different angle, and there was a brief break in them: islands. Different! They were not made from the same thumb. He indicated the photograph of the right thumb, and then pointed to another photo. 'Isn't the left thumb either,' he said with conviction. 'Of course, we don't know whose it was. Doesn't matter for this trial if we did. This is cause only for reasonable doubt.' He looked at Daniel carefully, to be sure he understood.

'Of course,' Daniel agreed, but he now had proof that Blackwell was not the murderer.

Ottershaw shook his head. 'Lot to learn, dear boy. Jurors are twelve ordinary people, not twelve enthusiasts for new adventures of the mind. Sitting still all day trying to concentrate on the arguments going on in front of them is enough adventure for most. They believe what they can understand. Trust me, I've tried to explain some finer points of science, and I might as well have saved my breath to cool my porridge. You've not only got to be right, you've got to be better than the other man. And Sefton is no fool. I know him. He'll try to make them think your chap's a trickster, a fraud. And that you are naïve. You won't win them over just with facts.' He shook his head as if he had said this many times before, but to no effect.

Daniel felt suddenly deflated. 'But you can see that that is not Blackwell's thumbprint!' he exclaimed.

'You can see that,' Ottershaw agreed. 'But if I don't want to believe that, then I won't.'

'Yes, you will,' Daniel contradicted immediately.

Ottershaw smiled widely. 'Yes,' he conceded. 'I will. Because Blackwell is a rogue, but I don't think he's a killer. And I'd like you to win. I like you. You're the future, open-minded, willing to learn, eager, and with sense to listen to what you're told — most of the time. But that isn't enough to win.'

Daniel was deflated. 'Then what is?'

'Make them want to believe you, and then show them why they should. They'll do it then, and Sefton won't argue them out of it.'

'But I've only got half a day!'

Ottershaw's eyes were bright. 'Then you'll have to be quick!'

'We both will,' Daniel assured him. 'I'm going to call you as a witness. I need an expert to swear to all of this. We haven't needed you before because there were no fingerprints.'

Ottershaw's face shone. 'Good. Should we have a cup of tea?'

'What?' Daniel was caught on the wrong foot.

'Do you want a cup of tea? I'm not working all night without a cup of tea and a piece of cake!'

'Oh — yes. Yes, please.' Daniel had not realised how much he would like that. 'Would you like me to make it?'

'Good idea. Then get ready to work, my boy. We've a lot to do. But we'll start by establishing the ground rules, eh?' He looked steadily at Daniel.

'Yes . . . '

'Good. They are simple. I'll do as you say, as to the law. You do as I say, as to science — and human nature.'

'I've — '

'You're agreed. Excellent.'

Daniel had been about to argue the point, but he looked at Ottershaw again and changed his mind. 'Yes, sir.'

Ottershaw waited.

'Yes, sir,' Daniel reaffirmed.

'Now, about that tea . . . '

★ ★ ★

Daniel slept on Ottershaw's sofa for a couple of hours, then rose and washed. He borrowed Ottershaw's razor at risk of cutting his throat; he had never used an open blade before. He borrowed a comb to make his unruly brown hair lie reasonably flat.

He then carefully packed the gun Ottershaw had lent him for the demonstration he planned in the courtroom.

After a hasty breakfast of porridge, they set

31

out for the courthouse. Ottershaw at least had a reasonable spring in his step. He did not know Blackwell enough to care deeply about saving his life. Daniel, on the other hand, knew both Blackwell and Mercy, even if he had met them only recently. He cared very much, not just that Blackwell might lose his life, and Mercy lose all that she cared about most, but also because they trusted Daniel to help them, whether it was a tactic to engage him or not. Although it might have begun that way, now it was real.

The trial began very much as it had adjourned the day before: the gallery was packed, the jurors expectant, and Sefton looked confident and very nearly triumphant. He could already smell the delicious aroma of victory, and the dish was set before him.

'Mr Pitt?' the judge said with his eyebrows raised.

'Yes, my lord.' Daniel rose to his feet. 'I call the only witness for the defence: Dr Octavius Ottershaw.'

Sefton rose immediately. 'My lord, Dr Ottershaw is well known to the court. He is a fingerprint expert. Possibly the best. We hardly need his expertise to tell us that there are no fingerprints on the gun that was used to murder Hinton.'

The judge looked at Daniel. 'I do hope this is not a diversionary tactic of desperation, Mr Pitt?'

'No, my lord. Far from it,' Daniel responded immediately.

'Then proceed. And please hold your remarks, Mr Sefton. I will not hang a man before I have heard his defence. Is that understood?'

'Yes, my lord,' Sefton said, with strained temper showing through his acquiescence.

Daniel called Ottershaw, who took the stand and swore to his name, place of residence, and some brief but impressive qualifications.

'Dr Ottershaw,' Daniel began, very aware that he must hold the jury's attention with every word he said. They were already convinced that Black-well was guilty, for which he could hardly blame them. They did not want to hear explanations, and above all they did not want to hear excuses. Sefton was aware of that and would play to it the instant he saw the opportunity. 'Are you quite sure all people's fingerprints are different?' Daniel asked innocently. He must keep it brief.

'Yes, sir, quite sure,' Ottershaw replied. Then he turned to the jury. 'You, sir,' he looked at a large, impressive man, very well dressed. It was easy to imagine he had a good opinion of himself. 'Your fingerprints are unique to you. They are not exactly the same as those of any other man on earth.'

The juror took it as a compliment, and it showed in his face.

'It matters,' Ottershaw continued. 'The whorls, the ridges, the islands, features and dimensions in the lines you can barely see with the naked eye, they are unique to you. More so even than your signature. I am sure you have seen many signatures that are illegible? Of course. Mine usually is, especially if I have been writing all day. But my fingerprints are always the same.' He produced a card about four inches square. 'May

I, my lord?' he asked, and assuming permission, he showed it to the juror. 'If you touch it, grasp it, you will leave your prints on it as well. Please . . .'

The juror took it, all the time watching Ottershaw's face. Then he looked at the card, and saw nothing.

Ottershaw held out his hand, and received the card back.

He drew a small brush out of his pocket and ran it over the card. A luminous smile lit up his face. 'There! You see?' He handed the card back to the juror.

The juror took it and his face too lit with delight. 'Those are mine?'

'Indeed, sir, they are. And no other man on earth, or woman either, can produce exactly those. You see that whorl in the centre? And the tiny islands? But I must proceed. Let me show you how this is relevant to the case on which you are required to render your verdict,' he hurried on. He turned and walked over to Daniel.

'Defence exhibit,' Daniel said loudly, handing Ottershaw one of the papers they had prepared during the night.

Ottershaw took it and walked over to the jury.

Daniel handed a copy to Sefton, who took it at first with interest, then seeing what it was, put it down again. 'My lord, this is a set of fingerprints unidentified, and therefore signifying nothing. And in case my . . . learned . . . friend has forgotten, no prints whatsoever were found on the gun. That has already been testified to. Mr Pitt is wasting the court's valuable time.'

'A man is fighting for his life, Mr Sefton,' the

judge said patiently. 'Allow Mr Pitt to make his point, if he has one. If he does not, I promise you I will stop him. Proceed, Dr Ottershaw.'

'Thank you, my lord,' Ottershaw replied politely. Then, as he passed twelve copies of the paper first to the judge, who then gave them to the clerk to pass them to the jury, his voice gathered enthusiasm. 'If you gentlemen would be good enough? You see many prints in front of you. Some are similar, some are utterly different, no two are identical. The differences may be small, but they are visible. Some are of a whole section of a finger or thumb, others are only part of a finger, as a man might leave on an object he had touched with the purpose of using it.'

Daniel looked at the faces of the jurors. They were fascinated. They wanted to be unique! They were ordinary enough men; it pleased them to think they were each unlike anyone else, as he knew Ottershaw was well aware.

The jurors were still sitting with their heads bent when Ottershaw continued. 'If you were to touch anything with your bare hands, and that thing had a clean, flat surface, you would leave fingerprints upon it. This was known to the person who shot Mr Hinton, because all such marks were removed — or else he wore gloves. With Mr Pitt's permission, I will show you what I mean . . . '

Sefton could not be silent any longer. 'My lord, it is perfectly clear what Dr Ottershaw means. And it is a waste of time, a diversion. There were no fingerprints on the gun! I have never argued that point. There is no purpose to this at all!'

At last, Daniel rose to his feet. 'There is a purpose, my lord. If I may demonstrate to the court for those who are unfamiliar with guns, just how you load a gun. If you will permit me to, I will be brief.' It was only half a question, As he spoke, he picked up the gun he had brought with him. It was not the weapon used to kill Hinton, but one exactly like it.

Daniel turned to the jury, holding the gun high, where they would all see it. Slowly, he opened the chamber, picked up the shells that lay on the table in front of him, loaded the gun, and closed it. He passed it to Ottershaw.

Ottershaw dusted it with a light powder in all the places where Daniel had touched it, and blew away the surplus. He was smiling.

'So? What is the purpose of that?' Sefton demanded. 'Why don't you polish it with a cloth, and then you will have nothing! And be precisely where, in fact, we are!' He pulled his handkerchief out of his pocket and offered it to Ottershaw.

'Thank you,' Ottershaw said. But instead of taking the handkerchief, he gave Sefton the gun.

Sefton took it and wiped it off, smiling. 'Satisfied?'

'Yes . . . yes, indeed,' Ottershaw said with an even wider smile. 'Didn't you forget something?'

Slowly, the look of satisfaction on Sefton's face slipped away. 'What?'

There was absolute silence in the courtroom.

'You forgot the shell casing,' Daniel answered

for Ottershaw. 'If you had loaded the gun, your fingerprint would be on the shell casing.'

There was a rustling of movement in the gallery. Sefton looked shocked. The jurors' attention was total. The judge leaned forward and spoke to Daniel. 'Mr Pitt, do you still have the shell casing from the crime, and are there fingerprints on it which are provably not those of Mr Blackwell?'

'Yes, my lord. We shall require your permission to take the prints of Mr Park, and anyone else we may reasonably suspect, but they are provably not those of Mr Blackwell. And if someone other than Mr Blackwell loaded the gun, I respectfully submit to your lordship, and to the gentlemen of the jury, that we may conclude Mr Blackwell did not fire the gun either.'

'Indeed,' the judge agreed. 'That would seem the reasonable conclusion.'

Daniel breathed in deeply, and then again. 'My lord, since the prints on the shell casing are not those of Roman Blackwell, may I humbly request that the matter is now put to the jury? If the prints are those of someone else involved in the case, it may take a little while . . . ' He looked at Park in the gallery, and then away again. 'The police will then arrest that person, and there will be a new case for another jury to decide.'

He shifted his weight, and then wished he had not. It made him look impatient.

'You seem in a hurry, Mr Pitt,' the judge observed.

Should he tell the truth?

'I wish to see the case to its conclusion, my

37

lord. But one of the lawyers in my chambers has met with a rather serious accident, and I am ordered to appear in his place as soon as possible.'

'I believe you told us that yesterday,' the judge said soberly. 'When are you due to appear, and where, Mr Pitt?'

'The Old Bailey, my lord. This morning . . . '

'Indeed. How are they managing without you?'

Sefton gave a snort. The judge looked at him, and he looked away.

'Then you had better finish your argument, Mr Pitt, and hope the Old Bailey manages without you for a little longer. I imagine the jury will not keep us too long, but will hasten with their proceedings.'

'Yes, my lord, thank you,' Daniel said humbly.

★ ★ ★

Indeed, it was not long. The verdict was delivered before noon: a unanimous not guilty. Daniel stayed long enough to receive Blackwell's overwhelming gratitude, and Mercy's thanks almost to the point of tears, which infuriated her. But she had been badly frightened, and she knew how close she had come to losing the son she loved.

Sefton was generous about it, but it cost him dearly. For him, the matter was delayed, but far from finished.

Ottershaw had enjoyed himself enormously, and promised to take Daniel to the best luncheon he had had, at some time convenient to him.

Daniel raced out to catch a cab to the Old Bailey.

3

Daniel had been to the Old Bailey before. How could he resist it? But he had only been able to visit as a member of the general public. It was one of the most famous courts in the world, certainly within the British Empire. But this was an entirely different situation. He was probably not going to say anything, just do errands and take messages for Kitteridge. He would also be looking up legal references, and would have to be both quick and accurate. Kitteridge would tolerate no mistakes or delays.

Kitteridge was a gangly man, with a most unusual face and a curious taste in neckties, or cravats. He had once been a junior himself, and had worked hard to improve his standing in the firm. He deserved his position, he cherished it, and he believed that Daniel had to prove his worth before he could aspire to anything like it. Kitteridge's father had been a well-respected headmaster of one of the better private schools for boys, but he was very well aware that Pitt's father was Sir Thomas Pitt, the Head of Special Branch. Kitteridge felt Daniel had benefited from nepotism, and did not approve.

Daniel explained to the usher that he was assistant to Mr Kitteridge, counsel for the defence.

The usher looked him up and down with disfavour. 'You are very late, sir.'

Daniel wanted to tell him that he was fresh from achieving a seemingly impossible victory in another court. However, he saw in the man's eyes that no other court was worthy of mention, and instead merely apologised for his lateness.

The door opened for him and he was permitted into the packed courtroom.

He walked up the aisle between the rows of the crowded gallery, without once looking at the judge, and found his place in the front, beside Kitteridge. He slid into the seat silently.

'Pitt, where the hell have you been?' Kitteridge hissed at him. 'You'd better have a damned good excuse. If you slept in, I'll have your head on a plate. I don't care how late you were last night, or in whose bed you slept, you're not at university now. This is reality.' He turned away and studied the papers in front of him.

'I was in court, in Greenwich,' Daniel replied.

'For what? Drunk and disorderly?' Kitteridge asked with an edge to his voice.

'The trial was for murder,' Daniel answered.

Kitteridge swung around to look at him. 'What were you? A witness?'

'Appearing for the defence,' Daniel said.

'And what? You left the poor bastard to swing?' he said with incredulity.

'I got him off — with forensic evidence.' Daniel kept the smile from his face with difficulty. 'Reputation of the firm, and all that. As you constantly remind me.'

'We are waiting for you, Mr Kitteridge,' the judge interrupted sourly. 'May we take it that you have nothing to ask of this witness?'

Kitteridge rose to his feet, biting back his anger. 'As a matter of fact, my lord, I do. My assistant has only just arrived. He was held up by unforeseen circumstances.'

'Not another traffic accident, I hope,' the judge remarked with barely concealed sarcasm.

Kitteridge flushed, but he knew better than to antagonise the judge, or to attempt humour, although he was not without a sense of the ridiculous. 'No, my lord. I did not ask for details.'

'Very wise.' The judge gave Daniel a scorching look. 'Please proceed. If you need reminding, Mr Tranmere has just drawn from Major Lydden his professional opinion of the accused, and of the victim.'

'Yes, my lord. Thank you.' Kitteridge faced the grey-haired man standing to attention in the witness box. He was dressed in a perfectly ordinary suit, such as any gentleman of means might wear, but a regimental tie made it appear a uniform. 'Major Lydden, I believe you live less than half a mile from the home of Mr and Mrs Graves, and you were socially acquainted?'

'With Mr Graves, yes. Yes. Good historian. Accurate, you know, which very few are,' Lydden replied.

'Less so with Mrs Graves?'

'Do not speak ill of the dead. Don't you know that, young man?'

'You speak the truth in court, sir,' Kitteridge reminded him.

Lydden was unused to being corrected and he did not take it well. 'I know very little about her.

Women like that are a mystery to me. Plain man, and all that.'

Kitteridge was playing a losing hand, and he was only too aware of it. He tried another approach.

Daniel studied the jury. It was supposed to be a jury of one's peers. He knew nothing about Graves at all. There had been no time even to take a curious look at the notes last night. He was charged with killing his wife, that was all Daniel knew. And all London knew that!

What he did not know was what on earth Kitteridge was offering as a defence. To judge by the jurors' faces, it was not going over-well.

Kitteridge tried again. 'In fact, an officer in the Indian Army?' he said, looking impressed. 'A major?'

'Retired rank of major. Acting colonel, to be precise,' Lydden corrected him with quiet satisfaction.

'In command of an entire regiment of men?' Kitteridge asked with respect.

'Yes, sir.'

'A pretty good judge of men, then. Know who's capable of what, and who will stand their ground under fire, and all that?'

Lydden would rather have been stripped naked than deny such a thing. He stood even taller. 'Yes, sir. I believe so,' he replied.

Daniel hid a smile. Kitteridge had made a good opening. But what could he put into it?

Pretending to be searching for a piece of paper he had dropped, Daniel bent over. In straightening up, he glanced to his left, high up where the dock was, placed above the courtroom, and reached by a different stair. He looked steadily at the man sitting between the warders.

Russell Graves was a big man, at least average height, and solid. He was quite handsome, with hair greying at the sides, but still thick. He had a fleshy face; not coarse, but perhaps insensitive. But how could any man be looking his best in a hostile court that had accused him of murdering his wife? He did not look like a grieving widower, but then why should he show his feelings to a prurient and alien public?

Daniel brought his attention back to Kitteridge and Major Lydden. He was eliciting details of the kind of man Graves was, his place in the community.

'Excellent chap,' Lydden repeated. 'Quiet, Not one of those who arrives in a place and instantly expects to be taken notice of. Too many like that. Think they know better how to run a place than those of us who've lived there all our lives.'

Kitteridge drew everything he could out of Lydden's testimony; it proved nothing. He sat down at the end weary and, in spite of his best effort at courage, defeated.

* * *

They adjourned early that afternoon.

'You look asleep on your feet,' Kitteridge said testily to Daniel as they left the court. 'You are not much use to me like that. Would a meal put some stuffing into you?'

Daniel thought not. What he wanted was

about ten hours' sleep. 'Yes,' he said firmly. 'I got about two hours' sleep on Ottershaw's couch last night.'

'Who is Ottershaw?' Kitteridge asked, matching his stride to Daniel's as they went down Ludgate Hill towards one of the best pubs in London.

'Fingerprint expert,' Daniel replied.

'Won't need him for this.' Kitteridge shook his head. 'Do you know anything at all about this case?'

'Beyond the fact that Graves is charged with having killed his wife, no I don't.'

They turned into Fleet Street.

'We'll go to Ye Olde Cheshire Cheese. There are plenty of private corners there,' Kitteridge said.

Daniel looked sideways at him. He appeared tired and disappointed, the beginnings of defeat showing in the twist of his mouth. He was surprisingly vulnerable for one who usually seemed sure of himself, to the point of arrogance.

Kitteridge was losing the case, and he knew it. A defeat in front of Daniel was going to be doubly difficult for him to bear. He didn't lose often.

'Do you think Graves is innocent?' Daniel lengthened his stride to keep up.

'Not really,' Kitteridge admitted. 'I looked at the evidence and I don't think there's a cat in hell's chance. Then I look at the man, and something in me believes him — I think.' He sounded surprised at his own conclusion.

45

Daniel was still trying to think of a reply when they entered Ye Olde Cheshire Cheese.

Kitteridge held the door open for Daniel, and they found a quiet table. A waiter appeared immediately and welcomed Kitteridge by name. Daniel was determined not to show it, but he was impressed. He was also quite sure that Kitteridge intended him to be.

'I suppose I'd better catch you up,' Kitteridge said. 'Since you did not catch up last night, as I had hoped.'

Daniel was tempted to say that he had already gathered that Kitteridge was losing. Kitteridge was losing his temper in a way he had not seen before. Daniel had had that same feeling of near panic only yesterday, thinking he was going to let Blackwell down disastrously. Did Kitteridge care that Graves did not hang, or only that he, Kitteridge, did not lose?

'What is the evidence against him?' Daniel asked.

'It's all against him,' Kitteridge said with sudden bitterness. 'His wife's body was found in her bedroom, her skull cracked at the back, and a good deal of her face and upper body burned to the point of total disfigurement. It was appalling. There is no sign of anyone breaking in. No strangers seen by the resident staff, or by the daughter, Sarah, who is nineteen, or the son, Arthur, who is sixteen and an invalid.' He stopped abruptly, staring at Daniel, waiting for his reaction.

Daniel looked back at him, and saw distress in his face, imperfectly masked. No wonder Kitteridge was afraid he was going to lose; it seemed

46

impossible to win. 'Why did you take the case?' he asked. Kitteridge was ambitious, clever, self-assured. Everybody was vulnerable, but Kitteridge seldom showed it. Or perhaps Daniel was not wise enough yet to see beyond the surface.

'You wouldn't have?' Kitteridge asked curiously.

Daniel did not know the answer to that. He had taken on Blackwell's case because his father had asked him to. And he had immediately liked Blackwell personally. He liked his quick mind, his imagination, and his throwaway sense of humour. Blackwell was an adventurer, but he was not violent. He was a teller of tall stories, largely to entertain more than to deceive. He was generous, both with his means and with his judgements of others.

Kitteridge did not like Graves; that was apparent.

Now Kitteridge was waiting for a reply. 'Well?' he asked.

'I don't know. Why did you? Did you have no choice?'

'Well done!' Kitteridge acknowledged with sarcasm. 'How long did it take you to work that out?'

'I suppose I have no choice either,' Daniel replied.

'Not if you want to stay at fford Croft and Gibson and eventually prosper. One day, you could be in my position.' There was a slight twist in his lips as he smiled, his eyes studying Daniel carefully.

'When you are in Mr fford Croft's position.'

Daniel finished the thought for him.

'Precisely.'

'So, he asked you to take the case?'

'Right again.'

'Does he think Graves is innocent?'

'That is a very interesting question.' The light had gone from Kitteridge's face.

Daniel hesitated. Marcus fford Croft was a friend of Daniel's father, but in what circumstances he did not know. His mother was not acquainted with him, so it was not a social connection. The alternatives were numerous, and not all of them pleasant.

'He didn't say. I got the impression he didn't know, and didn't care,' Kitteridge replied. 'But I have no doubt he wants me to win.'

He did not need to add any more for Daniel to understand. The firm was small, but one of the most respected in London. Marcus fford Croft himself had been one of the best lawyers in the country, in his time. Now he was head of chambers, but no longer appeared in court. He was an inexhaustible mine of legal information, and he knew the secrets of three-quarters of London's rich, famous, and infamous aristocrats and thieves. His manner had always been eccentric, but now his memory was as well. He had handed over the litigation to a number of chosen rising stars. Kitteridge was a leader among them, but there were others, young gentlemen who had chosen to follow the law, with more or less skill. Time and hardship would determine the successes.

'Did he tell you anything about Graves?'

Daniel asked, since Kitteridge had offered nothing further.

'No,' Kitteridge said testily. 'Including why he took the case at all. But I have the feeling that it matters to him. He was not being bloody-minded to see what I would do.'

'You mean whether you would give it your best shot, fight to the bloody end?' He meant the *bloody* metaphorically. 'Rather than fight a losing cause gallantly, but give in once it looked hopeless?'

'You're learning,' Kitteridge said drily.

The waiter returned with the menu. Kitteridge took his and passed the other to Daniel. They both ordered, and then Daniel went on questioning Kitteridge.

'So, she was found in her bedroom, her head severely injured, and worse than that, burned? Is there any explanation for that?'

'No, there isn't. So, a fall, or any other kind of accident is out. You can't disfigure a dead woman with fire accidentally.'

'Male servants in the house?' Daniel tried another tack.

'A bootboy, and the elderly butler who doubled as a valet for Graves.'

'Gardeners?'

'Well spotted. An old boy of seventy-odd, and a couple of lads here and there. None of them had access to the house.'

'Maids who might have let someone in?'

'Highly respectable housekeeper, a woman of 'a certain age'.' Kitteridge's smile was very brief. 'A cook and a scullery maid, a parlour maid, and

Mrs Graves' own lady's maid. All of them accounted for. Of course, someone might be lying, but it would take two telling the same lie. Which could be possible, but if you saw them you'd know it's unlikely.'

'That leaves only Graves — or someone he let in?' Daniel concluded, but he made it a question rather than a statement.

'Bravo,' Kitteridge said bitterly.

'What does he say?'

'Only that he's innocent,' Kitteridge answered, taking another sip of his drink.

'Doesn't he offer any alternative?'

'Not specifically. He has little good to say about his wife. Apparently, to him, she was light-minded, eccentric,' Kitteridge replied. His gaze did not waver from Daniel's face. He had clear eyes, pale blue, not what one would have expected, considering that his brows and his hair were quite dark. He was waiting for Daniel to offer an opinion. Was it curiosity? Or was he hoping for help, and concealing how desperately he needed it?

'What do you plan to do?' Daniel asked finally.

Kitteridge sighed. 'I have no idea. Between now and tomorrow morning, we must come up with an alternative answer — and I doubt Graves will be of much use.'

Daniel had not even seen Graves, and already he disliked the man. 'What do we know about her?'

'Very little. There's a photograph of her. Very handsome indeed. Jet-black hair, dark eyes, pale skin. I imagine her parents named her well after she was born. Or else she took the name herself.'

'What name?'

'Ebony. Ebony Graves.' This time Kitteridge really smiled. It altered his face, suggesting a quite different nature: something gentler, and far more vulnerable to being liked, or disliked.

Daniel thought for a moment. 'Have we got anything at all to go on, really?'

'No,' Kitteridge replied.

'So, what are you going to do?'

'Reasonable doubt is about all we have left,' Kitteridge said miserably. 'We'll have to think of all the ways someone could have got into the house — '

'That's definitely where it happened?' Daniel interrupted.

'Yes. There's blood on the floor and half the carpet is singed or downright burned.'

'Sounds like hatred.'

'Looks like it,' Kitteridge agreed. 'Whoever did it knew her well enough to have hated her very deeply.' He sat forward a little. 'Graves doesn't appear to be a man who would feel that degree of passion. He's a cold bastard. If she had a lover and he found out, he'd be more likely to kill the lover than her. If he did that, she'd not stray again in a hurry!'

This was going nowhere. 'Maybe if we question him again, he has something to give us, or at least another person to suspect,' Daniel concluded a little desperately. 'What's his reputation locally? Anyone willing to speak up for him, more warmly than Major Lydden?'

'A few,' Kitteridge replied, but there was no lift

51

in his voice. 'But he doesn't . . . ' He raised his shoulder in a slight gesture. 'He's good at what he does. He's honest in his dealings, as far as we can tell. He's arrogant, and I don't like him, and I can't find anyone who does. I don't know how to make the jury want to acquit him.'

Daniel understood. 'What do you want me to do . . . as long as I can stay awake . . . ?'

'If I knew, I'd do it myself,' Kitteridge said tersely.

Daniel did not reply. There was nothing about this case that he liked. He could see no way of defending Russell Graves from the charge of having murdered his wife. There was no defence. There was no alternative suspect. They had only reasonable doubt to suggest, and nothing to support it. Suddenly, he was overwhelmed with sympathy for Kitteridge. 'Right,' he agreed. 'We'd better start thinking.'

4

Daniel and Kitteridge began the following morning early by going to see the accused, Russell Graves. They were both tired after a heavy day and then, in Daniel's case, another night with too little sleep.

Daniel had taken a cab ride from his lodgings to the Old Bailey. He could not afford to risk being late by using the public omnibus. He fully expected Kitteridge to be washed out as well, not only from the long day yesterday, but also with anxiety about fighting when he had so little ammunition, and a very real prospect of losing. It was an important case, and a bad one to lose, because it was highly public and Marcus fford Croft obviously cared about it dearly.

Why? That was an interesting question. What stake had the old man in the outcome? Or in Russell Graves? Did Kitteridge know something important that he could not, or would not, tell Daniel? Something to do with Marcus fford Croft?

The cabby put him down on Ludgate Hill and Daniel thanked and paid him. He ran up the large flight of stone steps outside the Central Criminal Court, and in through the wide doors. Kitteridge was waiting for him just inside.

'Morning,' Kitteridge said, barely glancing at Daniel before turning on his heel and leading the way along the wide hall towards the back, and the small room where Graves would be waiting for them. They had already discussed their plans last night, actually in the small hours of this morning. There was no more to be said now.

Daniel had to stride to match Kitteridge's long steps. The man must have been around six-foot three or four, and loose-limbed, coordinated only with an effort.

They came to a door with a guard outside. He greeted Kitteridge and then unlocked the door. Kitteridge thanked him and led the way in, Daniel on his heels.

There was only one man inside. He was large, heavy shouldered, with a fine head of iron-grey hair. His features were good. Only a greyish pallor and an expression of discontent marred what would otherwise have been a striking appearance. He looked no different from how he had been yesterday in the dock, except even more strained.

Kitteridge introduced Daniel briefly, then sat down opposite Graves. Daniel took the other chair and remained silent.

'We haven't got long — only half an hour — so we will be brief,' Kitteridge began. 'I will call you to the stand first thing. Please answer me as we have already agreed — '

'What use is that going to be?' Graves interrupted. He had a good voice, deep pitched, and a well-educated accent without sounding affected, but his fear showed through in a heightened pitch and a certain abruptness. 'I don't know any details that haven't been sworn to by the police, doctors, firemen, and God knows who else.'

Daniel saw Kitteridge's face tighten and knew

that it cost him something to keep his own tone level.

'They need to see your reaction to it, judge your honesty for themselves,' Kitteridge explained. 'They need to see your grief over your wife's death, and hear you say you were not responsible. You know nothing you have not told the police — '

'Good God, man, of course I know nothing!' Graves said in ill-concealed exasperation.

Kitteridge clenched his jaw. '*I* know that. They need to hear it.'

'You told them . . . '

Kitteridge's fists were clenched in his lap under the table. 'They need to hear it from you.'

'I'm a . . . ' Graves began.

Daniel had agreed to keep silent but now he broke that agreement. 'Mr Graves, sir, it is not only what you say, but it is how you say it,' he interrupted. 'They have to want to believe you. They have to like you and to sympathise with you. For that, they need to feel some of your grief, your bewilderment at what happened — and believe that you don't know!'

Graves turned to look at him. 'I thought you were here as an assistant.'

Kitteridge drew in his breath to speak, and let it out silently. It was a mark of his anxiety that he let Daniel get away with the interruption.

'I am,' Daniel replied. 'I am trying to assist you to understand that your life depends on the twelve men of the jury being willing to believe that in spite of the evidence, there is reasonable doubt that you are responsible for your wife's death. Whatever the truth is, all the facts shown so far are against you. We've got this morning to convince them to look beyond those facts, and see a decent man, not unlike themselves, who's caught up in a tragedy not of his making. We have to persuade them that they do not want to convict you — they would much rather find a reason to acquit — so they will look for a reason.'

Graves raised his eyebrows, but his face was very white. 'Are they really so . . . guided by their emotions, rather than their reason?' There was a certain contempt in his tone. 'I did not kill her! Do you not believe in the justice system you serve, Mr . . . ? I'm sorry, I forget your name.'

'Pitt. And no, I do not believe it is infallible. Nobody who has studied the law could believe anything so — so fanciful. It is run by men. It is subject to all misconceptions and weaknesses that men have,' Daniel replied.

Graves looked at Kitteridge. 'Have you also such a jaundiced view of the law, Mr Kitteridge?'

Kitteridge did not look at Daniel. 'We are dealing with people, Mr Graves. People make mistakes.'

Graves looked back at Daniel. 'And where did you study law, young man?'

Daniel looked back at him without blinking. 'Cambridge, sir.'

'Really . . . ?' Graves was taken by surprise. 'And just what is it you suggest I do to get these twelve very ordinary men to believe that I am innocent? I did not kill my wife, and I have absolutely no idea who did. I am a very busy man, a leader in my field. I have no idea with

56

whom my wife consorted, who might have wished her harm. Perhaps I am guilty of pursuing my career to a degree that I did not go to parties, and local events, of such like with her. They bore me stiff, and I cannot afford the time. But I quite saw how she might enjoy them, and I gave her an ample budget, and the freedom to do as she chose. Perhaps that is something they would not understand?'

One thing Daniel did understand, and that was why they would dislike Graves' arrogance to the point where they would find it a pleasure to return a verdict of guilty. 'The butcher, the baker, the candlestick maker,' he said aloud. 'No, perhaps they would not, you being a man whose time is too important to attend their events.'

'Whatever you think of them, Mr Graves,' said Kitteridge, 'they have your life in their hands. If you don't want to hang, you'd be wise not to treat them so condescendingly. Their revenge will be all too easy. One word will do it . . . '

Graves look startled. 'One word? I . . . '

Kitteridge spoke it for him. 'Guilty.'

'But I'm not guilty!' Desperation raised Graves' voice almost an octave.

'Convince me,' Daniel said.

Graves looked at Daniel as if he were a rather tedious child who needed even the simplest things explaining.

'I wasn't even at home! I have no idea who her close friends were. I don't know whether she was having an affair, or even half a dozen. I don't know if she offended someone. She was outspoken, even rude. She had unconventional

57

ideas, unsuitable and eccentric friends. She gave her opinions far too freely, regardless of whom she offended. She was a beautiful woman, and dressed to show it off far too frequently. God knows how many enemies she may have made. I didn't restrain her activities at all.'

Graves' face was sad, and twisted with outrage at the injustice of the situation.

Daniel looked at Kitteridge. Oddly enough, it was not exasperation he felt, or even anger at the man's arrogance. It was something of the same feeling as he thought Kitteridge had: a genuine concern that the man might be speaking the truth. And, the moment after, the near certainty that the jury would be only too happy to convict him.

He glanced at Kitteridge and saw that same conclusion in his eyes. He also saw that Kitteridge had an idea, albeit a faint one.

Kitteridge rose to his feet. 'We will see you shortly, in court, Mr Graves. We will do our best for you, whether you assist us or not. That is our job.' And he walked past Daniel and went to the door.

Daniel stood also, but still looking at Graves. Whatever he felt, it was his duty to defend him. And it was very much in his interest to please Marcus fford Croft, whatever his reason for taking Graves' case. His feelings for Kitteridge were more mixed than before. He did not dislike him so wholeheartedly. It had been a very good dinner last night, and there was a pleasure in working with someone as clever as Kitteridge was.

★ ★ ★

The trial reopened exactly on time. The judge presiding was an elderly man with a thin ascetic face and a reputation for surprising wit. Daniel fancied he could see traces of it in the deep lines around his mouth. His face might look quite different if he smiled.

For the prosecution was Alister Tranmere, KC. It was a title any lawyer would aspire to: KC stood for King's Counsel. He was a formidable opponent for Kitteridge to face. Daniel wished he had taken the time to look him up. Not that he was going to do anything but assist Kitteridge in finding the right references at the right times. And it would take a lot more than that to keep Russell Graves from the gallows.

In a hushed court, Kitteridge stood and called Graves to the stand. Daniel could not help but contrast this with yesterday. Was it only twenty-four hours ago that he had been in Kitteridge's position, standing in a far lower court, with a gallery full of a noisy, jostling crowd, trying to save Blackwell's life? But then he had had a plan, and Ottershaw on his side.

Kitteridge, with his odd face, his well-cut suit, and his bony hands, looked far more afraid than Daniel had felt. He was facing a pillar of the establishment in Alister Tranmere, and Daniel would bet a week's rent that every one of the sober, well-fed jury already believed Graves to be guilty.

Graves crossed the body of the court, and walked with shoulders back and head high across to the steps to the witness stand. He climbed up with only one slight stumbling step when he was almost at the top. Daniel saw his muscles clench as he grasped the rail.

Would the jurors take his attitude as arrogance, or courage? What did Daniel himself take it for?

Kitteridge began very courteously. 'Mr Graves, you stand accused of having particularly violently not only murdered your wife, but then set fire to her so as to disfigure her face and upper body. The prosecution has not offered any reason why you should do such a thing. Can you tell the court something about your wife? She is not here to speak for herself. I do not wish to harrow your children by asking them to describe their dead mother. It might help the court to understand you and your family better, perhaps more fairly.'

Graves looked plainly distressed.

Daniel breathed out a sigh of relief. It seemed as if Graves would at last defend himself.

'What did she look like?' Kitteridge prompted. 'We have no way of knowing, since whoever did this to her destroyed her face . . . '

Graves winced. The jury must have seen it.

'She was beautiful,' Graves said quietly. 'In an unorthodox way. She had lovely hair, thick and wavy. Black as night. Marvellous eyes. She had grace in the way she moved, and the way she spoke. She had imagination, and she was original and funny.'

Daniel tried to visualise her. For a moment, she was alive in his mind, and he felt a grief that she no longer existed. He became impatient that they discover what had happened to her. It was more than not losing a trial. The truth mattered.

'Thank you,' Kitteridge answered. 'She sounds like a unique and valuable person. I imagine she had many friends?'

Tranmere was growing restless. If Kitteridge were not very careful indeed, he would appear cold to the jury's sense of outrage that such a woman had been killed, and so far they had no one but Graves himself to suspect.

Daniel knew what Kitteridge was trying to do: establish that Graves had loved her. He was playing with fire, but what else had they left to try?

'Yes,' Graves said.

'Was she always wise in the choice of friends?' Kitteridge could not keep a certain edge from his voice. Graves was doing nothing to help himself.

'No,' Graves said flatly. There was curiously little life in his voice. 'She failed to grasp that they did not always like her. I could see that many were hangers-on, people thirsty for excitement, and her way of life, her vitality, her possibility in certain circles, drew them in.' There was emotion, but also a certain condescension in his tone, even in the expression of distaste in his face.

Daniel wondered if that was what he truly felt. Would the jury see that too?

Kitteridge was addressing Graves again, asking more about Ebony, and then also her two children, Sarah and Arthur. Graves' expression was unreadable when he answered. Had the man not enough sense of his danger to let his feelings show through?

Daniel felt he should step in and say something. He could understand Kitteridge's desire not to embarrass the man, but a show of emotion was about the only thing that would save him! Did Kitteridge not understand that?

He looked across at Tranmere. Did he perceive the jury's regard for Graves' stoicism, and read it as indifference?

Daniel tweaked the edge of Kitteridge's gown.

Kitteridge ignored him.

Daniel tweaked it again, harder.

Kitteridge glared at him. 'What is it?' he hissed.

'Let me try! The man looks like ice,' Daniel replied.

'You'll ask the same things as I do,' Kitteridge answered.

'You're getting nowhere. I can't make it any worse,' Daniel responded.

'My lord!' Tranmere rose to his feet. 'If my learned friend has run out of questions, I will begin my own.'

'You will not!' Kitteridge snapped. 'My associate is going to question the witness.' He turned to Daniel again. 'This had better be good!' he whispered under his breath as he sat down.

Daniel stood and faced the witness. 'Mr Graves, tell us something about the day your wife was killed. Were you at home at all that day?'

Graves turned to Daniel, not completely masking his impatience.

'No. I was in the London Library for much of

the day. I arrived home early in the evening.'

'Did you see your wife, or greet her when you arrived?'

'The maid told me she was in her bedroom. I did not disturb her. I assumed she would come down when she was ready. I had notes to write up before I forgot any of the details that had been told me.'

'Who discovered your wife's body, sir?' Daniel knew that Graves himself had. He could not even imagine how terrible that must have been, were he not guilty. But the jury had to see his emotion and now was not the time to spare his feelings.

A wave of anger crossed Graves' face. 'I cannot imagine, sir, that you do not know it was I!' he said, his voice all but choking.

'We are not here to observe either compassion or good manners, Mr Graves,' Daniel answered. 'This is a place where only the truth counts. Are you telling the court that you discovered the body of your wife?'

'Yes.'

'Why did you go to her bedroom, when you had not done so earlier?'

'It was time for dinner.'

'And you did not wish her to miss it?'

'Of course!' Graves' patience was tissue thin.

'And you found her? Where was she?'

Graves' face was white now, and so stiff he had difficulties speaking clearly. 'She was lying on the floor; her head was near the hearth.'

'Did you know immediately that she was dead?'

Graves leaned forward over the railing, his body rigid, his skin devoid of all colour. 'God Almighty, man! She was covered with blood and her face was burned until there were no features left! Nobody could have lived . . . through . . . that.'

Daniel hated doing it, but the jury would have to see something other than the cold, arrogant man who felt only anger that they dared to question him at all. 'And you were naturally extremely distressed,' Daniel concluded. 'Horrified! Appalled?'

'Yes . . . ' His voice was almost strangled.

'Did you realise immediately what had happened to her?'

'I . . . I don't know. All I could think of was . . . how she must have suffered. Then I . . . ' His voice trailed off.

Was he going to lose the passion?

'How would you tell your children?' Daniel asked. It was cruel, but Graves' life hung on it. 'Your wife was very close to her children, was she not?' Daniel had no idea if that was true, but it was probable. It sounded good. 'I believe your son, Arthur, is an invalid. You must have feared terribly that the horror would kill him . . . '

Tranmere rose to his feet. 'My lord, my learned friend . . . ' He hesitated. 'My learned friend's assistant is leading his own witness. Is this . . . torture . . . necessary?'

The judge looked at Daniel.

'I apologise, my lord,' Daniel said. 'I fear Mr Graves is suffering a very natural distress . . . and needed some assistance. It is compassionate.'

The judge turned to Graves. 'Are you able to continue, sir?'

'Yes, thank you,' Graves replied. The brief respite had been sufficient for him to regain his composure, perhaps even to realise what Daniel was doing.

'Do you wish me to repeat the question?' Daniel asked.

'No, no, thank you. That is not necessary. God knows why, but you want me to tell you how I informed my children of their mother's . . . death.' And he proceeded to give a harrowing, even brutal account of telling each of them, and their deep distress. It was all that Daniel could have wished.

'Thank you,' he said quietly. 'I have only one more question.'

Graves glared at him. He had been humiliated by having to expose his emotions to this staring, speculating, accusing public.

'Did you kill your wife?' Daniel asked.

'No!' It was an incredulous answer, almost a shout.

Daniel sat down.

Kitteridge rose to his feet. He was pale, but totally composed. 'The defence rests, my lord.'

Tranmere considered for a moment, stood up, said, 'The prosecution has no questions for the accused, my lord,' then sat down.

'Then you may begin your summations,' the judge replied. 'We will adjourn for luncheon when you are finished.'

Tranmere stood up and faced the jury. He seemed less confident now. He described the brutality of the crime, and the fact that there was no other reasonable suspect. Even Graves himself had claimed to know very little of his wife's acquaintances and could suggest no one. It drew a picture of a very cold, disinterested man, and a distant marriage. But that in itself made it seem unlikely that Graves would have committed such a violent murder.

Kitteridge took his place and pointed that out. He did not labour anything but its inconsistency. He reminded them instead of Graves' obvious care for his children, attributing his apparent detachment to his deep care for his wife and his very private nature that did not wish to disclose his grief to the public to pry into. He also wished to protect what was left of his wife's reputation. Press comment had been vulgar, to say the least.

The jury retired and the court adjourned. Daniel was not at all sure how Kitteridge would regard his interference. His instructions had been plain enough. They walked out of the courtroom together, but without speaking. They could not go far. There was no way to tell how long the jury would be out. A swift return would almost certainly mean a guilty verdict, but the jurors themselves would at least have lunch.

Once Daniel and Kitteridge were out in the street, and walking down to the Magpie and Stump, one of the public houses that served a reasonable lunch, Kitteridge spoke at last.

'If you ever do that again, I will have you kept out of court for half a year,' he said. 'But as it happens, I think you probably improved the situation. We might even have a chance of winning.

66

You've no respect for anyone, have you?'

Daniel was not sure if he was referring to himself or to Graves. He chose to interpret it as if Kitteridge had meant Graves. 'He's an arrogant sod. They need to see him as human, capable of showing weakness or pain — like anyone.'

Kitteridge gave him a quick glance, then looked away again. 'He won't forgive you for exposing him like that.'

'If they hang him, it won't matter,' Daniel replied. 'And if they find him not guilty, he might even be grateful.'

Kitteridge gave him a frozen look. 'I am rather more concerned about what Marcus says, you idiot!'

Daniel had no answer for that, and he decided to say nothing for a while.

They had lunch largely in silence, Kitteridge buried in grim concentration on his food, pushing it around the plate and eating very little. Then suddenly he would look up, as if to say something, then change his mind.

Daniel ate, but he had no idea what it was on his plate. He had ordered steak and kidney pie, but it did not taste like anything. Had he ruined his career in fford Croft and Gibson? His father would probably be angry; without question, he would be disappointed. That is what would hurt. He had accepted his father's gift and squandered everything it offered him in one melodramatic and ill-judged attempt at — what? Getting an extremely unattractive, and publicly guilty man hanged!

Then what would Daniel do? He could explain all he wished that he thought the jury found Graves so cold as to believe anything possible of him. Perhaps he was wrong, and really the disobedience in not having kept quiet was all that mattered.

He looked up from his plate and found Kitteridge's blue eyes directly upon him. 'What is it?' Daniel asked.

Kitteridge hesitated. 'Do you still think he didn't do it?' he asked.

'Then who did?' Daniel had previously avoided the question. He was not sure what his own answer was.

Kitteridge returned to his meal, pausing a moment to answer. 'Doesn't matter now. It's up to the jury.' When Daniel did not reply, he said with sudden savagery, 'Do you care about anything? Don't you care about the law? No, that's a stupid question. I know that you don't. Not really. You play around the edges, which is a sin, Pitt! Because you could be good at it. Do you even understand that?'

Daniel thought for a moment. Kitteridge's questions startled him. Kitteridge had talent, but he had worked hard for it, harder than Daniel did. Kitteridge loved it; he loved the idea that law was the elegant but imperfect servant of justice. It was up to them to defend a vision and its errors. It required dedication and, more than that, obedience.

'No,' Daniel admitted. 'I don't see the law first, I see the people.'

'How incredibly stupid,' Kitteridge replied.

'You're not supposed to be the judge, you . . . child! You have to serve the law. You are the advocate, or the prosecutor, if you ever get far enough for the Crown to trust you. The judge knows the law and sees that we all conduct ourselves accordingly, and the jury decides who to believe. Didn't they teach you anything at Cambridge? Did you actually study?'

Daniel was stunned. He had actually studied very hard. He had had to, in order to pass the exams with a decent degree. He said the first truth that was burning a hole in his head. 'You think that we'll lose, don't you? And you're afraid old fford Croft will blame us because they'll hang Graves. You believe he's not guilty because you want him to be, so we'd be justified in getting him off? It might be very clever to win a case like this, but it won't help you sleep at night to think he did that to his wife and you helped him walk away from it. And that will go on a lot longer than fford Croft's satisfaction!'

Kitteridge stared at him. 'You bastard!'

'Is that your best argument?' Daniel asked incredulously.

'Shut up and eat your lunch.' Kitteridge bent and took a mouthful of cold roast beef and potatoes.

Daniel ate, too. There didn't seem to be any point in going on talking. He knew that Kitteridge was really afraid. And Daniel might well have ruined the case for him, although he thought it may have been beyond saving anyway.

They went back to the courtroom in silence. The jury had not returned.

69

By five o'clock, they still had not returned. They would be accommodated overnight, and continue their deliberations in the morning.

'I'm surprised,' Kitteridge remarked as he and Daniel went out into the street. 'I thought we hadn't a chance. I expected them to come back after an hour or two. I hope to hell we don't get a hung jury and have to do the whole damn thing again.'

'Do you want to go and have dinner?' Daniel suddenly asked, then wished he had not.

'Are you asking?' Kitteridge enquired. Then before Daniel could answer, he replied, 'All right. But let me choose the place. It's going to be a long night.'

Actually, Daniel would rather not have spent it alone either, although he would not have chosen Kitteridge for company.

★   ★   ★

The next day seemed to drag interminably. It was four o'clock in the afternoon when the jury finally returned with a verdict.

Kitteridge stood up slowly, as if all his joints were locked.

Daniel could hardly breathe.

The foreman of the jury was asked and answered, 'Guilty, my lord.'

It seemed for a moment unreal, as if it had been Daniel's own imagination answering him. Then someone in the gallery started to cough. The rustling began again. The judge sent for the black cap. What a ridiculous charade! What did it

70

matter what he was wearing?

The cap was put upon his head and he formally pronounced sentence of death upon Russell Graves, to be carried out after three Sundays had passed from now. Hanged by the neck until he was dead. That would be in twenty-one days.

5

Daniel and Kitteridge travelled back to the office in silence. They took a cab because it was late, and they wished to get to fford Croft before the verdict was in any newspaper, or someone else told him. They rode in silence because there was nothing to say. There were no excuses. In fact, Daniel faced the truth that the momentary flashes of thought that Graves might be innocent were probably born of pity rather than a matter of reason. As Tranmere had said over and over, if not Graves, then who? They had failed to provide a solid, believable answer.

Daniel knew that his success in saving Blackwell could be swallowed up in his failure to defend Graves, whom Marcus had personally required him to represent.

For Kitteridge, it would be far worse. He was considered the firm's best man in court. It was his responsibility. The fact that Graves was probably guilty was not an adequate excuse.

They arrived at the chambers in Lincoln's Inn, and were greeted by the chief clerk, Impney, who read their expressions instantly. It was his greatest skill, along with an encyclopaedic memory.

'Oh dear,' he said sympathetically. 'I imagine you would like to tell Mr fford Croft as soon as possible. Shall I bring tea?'

'Yes, Impney, it wouldn't hurt. Thank you,'

Kitteridge answered.

'Yes, sir. Will you be going in too, Mr Pitt?'

'Yes, he will,' Kitteridge said without turning around.

'Very good, sir.' Impney led the way to fford Croft's door, knocked, and waited a moment, then opened it. 'Mr Kitteridge and Mr Pitt have returned, sir,' he announced, and stepped back for them to enter.

Kitteridge went in; Daniel followed and closed the door behind him.

Marcus fford Croft was not physically a large man, but he had a big presence. Now that he no longer appeared in court himself, he dressed to suit his own tastes. He often wore velvet jackets. His shirts were immaculate, but of all sorts of styles and colours so that Daniel had considered whether or not he might actually be colour blind.

He had thick white hair, which he had cut when he thought of it, but which now appeared to have been some time ago.

He looked at their faces, and his own expression dimmed. All happiness faded. 'Well?'

'Guilty,' Kitteridge said quietly. 'They considered it for a long while, but they found him guilty.'

'And?' fford Croft asked.

'They sentenced him to death,' Kitteridge replied, lifting his chin a little.

Daniel did not have to look at him again to know that his jaw was set and his face white.

Kitteridge cleared his throat. 'In . . . in twenty-one days, sir.'

'I know what day of the week it is!' fford Croft

73

snapped. 'He has three Sundays clear. It is the law. Then that is how long we have to find a cause for appeal, and to get a stay of execution.'

Kitteridge looked profoundly unhappy. 'Yes, sir.'

Daniel was sorry for him, and sorry that he was here to witness the situation. He thought that was an error on fford Croft's part, the first he had recognised. You never found fault with a man in front of those who are junior to him. It humiliates him, and reduces his ability to lead. It also makes him dislike the junior, although he may find it as embarrassing as anyone else.

'It was my fault,' Daniel said, taking a step forward. 'I tried an experiment, although Mr Kitteridge told me not to. Graves seemed very cold and arrogant, sir. He showed no distress, even when the description was given of his wife's body. I asked him how he told the news of their mother's death to his children. He was very angry — but he did show grief at last.'

fford Croft sat still. 'Against your orders, Mr Kitteridge?'

Kitteridge was caught, he hesitated.

'Yes, sir,' Daniel replied.

fford Croft blinked several times. 'Why, Mr Pitt?' he said at last.

'I wanted to show the jury that the man was human, just under very tight control. That he was proud — not heartless.'

'I see,' Marcus replied. 'And did you think him innocent, Mr Pitt?'

'I thought it a possibility, sir. Not a likelihood.' That was the truth.

fford Croft turned to look at Kitteridge. 'And do you support your junior colleague in this, Mr Kitteridge? Or is he stepping forward to take the blame for you?'

The colour flamed up Kitteridge's cheeks. 'He is taking the blame for himself, sir. And for me, for allowing him to speak up.' He cleared his throat. 'And actually, sir, I think it may be the only thing that made the jury hesitate at all. I think without it they would have come back in less than an hour — sir.'

fford Croft pursed his lips. 'I didn't think you'd work well together. Wouldn't have put you together, if I'd had any choice. Looks as if I may have been wrong.' He turned to Daniel. 'I thought it was a mistake your representing Blackwell, but your father asked me to have you do it. What happened?'

'Not guilty, sir,' Daniel said as firmly as he dared. 'Someone else's fingerprints on the shell casing.'

'Whose?' fford Croft asked.

'I don't know, sir. I couldn't stay, because I had to go to the Old Bailey.'

'Would you like to know?'

'Yes, I would!'

'It was as you thought: Parks. The witness was guilty.' fford Croft's face was unreadable. There was a quirk at the corner of his mouth. It might have been a suppressed smile, or simply a nervous tic.

'Thank you, sir,' Daniel replied.

'Disobedience won't always turn out so well,' fford Croft warned, shaking his head. 'Well, between the two of you, you have a disaster to rescue.'

'Sir?' Daniel and Kitteridge said almost in unison.

'Only an appeal can save Graves and it needs to be lodged in good time. You have twenty-one days in which to get Graves out of the noose. Twenty days, tomorrow. You, Mr Pitt, know very little of the law. Mr Kitteridge, on the other hand, is possibly the best student of the law we have in this firm. He knows the law, as other men know their own minds.' He ignored the hot colour in Kitteridge's face and the fact that he was acutely uncomfortable. 'You will leave all examination of every aspect of the law to him, from every view whatever, is that clear, Mr Pitt?'

'Yes, sir.'

'Mr Kitteridge.'

'Yes, sir.'

'You will examine the records of the case. You will find if there is an error in anything whatsoever. Anything! Do you understand me?'

'Yes, sir.'

'Mr Dunham is in a plaster cast and likely incapacitated. Nevertheless, if you take him the necessary books, he can research for you. That will give him something to remove his mind from his misfortune. And possibly justify my paying him to sit in his own house! Are you clear?'

'Yes, sir.'

He turned to Daniel. 'And you, Mr Pitt, will play detective. Your father was one of the best detectives the London police ever had. Even in Special Branch he outthought many who would have brought about the destruction of this country's peace and prosperity. You will find out, beyond reasonable doubt, precisely who killed Ebony Graves, and how. If possible, you will also find out why, although that is less important.'

Daniel drew in his breath to say that was preposterous. Then he saw fford Croft's unblinking blue eyes staring back at him and knew that any protest would be taken as rebellion, or simply cowardice. 'Yes, sir,' he said very quietly.

'Well, get on with it! Time's wasting!' fford Croft banged his hand on the surface of his desk.

Kitteridge and Daniel turned in one movement and went out of the door, just as Impney appeared from the pantry with a tray of tea.

'We'll take it in my office,' Kitteridge said, after a momentary hesitation. 'Thank you.'

Daniel did not have an office, just a desk in the corner of the main room. He followed Kitteridge. Impney laid the tray on the desk and left.

Kitteridge sat down behind the desk, and Daniel sat in front of it, in the client's chair. 'Is there any legal error that you can find? One that would make any difference?' he asked.

'I don't know. None I could see at the time, or I'd have said,' Kitteridge replied. 'I might be able to find some precedent.' There was no life in his voice. 'I suppose. I know several people I can ask. One thing is clear, either there is or there isn't. Your task is a great deal harder. Somebody killed the poor woman, and she certainly didn't burn herself like that by accident, especially since it seemed to have happened after she was dead.' A wry smile touched the corner of his mouth.

Daniel shuddered in spite of himself. What kind of hatred disfigured someone till they were almost unrecognisable, as if death were not enough? 'He hid it very well . . . '

'What? How much he hated her? We're trying to prove him innocent, you ass! The jury's already found him guilty.'

'We can't find him innocent, if he isn't,' Daniel argued. 'fford Croft can't be asking us to do that.'

Kitteridge's eyebrows rose. 'I think that is exactly what he is asking us to do.'

'No . . . not exactly. He said to find someone else to suspect, although it will have to be more than that. It will have to be absolute proof, and even then their lordships won't be keen on reversing the verdict. A legal fault would be better.'

Kitteridge gave a sharp bark of laughter. 'That's because you think I'm going to do that. I don't think there is a fault to find. And to get anywhere, we will have to have both. A legal fault might earn a retrial, but what the hell difference will that make, if he's still guilty?'

'Do you think that he is?' Daniel asked, watching Kitteridge's face. He saw the shadow, the sadness, and also the desperation as Kitteridge foresaw his own career jeopardised because he could not save a guilty man from the gallows. 'You don't need to consider that,' Daniel said before Kitteridge could speak. 'You think he's guilty. So do I. But we've got to give this the best shot we can. Mr fford Croft must have his reasons for wanting Graves to be spared and it means he knows something he can't tell us — maybe for national security or something like that.'

Kitteridge sat forward suddenly. 'Do you think he does?'

'Why else would he insist on us pursuing this, even though the verdict is in?' Daniel said reasonably.

Kitteridge thought for a moment. 'What could it be? A debt? A secret? But whose?'

'I've no idea,' Daniel replied, 'but he's protecting someone.'

'We'd better make plans, and keep each other up to date.'

'One of us may find something that will help the other,' Daniel suggested.

'Highly unlikely, but we need to try.' Kitteridge gave another twisted smile. 'Where are you going to start?'

Daniel smiled back, and then said, 'I'll go and see Graves again. He must know more than he's told us.'

'He won't tell you anything,' Kitteridge replied. 'I've spent weeks trying to get him to open up.'

'Well, I can't find a hole in the law,' Daniel responded. 'To me, it is as full of holes as a lace collar.'

For some reason, Kitteridge thought that was funny. Daniel could still hear him laughing as he went out of the front door into the street. The sound haunted him: there was so much fear in it, and anticipation of defeat.

* * *

Daniel went back to his lodgings, although it was a little late for dinner now. He apologised to Mrs Portiscale, who forgave him, as she always did, and made him some scrambled eggs on toast, and a fresh pot of tea. He ate his meal, still contemplating the case.

Where would his father have begun? As Marcus fford Croft had reminded him, Thomas Pitt had been an extremely good detective. Still was! That didn't mean that Daniel had any of the same gifts; he certainly hadn't got the same history.

His features and his colouring were more like a masculine version of his mother, so he had been told. But his build was tall and lanky, like his father's, and the way he walked was the same. A big difference was that he did not stuff his pockets with everything he might need one day! Perhaps he had a little more vanity.

He took his tray to the kitchen, and thanked Mrs Portiscale again, then returned to his room and lay back in the armchair, looking at the ceiling.

He may learn nothing if he gained permission to see Graves, but they had no new questions to ask him. Graves had already said he was innocent, and had no idea who might be guilty. Had he expected to be acquitted? Would the shadow of the noose now hanging over him sharpen his mind to the reality that no one could save him without his help?

It was Ebony Graves who was dead. Someone had hated her — terribly. Could such a hatred remain secret? Somebody must know. Or had the police been so certain her killer was Graves that they had not looked very far into her life?

What advice would Pitt give? Daniel tried to remember the cases he knew something about: the older ones that were domestic murders. When Pitt joined Special Branch, so much of it became political. He had talked about some of the cases to Daniel, occasionally, when he had asked. Not the details, but how the investigation was proceeding. Daniel had listened with rapt attention. What little boy doesn't want to share his father's adventures?

What could he remember now?

Observation! Listen to what people say, but also how they say it. And watch their expressions: faces give away a lot. Remember what they tell you that you didn't ask them. And remember what they avoided telling you. It was coming back now: memories of sitting at the kitchen table with his father and mother. His mother was always part of it, and quick with helpful insights, particularly in her understanding of society's rules and limitations. And long ago, the little maid, Gracie. She had been barely five foot tall, but with a mind as sharp as a needle.

And later, Great-aunt Vespasia — Lady Vespasia Cumming-Gould. Actually, she was Aunt Emily's first husband's great-aunt, but she became an indispensable part of the whole family — and vital to Thomas Pitt's career as well — long after Emily's husband died.

Daniel smiled as he remembered Vespasia. She was quite old, but he did not realise it at the time. She was beautiful, highly intelligent, and very witty. His mother had said that Aunt Vespasia was who every woman wished to be, in her dreams. But what mattered was that she was brave and vulnerable, honest, frequently to a fault, and that she loved with all of her heart.

But what about Ebony Graves? What did she believe in? And who wanted her dead?

Graves had suggested Ebony was eccentric, that catchall word for everything that was out of the expected, good or bad. Graves' expression when he said it had suggested the bad. The servants had said no one outside the family had entered the house the day she was killed. But would they lie to protect her reputation, even if it meant implicating Graves? Or to protect the children? Probably. Maybe Graves was not liked, and had earned less loyalty than she?

Sarah was nineteen. In her case, at least, that was definitely adult. Or at least old enough to have a lover. If so, one she dared not tell her father about? An unsuitable lover?

Arthur was sixteen, and probably still being educated. Did he have a tutor? How much of an invalid was he?

The police would have looked closely at the servants, even if only to exclude them. Someone could have let a stranger in. They had said there was nothing missing. Perhaps they didn't know

82

at the time, being too shocked by the murder to notice. Or too ashamed at having let in a lover, a friend, a brother or father in trouble? There were possibilities that might look different now that the master was on the way to the gallows.

Daniel would have to be gentle enough to get someone to tell him the truth when they had already lied about it to the police. But to cause a man to be hanged on false testimony was a guilt that could stain the rest of their lives indelibly.

Daniel's mother, Charlotte, and her sister Emily, had meddled in Pitt's earlier cases, and been of some considerable help, because no one thought to connect them with the police. Perhaps he would go home for dinner one evening, when he had a little more information, and see if his mother could offer any light on Ebony Graves. She knew an extraordinary number and variety of people.

He suddenly sat up straight. He could ask Mercy Blackwell! She was a woman with a lively interest in London life, and a sharp mind. It was possible that she had heard of Ebony Graves, maybe had even encountered her. Women were gathering at meetings and rallies to discuss their rights all the time these days, and Ebony, by all accounts, was not someone to keep her opinions to herself. Mercy might know of Ebony, or have heard something. She would at least have advice. What she did not know, she could enquire about. She was sufficiently grateful to Daniel for doing the seemingly impossible in saving Roman Blackwell. Somebody, somewhere, knew something. It was up to him to find them. He had twenty days — very nearly three weeks. A good night's sleep, the first one since well before the verdict, and he would face the morning with a clear head — and a clear purpose.

6

Daniel set out very early in the morning to see Graves. The day was cool and the fresh wind added to the chill. The streets were still quiet. Grimy prison walls rose above him, adding to his sense of claustrophobia once he was inside, and emphasising the futility of trying to escape.

He was permitted in, but a dour-faced guard told him he had to wait until the prisoner had finished breakfast.

'You wouldn't want 'im to go 'ungry, would yer, Mr Pitt? Not got many breakfasts left.'

'I'd rather . . . ' Daniel began, then realised the emptiness of what he had been going to say. There was little enough chance that he would succeed in finding cause for appeal. Was false hope really better than none at all?

His stomach was churning, as he realised how ill-prepared he was to speak to a man who was facing certain death in twenty days. Daniel would walk out of this place at the end of their meeting. Graves would see these stone walls for a few days, and only leave them to face his death. Hanging was supposed to be comparatively painless: a civilised thing to do to those who had committed capital crimes, such as murder, piracy, or treason.

But nobody ever knew the whole story. Perhaps Graves was not guilty. After all, they had nearly hanged Blackwell. Maybe someone else had killed Ebony, someone she had known, and whom Graves himself had not even suspected. How frightened and alone he must feel!

'Want a cup of tea?' the warder offered.

Daniel thought he would choke on it. It was probably stewed. He shook his head, then changed his mind. Perhaps it would settle his churning stomach.

The guard brought it to him wordlessly, his face slightly amused.

'Thank you,' Daniel said, taking the enamel mug. The tea was black and very hot.

'Sorry,' the warder said. 'The milk is off, so I left it out. First time you come to see a bloke wot's going ter be 'anged?'

Was it that obvious? 'Yes,' Daniel admitted. 'The last man I defended wasn't guilty.'

'None of them are,' the warder said scornfully. 'You look very young ter me. Should yer be doing this?'

'I'm twenty-five,' Daniel said, knowing that to be so defensive about his age made him sound about eighteen. 'I meant that the last man I defended was found not guilty. He's probably eating eggs and bacon for breakfast in his own home. If he's even out of bed yet!' The image of Roman Blackwell reading his newspaper over a leisurely and elegant breakfast, being fussed over and sharing a joke and gossip with Mercy, passed briefly through his mind as he contemplated the mug of vile tea in the dreary room.

'You must be sharper than yer look, 'cause yer look sick as a parrot to me. 'Ere, drink that afore they come and get you.'

Daniel sipped it. It was stewed. It must have been sitting in the pot for hours. But drinking it was easier than talking to the guard.

Graves was brought to a small interview room, dressed in drab prison uniform, and with manacles on his wrists. He was unshaven and his skin beneath the greying beard was sallow. He glanced at Daniel, and sat down awkwardly in the wooden chair, as if his balance were affected.

'What do you want now?' he asked.

'Mr Kitteridge is looking to see if there is some legal error with which we can appeal . . . ' Daniel began.

'You mean he might have made a mistake?' Graves' voice was thick with derision, but he could not keep the hope out of his eyes.

'He's a very good lawyer.' Daniel instinctively defended Kitteridge. Anyway, it was the truth, whether you liked him or not. 'Something in the proceedings, a — '

The momentary light vanished from Graves' face. He let out a string of blasphemies.

'And I have come to see if I can find out who really killed your wife,' Daniel went on as if he had not heard. 'Assuming it wasn't you.'

'You stupid sod, do you suppose if I had the faintest idea I wouldn't have told you?' Graves said with acid disbelief.

'The difference being that I am free to spend my time enquiring into it, and you are not,' Daniel said tartly. 'If you want to waste your time abusing me, I really don't care. But if, on the other hand, you want a chance of getting out of here, you'll answer all the questions I ask you and see if you can give me something to investigate. The police may have missed something, not asked the right questions, not spoken to the right people. They wanted to prove you guilty; I want to prove you innocent.'

Graves stared at him with acute dislike. His desperation robbed him of dignity, stripped naked his fears and exposed the inner man far more than if he stood without the decency of being clothed. The humiliation burned in his eyes.

Daniel needed him to cooperate. 'It's your neck they'll stretch, not mine,' he said ruthlessly. 'Do you want me to stay . . . or go?'

'I did not kill her,' Graves said between his teeth.

'Well, someone did. I need to know a lot more about her. You can't protect her now, either her reputation or her life. I'm looking for the truth. I don't ask out of prurient curiosity, and I'm not going to tell anyone else, if it proves of no value in finding who killed her. Believe it or not, I don't find other people's affairs particularly interesting, and I'm good at keeping secrets. For one thing, I'm your lawyer; so I have to keep them, unless by following them up I can prove your innocence.'

Graves let out his breath in a sigh. It signified agreement, but the language of his body, slumped in a chair, made it seem like surrender.

Daniel felt a twinge of guilt. But this was no time to be gentle at the expense of truth.

Graves looked lost, as if he had no idea where to begin.

'You said she was eccentric,' Daniel prompted. 'In what ways? Did she do something that might have offended people?'

'Lots of things,' Graves said tartly. 'She was always offending people. But you don't kill a woman and burn her face so she's hardly recognisable because you don't like the way she dresses! Or because she keeps company you think beneath her, or because she walks in the room as if she owns it, or talks to the wrong people. For God's sake, man, we are not savages. Someone . . . hated her.' His face looked pinched, and frightened at his own words. He was angry, and he was weary of concealing it.

Daniel kept his patience with difficulty. Time was short, and he had little enough knowledge to work with. He began again. 'I'm trying to get an idea of what she was like,' he spoke slowly. 'At the moment, I have nowhere to begin. Someone did this to her. Do you think it was a chance robber who took nothing, but lingered long enough to disfigure her before escaping?'

'Don't be ridiculous! Of — ' Then Graves stopped. It was as if a shadow had suddenly passed over his face. His shoulders slumped in submission. 'I'll tell you what I can. She was a woman of strong opinions, and aroused strong opinions in others.'

'What about, that might have caused a quarrel?' Daniel asked. This was more hopeful.

'Politics,' Graves answered. 'She wanted to reform all sorts of things. But I don't know if anyone took her seriously. And of course she wanted women to have the vote, for heaven's sake.'

'So do quite a few people.' Daniel thought of his own mother, but did not say so. 'Did she offend anyone in particular?'

Graves made a gesture of distaste. 'She offended so many I lost count. She was highly in fashion sometimes, and wore her clothes well, better than Lady Midhurst, and the parson's wife, and the doctor's wife. But that happens in all communities where women have nothing useful to do with their time. Can you imagine killing another man because he has a better tailor, or can tie a cravat more elegantly?'

'I can imagine it being an outward sign of a much deeper rivalry,' Daniel replied. 'Or to show who is the leader of that community: whose word counts the most, not to mention who draws the most admiration from men, maybe one in particular.'

Graves looked at him with grudging agreement. 'It all seems so desperately trivial, but I suppose it's not. It depends upon the size of your world, doesn't it?'

'Was Mrs Graves' world so small? Who were her friends? Perhaps I should speak to them; they would know more of how she spent her time. If there was one who was jealous, even if for a futile reason, and there was a man involved? Money? A rivalry over something?'

Graves looked helpless.

Daniel leaned forward. 'It's happened! Think, man. Your life depends upon it!'

'I — I took no interest in local affairs,' Graves said helplessly. 'I'm a very busy man. It may not fall within your professional orbit, but I'm a biographer of some note. I write with great detail about men of the highest importance. I am noted for accuracy, even in the smallest details. I — I have no time to involve myself with the affairs of nobodies.'

'A biographer?' Daniel ignored the insult and affected an interest he did not feel. 'Then you must have learned to understand human nature, at its best and worst. You must know what makes a man give in to his weaknesses, or rise to his strengths.'

'Of course.' Graves looked as if at last Daniel had said something of worth. 'It is a high art, but also a most exact one. You have to understand people, to know what to seek that tells you their deepest secrets.' Some of the tension had gone from his face. It was as if he had moved his position in relation to the light.

'Good! Then speak as if you were doing a biography about Ebony! Describe her for me: her looks, her mannerisms. Tell me, what did she read, what did she care about? What causes did she fight for, and who did she fight against? Who did she admire? Who did she criticise? Who did she quarrel with, and what about? Somebody killed her. If it wasn't you, who was it? A biographer might be able to make a good guess!'

Graves was silent for so long that Daniel was about to speak again, and perhaps frighten him into some reaction, when at last he replied.

'She was a very attractive woman,' Graves said thoughtfully. 'She was interesting and alert. If I were writing about her in a story, I would say people were drawn to her because she was so alive. She felt more than most people do. She was never tedious, but she could be extremely irritating. She tried my temper sorely, on occasion. But I never grew bored with her.'

Daniel watched Graves' face as he spoke. It was not affection he saw, virtually no tenderness, but there was a certain admiration. Ebony had earned his respect, albeit unwillingly given. He did not interrupt.

'She loved music, colour, sensation, life itself. She loved flowers, open skies, electric storms, the flight of birds, the utter silence of a starlit night. And things made her laugh that I might have found ridiculous.'

So, he had noticed such things. She had been real to him, at least at times.

'She sounds like a woman who had both friends and enemies,' Daniel observed.

'Yes, I suppose so. I didn't know them.'

Daniel kept his temper with difficulty.

Graves seemed to show some appreciation of his wife, but more like the appreciation of an artist for a subject to paint than of a man for the woman he had married, and who had borne his two children. Daniel wondered what question he could ask that would bring out the humanity in him.

'Is your daughter like her mother?'

'Who, Sarah? No, nothing like her at all. Sarah looks like my mother. Fair-haired. Blue-eyes. Arthur is more like Ebony, or he would have been, were he . . . were he well.'

Daniel tried to catch the emotion in Graves' voice, or his face, or even the tension in his body, but he saw nothing. He could have been speaking of a stranger, not his son.

'Has he always been ill?' he asked.

'No ... he was perfectly normal until he caught an illness when he was about ten years old. Now he will always be ... dependent.' He still hid all feeling. 'His doctor is hopeful, if he gets constant treatment. But if you are looking to Arthur for any explanation of his mother's murder, you will not find one. He never leaves his room. Sarah is very good with him. She's very patient. Dedicated much of her life to him.' For a moment, there was something in his voice, perhaps admiration, but it disappeared before Daniel could be certain.

'Rather than his mother?' he asked.

'Yes. Ebony looked after him well enough. And we have very efficient household staff. There really was not anything I could do. I have tried.'

'You've only told me what she looked like,' Daniel said rather sharply. 'But what was her life like? How did she spend her time, who did she like or dislike? When she went out, where did she go? With whom?'

Graves could shed no light at all on Ebony's inner self. Daniel could have revealed far more about his mother, her curiosity, her quick temper at injustice, her humour, than Graves said about his wife. Graves seemed to recall no memories of shared experience; no flashes of insight appeared.

Daniel tried to think back on his own moments of closeness to someone, small truths that made him understand the greater ones. They mostly concerned his father. On one occasion Pitt had

93

been helping Daniel with a school project. They were building a sort of machine with wheels and chains and cogs. Pitt kept doing it with one piece backwards. Finally, Daniel thought very hard and realised what was wrong. He did not want to tell his father his mistake, but they were getting nowhere. As tactfully as he could, he explained, giving the reasons why they needed to do it again the new way. It worked. And then he saw the amusement in his father's face and had realised that he misplaced the piece on purpose in order to make Daniel not only do it, but understand the mechanism.

Maybe Graves never understood his wife. He saw her in lots of detail, but with little sense of her as a whole, as a woman who would stir passions of any sort, let alone ones that led to murder so violent and destructive. Could the man really be a good biographer with so little feel for the passions within the physical presence, the need and the heart behind the deeds?

'Was she interested in your work?' His work was the one subject Graves showed emotion about.

'Ebony?' Graves looked surprised. 'Not in the slightest. She liked that I met famous and powerful people. I suppose it gave her some standing in the community. But she never wanted to read any of my books.' His voice dropped from vitality to a lower note, which was laced with contempt. 'She liked the fame, thought it the completed result, but she showed no interest at all in the active labour, and refinement of detail, the learning of the truth about people.'

Daniel heard the real bitterness in Graves'

voice, and saw it in the sudden anger in his eyes. What was he angry about? That she had lived in such a way that someone had killed her, and Graves was going to take the blame for it, die for it? Or had she driven him to the point where he had lost his temper and killed her himself?

'Could her murder be to do with your work?' he asked. He had to get something from this interview. They would not give him much longer, and he had little enough to work with. 'Could she have been indiscreet?'

Graves suddenly stiffened. He raised his head slowly and stared at Daniel. 'Damn her!' he said between his teeth. 'Yes! Yes, she could. I'm dealing with important people. Dangerous people. Some of them are dead, but their power stretches beyond the grave. Others can be affected.' He drew in his breath, then spoke in a low, fierce voice, barely in control. 'Damn her! Damn her! How could she be so stupid? I deal with private lives, but also with public ones. It goes as far as state secrets, even high treason.' He looked up at Daniel. 'I never told her anything confidential — of course I didn't. But she could have heard a name, caught a thread of . . . some people I write about. I'm only just touching the edges myself — and it could threaten all kinds of people, the heads of government, even the Throne. Oh God! What an almighty fool!'

Daniel did not know whether to believe him or not. It was a perfect opening for believing that someone else was responsible for her death. With a careless word, had she been indiscreet? Had she led somebody to believe that she knew secrets about them that were dangerous . . . dangerous enough to kill for?

'But they didn't attack you?' he said to Graves. 'Why not? You are the one writing the book.'

Graves stared at him.

'Well?' Daniel pressed.

'Perhaps it was a warning,' Graves suggested. There was a rough edge to his voice that was almost certainly fear.

'And you are supposed to read it, and know what it means?' Daniel's tone was heavy with disbelief. 'Did you get any letters, or anything else to make you think that was what it was? No point in warning you if they don't say what they want you to do, or not to do!'

'No need to say, if they get me hanged!' Graves said back at him. 'I can't come back and tell any secrets if I am dead!'

Daniel was torn between anger and pity. He looked at Graves sitting in a wooden chair, his hands manacled. The prison uniform made him look like every other man awaiting death, ticking the days away, then the hours, finally the minutes.

'Anyone in particular whose secrets you were going to expose?' he asked. He must get to something practical, something he could use.

'Who knows where the threads of treason run?' Graves answered. 'And how do you imagine you are going to trace them? What are you? A newly graduated lawyer who's tried half a dozen cases, and those as second chair? I was your first big case, and you lost it. What do you imagine you can do against the Establishment? You are absurd. I would laugh at you, if it weren't my life at stake.'

'What did you imagine when you started doing biographies like this?' Daniel lashed back at him. 'That they were going to let you write whatever you like, and they'd do nothing about it? It must have crossed your mind, in among all the thoughts of how clever you were.'

'The men I am writing about are dead! At least the most powerful ones are!'

'But you said yourself their power stretches beyond the grave. Someone who cares is still alive. Are you going to tell me who I should start looking at?'

'So you can destroy my writing? How do I know you aren't paid by them?'

'Because I wouldn't be trying to clear your name, you fool! I'd let you hang,' Daniel replied.

'For all I know, that's what you are doing.' Graves rose to his feet, chains on his manacles clanking together.

Daniel thought for a moment before he answered, then he spoke deliberately. 'You are quite right. You don't know. But if these people really were guilty of treason, the Government would want to know. That might halt your death sentence long enough for us to find out more.'

Hope flared in Graves' eyes, then died again as Daniel looked at him. In spite of himself, he felt a kind of pity.

'I'll find out what I can about whether Mrs Graves was speaking unwisely. And Mr Kitteridge is working on the legal side of it. If there was any flaw in the proceedings whatever, he'll find it.'

'Will you come back and tell me?'

'If I have anything to tell. Or to ask.'

Graves did not reply. He turned away, so Daniel could not see his face. It was dismissal.

★　★　★

It was still only the middle of the day when Daniel went out of the grey shadow of the prison into the light on the pavement. He was going over in his mind what he would, or could, do. He was not sure how much he believed of anything that Graves had to say.

Perhaps the first thing was to find out if Graves was actually anything like the writer he claimed to be. He should exhaust his own resources first. Surely fford Croft would know. He was the man who had involved them in the case in the first place. But if fford Croft knew that Graves was a biographer who dealt in such dangerous subjects, would he not have told them that at the beginning? It was an obvious place to start looking.

To what purpose? Graves had nothing to gain in sending Daniel on a fool's errand. But perhaps he had nothing to lose, either. Would he rather have Daniel think he was a threat to some traitor than guilty of a sordid domestic murder over jealousy, humiliation, or greed? That was believable, too. Perhaps Ebony had mocked him, and his pride had led him to such hatred that he had killed her, and he had to destroy the beautiful face that had made a fool of him?

It sounded more likely than his writing an exposé of some famous figure whom he had previously suspected of . . . what? An unknown treason?

98

He passed a fairly large bookshop and decided to go in and enquire about Graves' work.

'Yes, sir, may I help you?' the elderly gentleman at the counter asked him.

'Thank you. I have had a certain author recommended to me, and I wondered whether you carried any of his work, and would advise me where to begin.'

'If you will tell me the name of the author, sir . . . ?'

'Yes. Russell Graves. I believe he is a biographer of some note.'

'Oh dear.' The man's face assumed an expression of piety. 'I dare say you have not heard. I'm afraid he has met with . . . a catastrophe.'

'Yes. I had heard. But he will perhaps appeal. And it does not alter his work. I am told he gets very much to grips with his subjects.'

'His research is exhaustive. Personally, sir, I prefer to leave my heroes their privacy. We are all weak at times, and I dare say there is no one who could stand the closest scrutiny. But I believe his biography of the Duke of Wellington was less scathing than some, and told us a few incidents that are little known, particularly of his political career, long after the Peninsula War or Waterloo. I can see if have a copy, if you like. We have sold one or two of his works lately, but I may have one left.'

Daniel had no money to spend on rare and expensive books he was not going to read, certainly not in the next nineteen days. 'No thank you,' he said, shaking his head. 'I'd like something more contemporary. If I change my mind, I shall return.'

'Yes, sir,' the man nodded, understanding exactly what Daniel meant.

★ ★ ★

Daniel checked in with fford Croft, and told him of his progress, or lack of it, but that he had a line of enquiry to follow. Apparently, Kitteridge had not yet discovered anything worthy of comment. That was no surprise. There probably was not anything to find — it was simply obligatory to try.

In the middle of the afternoon, Daniel went to see Mercy Blackwell. He had no idea whether she would welcome him or not. He had been to her house before, when consulting her regarding Roman's trial, and during the struggle to find any proof of his innocence. She knew perfectly well that Roman had lied about many things, but she also knew exactly when he was lying and when he was telling the truth. Daniel wondered if Roman was aware of quite how little he ever fooled her. He thought not. But it was a totally comfortable relationship, of that he was certain. There was a warmth in it, a natural friendship of two people who understood each other very well and, beneath any squabbling on the surface, held exactly the same values as to the kind of honesty that was important, and the jokes that were trivial. Above all they held a loyalty to each other that had no price.

Daniel had also been certain that Mercy was

one of the most vividly alive people he had ever known, and that her son's death would have robbed her of all heart. For him to be hanged might even have taken from her the will to live.

If he had not seen her vulnerability also, he would have been a little afraid of her. As it was, he had no hesitation presenting himself at her door early in the afternoon. He thought it was a time when she would be there, although he was prepared to wait as long as necessary, should she be out. He had to find out more about Ebony Graves, and not from her family, who may have actually known her less than anyone else.

The house was on a quiet street in Pimlico, and from the outside it looked ordinary enough. He ascended the steps and knocked on the front door. He would not have been surprised if there were no answer, but he realised how disappointed he would be.

Silence.

He knocked again.

This time, the door opened almost immediately. Mercy stood in the hallway. She was completely different from the exhausted woman he had seen the day the trial finished. Today, she radiated energy. The pallor was gone from her skin, and there was vitality in every aspect of her. She was quite small, a couple of inches over five foot, at least a foot shorter than Daniel, yet she carried her head so high that from a distance you would have sworn she was statuesque. Her magnificent hair was coiled on top of her head, giving her another two inches. Roman had told him that when it was loose, it was long enough that she could sit on it, and all shining black, except for the white streak in front.

'Well!' she said with pleasure. 'I did not expect to see you so soon. Are you in trouble?'

Daniel wondered if something were emanating from him, like an aura she could see, or if she felt he would not have come otherwise. He smiled, and stepped into the hallway. It was exactly as he remembered it. There were large mirrors, so placed as to make the space seem far bigger than it was. There appeared to be too many doors. He could see a dozen pictures, yet he knew there were only five. Two hat racks held an enormous number of hats, not obvious reflections of one another, because they looked more varied seen from different sides. Some brims were at unusual angles, some had feathers, others had flowers. All were in jewel colours.

Daniel found himself smiling. This house always affected him that way. It was an exercise in the art of illusion — or, as he preferred to think of it, as dreams, extensions of reality.

'Yes, I am in trouble,' he said, and the admission made the reality so much easier to cope with. 'I have a case much more complicated than your son's, because I don't know if the man is guilty or not.'

'But you are defending him?' She turned and led the way to one of the rooms off the hall.

'No, not really.' He followed her into the room, which was also familiar. For once he was not interested in the wild collection of things in it. Nothing matched, but because there was no pattern, there was no sense of dissimilarities either. At least there was none to him. He knew that each piece had history and represented some friendship or adventure. She had kept many memories sharp by having around her a Chinese screen exquisitely painted, next to a Persian hookah complete with pipes and a delicately carved glass bowl. It was easy to imagine dreams while seeing the painted birds on the porcelain dish on the wall, and half a dozen Delft figurines on the side tables.

'He's already been convicted. The head of my chambers is determined that we should appeal the verdict. I have nineteen days left,' he told her.

She gestured for him to sit down in one of the plush-covered chairs, and she took the other. They were not a pair, but the rich colours complemented each other surprisingly well. How could anyone have foreseen that crimson and plum would do anything but jar the senses, or that a purple cushion would make it seem natural? The sheer unlikelihood of the room pleased him.

'I need to know more about the victim,' he said, without waiting for her to ask. 'I think you may be able to find out, or actually already know. Her name was Ebony Graves.' He saw the immediate sorrow in Mercy's eyes. 'You knew her,' he said.

'No. Not really. I knew of her. I met her once,' she corrected him. She was sitting in the crimson chair, and she slowly lowered her head until he could not see her expression. It was unnecessary to ask if Mercy had liked her. It was there in the grief of her gestures.

'I want to know what she was like,' he went on quietly. 'I need to find out who killed her and, if possible, why.'

She looked up. 'But they are going to hang her husband. Do you really think he is innocent? Or is it your job to speak for the condemned,' she answered herself, 'so they can hang him and go home to sleep in peace?'

'He is an unpleasant man, but that is not necessarily the same as being guilty,' Daniel replied. 'And if by some chance he is not guilty, then someone else is.'

Mercy straightened up and looked at him for a long time without speaking.

He waited her out.

'She fought a lot of causes,' she said quietly. 'The world is changing very fast. Too fast for a lot of people, but not fast enough for others who have already caught the scent of change, and become intoxicated. Change does that to some. They fear the new. It seemed that Ebony was not afraid of anything. Not afraid enough to run away, poor creature. She wanted not only women to vote for Members of Parliament, but to be Members. She wanted education for girls. But academic, not just to speak foreign languages, and play the piano. She wanted them to read books, not just walk with a pile of them on their heads. And to practise the sciences. And she knew it would upset society. Equality always does, but I don't think she realised how much. We talk splendidly about equality, but the reality of it appals us. We want change, but it must start tomorrow, not today, and above all, not here.'

Daniel smiled, not because it was either good or funny, but because it made him think well of Ebony. 'She was a crusader,' he said.

'Yes,' Mercy agreed. 'But she made many people dream, too. And one man's dream is another's nightmare.'

'Did her husband agree, or not?'

'He was too busy writing his stories revealing the weaknesses of other people to care, I understand. He believed she would never achieve anything except a degree of unpopularity. At least that is what I think.'

'And he did not mind that? It did not bother him?' Then a new thought came to his mind. 'If he exposed people in his biographies, did she discover any of the facts for him that he used?'

Mercy weighed her answer for so long, he thought she was going to refuse to respond. Then, at last, she spoke. 'I suppose that is possible. She had opportunities, connections that he could never aspire to. And certainly she was both clever and observant. But I would prefer to think she did not repeat secrets to him. In fact, I choose to believe she despised gossip. Besides, for all I know, she was far too clever to soil her own reputation.'

'Clever?'

'Sometimes you are so very young.' She sighed. 'My dear, a secret exposed is a secret you can no longer use. It is an opportunity wasted, is it not?'

'You mean Ebony blackmailed people?'

'That is an ugly word. But I think she might have made suggestions to people that they help certain causes — in their own interest. I don't know. As I said, I only met her once. But I have friends who knew her better than I did. Do you want me to make enquiries?'

Daniel was not sure. She had the air of not being in the least discreet, nor able to keep a secret, let alone be inclined to keep one. He looked at her bright dark eyes, and half-smile on her lips, and realised that it all very well might be an act. She had never actually told him anything that was secret, only things that were entertaining. He had thought he knew her well, but perhaps what she presented was a deliberate illusion.

'Time is short,' he replied. 'Very short. Nineteen more days. Ebony was not only killed, but disfigured by fire, deliberately. I don't want the case closed and her husband hanged, if he was not the man who did this to her.'

'I will see if I can find information for you,' Mercy replied. 'Either about her — or him.'

'Thank you.'

'Now, tea?' she offered. 'I have the most excellent cake.'

7

Daniel went over all the evidence again, later in the afternoon, and had a brief supper with Kitteridge, who looked tired and disappointed. They sat in the darkest corner of a familiar public house and ate hot cottage pie with plenty of onions.

'So, what have you got?' Kitteridge asked miserably. 'I read and reread the transcript and all my notes. I'm going to start to look up precedent tomorrow, but I don't think I'll find anything.'

'Are you going to look up cases that were appealed and succeeded?' Daniel asked. He wanted to encourage Kitteridge, but he also thought Kitteridge's mission was pointless.

'I don't think it will help, but there's nothing else,' Kitteridge replied. 'I wish to hell I'd never been given the case.' He took another mouthful of the mashed potatoes.

'If fford Croft didn't put his best man on, Graves would have crucified him,' Daniel pointed out. 'For some reason we don't know, he really wanted to get him off.'

Kitteridge looked up, almost as if he suspected Daniel of being sarcastic.

Daniel held his gaze with complete innocence. 'He must have reason for defending Graves,' Daniel argued. 'He knows something that we don't, but why wouldn't he help us if he wants us to succeed?'

'He knows a lot of things we don't,' Kitteridge said with an edge to his voice. He reached for the salt, then changed his mind. 'That's why he's head of chambers, and we are its employees. What have you found out, anyway?'

'Apparently Ebony Graves was active in fighting for social change,' Daniel replied. 'But rather more interesting than that, Russell Graves really is a well-known biographer, if we're bent on dissecting people rather than recording their lives in an even-handed way. I wanted to find out whether she did any of his research . . . betrayed anyone's confidence.'

Kitteridge looked more interested.

Daniel went on, 'I'm going to the house tomorrow morning. I want to see where it happened. Talk to the servants. Hear what they say. I know we've got police reports, but they may not be exact. And they don't tell us expressions, how people looked when they answered. Perhaps they didn't ask the same questions I'll ask. I have the advantage of having seen Graves in court. And then afterward, in custody, to see what an intimidating bastard he can be. They might say to me things they would dare not say in his presence.'

'You don't think we'll win, do you?' That wasn't a question. Kitteridge's face was without hope, without its usual energy and black humour.

'Probably not,' Daniel agreed with a grimace. 'But, like you, I have that shred of belief that he really didn't do it.' He shrugged. 'There's something missing.'

'Very precise,' Kitteridge said sarcastically. 'Very lawyerly. You remind me of my mother, when she's arranging flowers in the church. 'Very nice, my dear, but there's something missing. I think something purple, don't you? Purple always ties it together, you know.'' He looked away. 'Sorry. By all means, go out to his house and ask the servants. Tell them you're looking for something purple to tie it all together.'

Daniel did not bother to answer. He finished his cottage pie and considered asking if they had any more.

★ ★ ★

The following morning, with nineteen days before Graves was to be hanged, Daniel set out immediately after breakfast on an early train to Herne Hill, on the southern outskirts of London.

From the station, he had to find a taxi, and it took him some time. Eventually he stepped out, paid the driver, and turned to look at the garden that stretched beyond the front gateway, out of sight around the house, and what looked to be a large orchard. There were trees, most clipped, and flowerbeds in early bloom. It was easy to believe it would require the full-time services of two gardeners to keep it in this immaculate condition.

It was an impressive house, built for both comfort and grace. There might have been at least eight bedrooms, apart from servants' quarters in the attic. There was also a carriage house, although whether it was used for carriages or automobiles these days was an option. Probably Graves preferred automobiles. It would save him the cost of keeping a stable staff, feeding horses, and paying vets' bills.

Daniel approached the front door, suddenly a little self-conscious, aware of the sensitivity of his purpose. He had no police authority, but then, on the other hand, he had now the enormous burden of saving Graves from the rope, if it was even remotely possible.

He knocked on the door and stepped back.

Had the household been bothered by the press and maybe would not even answer to a stranger? He could not blame them. He must be prepared to insist. Graves had been found guilty, but this was still his house. He would expect his children and his staff to serve his interests while he was alive. Another nineteen days!

The door opened and a tall and portly man stood just inside. He wore a dark, formal suit. He looked Daniel straight in the eyes. 'Yes, sir?' he enquired coolly.

'Would you be Mr Falthorne?' Daniel asked.

The man's grey eyebrows rose slightly. 'Before I answer any questions, sir, I'll ask who wishes to know. We have been troubled by insistent and intrusive persons lately, and I have no intention of allowing the family to be further harassed.'

'Neither should you.' Daniel smiled bleakly. 'I am Daniel Pitt. I represented Mr Graves in court when my predecessor was unfortunately injured in an automobile accident. Or should I say I assisted Mr Kitteridge. He is presently doing all he can to see if there is an error in the law

110

sufficient to form grounds for an appeal. I am endeavouring to find some solution to the tragedy of Mrs Graves' death other than the one the police proposed.' He saw the butler's face darken. 'At the request of Mr Marcus fford Croft.'

Falthorne was clearly confused as to what his decision should be. From his sombre appearance, he had lost all hope of a successful verdict. Now he was presented with hope. Was it a cruel trick, or a brave one? 'If you would care to come inside, sir, it would cause less speculation, should someone pass by in the street.'

'I'm sorry to distress you,' Daniel said, 'but time is short. I imagine you would wish us to make all efforts to find another less tragic solution, for the family's sake.'

'Yes, sir. If you will follow me?' Falthorne stepped back, into the hall, and stood aside to let Daniel come after him. Falthorne turned. 'I will not allow you to distress Miss Sarah. Do not offer her false hope that the facts are other than have been presented. It would be a very callous piece of cruelty. And I . . . I will not permit it.' He stood very straight and faced Daniel with a slight flush on his cheeks. He was exceeding his duty, yet he was doing what he perfectly, clearly believed to be right.

Daniel thought it was not only a matter of this man taking his position in the house as effectively head of it. Certainly, he had the responsibility for all the servants, both male and female, but also there was no parent to care for the young people who had lost both their mother, and were about to lose their father. Possibly he had known them all their lives.

Daniel was perfectly aware that he was going to hurt them more, and he could not see any way out of it. Momentarily, he hated Graves for putting him in this position. Had he no thought at all beyond his own self-interests?

'Would you prefer that I did not try?' Daniel asked. 'I admit, the hope is small.'

'Certainly not!' Falthorne said immediately. Then his expression changed, as if the light had moved and illuminated a different part of his emotions. 'The guilt will be terrible, whatever the truth may be, if we did not do our best. If you will come with me, sir, you can start with Mrs Warlaby, the housekeeper, while I prepare Miss Sarah to meet with you. She will probably wish to make sure Mr Arthur is well taken care of before she sees you.'

'Thank you,' Daniel accepted.

Falthorne offered him a cup of tea, and he declined. He settled himself in a small but very comfortable sitting room. He should be offered hospitality, and yet he could not very well interview the staff in the formal withdrawing room.

It was only a few minutes before Mrs Warlaby came in, closing the sitting-room door quietly behind her and remaining standing.

Daniel did not know what he expected, but not this dignified, slender woman with her black dress and white apron, and her ring of keys hanging from her belt. He had not grown up with a housekeeper, although he was used to servants. Some of them had been almost like members of the family. Ridiculously, he remembered the one maid of his childhood. Gracie Phipps was barely five foot tall and had unlimited courage, and opinions about everything. Later, when he was a young man, they had had a cook, a housemaid, and a manservant. Gracie was the one who stayed in his mind and later, Minnie Maude.

He stood up. 'How do you do, Mrs Warlaby? Thank you for sparing your time.'

'Mr Falthorne said you are trying to find some explanation of Mrs Graves' death that does not blame Mr Graves,' she said with a very direct stare. She had grey eyes and fading fair hair. She must have been a handsome woman in her youth. 'I hope you are not going to raise false hopes for Miss Sarah and Mr Arthur. They are just beginning to accept this . . . this appalling situation . . . '

'They were close to their mother?' He gestured to the chair opposite her, but she declined, preferring to stand. It left him no choice but to stand also.

'Yes,' she replied. 'Very. What is it you think I may be able to tell you, Mr Pitt? If I knew anything relevant, I would have told the police.'

'I'm sure you must have answered their questions. But I shall ask you different questions. I believe Mrs Graves was involved in various social issues? Such as female franchise, for example.'

Mrs Warlaby's expression hardened and her chin came up a fraction. 'Do you disapprove of

113

that, Mr Pitt? Think it is deserving of death?' Her voice shook a little, and she was unable to control it.

He made an instant decision. 'Not at all, Mrs Warlaby. On the contrary, my own mother is a very strong fighter for such rights, and has been considerably more outspoken than is socially acceptable, in spite of my father's position in the establishment.' He said it with a rueful smile. It was perfectly true. But then his mother had been in a far higher situation in society, and her sister was both titled and extremely wealthy. It had never been sufficient to silence Charlotte Pitt's opinions, especially where she felt injustice was involved.

Mrs Warlaby's face softened, but she still looked dubious. 'Really?'

'Yes. Unfortunately, some of those most vehemently opposed are other women. I have asked my mother why, and she has a very dark opinion of them. Had she known Mrs Graves, I think she would have liked her, from what I have heard.'

There were tears in the housekeeper's eyes, but she ignored them. 'Oh, she would. She had a very fine, rich spirit! She never attacked people, or spoke ill of them. She used to make fun of them instead. But that can make you far more enemies than outright argument. She told me some of the situations, and we laughed till we cried.' Mrs Warlaby sniffed and hunted for a handkerchief in her pocket.

Daniel gave her a moment in which to regain her composure. He gestured towards one of the chairs, and this time she accepted and sat down. 'Tell me something about her,' he requested. 'I would like to be able to tell my mother something that was real, not just the usual good intentions.' He settled to listen, not only as his job, but as his pleasure,

The picture Mrs Warlaby drew was far more vivid than anything others had said. She saw a woman who was passionate about causes, to the point of foolhardiness, sometimes beyond, scaldingly honest at times, but often extremely funny. The housekeeper was obviously very fond of her, and Daniel thought more loyal than accurate.

'I wish I had known her,' he said simply, when Mrs Warlaby drew to a close.

'You would have liked her, sir,' Mrs Warlaby said, and Daniel realised that that was a high compliment from the housekeeper.

'We must be quite certain that we have the truth of her death.'

'Yes, Mr Pitt,' she agreed immediately.

'Then tell me of the people who visited her here, in case there is someone who felt very violently against her cause. It must have been somebody she trusted, to have allowed them into her private rooms. They could not have followed her to her bedroom unless they were in the house and knew the way.'

Mrs Warlaby looked startled. 'I suppose — I suppose you're right. What a dreadful thing.'

'Somebody did,' he told her, curious that she should feel that even more deeply than that it should be her husband. That was a thought to investigate more fully.

He noted down the names that she gave him, and the causes they were allied with. Then he thanked her and promised to look into it. She stood up to leave, and he rose to his feet as well, as if they were of equal status.

She gave him a brief smile.

'Mrs Warlaby, has anyone ever attacked her before? Struck her, or threatened to, that you know of?'

'No . . . ' she hesitated.

'Anyone at all . . . ?'

'Well . . . '

He guessed. 'Mr Graves?'

'Yes,' she said slowly. 'But that's not a crime. She was his wife. And I thought you said you believed he was innocent . . . '

'I believe he might be,' he corrected. 'And as you say, hitting someone and killing them are two quite different things.'

But when she had gone, he wondered how very different they were, actually. He could not imagine his father hitting his mother, no matter what she might do. And she was exasperating at times, when she was fighting for a cause she believed to be right and just. Quite often she was correct, too, but so far as Daniel knew, she did not remind Pitt of it.

He saw the cook, Mrs Hanslope, who could add nothing, except that Mrs Graves was a very good mistress, never one to interfere in the kitchen, or to expect miracles at short notice, like a dinner for twelve with no warning.

The kitchen maid had nothing to offer,

likewise the bootboy and the housemaid. Daniel went outside to see the two gardeners. However, they offered only that Mrs Graves appreciated their work, and knew quite a lot about flowers. Daniel had gone through all the names of the flowers he knew, and accepted their corrections when he got them wrong.

Salcombe was the elder of the two. 'Bless you, sir, put out in the sunshine and it'll do fine, but give you nothing but leaves. Need shade, they do. Here . . . ' He led the way to a corner of the garden where the shade was deep. 'See! There's the best.'

'Quite a hidden spot,' Daniel observed.

'Got to walk a garden to appreciate it,' Salcombe nodded sagely. 'Don't just look out the window.'

'Did Mr Graves look out of the window?'

Salcombe shook his head. 'Walked through the garden without seeing it.'

That was disapproval. Daniel could not get him to express any further opinion. He thanked him and went back inside. Now he must face speaking to Ebony's daughter. That was going to be difficult, and even though he had thought about it for some time, he had no ideas in his mind. What do you say to a young woman whose mother has been murdered, and whose father is to be hanged for it in a matter of days?

For propriety's sake, Miss Purbright, the lady's maid, sat silently in the corner. She was the one member of staff Daniel had yet to speak with. She must know Ebony better than anyone else. Just as no man was a hero to his valet, no woman had secrets from her lady's maid. His mother had grown up in a house where there were valets and lady's maids. Aunt Emily had always had one. Daniel was familiar with the custom, even if he had never experienced it himself. His father was first a policeman, in the days when the police were of a social standing with the bailiff or the rat catcher. His mother had married for love, and love only. She had given up her social status and the money that went with it. In return, she had received comparative poverty but endless interest, admiration, and a deepening love.

What had Ebony Graves received? Only an early and scandalous death.

Miss Purbright remained in the chair nearest the door, sitting uncomfortably. Daniel presumed she sat at all only because to stand would have drawn attention to her, and perhaps make Sarah even more tense.

Sarah Graves was a handsome young woman, in a very quiet way. She had nondescript fair colouring, and regular features. She was of average height and a pleasing enough figure. The only things remarkable about her were the grace of her composure, and her unusually dark blue eyes, dark-lashed, and very direct. It was her gracefulness that reminded him in some way of his sister, Jemima. She was now a mother, and lived in New York, and he missed her.

'Good afternoon, Mr Pitt,' Sarah said calmly, coming into the room, glancing at the maid, and then at Daniel. 'I don't know what I can tell you, but I would like to lay to rest some of the spiteful things that are being said about my mother.' She sat down in the chair opposite him.

Miss Purbright had risen when Sarah entered, then she resumed her seat in the corner and sat silent guard. Daniel made no comment to Sarah on the fact that it was Ebony's reputation she was here to protect from ill-informed gossip, not her father's from the charge of murder. He drew in his breath to say so, then changed his mind. There were far more subtle ways to draw out explanations. His instinct was to be gentle, both personally and professionally.

'I cannot imagine how distressing it must be for you to hear irresponsible things said about her, and you cannot defend her,' he said gravely. 'I have heard my own mother criticised unjustly, and it was horrible.'

She looked surprised. 'Did they say she was strident, malicious, wanting to have roles that rightly belonged to men?' she asked with a hard edge to her voice.

He heard the tension as she sought to control it.

'That she was unnatural? And suggest all kinds of . . . disgusting things?' she went on.

'People say that when they are frightened . . . '

'Of what? What is frightening about women having the right to vote for the Government?' she demanded. 'We have to obey the laws, just like men. Shouldn't we have a say in what they are?'

'Yes,' he agreed. 'But it is a change. For women, it is a responsibility some of them don't want. For men, it is a loss of control, and people always hate giving up control, going into a new

119

situation they can't predict, losing power, status . . . '

'Would you like it if your mother did that?' she asked, raising her eyebrows a little.

He smiled. 'She didn't ask me if I minded or not. And, honestly, I don't think it would have made any difference.'

Sarah was silent for a moment, surprised. It was obviously an answer she had not foreseen.

'Did it frighten you?' he asked.

'No! Well . . . a bit. But I think she was right! And brave . . . '

'Yes,' he agreed. 'I understand women's suffrage was not the only cause she fought for.'

'No.' Her cheeks flooded with colour. 'There were other things, to do with having child after child, with no way of . . . stopping . . . '

He realised she was terribly embarrassed, discussing such things with a young man she barely knew, yet she was proud of her mother for fighting so controversial a battle, and she would not back down from defending her.

What could he say to put her at ease? And possibly learn more about people who might have hated or feared Ebony Graves enough to kill her?

'It is a subject which arouses deep feelings,' he answered. 'But it doesn't excuse violence.'

Her eyes widened. 'Do you think someone might have killed her over that? But how could they break into the house? And why would they? The police said no one broke in — wouldn't they take the opportunity to attack my mother in the street somewhere? When she was maybe alone, leaving a meeting or . . . or . . . '

'Not someone she knew in other circumstances, and would let in herself, not fearing
anything except perhaps an argument?' he asked.

She hesitated. 'Perhaps . . . '

'Did your father have views on such things?'

'You mean he let someone in who . . . or that
that is why he killed her?' She did not seem to
have any difficulty framing the question. 'He had
a temper,' she added. 'Could it have been an
accident?'

Should he lie? There would be no way back,
and every instinct told him not to try deceiving
her. She would resent it, and turn him into an
enemy.

'Her death might have been, but not the fire
afterwards,' he answered.

She winced, and the colour drained from her
face. She hunched a little further down in her
chair and hugged her arms around herself. 'I
really don't know. I hate to think of my father
doing that, but no one broke in. The police said
so. It has to be someone she let in, or . . . one of
us. That can only be my father.' She glanced at
Miss Purbright. 'All the staff are good, and they
are honest. The only men inside the house are
Falthorne and Joe, the bootboy. He's only
fourteen, anyway.'

'And your brother . . . '

Her head jerked up. 'Arthur's in a wheelchair!
That's ridiculous. He adored Mother, anyway.
How dare you — '

'I wasn't suggesting he did such a thing,'
Daniel said. 'Only that he might know

121

something. People who are restricted in participation often notice more than other people.'

'Oh.' She crumpled up again. The pain was marked clearly in her face.

He realised that she had to be exhausted by the circumstances of her mother's death, her father's arrest, the trial, and now the hanging looming up in days, and a sick brother to look after, perhaps to comfort. 'I'm sorry, Miss Graves,' he said. 'I pushed you too far. I'm trying to find any answer other than your father's guilt.'

She looked at him. He was extremely aware of the burning blue of her eyes.

'Why?' she asked.

Did she believe he was guilty because of the weight of evidence against him? Or did she wish to? Did she know something further than the police had found?

'We must not execute the wrong person.' He avoided the word 'hanged'. 'If there is any doubt at all, we must find it.'

She was trembling a little. She rose to her feet, and after a quick glance at Miss Purbright, she walked stiffly to the door. 'If you will come with me, I will take you to Arthur. I believe you want to speak with him, too. You do not need to come, thank you, Miss Purbright. I will be quite all right.'

'Yes, Miss Sarah,' the lady's maid conceded.

Arthur Graves was a striking-looking young man. Had his health been normal, he would have been handsome. He had his mother's good looks, with black hair and eyes almost as dark. His regular features were marred only by extreme pallor, and the marks of chronic pain. He was seated in a wheelchair, with a rug over his legs, even though the day was warm.

The room was interesting, although Daniel had little time to do more than notice it. It faced east, but had a skylight to the north that filled it with light. There was only just time to glimpse on the walls several almost impressionistic pictures of birds in flight. At a glance, Daniel knew what they were. In pen and ink, details in heads and many feathers, the rest was only a sweeping suggestion to the mind of speed and freedom, endless possibilities of movement.

Those that were painted had only a limited palette: blue and grey, denoting windy sky, shreds of cloud and, again, movement.

Sarah was introducing him to Arthur and he had paid less attention to her than was polite.

'How do you do, sir?' Daniel replied. 'I'm sorry, my attention was taken by the beautiful room.'

Arthur smiled. 'Yes, isn't it? Mother and Sarah designed it for me.'

Daniel heard the slight tremor in his voice when he mentioned his mother. How much had they told him of the truth?

He felt Sarah's presence almost at his elbow. She was going to be head of the household soon. In practical terms, she was already. Daniel knew, without any word from her, that she would defend her brother at any cost whatsoever. How had Russell Graves taken to his only son being an invalid? Was he angry, ashamed? Or willing to defend him even more than Sarah was?

Somebody had paid for this beautiful room. Did Arthur ever go out, or was this his world?

Had Ebony and Graves quarrelled over cost? And what treatment he should receive, or was best for him? Perhaps they had not agreed. He did not wish to ask Sarah. The butler would know.

'May I sit down?' he asked Arthur.

'Of course,' Arthur replied immediately. 'Falthorne came up and told me who you are and what you are here for. I'm afraid I won't be much use to you. I've really got no idea what happened.' He had a nice voice, deeper than Daniel would have expected, and his diction was beautiful. No doubt he had been privately tutored. Being too disabled to join any community activities, he had all day to learn those things of the mind. Anything to take his thoughts off the pain, and to enlarge his limited world.

'I understand,' Daniel said quietly, his mind racing as to what he could ask this young man. 'Were you aware of your mother's battles regarding female suffrage, for example? My mother doesn't allow me not to know.'

Arthur smiled. 'Sounds like my mother. Yes. And I think she is right.' He spoke instinctively in the present tense. He had not absorbed the idea that she was gone. 'They'll win, in the end. Have to. They are half the human race, after all. But most people cling onto the past, as if it were a life raft, and all of us on a sinking ship.'

'That's a grim analogy,' Daniel remarked.

Arthur gave a rueful little gesture, infinitely expressive.

'Father didn't approve, and he made it very heavily known.' He glanced quickly at Sarah, and then, assured of her approval, back to Daniel again. 'Is your father like that?'

Daniel tried to think clearly. 'He keeps his rebellions pretty quiet. They are more effective that way.'

'Are they?' Arthur looked doubtful.

'Yes. I think so. You see, he has the power to actually do something. So, it's better if he says nothing, and takes people by surprise.'

This time Arthur's smile was wide, showing beautiful teeth. 'Your father sounds like a fine fellow. I think I should like him.'

'Is your father not the same?' It was a delicate question, but as soon as Daniel spoke, he felt it was too obvious.

Arthur shrugged. 'I would have said devious, rather than subtle.' It was a candid admission — and Arthur's eyes were on Daniel as he made it.

Sarah was watching Daniel. He could feel her gaze. The moment he threatened Arthur in any way, even emotionally, she would shut down the interview. He knew it as surely as if she had said so.

Was Graves a bully? How could he find out? Surely, he would not be a physical one — strike a crippled son? No. Ebony would have fought him if he had. Or was that what had happened? And she had lost? Mrs Warlaby had said that Graves had hit his wife . . .

They were waiting.

'He's a writer, isn't he?' He looked from Arthur to Sarah, and back again.

'Yes,' Arthur agreed.

'Biography, not literary work,' Sarah added.

'I think you underestimate him,' Arthur said with a bitter edge to his voice. 'There's more art than truth to some of his work.'

'Creative?' Daniel asked. He chose his word with care.

'Not really,' Arthur said. 'You can stick very strictly to the truth, and as long as you omit the right points, tell a completely different story. The best lines are those that are implied. Everything you say is true and proven, and yet it doesn't add up the way the real truth does.'

Daniel thought that was correct. There was a lot more wisdom to that than at first appeared. 'Do you think that is what the police, and the courts, think about the cause of your mother's death?' he asked.

Sarah cut across him, her voice sharp. 'Arthur doesn't know! We don't know, either of us. There wasn't anybody else here, apart from the family, and of course the staff.'

'It's all right, Sarah,' Arthur assured her. 'He just has to make certain.' He turned to Daniel. 'Do you think there is any chance that my father is not guilty, Mr Pitt? You don't suspect Falthorne, do you? If he was going to do anything against Father, he would have done it ages ago. The first time Father took a horse whip to the groom, when we still had horses.'

'Arthur! Stop it!' Sarah said sharply. 'Mr Pitt, that was years ago, and Falthorne would never attack anybody unless it were to protect us.'

'And did he?' Daniel asked.

126

'What?' She looked as if he had struck her.

'No!' Arthur said fiercely. 'Of course, he didn't!'

'Excuse me, sir, but how would you know?' Daniel asked.

Arthur's faced flushed, but it was with shame rather than anger.

Daniel felt appalling for having asked, but the idea was not out of character with the man Daniel had seen in court, and in prison: quick-tempered, arrogant, defensive.

Arthur struggled for an answer and was left speechless.

'Will you please leave?' Sarah meant it as an order, but all she could do was plead. 'Arthur is quite right. He would know if Falthorne had been in a fight with Father. Father is heavier and stronger. Falthorne is sixty, and not used to violence. He looks after Arthur, doing the things . . . a . . . man needs to do to help him. Looks after him with . . . ' she swallowed, 'a little dignity. Father would have half killed him if he had raised a hand against him. Please go!'

Daniel felt shaken, ashamed of having ripped the bandage off such wounds. And yet he was not surprised. Perhaps he should even have been prepared for an error like that. 'I'm sorry, Miss Graves. I've met your father. I do not think he is innocent, but it is still my duty to fight for him, in the chance that I am wrong.' He stood up and walked towards the door. He turned back and looked at them. 'I love the birds. Who is the artist?'

'I am,' Arthur replied. 'In my imagination, I can fly.'

127

8

Towards the end of the afternoon, after a late lunch of sandwiches, Daniel at last looked at the room where Ebony Graves had died. It was a large and gracious room, furnished as a place where she could receive family members and other women she knew well. He knew it as a boudoir. His mother had never had one, but his aunt Emily had, both in her London house and in Ashworth Hall, her country residence.

Ebony Graves' boudoir was charming. He stared at the curtained windows looking out onto the side garden with its carefully tended flowering trees and shrubs. There were flower-beds not far from the window, and early yellow climbing roses in bloom immediately outside.

There was much yellow inside the room also: pale yellow walls like sunshine, and yellow cushions on the floral chairs, and one on the dark green sofa. It was easy and restful. How could such a violent and terrible thing happen amid such peace?

He looked at the pictures on the walls, interesting studies of trees and flowers, caught for beauty rather than botanical realism. In some, they were named.

There was a large bookcase, five series of shelves, fully packed. Some books were lying sideways, on top of the upright ones, where there was room. Mostly he could see novels, memoirs, and histories.

Lastly, he forced himself to look at the fireplace and the hearth, and the small section of the carpet next to it. It jolted him with the stains, and a mental image of the violence that had left its marks here. Maybe no one had been detailed to remove them? Or maybe the police had insisted that they be left in evidence, and never thought to lift the restriction so that they could be cleansed, now that the case was over. Perhaps no one could bear to. Daniel could easily imagine neither Falthorne nor Mrs Warlaby sending in any of the young maids to perform such a task.

There was a brown stain of blood on the hearth stone, which otherwise was a warm yellow sandstone, porous, unpolished, very natural-looking. The carpet beside it, to the right as one faced it, was also stained with blood. There was just the one stain, but deep, as if there had been a single wound that had bled profusely.

Next to the stain was the charring. The soft colours of the carpet were scarred with burns deeply enough to show the canvas in places. In other places, the entire carpet had been destroyed, and the wooden floor beneath was also scarred. The fire had been small, localised, and extremely hot. Created to destroy evidence? Of what? What could she have in her hair or on her face that might ever be evidence?

Or had it been done simply out of hatred? The wish to destroy the beauty, the character, the very identity of the dead woman?

That took a very particular kind of hatred.

Daniel shivered, as if the room had suddenly

dropped in temperature. Was there anything here he could learn that would oblige him to stay?

He forced himself to go into the bedroom next door and look at that. The bed was made up, as if they still thought she might return. It was furnished in the same design as the boudoir, and largely with the same colours, but fewer pictures on the wall. There were photographs here, several of Sarah and Arthur at different ages. Arthur seemed to have been well until about eleven or twelve years old. After that, he was always seated, and he looked like a memory of the child he had been.

It hurt Daniel to see the damage in him. It must have wounded his mother appallingly, and yet she had kept the earlier photographs there, where she could see them every day.

There were none of Russell Graves, not even a wedding photograph. Had there ever been any, in the earlier years? And had she destroyed them? Nor were there any of those who might have been her parents, or other members of her family.

He opened the wardrobe doors and saw clothes fairly tightly packed together, and several drawers of stockings, leather gloves, carefully folded undergarments of silk, or something that looked like it. He felt intrusive looking through them, and yet they told him something about her. She clearly loved clothes, and had had plenty of money to indulge herself. He put out his hand and tentatively stroked a dress. The silk was so soft he saw rather than felt his fingers touch it. The dresses were of several different colours, muted shades, subtle ones, with here and there something bright.

Reluctantly, he closed the door. Seeing her personal belongings, the clothes she had chosen and worn, somehow had made death seem more immediate. He was aware of her life rather than other people's descriptions of her. These had been hers.

He went out of the room and onto the landing, and found Falthorne waiting for him.

'Is there anything else I can help you with, sir?' he asked.

Daniel wondered if the man had been waiting there for him all the time he had been in Ebony's room. Was he watching discreetly, to see that nothing was removed? Or merely guarding the things that had been hers? Daniel wished he had not felt it necessary to search them. Yet the more he knew about how Ebony had lived, the closer he would come to discovering how she had died.

'Yes,' he answered. 'If you please, I would like to see Mr Graves' study.'

Falthorne hesitated. 'I'm not sure if he would like that, sir. He is a very private man, especially about his work.'

'He suggested to me that it is his work that may have made him enemies,' Daniel pointed out. 'Some person wishing to destroy him, in order to prevent his exposing their very serious behaviour, even crimes. He said they may have made him look guilty of Mrs Graves' death in order to silence him. I think he would wish us to look into that possibility.'

'Yes, sir, I think that is likely,' Falthorne

131

conceded. 'I just felt that I should say something. It is my . . . duty . . . to do so.'

Daniel was surprised how easily he had given in. He would have expected much more resistance, even an argument.

Perhaps Falthorne wanted him to discover something? All the staff seemed more shaken and grieved by Mrs Graves' death than by Graves' conviction for her murder. Maybe they had expected it.

'Sir?' Falthorne interrupted his thoughts.

'Yes?'

'Perhaps considering the lateness of the hour, and the volume of papers, you would like to have a little supper first? Mr Arthur does not come downstairs, and Miss Sarah will eat with him. But you are welcome to eat in the servants' hall if you wish. Or I can bring you something in the dining room? However, it has not been heated recently, and may be a little cold.'

'Do you know what time the last train is to London?' Daniel only just realised how late it was, because this time of the year the sun did not set until eight, or even nine o'clock.

'No, sir, but we can look it up for you, or make enquiries. However, if you prefer, we can make up the guest room for you.' There was a mild, polite smile on Falthorne's face, completely unreadable.

Daniel hesitated only a moment. 'Thank you. That would be very kind of you, Mr Falthorne. And will save me a great deal of time. It's most thoughtful of you, and I will be delighted to have dinner with you, and the rest of the household.'

'Very good, sir. It will be served in half an

hour. I'll show you to Mr Graves' study, if you will be so good as to follow me, sir.'

Daniel went down the stairs behind Falthorne and crossed the hallway to the door of the study. It was a larger room than he expected, a cross between a sitting room and a library. There were extensive shelves of books, many of them leatherbound; some were sets of reference books, dictionaries, and a number of biographies of noted people. One section was devoted to his own works, several copies of each.

There was a large leather inlaid desk and a leather-seated chair to match. There were also three leather armchairs grouped around a handsome Adam fireplace, complete with gleaming brasses.

Falthorne noticed his glance. 'Have to keep it clean, sir, as if we thought he was going to come home.' His face was expressionless.

Daniel wondered what it would have shown had he allowed himself that freedom. His studied good manners masked everything, except the effort it cost him. Falthorne had been faultless all the time Daniel had been here. No emotion had betrayed itself but the natural gravity to be expected from a butler in a house of mourning — and scandal.

'You are admirable, Mr Falthorne,' Daniel said, looking directly at him. 'The family and the staff are very fortunate to have you to guide them at such a time.'

That broke Falthorne's composure. He blushed a deep pink. 'Thank you, sir. I will do my best. It has been . . . a very difficult time for us all.' He gave a slight bow.

Daniel smiled at him.

Falthorne avoided his eyes and gave the smallest of nods. 'In half an hour, sir, I shall send the bootboy to fetch you for supper. If you will excuse me, sir? If you need to look in the desk the keys are behind the clock on the mantelpiece'

'Of course. And thank you.'

As soon as Falthorne was gone, Daniel took the keys and opened the desk drawers one by one.

In a large central drawer, Daniel found a working manuscript. As Graves had said, he was clearly well advanced in research, and a preliminary draft of his new work. *A Modern Machiavelli* was the provisional title. It piqued the interest, if nothing else. The name of the Florentine Renaissance master political scientist had passed into the language. His work *The Prince* was legendary for its advocating intrigue, deception and ruthlessness. Daniel wondered who Graves was referring to. He did not know of anyone with that refinement of deviousness.

He began with the notes written in a bold, sprawling hand. A lot of dates were mentioned, along with initials. The letter N occurred many times. It appeared to be the record of someone who had had several changes of career: a brief spell in the Indian Army, then university to study law, and a period practising before being seconded into the civil service, in some position not specifically named.

What was clear was that Graves did not like him. There was to be the exposure of a ghost-like

134

figure who manipulated others from the shadows offstage, rather than a man who showed himself, and took the praise or the blame openly.

The more Daniel read, the less he liked the man who was the subject of these notes. Graves clearly took pleasure in the thought of unmasking him.

Could he be to blame for Graves' present situation? If the man were the master manipulator Graves believed him to be, it would not be beyond his power, or his morality.

Could Graves, dislikeable as he was, actually be innocent of the murder of his wife?

Why the burning of her face and upper body? To make sure her death was regarded as a murder, and not some sort of an accident? Daniel actually felt a twinge of pity for Graves.

And then the moment after, he wondered why Graves had not mentioned his current biographical work to Kitteridge before his trial. Could he have been so arrogant, so stupid, as not to see the relevance? It would have created at least a reasonable doubt, in the hands of a good lawyer. And Kitteridge was good.

Who was the Machiavelli that Graves was writing about? Could Graves be afraid of him? Or afraid of someone that 'Machiavelli' had power over?

There was a knock on the study door. 'Come in,' Daniel called.

It was the bootboy, Joe, to say that dinner was served, if he'd be pleased to come.

'Thank you,' Daniel said sincerely. 'I'd be delighted.'

Dinner was a delicious meal, and Daniel had not realised until he smelled the fragrant steam rising from the table how hungry he was. He had never dined in a servants' hall before. He imagined that most people who were not themselves servants had not done so. No one ate with their own servants.

But Daniel was not master here. He was their guest, and possibly considered something closer to their level than a man who might have servants himself. Daniel had a landlady who looked after him very well, but his father, although knighted by the Queen, never forgot that his father had been a servant, albeit a gamekeeper, not an indoor servant.

He watched the exchanges across the table with interest. Falthorne was very obviously the head of the family — and 'family' was not too intense a word for their relationship. He would have been the senior servant, even before Graves' arrest, but now he had the extra responsibility of being the only adult man in the house. Daniel saw that he was handling it with grace.

Everyone deferred to him, except perhaps Ebony's lady's maid, Miss Purbright. She had the relationship with the rest of the servants that a visiting maiden aunt might have had. She was treated with respect but never completely included.

The housekeeper, Mrs Warlaby, contested with the cook, Mrs Hanslope, for supremacy. The kitchen maid, Bessie, was about sixteen, and answered to the cook. The housemaid, Maisie, was eighteen and made a point of the fact that she answered to Mrs Warlaby.

The bootboy, Joe, aspired to being a footman when he was older and he answered to the butler or the housekeeper, whoever got to him first.

It did not take Daniel long to realise that Joe played one off against the other, with considerable advantage, as an inborn skill.

Strict discipline was kept at the table. Falthorne said grace before the meal. No one fidgeted, and certainly no one tasted the food before he had finished.

'You may begin,' he gave permission.

Everyone reached for knife and fork, Daniel included.

Joe was clearly too hungry to think of anything else. But the kitchen maid, Bessie, stared at Daniel quite openly until Mrs Hanslope told her not to. Bessie murmured something that sounded like an apology, flushed scarlet, and bent her attention back to her plate.

The meal was beef and kidney pudding with a suet crust, with cabbage and early green beans. Everyone else was served, but Daniel was permitted to serve himself, which he accepted with thanks. He took one mouthful and complimented Mrs Hanslope sincerely. She accepted it graciously, but as her due.

Daniel began to feel surprisingly comfortable, as gradually they forgot his purpose and began to behave as if he were one of them. They teased each other, especially the younger ones. They gossiped about trivia, people they knew, servants in other nearby large houses.

They finished the main course. Joe, the

bootboy, was permitted to eat the remainder of the pudding after Daniel had declined a second helping with thanks. Daniel was served apple pie freshly from the oven, probably with apples stored over the winter. The crust was crisp and it was accompanied by hot custard.

This time, Daniel did not compliment Mrs Hanslope; he merely took a mouthful and smiled at her, an expression of pure delight. She was more than satisfied. There was a flush of pleasure on her cheeks.

As they all relaxed a little more, Joe began to tease the maids, and the banter was quick, and forgetful of the underlying tension. The cook looked on benevolently and even Mrs Warlaby smiled.

Daniel realised how much all of them were alone, and far from their families, if they had any. This was their family now. This was where they lived and worked, their safety, belonging, and purpose. They were deliberately avoiding saying what they all feared: that soon it would come to an end. They would have to find new positions in places as yet unknown. But more than that, they would inevitably be separated. And, once again, be alone.

It was Maisie, the housemaid, who gave words to it. She looked at Daniel. 'Joe says you're here to find something as'll save Mr Graves, and 'e'll come 'ome. That true, mister?'

Daniel felt all the desperation that was behind that question.

'Don't be daft!' Bessie the kitchen maid said a little roughly. ''E dunnit. Nothing can save 'im.

You want 'im 'ome, anyway? Remember poor Mrs Graves, yer daft little ha'porth. In't you got no sense at all?'

Daniel thought of Gracie, and for a few seconds he was back at the dinner table of his childhood. Gracie's scathingly honest opinions had been so often right.

He wanted to interrupt, comfort both of them, and protect Bessie, who looked so crushed, but he could learn so much more from letting them talk.

Falthorne was obviously uncomfortable. 'You are speaking out of turn, Maisie. Justice must be done. And you, too, Bessie. It is not your place to give your opinions at the table. Or at all, for that matter.'

The housekeeper gave him a quick look, but she did not speak. Order must be preserved. It was the only kind of safety they had left. They had to cling onto it for as long as possible.

'Mr Arthur and Miss Sarah will have to live somewhere,' Mrs Warlaby said. 'They may stay here, and if they move somewhere else, they could take us with them . . . ' Her voice trailed off. It was a brave hope, and nobody argued with her.

Daniel wondered what would happen to the estate if Russell Graves were hanged. Did it go to his heirs? Was it another reason to hope to find some grounds for appeal?

Falthorne took a deep breath and composed himself with an effort. 'Best we not think about it until necessary,' he said. 'But if there is anyone who is offered a post, and wishes a letter of good character, I will be happy to write one. There is no one else in a position to do so.' It was duty, the least he could do. There was no lift in his voice.

'Thank you, Mr Falthorne,' Mrs Warlaby said quietly. She turned to Daniel. 'I hope your room is satisfactory, Mr Pitt.'

'Thank you, Mrs Warlaby. I'm sure I shall be most comfortable,' he replied.

'Would you like coffee, and perhaps a cigar, Mr Pitt?' Falthorne offered.

Daniel was startled. He was being treated as if he were a true guest, not a young lawyer down here after a tragedy, and to search for information in an act that was, in itself, necessarily intrusive. Or was it largely to get him away from the table and perhaps into the study, to leave them in peace?

In that case, he should accept.

'Thank you. That is very courteous of you.' He rose, thanked the cook again, inclined his head to the housekeeper and lady's maid, and said good night to the younger ones, who were little more than children. He had been at school at their age. But then he had started earning his living at twenty-four, not at fourteen. 'Good night.'

'Good night, sir,' came from all around the table.

He went back to the study, as Falthorne had suggested, and sat in the largest armchair. Ten minutes later, Falthorne came in with a tray of coffee and set it down on the table at his side.

'Would you like me to pour you a glass of brandy, sir?'

'No — no, thank you. And I don't smoke cigars, either. I thought perhaps you might prefer to be alone. You have a large task ahead of you, helping them . . . to . . . ' Suddenly, he did not know how to finish.

'Yes, sir. There was something I was wondering, if I might ask your advice, sir?'

Daniel felt a sudden chill. Had he the knowledge to give this man counsel that was accurate, helpful, worthy of his trust? 'Of course, Mr Falthorne. Please sit down.'

Falthorne sat very carefully, moving the tails of his coat so as not to crush them. Appearance was never to be forgotten. 'Thank you, sir.'

Daniel sat forward a little, trying to look attentive, aware that the man was more than twice his age.

Falthorne cleared his throat. 'We must be practical, sir. It is not at all likely, even with your best efforts, that you will be able to find evidence that clears Mr Graves. I do not mean to . . . to doubt your skills, sir. I do not think the evidence exists. Forgive me for saying it, but I am responsible for these people . . . '

'I understand.' Daniel could see his difficulty and his embarrassment. He was a man who took orders every day, but beneath the obedient exterior he was proud, and he took his responsibilities very seriously. The rest of the household was as much his trust as if they had been literally his family. 'You have to face the possibilities.'

'Yes, sir. I am grateful that you think it not . . . disloyal of me. There is hope, and there is reality.' He met Daniel's eyes with momentary grief, and then he looked down.

'What is it you wish to know, Mr Falthorne?'

Falthorne cleared his throat again. 'Before Mrs Graves' death, sir, I came across a piece of information, quite accidentally, while fetching a book from Mr Graves' desk. He was in the withdrawing room and required it.'

'I understand. What is this information?'

'There is a very handsome estate in Huntingdonshire, many miles the other side of London. Lord Epscomb, sir. A fine house, and a hundred or so acres . . . '

'Very handsome,' Daniel agreed. He could not imagine Graves had the money to purchase such a place, and anyway, it was possibly a family estate. 'And Lord Epscomb?'

'Very recently deceased, sir.' Falthorne cleared his throat again. 'Without issue. The estate, the title, and the money go to his nearest relative, which is actually a cousin.'

'And Mr Graves' interest in this? Lord Epscomb is not one of his biographical subjects, is he?' The knot grew a little tighter in Daniel's stomach. He thought of the book for which Graves had made side notes. It was surely intended to ruin someone. He had never heard of Epscomb, but the man might have been of such hidden power that his name was not generally known.

'That is it, sir. The cousin is Mr Graves. He was set to inherit it all.'

'What?'

'Yes, sir. There was a lawyer's letter accompanying the photograph of the house, and a

142

description of the surrounding acreage. I admit, I read it. There is no doubt. The family connection was all there, through his mother. The will was in probate, but there was no doubt that he is the heir. What I want to know is, will Mr Arthur now inherit? Or does the fact that Mr Graves may be hanged in . . . I believe it is in less than three weeks . . . mean that the title goes elsewhere? And if it means a battle of some sort, will you accept the task of fighting for Mr Arthur? I do not believe he is aware of it at all. He and Miss Sarah face possibly a bleak and uncertain future, with their mother dead and their father . . . hanged. They have no one else to fight for them. I doubt Mr fford Croft is even aware of the inheritance, sir.'

'Yes, of course I shall inform Mr fford Croft of the situation, if he is not aware already, and he will put whoever is the firm's most skilled man in this field on the case. I am only a beginner, but I will do all I can.'

'Thank you, sir. It is not only for Mr Arthur, and of course Miss Sarah, it is for the whole household. It will not be easy to see them all settled anew. Not everyone wishes to be connected, however loosely, with such a . . . a scandal.'

'No, of course not. But if it should come to the necessity, my mother may be able to help.'

'Your mother . . . sir?' Falthorne could not conceal his doubt.

'She knows very many people in society who might appreciate well-trained staff. Her sister even more so.' Daniel preferred not to tell

Falthorne his exact family position.

Falthorne rose to his feet. 'Thank you very much, sir. Please ring the bell if there is anything else you wish. Otherwise, good night, sir.'

'Good night, Mr Falthorne.'

★ ★ ★

Daniel had expected to sleep well, but he turned the new information over and over in his mind. Had it anything to do with Ebony's death? Or to do with Graves' new book? He almost got up at about two in the morning, to search Graves' papers for more information, but he was afraid of disturbing the whole household. Perhaps, rather more honestly, he knew he was too tired to do the job properly. He could see the facts on the page, and still miss them.

He finally fell asleep, and it was daylight when he woke to see Falthorne standing beside the bed with a tray of hot tea in his hands.

'Good morning, sir. I hope you slept well. Breakfast will be in half an hour. I will serve you in the dining room, if you wish?'

'No . . . no thank you.' Daniel rubbed his eyes and sat up slowly. 'I will eat with the rest of you, if I may?'

'Yes, sir. Will that be all, sir?'

'Yes, yes, thank you. Thank you for the tea.'

'Yes, sir.' Falthorne excused himself, and after opening the curtains on a bright morning, went out and closed the door softly behind him.

Daniel got up immediately. Thirty minutes later he was washed, shaved and dressed, and joined the staff in the kitchen for breakfast of bacon, eggs, sausages, and then toast and marmalade and a second cup of tea.

By nine o'clock, he was back in Graves' study reading his research papers. He needed to find who it was that he was writing about, and if that person had anything to do with Epscomb. Perhaps Daniel needed to know anyway. The more he read, the more it was plain that Graves considered his subject morally deplorable, a man who used his office to gain painful, intimate information about people, and then forced them to do things that were sometimes close to treasonous. He was driven from office by a scandal that he managed to conceal, but it was too close to being criminal for him to remain — someone had stood up to him! But he managed to choose his successor, a weak man promoted beyond his ability. He then married his long-time mistress and retired to the House of Lords; such was the corruption that Graves would expose.

Daniel read his notes with a feeling of increasing distaste, as if he had covered himself with filth in being obliged to look into it. It would distress many people, both those who believed it, and those who did not. Accusations like these would not easily be forgotten, and they might well provoke the violence of which he had seen evidence in Ebony's bedroom.

Why kill Ebony, unless she had something to do with it? Was the murderer so sure of seeing Graves hang for it? Indirect, oblique! But it had proved effective. But was that by luck, or skill?

What was Marcus fford Croft's part in it? Did he know any of this?

That made Daniel wonder if it was true, at least in part.

What damage would it do if this and the reasons for it were exposed? If the man was as important as Graves implied, immense!

Was that what fford Croft was afraid of? For that matter, was he seeking to expose it, or to make sure it was not exposed? Where did his loyalties actually lie? Or was he pressured also from some earlier act of indiscretion?

Did fford Croft want Graves saved, or hanged?

Daniel went back to the papers. Some of the notes were passages copied from other sources, with ideas written on them, which were often crossed out, or scribbled sideways up the margins of the pages.

At last, after what seemed like hours, he came across a name written in very small but neat writing in the margin.

The papers slid from Daniel's hand onto the floor. He found he was shaking so that he could not grasp them again. They lay on the floor, but he could still see the words. He was not mistaken. Victor Narraway. Graves was writing of his father's predecessor at Special Branch, Victor Narraway. And Narraway's wife, Vespasia Cumming-Gould. Daniel dropped to his knees to pick up the papers one by one. One page with notes leaped out at him. As he read, his heart pounded so hard that he was shaking. The corrupt man following in Narraway's footsteps, covering up crime, even murder, for his own benefit, was Daniel's father, Sir Thomas Pitt himself.

Graves must have concocted a mountain of lies! He must have. None of this could be true. Daniel knew all these people. It was Graves who was asserting Narraway was guilty of treason.

If this book were ever published, the damage it would do would be immeasurable. Thank God Graves was going to be hanged — and all these lies would perish with him.

No — that was not good enough. These lies must not be spread. Rumour had wings; the more scandal, the stronger those wings, the greater the damage it did to the victims. And in this case, both Narraway and Vespasia were dead, and could not defend themselves. But Thomas Pitt was very much alive! He would be ruined.

It was so unjust that Daniel could not stop shaking. He would have put the rope around Graves' neck himself, and pulled the lever to let him drop.

Then another thought formed itself in his mind: had Graves told anyone else about this? If he was framed for Ebony's murder, and was not actually guilty, who could have done it? Special Branch, of course! They would be the obvious suspects.

Daniel knew that he must find the answer. He must do everything possible to force the truth into the open — not to save Graves, but to see who was really guilty, without question, before they hanged him.

He stared at the papers. He even thought of burning them, destroying all mention of Narraway's name. Then he reminded himself that Graves could recreate his work. But Daniel's father would never have done such things; he knew that absolutely.

But could any of this be true? Pitt was not someone who would collude in the murder of anyone, a man doing as he was bidden in order to hang onto a job too large for him, as Graves said. But Daniel knew many of his cases had been complicated, very difficult to solve, and not always a simple answer of innocent or guilty. He could remember long days and nights of his father's anxiety. Both his parents talking earnestly, and suddenly falling silent when he or Jemima came into the room.

Narraway had trusted Pitt. They had both trusted Vespasia. Had she been Narraway's mistress all along? He did not believe it. No doubt, he was charming. He had been very dark, lean and elegant, and brilliant, such a biting wit. Daniel had been afraid of him when he was younger, but had grown to trust him later on.

Vespasia he had always loved. She had been the greatest beauty of her age, when she was younger. But that did not matter to him. He had not known her then. She was always magnificent to Daniel, a magical figure to a small boy. She wore her hair like a crown, had dark silver eyes, and grace like no one else, not even the queen. Actually, the queen was quite ugly. So was everyone, compared with Vespasia. And she was funny, too, with a quicker wit than anyone else he knew, even Narraway. And she said what she believed.

No, Graves had to be wrong.

Daniel would prove it.

He stood up, still shaking a little, put the papers at the bottom of the pile, and the whole manuscript in a drawer of the desk, and relocked it. He went to find Falthorne and ask him to lock the study door, then if he would be good enough, find Daniel a taxi to take him to the railway station. He must return to London immediately.

'Are you all right, sir?' Falthorne asked with concern.

'Yes . . . thank you. I . . . will not forget your . . . anxiety about the staff. I'll do what I can.'

'Thank you, sir,' Falthorne said grimly.

Daniel barely heard him as he went upstairs to get ready to leave. He needed to be alone to compose himself, away from observant eyes, no matter how well-meaning.

9

Daniel paced the platform at the station for ten minutes before the morning train came in with clouds of steam and a comforting roar of engine and clatter of metal on metal. No one got off, which he had expected, but half a dozen people got on. All of them he guessed to be workers in the city, such as bankers, managers of this and that, people who did not have to report for duty at an early hour.

He climbed up the steps and found a seat immediately. He had bought a newspaper, not to read, but to hide behind, so he would not be expected to converse with anyone. He could not face polite exchanges of any sort. His mind was in a state like the proverbial Gordian knot: everything was tied to everything else, and there was nowhere to begin or end.

Did the news of Graves' inheritance — completely unexpected — somehow trigger the death of Ebony? But how? Must he silence her to protect his new place in society?

Or was it the biography? Who or what would it destroy? Marriages? Fortunes? Reputations? Daniel sat up, clenched his fists, and took a deep breath. The answer was obvious: Special Branch. His father.

Was it a Special Branch agent gone rogue? But again, why?

Why had the killer obliterated Ebony's face?

Everyone knew who she was. Was it just hatred? Would anyone linger in order to do such a hideous thing without a compelling reason?

A sudden thought came to him. What if he let Graves hang? Then all of the papers could be destroyed, all the questions and accusations would disappear. A sudden warmth returned to his limbs, and he relaxed back into his seat. It would be the answer to everything! It would all be so easy.

Then a wave of nausea swept through him. My God, what was he thinking? It was hideously plain: he thought his father could be guilty! How could he ever face him again? He would have betrayed everything he had been taught. How far would he go to protect those he loved? Far enough to let them hang a man who was possibly innocent?

Pitt would never want that! Daniel must find the truth, whatever it was, and trust that he could live with it.

Daniel wished that he had never been called onto this case. He had thought for an instant that it was an honour, a step up in the hierarchy. Then he realised that there had been no one else to take it on. He was merely the least busy, and had not even expected to do anything more than fill a position that would be noticeable if it were left empty. Kitteridge was the one to do battle, and that was deservedly so.

Was there really any chance that there was a legal error sufficient to allow an appeal? Daniel doubted it. Kitteridge was meticulous. But that was only the first thread. There were others far more important, and dangerous. Was Graves guilty? Or, as he had said, was someone trying to blame him and discredit him so that even in death his work would not be worth publishing?

Actually, given human nature, scandal and the fall of the mighty, or those who were perceived to be so, was always news. The suggestion that Graves had been framed in order to silence him would multiply his sales tenfold! A judicial hanging, connived at to silence him, would give his accusations the power of a dying declaration! They would be carved indelibly into the public mind. People would pay black-market prices for copies of his book.

Had he thought of all that? Even planned it?

Surely not, at the cost of his life! He had not struck Daniel as a crusader of anything that would come at such a price. He was an arrogant man, self-serving. Hanging was a terrible death.

But of course Graves had not planned that! He had not imagined it. He must have known that if those he intended to expose were as corrupt as he said, they would retaliate. But perhaps he had expected to escape them? Why no accusation at trial? It was the ideal place to have exposed them to the world. He would never again have such a stage on which to speak. It made no sense to forego it. Narraway and Vespasia were both dead, but Pitt was very much alive. Why not accuse him? Pitt would have done his best to defend two of the closest friends he'd ever had. Loyalty, friendship, his own passion would have compelled him.

The train jolted forward again. Daniel had not

even realised that they had stopped at another suburban station. Where were they? He looked around and could see nothing he recognised. Then his alarm subsided. The stop he wanted was the terminus to the south of central London.

He was glad he was not there yet. He leaned back in his seat. He had a lot to sort out in his mind before he faced Marcus fford Croft. For a start, how much did fford Croft know? Why was he insistent on defending this man? It couldn't surely be for any personal like of someone so basically unpleasant. Even his own household had seemed united in loyalty to Ebony, and dislike of Graves. Or perhaps it was, even more, care of Sarah and Arthur? And of course the desire to stay in their present positions in the house, together, being as much of a family as they knew. Death was always hard, and one with as much violence as this was doubly so. And with the scandal on top of it, it would be hard for them to find other situations. Even if they did, there was always the uncertainty of settling into a new household. For the younger ones, it was sending them from the only place they had ever known, apart from wherever they had grown up. Daniel could imagine the anxieties and the fears that crowded their minds.

None of which was likely ever to have troubled the thoughts of Marcus fford Croft. And now that it was so much more serious, and involved Daniel so intimately, he would have to ask fford Croft for his reasons. Daniel's own job might be in peril if fford Croft's motive for helping Graves in a case he could not have expected to win held dangerous secrets. How much did Marcus know? Would a man fighting for his life not tell him everything? That was a question to which Daniel genuinely did not know the answer.

He went back to the question he really did not want to face, but it lay at the bottom of all of it. Had Victor Narraway been as devious and corrupt as Graves believed? It was difficult even to quantify it. In order to do his job well as head of Special Branch, particularly in the years when Fenian bombers had been so active in London, he had to have as much information as he could about possible bombers and their targets. There was no room for delicacy. 'I didn't like to probe his personal affairs,' was no answer. A single dead body justified any intrusion, let alone half a dozen, and more shattered, with limbs blown off, and any of the other dreadful damage that bombs could do. Daniel did not know very much about Special Branch; it had to be secret to survive, and to do its job. Some people who were the loudest to criticise them for interfering in personal privacy were also the loudest to accuse them if a bomb were undetected and eminent people were killed or maimed for the misfortune of being in the wrong place at the wrong time.

It was a matter of scale.

Graves had accused Pitt of colluding in murder to benefit his own position. That stung to the point that Daniel would see him hang with pleasure!

No, perhaps that was exaggeration. But he would certainly have beaten the daylights out of him with considerable satisfaction. Should he even be trying to find cause for an appeal, given the circumstances? Daniel was compromised. He would be excluded from defending Graves in court again.

Did Marcus know that too?

What in hell was he playing at?

Someone touched his elbow and he was startled. He stared at the man. It was a moment before he recognised it was the ticket collector.

'Oh — what did you say?' he asked.

'Your ticket, sir,' the man repeated. 'Sorry to disturb you, sir.'

Daniel hunted in his pocket and could not remember whether he had bought a ticket or not. The man waited patiently. Daniel retrieved it and handed it to him. He clipped it and passed it back.

★　★　★

When he arrived at Lincoln's Inn and went into the chambers of fford Croft and Gibson, he asked Impney, the chief clerk, if he could see Mr fford Croft immediately. He added that he had just returned from Mr Graves' house. He waited impatiently, and Impney returned in less than five minutes to say that Mr fford Croft would see him straight away.

Marcus fford Croft looked perfectly composed, if a little earnest, when Daniel walked into his study.

'Sit down, dear boy, and tell me what you have learned,' he invited him. 'Thank you, Impney. See that we are not disturbed.'

'Certainly, sir,' Impney replied, leaving the room and closing the door quietly behind him.

'Good morning, sir.' Daniel sat down opposite the desk. He wondered briefly if everyone else had been so uncomfortable in what was supposed to be an easy chair.

'What have you to report?' fford Croft asked. 'You look troubled. I imagine the household were not able to be particularly helpful.' He looked bland, as if he had resigned himself to bad news. Maybe he was placing all his hopes on Kitteridge.

'They were as helpful as they could be, sir.' Daniel replied. 'Their hospitality was excellent. One can learn a lot about people from their staff, even if they mean to tell you little.' Why was he spinning this out? They were sitting here in highly civilised fashion, as if nothing were wrong, that Ebony Graves had not been killed and then disfigured, and that Russell Graves was not going to hang, that there was no book written about people Daniel loved that was going to rip his life apart. Above all, that right now fford Croft did not know anything about it.

fford Croft leaned forward a little. 'But did you learn anything?' he asked with a little of his patience beginning to fray.

How much did fford Croft know already? Had he accepted the case in an attempt to control the damage Graves could do? Daniel knew that fford Croft was acquainted with his father. Had he also known Narraway? Had he some motive for involving Daniel in this particular case?

Daniel could read nothing in his face.

156

He must answer.

'Do you know what the book is about that Graves was writing, sir? And if he is granted an appeal, that he will then complete and publish?'

fford Croft's white eyebrows rose. 'Does it really matter now? It's a biography of someone, but I don't know of whom.'

'Victor Narraway, Head of Special Branch before my father,' Daniel said. He did not mean his voice to sound so grating, but he could not control it. 'It purports to be an exposé — of corruption, greed, manipulation, blackmail, and extortion . . . '

Either fford Croft had not known, or he was the most superb actor alive.

'And the Lady Vespasia,' Daniel went on. 'As the most skilled and dramatic whore in the European aristocracy. Furthermore — '

'Stop!' fford Croft's voice was hoarse. 'Stop this moment! What on earth are you saying?'

Brilliant actor or not, no one could make blood drain from their skin the way fford Croft's had done now. He was almost grey.

'And it says that my father is also corrupt,' Daniel continued. 'Promoted so that Narraway could continue to use him, more or less to manipulate him, to run the Special Branch.'

'That is nonsense!' fford Croft shook his head. 'Are you sure you did not misunderstand — '

'Yes, I'm quite sure.' Daniel cut across him in a way he would not have dared even a day ago. 'I've read his notes. They are incontestable.'

'The staff let you?'

'They imagined I was there to save him, if it is

157

possible. They know that you are his lawyer. That is your job.' He looked straight at fford Croft without flickering or lowering his eyes.

fford Croft said nothing.

'What is my job, sir?' Daniel asked. 'To save the man, if I can? To see if he is being framed by Special Branch, or someone in it? Do we expose this frame, break it? Or is my job to see that it fits, and he's hanged, and his notes destroyed? All I have done so far is make sure they say what they seem to, lock them away and ask the butler to secure the study door, so no one else reads them.'

fford Croft stared at him as if he were some dangerous creature that had materialised before him without warning. He looked flustered, suddenly very much older and utterly confused.

Daniel felt guilty for talking to him this way. He could not now say he had not suspected fford Croft of some sort of complicity; it was all too plain in his manner that he had. It would add insult to injury for him to pretend.

'This is appalling!' fford Croft breathed out slowly. He seemed to have shrunk in his chair. 'I . . . I had no idea . . . '

Daniel had no right to ask, but he needed to know. 'Why did you take this case, sir? We had very little chance of winning it. The evidence is overwhelmingly against Graves, and I didn't find anything to mitigate it at all, except that he had enemies, well-deserved ones.' He did not add that he refused to believe Special Branch had framed him to silence him, although as it filled his mind, he knew the first suspicion would fall on his father, but it might extend further as well. His colleagues were very loyal to him and to the service in general. Or perhaps the detail Graves gave implicated others even beyond Special Branch.

fford Croft was biting his lip. He seemed to be having some difficulty in deciding what to say. He looked at Daniel, but Daniel did not look away, even though he now was embarrassed, even sorry for his employer. That might be something fford Croft would not forgive, from anyone, let alone someone as junior as Daniel. This could be the end of his job. How would he explain that to his father?

But then that might be the least of his worries.

'A long time ago,' fford Croft began, 'thirty years, perhaps — it doesn't matter now; some things are timeless . . . '

Daniel sat without moving.

' . . . I knew Graves' father. He and I were friends.' fford Croft looked down at the desk. 'He got into a spot of trouble. Rather serious trouble. I was newly qualified then, but I was good. I had a few notable victories. Not unlike you, maybe, in a year or two.' His smile was sad, regretful. 'He asked me for my help. I . . . I let him down. I made a mistake. Not a big one, but enough to lose the case. He was guilty, I knew that. But there were mitigating circumstances. In defending Russell now, I'm repaying that old debt.'

The seconds ticked by, and then he looked up at Daniel at last. 'I owe him this much. It is as simple as that. And before you say so, I know that my chief obligation is to the law, and not to what I may consider my own idea of justice. Andrew Graves lost everything. He need not have, had I been wiser and more diligent. I owe Russell Graves the best effort I have, even if I despise him personally and think him guilty. We are not judge or jury, Pitt. We are advocates. Russell Graves never told me he was guilty of his wife's death. He has always insisted he was not. It is my job before the law to defend him to the best of my ability. And that means of yours, too. This other . . . is monstrous. I know nothing of it. But it does not mean he killed his wife. In fact, it gives sufficient motive to several others to raise reasonable doubt. We have let him down also.'

'No, sir!' Daniel said loudly. 'He knew he was writing such a book. He did not tell any of us. I can well see why he did not tell me, but in honesty he should have told you.'

'I have known your father for years, Pitt, not well, but well enough to know that the suggestions you say Graves makes are not true. Unfortunately, the public does not know what Special Branch does. They do not know of all the disasters they prevent. That is the nature of the office.'

'And we are going to use it to seek another trial? Or is it too late?'

fford Croft's face lit with a bitter humour. 'That is surely the last thing you want? Apart from destroying your father's reputation, to open up the security services to such public review would be little short of treason. We cannot even

160

mention it in open court. And Russell Graves must have known that.'

'Then wouldn't it be treasonous to publish this book?' Daniel asked.

'Possibly, but it could be veiled in such implication as merely to be libellous, although Victor Narraway is dead, and so is Lady Vespasia. They cannot sue; one cannot libel the dead. And if Thomas Pitt decided to sue for libel, because Graves called him deceitful or corrupt, it would be pointless. Once you have lost the public's confidence, you cannot regain it.'

'Why would Graves write such a thing?'

'Possibly for money,' fford Croft said wearily 'To draw attention to himself. To have some imagined revenge.' He shrugged. 'It doesn't matter. The thing is to see that it is not published. And hanging him will not necessarily do that. There may be other pages, notes that the publisher already has.'

A coldness settled around Daniel's chest, almost too tightly for him to breathe. 'Apart from that, sir, if he did not kill Ebony Graves, then who did?'

Marcus looked at him.

'He could defend himself, sir,' Daniel went on, 'by saying he was being made to look guilty by someone in Special Branch. That would be his ultimate revenge. He can say that to anyone — to Kitteridge, next time he sees him. To an appeal judge, if we get an appeal. Even to a journalist! I suppose he could raise his father's case and say that you are trying to silence him

. . . if he's desperate enough.'

fford Croft started to speak, then faltered to a stop.

Daniel said nothing.

fford Croft began again. 'Do you want to be released from this case, Pitt?'

'No!' The answer was instant, and not thought out.

This time, it was fford Croft who was silent.

'No,' Daniel said again, leaning forward a little towards the desk. 'I have established a relationship . . . with the household of Russell Graves. I care what happens to his children. I gave them my word. And . . . and for my father. At least I know his nature, and that includes his integrity. And I can't leave finding this to someone else. My father may have made mistakes. It's a very difficult job, and there's not always a right and a wrong. I had . . . I have to know as much as I can to defend him, if it ever comes to that. I can't go and bury my head in the sand. This isn't going to go away, especially as we are trying to prove that Graves did not, in fact, kill his wife,' Daniel said.

'Yes,' fford Croft agreed. 'But at least let us say we have to find the truth. If it exonerates Graves of his wife's murder, then it might well implicate someone else. To summarise, it would seem to be either someone in the house, or someone who was allowed in by one of the servants. The police are certain there was no break-in. Of the people in the house, Graves himself is most likely. The alternatives are only the servants, or one of the children. Arthur is in a wheelchair. By every

162

account we have, Sarah and her mother were close. There is no word of any quarrel at all, let alone one terrible enough for a girl to have killed her mother and then burned her face and hair, till she was barely recognisable.'

fford Croft's voice held level, but Daniel knew the intensity of self-control he was exercising, because he saw the white knuckles of the hand resting on his desk and the pulse beating in his temple.

'Yes, sir,' Daniel said quietly. All the time his mind was racing over what he could remember about his father and Special Branch. He had memories of conversations. Mention of crime, often murder, of pretence and deceit. He could remember bombings, and his father coming home desperate to stop them. Frightened people wanted quick answers. If Pitt had taught him anything, it was that there were many sides to any story.

As Daniel had grown older, he had begun to realise how difficult it was to make a judgement, and that the answer often contained tragedy as much as any intentional evil. It was so much easier to be angry, to blame, rather than be drenched with pity.

'I have an idea,' fford Croft said. 'First, we must go back to the beginning. The police didn't give us much to go on. We need to know more about the science.'

'What science, sir? Fingerprints aren't going to help us. Everybody's prints are all over the place,' Daniel pointed out.

'There is more to the science of forensics than

that,' fford Croft answered. 'My daughter has studied medicine . . . and chemistry. Her name is Miriam. I've asked her to come in. Tell her what we have, and see if she has any ideas. Don't be put off by her. She's clever. Very clever, although her achievements are not recognised among her male peers and she was not awarded her degrees although she passed all her examinations.'

Daniel said nothing. He couldn't imagine that this was going to turn up any new evidence.

'I'll let you know when Miriam's here. We've only got another seventeen days left after today!'

'Yes . . . sir.' Daniel stood up slowly. He wanted to say something else, but his mind was whirling like a dust storm, everything banging into each other: Arthur in his chair, with the exquisite birds, all wings and dreams on his walls; the blood and the scorched carpet in Ebony's room. The servants facing the break-up of the only family they knew. Graves' pointless words about the people Daniel loved the most. And fford Croft wanted to call in his daughter, who was a doctor and a chemist!

'Yes, sir,' he said again from the doorway. And then he walked out and closed the door softly behind him.

10

Daniel worked at his desk, mostly making notes on what he had heard and observed at Graves' house. Kitteridge came in, looking tired and unhappy. Daniel was not surprised to learn that he had discovered no legal error of any size at all, let alone one sufficient to justify an appeal.

He sat down facing Daniel's desk. No one else in the same room took any notice of him. They were busy studying, worrying about their own cases.

Daniel did not want to discuss what he had learned, particularly the part about Special Branch, but Kitteridge had a right to know. If it proved viable and there was a retrial, then everyone who could read a newspaper would know. He realised with a profound sharpness, as only the first impact of the wound, what it would be like to have every person in the street aware of what you were accused of, but no idea of the reality of who you were, or your side of the story.

'Pitt!' Kitteridge said sharply.

Daniel realised that Kitteridge had spoken to him, and he had not heard. 'Yes? Sorry . . . '

'Did you learn anything at Graves' house? Do you think he did it? Have you got any other suspects at all?' Kitteridge's patience was short, and it was audible in his tone of voice.

'I learned quite a lot,' Daniel replied. 'Did you know he was writing a biography of one of the past heads of Special Branch?'

'No, is it relevant?' Kitteridge looked blank. Then suddenly it came to him, and he sat forward so he could lower his voice and be heard only by Daniel. 'That's your father's job, isn't it?'

'Yes. But this is mostly about the man before him, who's dead now. The notes are vile.'

'Can we still stop it?' Kitteridge asked. 'What a cowardly thing to do. I knew I didn't like the bastard.'

Daniel smiled with a sudden upsurge of warmth. 'Neither do his household staff, although they're very discreet about it. An expression on their faces, and extra polite language. But the point is, someone from Special Branch might have done this to frame him.'

'What? Kill his wife?' Kitteridge looked very sceptical indeed.

'Make it look as if he did.'

Kitteridge's eyebrows rose. 'Why not simply kill him? It seems a long way round about it.' Then suddenly he shook his head, as if he understood. 'Disgrace him, then ruin him. Probably effective. But then who did kill Mrs Graves?'

'That's the difficulty,' Daniel agreed.

'Do Special Branch go in for that sort of thing? Assassinations?' Kitteridge asked. 'It's a bit steep! Killing poor Mrs Graves. It's not her fault. It would be plain murder. I don't like the sound of that at all.'

'The way he paints Special Branch, or at the least the heads of it, that would be the least of their crimes,' Daniel said bitterly.

166

'What are you going to do?' There was a surprising gentleness in Kitteridge's voice, as if he understood the complexity and the pain of family loyalty, rivalry, complicated love, and the need for ties at the same time as freedom.

Daniel hesitated before he answered. 'I'm going to try to find out who did kill Ebony Graves. It still could have been Graves himself. We know no one broke in, and I can't imagine any of the staff doing it. None of them would have the strength, except the butler. If he did, he must have had a hell of a reason!'

'It must have been someone already in the house,' Kitteridge said. 'We've been through this. If Graves had let someone in, he'd have said so by now.'

'Or she let them in herself?'

'A lover? They couldn't find any trace of one.'

'So, he was clever, and careful.'

'Do you believe that?'

Daniel shrugged. 'I've no idea. But we have still got seventeen more days to find out.'

'Less.' Kitteridge climbed to his feet. 'We can't lodge an appeal on the last day. Not that we've got anything to appeal about. I wish I wanted to save him.' His mouth twisted with an expression of complicated regret. 'What you just told me makes me want to see him hang. I don't like being made to question my government. There's so much else in the world that's changing, or questioning everything. I want to have somebody to believe in.'

Daniel watched him retreat, and was aware with a sudden sense of pity that Kitteridge had not said he wanted to believe in his own family. But Daniel did, profoundly.

Sometime later, Daniel looked up from his note-making to see Impney standing in front of him. 'Yes?'

'Miss fford Croft is here to see you, sir. I've asked her to wait in Mr fford Croft's rooms, since he is not in at the moment. You will not be disturbed.'

Daniel rose to his feet, not feeling ready for this at all. 'Thank you, Impney.'

He knocked briefly on fford Croft's door, and as soon as he heard an answer he went in. He did not know what he expected, but it was not the woman who stood in the centre of the floor. Miriam was not tall, but she was slender, which gave the impression of more height than she had. Daniel had only ever known fford Croft with white hair, so he had no idea what colour it had been in his youth. Hers was bright auburn; one might say less politely, red. She had the fair blemishless skin that sometimes goes with that shade, and her eyes were unmistakably greenish-blue. She was not beautiful, which was a surprise, given her colouring. Her face was too strong, her nose too bold. But she was entirely unforgettable. On this occasion, she wore a business-like full-length skirt; there was no concession to fashion in it. Her jacket was tailored, and her blouse crisp white, but unadorned by lace or frills.

'You're Daniel Pitt?' she asked, as if surprised by his appearance. Perhaps she had expected someone older, like Kitteridge, perhaps, who was thirty-four, nearer to her own age, which looked to be just under forty.

'Yes. How do you do, Miss fford Croft?' he replied a little stiffly. This woman was a doctor and a chemist. Why, for heaven's sake?

'Please sit down, Mr Pitt,' she directed. 'Tell me everything you know about the case about which you want advice. And when I say *know*, I mean only those facts that are beyond dispute. I will sit at my father's desk so I may make notes.'

Daniel obeyed, slowly. In her own way, she was as intimidating as her father.

She looked at him enquiringly, pencil poised.

He tried to marshal his thoughts: definitely facts only, no conclusions. He told her what the police had reported about the finding of the body: when, where, who, how, and what they believed to be the cause of death.

She wrote many notes. She worked so rapidly that he wondered if she had her own form of shorthand.

'And Mr Graves was tried for the crime and found guilty?' she asked.

'Yes . . . ' He did not know what to call her, whether she was Doctor or Miss, so he left it open.

'What evidence is there that it was he?' she asked.

'There was no break-in, and he was the only one in the house unaccounted for at the time she died. The body was discovered at ten in the evening. There were no other people present except the family, and the household servants.'

'So, could she not have let someone in, or it

was someone already in the house?' she said quietly. 'Interesting . . . and sad. It is always sad when someone is killed by a person they know well, a family member. But I believe it happens quite often. Tell me about the burning you mentioned.'

'All I know is that there was blood on the corner of the hearthstone, and a lot of the carpet was burned where her head and upper body must have been . . . where they said the head and body were.' He would be as precisely accurate as she had requested, although he could not think of any way in which she could help.

She looked down at her notes, and then up at him. She met his eyes with complete candour. 'Precisely what is it you wish me to do, Mr Pitt? Do you believe that there is any doubt about his guilt?'

'Very little,' he answered. 'When you look at all those facts, I think the jury came to the only conclusion they could.'

'But . . . ?'

'There were other facts that they did not know. Graves knew them, so I don't know why he didn't raise them then. He mentioned them to me privately, and I found proof when I searched the study in his house. He is writing a book that is a complete destruction of the character and reputation of two very important people, both now dead, so they cannot defend themselves, nor could he be accused of libelling them. There is another in the biography who is alive, and in an important government position. Graves accuses him of corruption and covering up serious crimes. Leaders are always subject to such charges. I suppose they have to be . . . '

'So, he guided his way well between maligning the dead, whom he cannot libel, and accusing only of duplicity the one man he could,' she concluded. 'Are you suggesting that someone, on their behalf, could have killed his wife? Is that what he suggested?'

'I don't remember exactly what he said, but yes, he suggested it.'

'Do you think there is any truth in it?' She frowned slightly. Whether she doubted it, or simply found it distasteful, he could not tell.

He smiled wryly. 'Since I knew the two people who are dead very well, from my early childhood, and the one still living is my father . . . '

He saw her startled reaction, and sudden sympathy.

'I am not in an impartial position,' he went on. 'Personally, I would see Graves in hell, with pleasure. But that is neither a legal defence, nor a moral one.' He heard the emotion thick in his voice, but he could not control it.

'So, the only solution is to find out who did kill Ebony Graves.' Her voice was soft with regret. 'And hope that it is indeed Russell Graves. I doubt, Mr Pitt, if it was someone in defence of the people he maligned. It is an oblique and rather inefficient way of dealing with it. Has his publisher any notes, or a rough draft of the manuscript? It would be interesting to know if anyone else has commented on them, to keep the book from publication.'

171

'I don't know,' he admitted. 'I . . . I found them only this morning. And I don't want any more people to know about it than have to. We must find out who the publisher is.' That was not a task he was looking forward to. It was very easy for the Duke of Wellington to say, 'Publish and be damned'. He was a good deal safer in his position than any of the people Daniel cared for. Arid, if he remembered correctly, that was only about having a mistress. Not a sin, compared with those supposedly exposed in Graves' book, such as profound corruption.

Miriam fford Croft was smiling, but it was with considerable sympathy.

'It sounds as if Mr Graves is a man who made many enemies,' she observed tartly. 'He may be about to add one more to the list. You sound as if you have been to the house yourself?'

'Yesterday and I came back this morning,' Daniel agreed. 'Do we have to return there? I did not tell you much about the family, or the staff. I don't think they can help. I . . . think they would, if they were able.'

'Then there is no evidence to look at here, Mr Pitt. We can only learn more from studying what is there. Her body has already been buried, I presume.'

'Yes. Several weeks ago. But she died of a blow to the back of her head. I can get you the police reports, if you wish?'

'It would be useful to read them,' she conceded. 'I will ask my father to obtain a copy. First, I think we *will* go to the house, and have another look at the scene. Are her belongings still there? Her clothes, for example?'

'Yes.'

'Good. One may sometimes learn a great deal from clothes.'

Daniel doubted it, but he did not argue. He was beginning to think it was a complete waste of time. What did this woman think she could learn? He must not forget to see if Mercy Blackwell had discovered anything. It was a faint hope. His mind was filled with fear that the scandal Graves had invented was at the heart of the crime. It was too urgent, too big, and too ugly to be an incidental thread. It was the kind of thing that would very easily inspire murder.

But why Ebony? Then another thought occurred to him. Had she somehow been the one who had found the information and given it to Graves? Yet he could not see how her crusading for various rights and privileges had taken her into where she had learned about Special Branch.

Miriam fford Croft was waiting for him.

He followed her out into the front of the office. A few moments later they were in a taxi on their way to the station. They took the next train south and settled down for the twenty-six-minute journey.

Daniel had been afraid that she would ask him for further information about his father, and especially about Narraway, but instead she talked of the great prospects she believed science had in the solving of crime. In spite of himself, he found he was interested. He began asking her questions, especially about the problems she

173

seemed to see already making themselves apparent.

'The greatest difficulty?' she said with a twisted smile. 'Of all?'

He was surprised. 'There are so many?'

'Oh, yes. For example, to understand that things can be weighed and measured, and you can come up with a definite answer. But that in itself may prove a thing is possible or impossible. It seldom proves that that is the only answer. Some things are individual, for example, fingerprints. But it still is a skill to see the tiny differences. We are only just learning and categorising them. Another is bullets. Some have left-hand rifling, some have right-hand, some, like shotgun pellets, have no distinguishing marks at all. We can tell if bullets don't match a particular gun, and that if they do it only means it could be that gun, not that it was.'

'So, more negatives than positives. As a defence lawyer, I can't fault that!' he said very regretfully. His thoughts were darker than such details, and he could not hide it.

'There are small limitations,' she went on. 'And in time we may be able to tell very much more. The struggle is to prove it to a jury. They are highly suspicious. They don't like to be condescended to. They are ignorant but they do not like to be told as much.'

'Not many of us do,' Daniel pointed out.

She gave a half-smile. It softened her face. 'Indeed. I'm afraid some of it depends upon who you are, not upon what you say. There are experts they will trust, and those they will not.'

She gave a somewhat wry gesture. 'They do not think we can count, never mind understand science. Most people, women included, judge according to their own experience. We think what we need to think, in order to hold onto our own world view and validate what we must believe. It is a matter of survival, although it may seem merely to be prejudice to someone else. It takes a lot of courage to turn your world upside down and start again. Most people have enough practical worries of survival not to look for philosophical ones.'

He looked across at her face, which seemed quite calm and composed. There were only tiny lines around her mouth, and shadows in her eyes. She was old enough that experience and emotion had marked her features.

Quite suddenly, he liked her better for it.

They discussed trials, jury and evidence a little longer, then when they arrived at the station he found a cab and they set out towards Graves' house.

She was impressed by it, as he had been. She said little, but he saw it in her expression. For the first time, he wondered where Marcus fford Croft lived. He knew the area, but not the particular house. Surely it was at least as fine as this? But of course it would be full of memories that coloured every thought of it. Just as there were for him in the house on Keppel Street, Bloomsbury, where he had grown up. It was in the heart of London, not the spacious suburbs, but even so, the squares were tree-lined, grassy, and houses had a certain elegance. But the important thing was the comfort of the mind, the knowledge of warmth not only in the literal sense, but in the heart, certain beliefs not only about the past, but about the future also.

He must pay attention to his job.

The front door was opened by Falthorne.

'Good afternoon, Falthorne,' Daniel said immediately. 'May I introduce Miss fford Croft? She has come to help me try to learn exactly what occurred here regarding Mrs Graves' death. She is a scientist, and may learn things that we cannot.'

'Good afternoon, Miss fford Croft.' Falthorne inclined his head. 'If you would care to come in? Would you like tea served, sir? Will you be in the morning room?'

'Thank you, Falthorne, I think we will begin right away in the bedroom, if you don't mind. Time . . . is short.'

'Yes, sir, ma'am,' Falthorne closed the door and led them upstairs to Ebony Graves' bedroom. 'If there is anything you wish, sir, just ring the bell. Perhaps you would care for tea and sandwiches later? I'm sure Mrs Hanslope would be happy to make something.'

'That would be very nice,' Daniel accepted. He was sorry to miss the familiar lunch in the servants' hall, but there was no time for that now.

Falthorne conducted them upstairs, then excused himself, leaving them in what had been Ebony's room.

Daniel turned to Miriam. 'How can I help?'

She was gazing around in interest, and there

176

was a sadness in her face that she was probably unaware of. She looked younger and more vulnerable than when she spoke of science. Was she imagining Ebony Graves here, and the last unsuspecting moments of her life, before she knew that person there with her was about to kill her? To be in the bedroom, surely it had to be someone she loved, or at the very least trusted? This was a place you imagine yourself apart from the world, when you let down your guard.

Except, of course, if the person most dangerous to you was in your own family! Then it was anything but a place of peace. It was where you were most vulnerable. There would be nowhere to run to, no one who could help.

Was that how it had been?

Miriam walked over to the hearth. One did not have to look around in order to find the place where the murder had happened, especially when no attempt had been made to clean it. Indeed, the carpet was ruined. She kneeled down and looked very carefully at the blood on the cornerstone. Daniel had no idea what she could tell from it, other than that was the place where Ebony had sustained her fatal injury.

Miriam was silent. Could the blood tell her anything that they did not already know? It was possible now to differentiate human blood from animal blood, Daniel knew, but not one person's from another's. Perhaps venous blood from arterial? But if so, what would that help? They knew the injury was to the back of her head.

She looked up at Daniel. 'The problem is, juries dislike anything they cannot understand,

and think we are trying to trick them.'

'Do you mean they see the science as magic?'

'Yes, unfortunately.'

She moved from the blood to the burned carpet. She stared at this silently for what seemed like minutes. 'There must have been quite a fire here,' she said at last, rising to her feet. 'How badly was the body burned? Do you know? Did you see it, or photographs of it, perhaps?'

'Yes, they were appalling. She was badly disfigured, from the chest up. Would they help?'

'I don't know,' she said frankly. 'She didn't fall into the fire. Coals from it must have been placed onto her deliberately. But why?' She frowned. 'And how did it continue to burn? Fire burns upward, not downward. There had to be something to fuel it, or it would have gone out.'

'Something? Like what?' Daniel was confused.

Miriam said nothing for several moments, clearly examining the possibilities in her mind. 'Perhaps something like cotton, or linen,' she suggested. 'A towel? But more likely something like fat, or oil, as well. Perhaps whoever it was went to the kitchen . . . or spirits? Yes, a whole body of whisky or brandy, on a towel — that would burn for a while and get quite hot.'

'Is there some way you can know?' Daniel asked.

'If I could see the body, yes. The photographs might be of help, but I doubt it. Maybe the coroner's report? But only if they tested for something highly combustible. Otherwise not. The carpet is badly charred, but somebody has swept away the ashes from whatever was left, and the blood is quite plain on the hearthstone.'

'The body is buried,' he reminded her. 'Even if you found where she was burned, and what caused it, would it tell you who did it?'

She looked rueful. 'Probably not. In fact, almost certainly not. But if it was with alcohol for drinking, say, whisky or brandy, it suggests someone who knew where such things were kept. But why? It was done on purpose, so far as I can see. What does it mean?'

'Hatred?' He thought aloud. 'A sort of revenge, even on what was left of her.'

Miriam bit her lip. 'That's a very terrible sort of hatred, to destroy a dead woman's face.'

'If you met Graves, you might believe it. But you're right, it's insane.'

'What was she like?' Miriam looked directly at him, as if it became suddenly very important to her to understand Ebony. Perhaps she was imagining what it would be like to die in this room at the hands of a man capable of that kind of hatred.

Daniel was imagining it, and it chilled through to the core of him. 'Apparently, she was a passionate fighter for women's freedoms, and other things such as better medicine for women, some form of birth control . . . '

He found himself blushing ridiculously at mentioning such a thing to Miriam, a woman he barely knew, and yet found himself admiring. Maybe Ebony had been something like her, trying to break ground for greater freedom for other women. His sister, Jemima, would approve

179

of Miriam. She always wanted more than was permitted her, as a girl.

'Let's look at her clothes.' Miriam started moving as she spoke. She went over to the first wardrobe door and opened it. 'They can tell us much about a person,' she said, touching the long sweep of an afternoon gown in lavender silk. 'Good quality.' She started taking them down, out of the cupboard, and laying them on the bed, and then returning for more.

'What are you doing?' Daniel demanded. He could see no relationship between a woman's taste in clothing and the cause of her being murdered.

Miriam gave him a cool look, her eyebrows slightly raised. 'Clothing tells us a lot about someone. How her appearance matters, what impression she wishes to create, and the kind of events she attended. Fetch the next one for me, please.' And without turning to see if he would obey, she started holding the clothes up one at a time, and looking at herself in the glass to establish how they would have looked when worn.

'What does that tell you?' Daniel asked, taking more gowns and laying them on top of the others.

'Her budget,' Miriam replied. 'Which was generous. A lot of afternoon dresses here, very few evening, which suggests she did not go out with her husband.'

'I wondered what Ebony had looked like. Apart from being dark, and beautiful.' He had not even seen a photograph of her and he had

180

tried to imagine her. He saw her as vulnerable, too, a dreamer, someone who wanted far more than she had ever received.

'Most of them have been worn several times.' Miriam interrupted his train of thought. 'Like these, for example.' She held up one in dark grey-coloured wool. 'It is even a bit thin in places,' she went on, her interest piqued. 'I wonder why, because it's not particularly attractive. Of course, it may have been better when it was on. Some dresses are. In fact, the best of them. The secret lies in the cut, not the fabric.' She ran it through her fingers, feeling the quality of it. 'But this seems very ordinary.' She looked at the seams and stitching. Then she put it flat on the bed and picked another dress, and compared them for size. She looked up at Daniel, puzzled. 'The dark wool is longer by at least a couple of inches, maybe three. And it's not of the same quality. And yet it's well worn. I wonder why that is?'

Daniel could think of no reasonable answer.

'Is there anything else like that?' Miriam went on. 'Shoes? Boots?'

Daniel turned and looked in the bottom of the wardrobe. He could not tell at a glance, but kneeled down to look more closely. There was one pair that looked more used than the others, and plainer.

'How about these?' he asked, holding them up.

Miriam put down the clothes she was considering and came across. She took the boots from him and looked at them closely. Then she took a pair of shoes, which were of good quality leather, with heels. She examined them thoroughly, then stared up at Daniel. 'You might keep an old dress from when you were heavier,' she said thoughtfully. 'Though I can't think why. It's not attractive, and it would take far too much room to be worth it. And why only one? All the others I can see are roughly the same, a smaller size. But the boots are another thing. Your feet don't change in size that much, in fact hardly at all, no matter how much weight you might lose. They get thinner, but not shorter.'

'These things are not hers,' he concluded.

'It would seem not,' she agreed. 'But whose are they? And why are they here?' She looked up from the boots. 'Did she dress up as someone else? Did she have a secret life her husband knew nothing of? These boots are larger than hers. She could have put thick socks on, and worn them.' She took a deep breath. 'I think there may be a side to Mrs Graves that we do not yet know. You said you had a friend you enquired of, if she knew anything of Ebony Graves. Although it may have nothing to do with the manner of her death.'

'But do you think if we learn whatever these clothes are about that might lead us to who killed her?' Daniel was not sure that he wanted to know, but there was no escaping it. 'I don't want Russell Graves to hang, if he really is innocent . . . '

'I doubt he's innocent,' Miriam said with a dark tone in her voice. 'And even if you discover where she wore those clothes, or if she wore them at all, it doesn't prove he was not involved in her death. It just suggests that there is a better reason than a marital quarrel.' She put the boots down. 'I suggest you ask Mr Falthorne to lock this door. Not that I imagine there is anyone likely to come in. But we must take precautions. This is becoming more . . . complicated. There is little here for us to work with, but I will take a small piece of this carpet, which must have been roughly beneath her head, and see what I can find. I wish we had the body.'

'What do you expect to find?'

'Some tiny traces of alcohol . . . although it may well have burned away, if it was ever there,' she answered. 'But something was very hot. It burned a part of the carpet, and even the canvas beneath. And it burned human flesh.' She looked at him with a wince of pain. 'There is something terribly ugly here.'

That evening, before he and Miriam caught the train home, Daniel asked Falthorne to unlock Graves' study door. He went to the desk, unlocked it and removed the copious notes and manuscript — in fact, all he could find of Graves' book — and put it in his briefcase. He foresaw that he would need it to hand, convinced as he was that it had some bearing on the case. The question was what exactly that was.

11

The morning after returning from Graves' house to London, Daniel went again to see Graves in prison. He needed more information about the biography, particularly what Graves' sources had been.

There were only seventeen more days before he would hang, if they did not find cause for the appeal.

Kitteridge had found nothing so far. All the evidence regarding the potential unpopularity of Graves' proposed book may not have been known to Kitteridge, but it was definitely known to Graves himself.

Why had Graves not spoken of it before? That question had gnawed at Daniel since he had heard of it. It was Miriam, on the train journey back to London, who had suggested the answer. Graves had been indiscreet in his suggestions of corruption, blackmail, and sins of passion that might stretch to include suspicion of treason. No one knew how far it stretched, what damage it might do, or whose lives it would touch and stain.

Miriam had reminded Daniel that that was what had finally brought Robespierre down, and brought to an end the high terror in the French Revolution. Spread the fear widely enough, and no one was safe. Someone would silence you. Certainly no one could afford to let you speak.

Someone they cared for, even if not they themselves, would be touched by it.

'Graves has been too wide in his threats,' she said with a bleak smile. 'Anybody siding with him will make himself a hundred enemies.'

'Graves will get very specific.'

'Yes,' she said quietly. 'We had better find something before then. Perhaps he will at last realise his danger?'

'Then I shall tell him!' Daniel promised.

He did not want to see Graves, but it was unavoidable. It was his duty, at the very least, to advise him regarding the facts of the case. There was no realistic chance that Kitteridge would discover cause for appeal, as Kitteridge had reminded him, although he was still looking. Graves' last chance was to present a viable other suspect, along with any possible evidence of their guilt. It might be enough to get a stay of execution.

This he told Graves when he saw him.

'They got me tried and convicted, what the hell is likely to make them keep me alive now?' Graves demanded furiously. Today he looked haggard. His hair was unkempt, and was in need of washing and cutting. His skin was pallid, sagging a little around the jawline, and unsurprisingly he was not allowed a blade to shave himself.

Daniel kept his own temper with difficulty. 'I'll ask the questions. I've been to your house, interviewed your servants and looked in your desk. I've seen the notes for your book, too. It's time for you to tell me what your information is, and where you got it! If anyone is involved with as much treason, blackmail and murder as you say, they'll want to kill this book before it's born.'

'You expect me to tell you my sources, so you can destroy them?' Graves snapped back. 'I will go to my grave with my secrets.' He glanced at Daniel. 'Don't think I don't know who you are, Pitt! Clever, aren't they, giving me Thomas Pitt's son to keep me from telling the truth? You may think you've succeeded, but you haven't.' Suddenly there was life in his face, in his eyes.

'Won't do you any good if you're dead,' Daniel said. 'I want to find a believable suspect of who could have killed your wife and framed you. Since that is what happened, according to you.'

'Of course it is, you fool! Why would I kill her? She bored me with her endless causes, but she was doing no one any harm. If I had killed her, you wouldn't have found her body there, in the bedroom, and at a time when I couldn't prove myself elsewhere. Do you think I'm stupid?'

'No,' Daniel said honestly. 'But I think you've got a hell of a temper, and you are certainly not above losing it with someone. You could have hit her, harder than you meant to, and found she was dead.'

'They said she was burned,' Graves retorted immediately. 'Why in hell would I do that?'

'Why would anybody?' Daniel asked.

The scorn in Graves' face was quite open. 'To make it more horrific, of course. And to prove it wasn't an accident. Don't pretend to be a fool! You must have thought of that. God! Why did they give me such a novice?' He sat back in his chair, straining for a moment against his manacles, his shoulders bunched with the effort.

'Because Kitteridge is busy, still looking for a loophole in the law,' Daniel replied, trying to keep the anger out of his voice. 'You're lucky we're trying at all! The world thinks you're guilty.' The moment he said that, he wished he had not. It was part of his job to keep Graves still hoping, still fighting. Was it cruel, when there was so little chance? Would it be kinder to help him come to terms with death? That was a priest's job, but Daniel did not envy him that.

He couldn't take the words back now, and apologising was useless.

'You're right,' he admitted. 'It doesn't make any sense for you to have disfigured her face, except hatred. Since indisputably someone did, what reasons do you think they had? It must have taken some time. They risked being found, so they must have wanted to very much.'

'To make everyone hate me,' Graves answered. 'So I'd look like a monster! Did you really need to ask that? God — you are a fool! Listen, you idiot, those behind my wife's murder need to destroy me in order to make all my work seem like delusion, invented, instead of uncovering the corruption behind the face of power. Don't you understand that?' He looked at Daniel with a most profound contempt.

Said that like, it looked believable, even likely.

But it all depended on the charges that Graves' book detailed being true.

Slowly, Daniel was being forced to accept the possibility that Graves thought it was true, however detached he was from reality.

'All right,' he said cautiously. 'Who else knew about this book?'

Graves did not answer.

'They had to know,' Daniel pointed out. 'Otherwise why take the risk of framing you for your wife's murder? Actually, why not simply kill you? Then frame her, if they had to?'

'Because I'm prepared,' Graves replied. 'Pretty obvious, really. I'd be a lot harder to kill.'

Daniel raised his eyebrows. 'With all the skills they have? I don't think they'd hesitate to kill you. Maybe with a blow to the head, or perhaps with a knife, or a gun. This seems like a long way around it.'

'It wouldn't stop my book being published,' Graves answered.

'And will this?'

'No. I took precautions.' Graves smiled slowly, a sour, malicious smile.

'So, you don't care whether you get hanged or not, as long as the book comes out?' Daniel concluded.

Graves slammed his manacled fists on the table. The jolt of the steel against his wrists must have hurt appallingly. He would have bruises there in the morning.

'Of course, I care! But I can't let them win. When they've got my death on their consciences as well, it will only add to their infamy.'

'Well, I'd like to see it averted before then,' Daniel lied. 'It's my job to save you, and to expose the truth, if I can, but I can't do it without you. Somebody killed your wife. And it

188

wasn't Narraway, because he's dead himself, and so is Lady Vespasia. Then who killed Mrs Graves?'

'You should ask your father!' Graves spat the words.

Daniel felt as if he had been struck. Nausea overwhelmed him. His mind raced. He had expected this, but it still hit him with a shock, like a bad fall, as if he was sprawling on the ground, bleeding, skin torn and bloody.

'Do you imagine he will tell me?' he asked. 'With no proof at all, just the desperate word of a man facing the gallows for the brutal murder of his wife? Really, you can do better than that! You'll have to.'

Graves stared at him with hatred. The look on his face was that of a cornered animal, frightened and dangerous, nothing left to lose except his life.

'Giving up?' he said with contempt in his voice. 'You're not! You're backing out because you're afraid of what you'll find. You look into all that past stuff, you'll find that Narraway kept a file of all the things he learned in his job: all the debts, the sins, the mistakes of everyone he could one day blackmail. And since they'd given in, he'd got them for ever. Your father inherited that file and, believe me, when he gets tightly enough trapped, he uses it. Just a little bit at first. A small favour to solve a bad case. Then a little bit bigger one the next time, and bigger again.' He smiled very slightly, an ugly, knowing gesture. 'He can't afford to fail! Not coming after the great Victor Narraway. And your father hasn't got a Vespasia,

who learned everybody's secrets in the aristocracy, not only here, but in Europe, too.' Graves'
face shone with malice. 'No wonder she was
never out of money! She earned a fortune in
favours, one way or another. Mistress to half the
crowned heads of Europe — and their enemies,
no doubt. Blackmail for life, that!'

Daniel snapped at last. 'I don't believe you.'

'Not yet,' Graves agreed. 'But you'll have to
find out. You won't be able to ignore it, not for
ever. Little bits of evidence will turn up, old
tales, and when there's enough of them, you'll
see that I was right. The image will be there in
your mind, a bright silver one, all glittering with
light. But as you see it more and more often, it
will be a little more tarnished each time, until it's
grey and yellow, corroded over, as ugly as it once
was beautiful.' His eyes never left Daniel's face.

That was a stab that hurt. Daniel could
remember Vespasia from his earliest childhood.
She was beautiful, and she made him laugh. She
always had time to talk to him. Once or twice she
had given him books and sat with him to discuss
them. He remembered long talks about Ivanhoe
and Hereward the Wake and his long battle
against the Normans.

And she was funny. He remembered her
remarks that often he did not understand, but
made everybody laugh.

When a case was very bad, seeming impossible
to solve, she and Narraway would come to the
house and they would sit around the kitchen
table and work out all the ways to solve it. He
remembered creeping down the stairs with

Jemima and sitting on the lower steps listening at the kitchen door. They knew from the voices that it was serious, although they didn't understand very much. They knew when a decision had been made, and more than once had had to hide very quickly in the pantry, or get caught.

These were good memories, ones he would not let Graves spoil. He knew that the cases were serious, often to do with treason, or murder, but he refused to believe that they fought for their own gain and not for a just cause, or to save the lives of those who were guilty of no more than foolishness, or being in the wrong place at the wrong time.

He looked at Graves' sneering face. 'I think most of her lovers would be dead by now,' he said as levelly as he could. He heard the strain in his own voice. 'Although perhaps their sons are not. You have certainly made a lot of enemies. I wouldn't know where to begin. You'll have to do better than that. It would take me years to go through all of them.'

Graves' eyes widened. He saw his own tactical error, as Daniel recognised before a look of hatred filled Graves' face.

'I agree,' Graves said softly. 'Forget about Lady Vespasia, and Narraway, for that matter. His extorted help, money from too many people; betrayed his friends. And those from his early years would be dead, too. Concentrate on your father. He's still alive, and has fifteen years left in office, more or less. The lists of victims to blackmail are his! Lots of them are still alive. Look into those he trusts to do something like kill my wife and blame me! Ask him about Portugal! Then you won't think he's such a damn hero!'

Daniel frowned. Puzzled. What did Graves mean about Portugal?

'You're no more of a hero than your father.'

Daniel was confused, but he would ask his father, not Graves.

'It's common knowledge that he paid old fford Croft to take you on. You are his man inside one of the most discreet and trusted law firms in the country. Think of the secrets you will know — one day,' he said with contempt. 'Will you be Sir Daniel when he's gone?' Now his sneer was undisguised. 'Was it not that kind of knighthood? Bought and paid for by turning a blind eye to all the right things! As I said in my book — weak! And weakness leads to corruption. And corruption leads to murder. Got to solve the case, no matter how, no matter who hangs for it. Runs in the bloodline, doesn't it? His father was a poacher, he's a lackey to Narraway, and God knows who else now. What are you going to be?'

Daniel rose to his feet. He was shaking. 'The man who finds out who killed your wife,' he replied without hesitation. 'Whether it's you or not. If it isn't you, I'll get you out of here. And if it is, I'll see you hang with pleasure.'

Daniel went to the door and banged on it to be let out. He did not look back at Graves when the guard came, but walked away.

12

Daniel made up his mind that he must go and see his father that evening. He set out with the intention of arriving about six o'clock. It would be before dinner, and it would be an interruption to his parents' evening, but it was the best time to catch him, in the event that they had planned to go out. If so, their plans might have to be cancelled. This matter would not wait.

Several times on the way there, he wondered if it was wise to appeal to his father, and if it was even necessary. It could be left until he knew more, in fact until after he had found out who might be behind Ebony's death. But he did not hesitate in his stride. He knew these were all excuses, because it was going to be difficult. Unpleasant, at least; at worst, disastrous.

He turned the corner into Keppel Street. Every house was familiar. He had walked this way almost every day since he was four or five years old, right until he went up to Cambridge. He did not hesitate, although he was forcing himself in every step.

He was glad they had not moved to a newer, grander house with Pitt's promotion, and higher salary. This was home. He pulled the bell rope and stepped back.

It was answered almost immediately. They had a manservant now. That was fairly new. They'd always managed before with one maid, and a woman a couple of days a week for the heavy work.

'Good evening, Mr Daniel. Is Sir Thomas expecting you?' The servant opened the door wide and moved aside to allow Daniel in. He must know that Daniel was not expected, but it was a courteous way of asking.

'No, Yeats, he isn't. And I'm sorry if it causes inconvenience, but it's really urgent. Will you please tell him I'm here? And I'll say hello to my mother.'

'Yes, sir. Lady Pitt is in the sitting room.' Yeats went ahead of him, knocked on the sitting-room door and went in immediately. Daniel heard him say something in a murmur, and the next moment Charlotte was in the doorway.

'Daniel!' Her face was alight with pleasure and she hugged him immediately. He felt the warmth of her and responded. Since he had lived away from home, he had missed her enthusiasm, her interest in everything, even her desire to be involved in whatever was his latest interest. He had never known anybody more alive. It had driven him frantic, and frequently embarrassed him when he was a child. But he looked back on it now with pleasure.

He hugged her in return. 'Hello, Mama. Sorry to come without warning, but I have to talk to Father rather urgently about something very serious. And it's a case I can't tell you about, so don't ask me. I know I'm interrupting, but it won't wait.'

'Oh!' She seemed about to add more, but the gravity in his face, even perhaps a degree of pain,

194

kept her from arguing. She could be amazingly discreet at times, which still surprised him. 'I'll fetch him. He's in the study.'

'I'd rather go in to him there,' he said. 'It's . . . '

'Serious?' she asked, the light slipping out of her face. 'Before dinner?'

'Please.' He wanted to talk as if everything were normal and not tell her he was too nervous to eat. He thought he had more control than that. He had stood up in court and defended a man, knowing that the man would live or die, depending on his success. He might even have turned the tide for Graves, temporarily. Was that an achievement, or a disaster? But telling his father about Graves' accusations was different. It struck at the root of who his family was, who he was himself. And Graves knew it! He had seen that in his eyes, the knowledge of leaving a deep wound. It was what he had meant to do.

Charlotte did not press him any further. She might ask Pitt afterwards, but that was up to them.

She took him to the study door, knocked, and then went in. 'Thomas? Daniel is here to see you about something very important. He says it's better to get it over with before dinner.' She held the door open for Daniel.

Pitt was sitting at his desk. As usual, there were papers spread all over it. None of them would be secret. Those did not leave the office. Even so, Daniel did not glance at any of them, but straight at his father.

Pitt was tall and loose-limbed. He had

improved on his natural untidiness a little over the years, but not a great deal. His hair was still too long and unruly, and lately there was a good deal of grey in it. Actually, it became him. It gave him a certain gravitas he had lacked before. He looked at Daniel steadily for several seconds.

'You'd better sit down and tell me what it is,' he said at last. 'And if you are going to ruin your mother's dinner. I hope you have already informed her?'

'I don't know . . . '

Pitt saw the concern in his face. 'Tell me . . . '

Daniel sat down in the chair opposite the desk. He still did not know how he was going to approach this. He had thought of half a dozen ways on the journey here, and cast them all aside. Was the whole thing foolish, and he should not bother his father? Or was this going to be a turning point in the family, the beginning of a damage that would never be undone, never be completely healed over?

Pitt was waiting, a shadow in his face now.

Should Daniel start with Marcus fford Croft? Or defending Graves, and the outcome? Or go straight to Graves' accusation?

'Daniel?'

'I have a defendant accused of a murder,' he began. 'I was only assisting at the trial, because the lawyer who was doing it had met with a street accident.' He was making a mess of it already.

Pitt did not interrupt.

Daniel took a breath and started again. 'The accused was found guilty and sentenced to be hanged. There are seventeen days left. Sixteen, tomorrow. Marcus put the senior lawyer into finding grounds to appeal in law, and me on finding grounds in fact . . . like another major suspect . . . '

'And have you found one?' Pitt asked quietly.

It was the moment when Daniel had to tell him the truth. There was no evading it, other than lying.

'Not by name, but by a major motive, which I'm afraid makes a lot of sense.'

'Afraid? Why? What is it?'

This was the moment beyond which he could not retreat.

Daniel looked away, and then back at his father. 'Have you ever heard of Russell Graves?'

'No. Who is he?'

'You've never heard of him? No one you know has ever even mentioned his name?'

'No. Why should they have? Who is he?' Pitt asked. A flicker of anxiety crossed his face.

Daniel saw it. 'He is a particularly unpleasant biographer. Likes to rip the mask off people we have regarded as heroes, for one reason or another.'

'It happens,' Pitt replied, his voice almost without inflection, giving away nothing. 'Every good man, or woman, has their detractors. Some see them as saints, and rob them of their humanity. Others cannot believe in a quality they don't have themselves, and want to force us to see their flaws. Usually, we sort them out. But you cannot suppress opinions, and we shouldn't try. Why do you mention Graves in particular?'

He frowned. 'Isn't that the man who murdered his wife, and then disfigured her face?'

Daniel swallowed. 'Yes. Except he claims he didn't. But whether he did or not, the book he's planning to write will have given him a great number of enemies who would be glad to see him hang, but even more than that, totally dishonoured. Although I'm afraid that his hanging may well make some people of a certain sort want to read what he has written.'

Pitt's face was filled with sympathy, which softened all the lines in it, making him look younger and much more vulnerable. 'There will always be people like that. There's nothing we can do about it.'

Daniel felt the sweat on his hands. 'There ought to be,' he replied. 'It's not just unpleasant. I have to investigate, in case it is true that somebody else killed his wife, in order to ruin him. Silence him permanently, by hanging.'

'You just said it won't save him,' Pitt pointed out.

Daniel was losing control of it. He could not back out now. 'The man he has exposed is Victor Narraway . . . '

Pitt looked incredulous, 'What?'

'Victor Narraway,' Daniel repeated.

'Exposing him as what?' Pitt asked incredulously. 'Head of Special Branch? For God's sake, everybody who mattered knew that. And Victor's dead. He hasn't got any family to pay . . . or whatever this man wants.'

'He's not looking for money. He's just inherited a whole fortune. Lands, money and a title. But it isn't only Narraway . . . ' This was hard to say. Pitt didn't seem to have understood it — not really.

Pitt waited, his face paler now, the tension apparent in the way he sat.

'Graves has painted him as corrupt.' Daniel swallowed. 'He says Narraway had a file of information on people which he used to blackmail them, to give himself more and more power. And he also said . . . ' This was even harder than he had foreseen. He felt as if it would make it sound believable, just by repeating it. 'He says that Aunt Vespasia slept with all sorts of people to get information . . . personal information about important people, that she was . . . a high-class whore.' He watched Pitt's expression move from incredulity to understanding, to fury, then to grief.

'I'm sorry . . . ' Daniel began.

Pitt put up his hand, as if that could silence Daniel.

'I had to tell you!' Daniel said, his voice shaking with emotion. 'And he says you use the same file of names to keep power. He . . . ' He tailed off. He could not repeat Graves' words about Pitt. Even to say it sounded as if Pitt had to justify himself to Daniel. He could not do it. 'He is suggesting that someone in Special Branch killed Ebony Graves, to keep anyone from publishing Graves' book. I have to prove that is not true! It's . . . it's his only defence. And they're going to hang him in less than three weeks. I don't believe it, but that isn't good enough . . . '

Pitt seemed to be stunned. He blinked once or twice. 'Did he say where he got his information from?'

'No. He knows that I'm your son. He seemed to take some pleasure in that.'

'So, he used it to manipulate you? Or to have some sort of revenge on you that you didn't save him?'

'No. He hasn't been home since I came onto the case. I'm only a replacement.'

'What difference does it make that he hasn't been home?'

Daniel was doing this badly. And Pitt was refusing to understand. Daniel wanted to shout at him that he couldn't evade it like that! Why wouldn't he see that this was real?

He took a deep breath. 'I went to his house. Spoke to his servants, who don't like him very much. They didn't actually say so, but it's there. They don't seem to have any trouble believing that he killed his wife. I don't know whether I believe he did or not. But Mr fford Croft owed him a debt of honour, and we have to . . . ' That was not what he meant. Start again.

'I have to investigate it,' he said desperately. 'He hasn't written a complete book yet, but he's done a lot of it, a lot of the preliminary work, and a draft of the complete manuscript. And I don't know who his publisher is yet and I don't know how much they know.' His voice was rising in exasperation. 'I've got to see if it's a credible defence! Somebody, anybody, might have tried to silence publication by framing Graves.' He went on. 'As he says, if he wanted to kill his wife, he could find a far better way of doing it than when he was the only suspect. And he could make it look like an accident, and no one would be the wiser. As it is, it's obviously murder, because she was disfigured afterwards.'

'Yes, all right!' Pitt said quickly. 'I see. And considering the material, the suspicion naturally falls on Special Branch. Narraway has no relatives, and Vespasia's are her grandchildren, who are largely abroad. And they are not likely even to have heard of this, and less likely to do anything so . . . violent. And so futile.'

'It's to ruin Special Branch,' Daniel said. 'And you.'

'Oh?' A black humour lit Pitt's face for a moment, and vanished. 'What do these notes say about me?'

Daniel did not answer.

Pitt's voice was stunned. 'Daniel? What do they say about me?'

Daniel felt the room sway around him. He clenched his teeth, and breathed in deeply. 'That you're no better than Narraway. That you'll do anything for power . . . even cover . . . murder.' He waited, watching his father's face as it changed from bewilderment to a flash of understanding, and then ill-concealed distress.

The silence prickled for a moment. Then Pitt spoke. 'And does he say whose murder this was, or only that I . . . covered it up?'

'No. Except that it was a woman, and it was very violent.' Why didn't his father deny it? Why was he asking questions? He must know: it was in his eyes, in every hesitation in his voice. There could not be more than one incident like this . . . surely. He tried to speak, but his voice would not come. He cleared his throat and began again. 'Do you know what he's talking about?' Instantly he wished he had not asked. It was already too late to take it back. He sat while the silence washed around him like waves.

'Yes,' Pitt said at last. 'But I don't know how Graves came to know anything about it . . . or to think he knows.'

Daniel was stunned. He fought to remain calm. 'I've only read his notes. I have a draft of the manuscript, with a lot of notes in the margins, and crossings out. I haven't had time to read it. I don't want to. Unless it wasn't Graves who killed his wife, and I can . . . raise a reasonable doubt . . . ' He heard his own voice as if it were someone else's.

'I know,' Pitt answered before Daniel could think how to finish. 'If you can, you must. You must be true to your word, and your obligation. I would never expect anything less from you.'

Daniel flinched. Pitt did not often speak of honour, or duty. It was implicit in everyday life, something that did not need to be given words. Daniel wished he had not come, had not raised anything of the issue. But it was too late to go back. He was now questioning his father's honesty. Which meant that he was questioning his whole life. He could not deny it.

Pitt was speaking again. 'I know what Graves is referring to, and in essence what he said is true. A man of high power in Portuguese politics, Luz dos Santos, here in London at the time, had a violent quarrel with his wife in their home. It ended tragically. He struck her hard and killed her. So yes, it was murder. He was a violent man.'

'You helped him? Why?' Daniel demanded.

'It was two years ago, just before the assassination of the King of Portugal.'

'What does that have to do with it?'

'It was a very turbulent time in Portugal. It still is. I hope there won't be any more, but there is a strong chance of another rebellion like the last one, but far worse. There is unrest all over Europe, particularly Socialists uprisings. I can't say I entirely blame them.'

'What? Assassinations? Riots?'

'I am not approving of them, Daniel, I'm saying I understand why they rebel against poverty, oppression, and a rule that has no fairness and no room to appeal.'

'And was this man's wife oppressing him?' Daniel asked, and then wished he could have left the sarcasm out of his voice. Should he apologise? He had not intended the rudeness, but the disbelief was real.

'You have to follow the exactness of the law,' Pitt said. He, too, seemed to be keeping his temper with an effort. 'I can't always afford the luxury of having what I do dictated by statute. Revolution is essentially about breaking laws.'

'Murder?' Daniel challenged. He hated this. He wished he had never begun, but he could not leave it now. His father's beliefs were the framework of all he believed himself. Fairness, innate decency, following the rules when they suited you, and even more scrupulously when they didn't. It was what his parents had taught him all his life. How could it be changing now? He felt utterly lost, more than ever before.

'Daniel!' Pitt's voice was sharp.

Daniel looked up.

'I didn't kill the woman. I would have saved her if I could, but when I arrived she was already dead. The man knew too many secrets that he would tell if I let him be taken into police custody, and charged, then stand trial. I hated saving him, but the alternative would have cost many lives that I was not too late to save.'

Daniel felt hope surge inside him. He wanted that to be true, wanted it so badly it was like gasping for air when you have been under water. 'What did you do? Lie to the police?'

'Yes.'

'Did anyone else get blamed?'

'No,' Pitt said stiffly. 'Of course not. We managed to disguise it to look like an accident. She fell down the stairs.'

'And what happened to him?'

'I got him out of the country.'

'But the assassination happened anyway?'

'Yes.'

'And the people whose deaths he would have caused, they are still alive?' Daniel asked slowly.

'Daniel, I'm not trying to change the political situation in other countries,' Pitt said patiently. 'I'm trying to stop the violence from coming here. Half the social extremists in Europe — that is, the revolutionaries — are in London, one time or another. Spanish, Italian, German, Russian, they feel safe here, some of them even live here. God knows what they are planning. And I like to know as much of it as I can. That's what Special Branch is about. Safeguarding us against violence, terrorism, change by force.' His grimace was something short of a smile.

'I see . . . '

'Do you?'

'I think so. Something, anyway. This biography that Graves is writing — it's pretty . . . nasty.'

'I damn well intend to find out,' Pitt answered. 'We should have known someone was writing a biography like this. He must have had to do a great deal of research into it. And if someone at Special Branch answered his questions, I will need some good excuse if they expect to keep their job now, and an account of exactly what he asked, and exactly what he was told. They're going to have to earn their redemption.' He pushed his hand through his unruly hair, making it worse. 'It must have been difficult for you to tell me.'

Daniel felt a mixture of pity for those accused in Graves' book, guilt that he had told Pitt about it, and the fierce wish that he could do something to help. Mostly he feared that all the certainties in life that made sense, and the values of everything, even his own identity, were beginning to unravel in front of him.

'I'm sorry . . . '

Pitt jerked his head up. 'You'd be a damn sight sorrier if you'd said nothing, and passed this case on to someone else. Graves is your client?'

'Yes . . . but — '

'No *buts*. You can repeat nothing you know in confidence that is against his interest,' Pitt replied. 'You must investigate this wherever it leads, but if you find out anything that is a threat to the security of the nation, you will tell me. I don't imagine that will happen. If it does, you may have a conflict of interest. Ask fford Croft, he'll advise you.'

'Would it be against the interest of the nation if you were not able to perform your job?'

Pitt's smile was bleak. 'That's a matter of opinion. I hope so. But no doubt there will be those who think it would be in the best interests of the country if I *were* to be replaced. A few for whom it would be very much in their interest!' His amusement was self-mocking.

Daniel did not know what to say. He would have given a great deal for this not to be happening, for it to be something else he had to tell Pitt, that his man, at least one of them, had let him down. He stumbled for something to say, but nothing came to him that was honest.

'There isn't anything you can do,' Pitt repeated. 'Once Graves told you, there was only one thing you could ever have done.' He took a moment to think. 'Tell me, what have you learned since then? I ask because I have to find out who could and should have known about this, and why he didn't. Is it carelessness, or design? Did someone know, and not set it right? And if so, why?'

Daniel could think of nothing useful to say. It was not his fault, and yet he felt as if it were. At every step, he could have paid lip service to the idea of saving Graves from the rope, whether he killed Ebony or not, and he surely deserved to hang!

Except you have to have faith, before you hanged someone, that you were right, at least in fact. The morality of it was not your judgement.

'What are you going to do?' he asked Pitt.

'Find out where the information came from,' Pitt answered. 'And you are going to help me. I want all the details you can remember of exactly what stories Graves was going to tell. He must have got some details — it's not a story without them. Tell me. What stories did he tell of Narraway, specifically? Then of Vespasia, something that's not just gossip that anyone knows? Although the days she was gossiped about are long past. Is it first-hand knowledge or second? And about me? I used to know the dates. I need to know the details.'

'It's ugly . . . ' Daniel avoided his father's eyes.

'The details!' Pitt said sharply. 'If I know the details he has, I can very probably trace it back to the source. The devil of truth is in the details, Daniel. Just what stories do they tell about Narraway?'

Daniel tried to remember exactly what he had seen in Graves' notes. 'There was something about a case in Ireland. A man named O'Neill, who was betrayed and died. A woman Narraway seduced, and then betrayed. Someone else who had betrayed Special Branch, and sent you on an abortive trip to France, to Paris.'

'You sure it was Paris?'

'Yes.'

'Interesting. It was Saint Malo, actually. Go on.'

'Wouldn't you go to Paris first?'

'No. Paris is inland, I took a ferry direct to Le Havre, and then to Saint Malo.'

Daniel felt a thin trickle of hope, like winter sunlight. 'And then there was a case about an addicted young man who shot a bystander and blamed the police, and Narraway told you to get him off.'

'Interesting details. Did they say how I got him off or why Narraway wanted it?'

'Narraway wanted to . . . something to do with the boy's father, who was very important.' Daniel struggled to remember more, and could not.

'Get me all you can — copies of Graves' notes, if possible,' Pitt told him. 'The cases are real ones. But the details are wrong. The boy was dying anyway. All I did was get him into a hospital for the last few months of his life, instead of a prison cell and a death in unbearable pain. And as for his father, I'd have seen the swine in hell, with pleasure. But his mother was a good woman. Go on.'

Daniel told him all the rest that he could remember, and promised to bring him more detail as soon as he could.

When he finally stood up to go, his mind was racing with ideas. All the facts he remembered, and any others he could add later, might well help Pitt to lead Daniel to whoever had murdered Ebony Graves and had framed Graves. On orders from someone in Special Branch? And was that person a traitor — or a patriot? Did that depend upon whether Narraway, or Pitt himself, had acted as Graves concluded? Or was that immaterial? And if it had all happened while Pitt was head of Special Branch, did that make it his fault?

Daniel stayed for dinner, even though part of him wanted to leave and think what to do next. First, he must study the material of Graves' book he had taken back to his lodgings.

But if he didn't stay, then he would have to explain to his mother why. It would frighten her. And then she would see through it immediately if he tried to look as if nothing were going on. He had learned that at the age of six. She knew him better than he knew himself. It wasn't completely true now, but the memory was strong, and she could still surprise him at times.

At dinner, they sat around the dining-room table, not the kitchen, as in so many years in the past. Perhaps if he had not been present it would have been in the kitchen this evening, too.

Daniel dismissed the whole subject of Russell Graves, and instead told his mother in particular how he had very nearly lost the case for Roman Blackwell, but in the end pulled it out of apparently nothing, like a magician's rabbit out of a hat. They all discussed the latest letter from Jemima in New York, and how her husband, Patrick, was faring, and, of course, all about her two little girls.

Daniel left after nine. He hugged his mother, as he did always, and shook his father's hand, feeling the warmth of his grip just a moment longer than usual. It was Charlotte who saw him to the door.

'Come back, if you can't handle it alone,' she said very quietly. 'We're always here.'

'Handle what?' He feigned innocence.

'Whatever it is,' she said impatiently. 'I've been a policeman's wife since before you were born, my darling. I know there's something very wrong. Just remember . . . we are here.' She reached up and gave him a quick kiss on the cheek, then almost pushed him out of the door.

★　★　★

He arrived back at Mrs Portiscale's, opened the front door as close to silently as he was able, and went inside. There was only the night light on in the hall. He went up the stair, avoiding the step he knew creaked, and into his own room on the next floor, overlooking the garden.

He saw the message on the desk, propped up, and written in Mrs Portiscale's painfully careful hand: 'Dear Mr Pitt, a Mr Roman Blackwell left a message for you to visit him. Sincerely, Mrs Portiscale.'

Well, whatever it was would have to wait until tomorrow. Maybe Mercy had heard something interesting . . .

Daniel sat down at the desk and unlocked the drawer. He took out Graves' notes for the book and started to copy them for his father. He studied them also for himself as he went. At last he knew where to begin.

It was nearly two o'clock when he finally went to bed.

13

Daniel woke with a start to find sunlight streaming in through the window. His mind had been in too much turmoil to remember to set his alarm clock, and it was already after eight. He might well have missed breakfast, and he had work that could not wait.

He washed, shaved and dressed, and hurried downstairs to see if there was anything left to eat. Then he changed his mind. Roman Blackwell's message had been delivered the previous afternoon. He should go straight away. With a hurried apology to Mrs Portiscale, he dashed out of the front door and then down the street to the nearest cab stand. He asked the driver to take him to Blackwell's address.

It was about nine o'clock and traffic was totally entangled at the busiest time of day. When they arrived, he paid the driver. The fare seemed an exorbitant amount, but the man had found backroads that avoided the worst blockages and left Daniel on the pavement sooner than he would have thought possible. He thanked him, and walked up to Blackwell's doorstep. Before he raised his hand to knock, it opened in front of him.

'Well!' Mercy said, looking him up and down. She refrained from straightening his tie for him, but only just. 'Come in,' she invited, stepping back. 'You look . . . frazzled!'

'I'm sorry,' Daniel apologised. He must not let her see, or guess, the real reason for his inability to command his thoughts. 'I am. I got Roman's message too late to call on you. I was . . . out . . . '

She grunted rather than spoke. 'Breakfast?'

'No, dinner last night. With my parents.'

'I mean would you like breakfast?' she offered. 'Nobody does their best thinking on an empty stomach.'

'Am I going to need my best thinking?' he asked, trying to invest some lightness into his voice, and failing. He did not want more nasty surprises.

'Yes,' Mercy said simply.

She took him through to the kitchen where Blackwell was sitting at the table nursing a cold cup of tea.

'Ah!' he said as soon as he saw Daniel. 'What news?' His dark face was crumpled, as if he were expecting something bad and trying to guess the nature of it before he was told.

'You sent for me!' Daniel said, sitting down in the chair opposite him.

'True,' Blackwell agreed. 'Ma, you'd better feed him. He looks bloody awful.'

'I can see that,' Mercy replied without turning round. She was already busy with slicing bread and warming up the grill. 'And watch your manners, Roman. I'm still your mother, and don't you forget it!'

Blackwell smiled and his face lit with genuine amusement. 'My one reliable pleasure in life is baiting Mercy. She never fails to bite.'

'Rubbish,' she said. 'Balderdash!'

'What have you found out so far?' Blackwell asked Daniel. 'I think I can add to it.'

'A lot,' Daniel replied, conscious of telling Blackwell less than the truth. But Blackwell admired Pitt so much, he would not want to know about the Portuguese murder and the compromise Pitt had felt he had to make. 'But without proof it all amounts to nothing,' he added, refusing to give Graves' manuscript the credit of belief.

Daniel felt a little like a moth pinned to a board, so piercing was Blackwell's gaze.

'Bad, eh?' Blackwell asked. 'You don't care if Graves hangs. He deserves to, if he did that to his wife. And by all accounts, he's a rotten sod anyway, quite apart from whether he killed her or not. So, what's eating at you? Old fford Croft going to throw you out if you can't rescue Graves? Or are you up to rescuing Kitchener, or whatever his name is?'

'Kitteridge,' Daniel corrected. 'He's looking for holes in the law . . . '

'Well, if he can't find a hole in the law, he's an ass! It's as full of holes as a sieve!' Blackwell said in disgust. 'Some you could drive a coach and horses through, but none that will save Russell Graves! Why does fford Croft want to? Have you worked that out yet?'

'It's a debt he owes. An old occasion when Marcus let Graves' father down. It weighs on him,' Daniel replied.

'So, was his father a rotten sod as well?' Blackwell's eyebrows rose, giving his face a startled look.

'A promise is a promise,' Daniel replied,

feeling even more cornered. 'It's about you, not whoever you made the promise to!' He could almost hear his father's voice in his head saying it for him.

'Have a cup of tea.' Blackwell turned in his seat. 'Is that kettle boiling yet?' It was an oblique observation, not a question as to fact. Blackwell turned to Daniel again. 'So why do we care so much? And don't lie to me. You're not good enough at it yet to get away with it. Not to me, anyway. Don't think you'll ever be. You care so much, it's got you all twisted up and cold inside, like a pig's tail in ice. Why?'

Mercy put a fresh pot of tea and a fresh, crisp bacon sandwich in front of Daniel.

Blackwell sat and listened, his face increasingly grim, while Daniel told him very briefly about Graves' intended book and its exposure of Narraway and Vespasia Cumming-Gould, who became his wife. He finished up by admitting it had to be the incontestable conclusion that the person most likely to destroy Graves was someone in Special Branch — either Thomas Pitt himself, or someone fulfilling his orders. He was uncomfortably conscious of omitting reference to Pitt, or the Portuguese murder.

Daniel wanted to choose his words carefully, understanding that his emotion was too strong for him. 'He didn't know anything about the book,' he said, and then realised how incompetent that made Pitt seem. 'He should have. Some of his own men must have access to that kind of information . . . '

Blackwell pursed his lips. His disgust was

214

plain, but he did not waste words on it. 'Has Graves a publisher for this thing?'

'He says so,' Daniel replied. 'Ah! I see. Why is the publisher prepared to set up a book like this, and ruin his own reputation? Are there damages the people in it will claim — if they're still alive? That's the thing. Most of them are dead. Lord Narraway is, so is Lady Vespasia . . . ' He felt a sudden tightness in his throat as he said that. It had not been long ago, and the loss was still fresh enough to hurt. There was a place in his life that felt as if it would always be empty now. 'Why would the publisher accept it in the first place?' he asked, struggling to stop the emotion from drowning him. 'I'll find out exactly who it is. They are hiding behind the company name.'

'You may be poking a stick into a hornets' nest,' Blackwell warned. 'Why don't you let me do it — sideways, like?'

'Can you?' Daniel asked, but he was really wondering if Blackwell already knew, or guessed, far more than Daniel did.

'You can do most things, if you know the right people to ask.' Blackwell smiled, pouring himself another cup of tea. 'And, of course, the right questions.'

Daniel thought of a lot of things to ask, and a lot of warnings and rules for Blackwell to keep, or at least not to break too badly, and ended up simply saying, 'Thank you.' He took a sip of his own tea, still very hot, and a bite of the bacon sandwich. It was so good he realised how hungry he was, and ate the rest of it before speaking again.

Blackwell was following his own train of thought. 'Wonder what axe the publisher has to grind. He won't be so stupid as to think he could avoid causing a furore.'

Mercy put down the piece of toast she was buttering. 'There could be a lot of interesting things to find out about that,' she said thoughtfully. 'And a lot of reasons for doing it, or not doing it.'

Daniel turned to look at her. The white stripe in her hair caught the light and shone dazzlingly, then she moved her head and it was shadowed again.

'Apart from money, what?' he asked. 'A personal revenge? Pretty deep hatred to take revenge on the dead, isn't it? Someone who was too scared to do it while they were alive?'

'Your father's head of Special Branch, right?' Mercy said thoughtfully, moving her own slice of toast away from the open door of the oven fire.

'Yes.'

'His intention would be protecting the reputation of his friends, not protecting his own. It's a good distinction. Oldest trick in the book,' she added.

'He'd see through that,' Daniel answered, but as he said it, he wondered if it were true. Friends, real friends who had fought battles beside you, after they were exhausted, but fought on to protect, stood by you. Even if the end was defeat, they did not leave you, they stayed with you. Friends knew your flaws, as you did theirs, but stood by you anyway. You laughed together, and mourned together, celebrated victories and

216

grieved for losses. Pitt would never let them down. Perhaps if they were guilty you could not protect them from the carrion creatures who dared not attack them when they were alive. But still you would protect what you could. That's what friendship is, not lies, sometimes not silence either.

He had seen it in his father, as long as he could remember. His mother, too. She was even quicker to defend the vulnerable. It did not often occur to her to wonder if they deserved it. In fact, he could not remember her ever doing that. She had defended him when he was wrong, but punished him herself afterwards! He smiled at it now, but he had been scared stiff of her anger at the time.

Strange thing, loyalty; defence of the vulnerable, whether right or wrong. Who to trust? Loyalty to what? Which were the ideals to follow? There were so very many! What were they worth, if mercy were not one of them?

He sipped his tea again, and another bacon sandwich appeared on his plate. 'Thank you,' he said appreciatively, and began eating it immediately.

'We must find out where Graves got his information, starting with those things that are true.' Blackwell resumed.

'There's not much of it true!' Daniel said too quickly.

Mercy patted him on the arm. 'Whatever is. It's the only starting place that we know of. Get those things, and you may get the people. And find something we would like to have been true,

217

and wasn't, and that's a point to fix the moving pieces!'

Daniel began to see what she was meaning. 'But if we do find out who was giving Graves the information, what good will that do us?'

Mercy was absolutely direct. 'What good do you want?'

Daniel hesitated. What he wanted most was to prove beyond doubt that his father was not guilty of concealing a murder dishonourably, that he had a compelling reason, one that any decent person would understand. Graves had implied that this reason did not exist. There was nothing to expose, if there were such a reason. He knew perfectly well that Pitt would never have sanctioned the killing of Ebony Graves. That was not even a question. Nor would he have intentionally looked the other way while some-one else did.

And did not that amount to the question, in the end, of whether Narraway was guilty of any of the things he was accused of?

Another thought occurred to him. If Narraway was guilty, had the person behind this known that at the time? Had they colluded in it?

And did he, Daniel, want to prove Graves innocent, or not guilty beyond a reasonable doubt? Or did he really want to see him hanged, but with a clean conscience?

Mercy was waiting, watching his face.

Perhaps the last was really the truth, and he wanted to see him hanged.

'I want lots of things,' he said. 'In order? I want to prove Graves killed his wife and we would be right to hang him. That if he didn't, I want to know who did, and prove that. And I want to prove that my father didn't — ' He stopped.

He had said too much already. Was betrayal really as easy as that — a careless word because you could not carry the weight of a secret alone? The doubt in it was too much for you?

'And you would like it in the next fifteen days,' Mercy said in black humour.

'Sixteen,' Daniel corrected, his own smile twisted.

'Fifteen,' she repeated. 'Eight o'clock in the morning, sixteen days from now, he'll be hanged.'

He did not bother to argue. He recounted briefly his visit to Graves' house in Herne Hill with Miriam fford Croft and what they had observed at the murder scene.

Mercy poured herself a cup of tea and sat beside him. 'If what Graves said is true, then Ebony's character is by the way and has nothing to do with her death. The purpose is to blame Graves and silence him.'

Daniel nodded. 'That is pretty brutal!'

'Yes,' she agreed.

He thought for a moment, forcing his mind to remain on the immediate problem. 'Then why burn her face? That makes it very personal.'

'All I could find about her, she was a woman who aroused deep feelings,' Mercy said thoughtfully. 'But more liked than disliked. She fought hard for what she believed in and she didn't hold her tongue, when perhaps she ought to have.

Enthusiast, you know? If you are enthusiastic, too, she's wonderful. If not — she would be very irritating. Rather an . . . irresponsible sense of humour, as one woman put it.' Suddenly her face filled with sorrow. As if the reality had suddenly reached her. 'I think I would have liked her.'

Blackwell started to speak.

Mercy held up her hand. 'I know.' She sniffed. 'I know for you to burn someone's face away because they irritate you, it was not easy to do. It requires a cold heart, an over-bearing need, and something to make it burn. Flesh does not burn by itself. And why?' She looked at Daniel. 'I tried to find something she knew that was dangerous. Nothing. It makes no sense.'

Daniel drew a deep breath. 'Then you think she could have been killed just to cause Graves to be hanged?'

Blackwell nodded slowly. 'Mercy's told me all she found out. No one had a reason to kill Ebony. Jealousy, yes, maybe.' His face expressed what he thought of that. 'Disagreed with her ideas, definitely. But I'm afraid none of the changes she wanted are likely to happen within the next ten years, anyway. And then, maybe, nothing will stop them. If she'd been slashed in a fight, I'd believe it. Another woman's jealousy, maybe. But finding a way into her house, when her children were at home — nothing was heard, no noise, no lock picked, no window broken — and burning her face?' He looked from one to the other of them.

'I see,' Daniel cut in. 'You are right. If it were a personal thing, it would have cleared up suddenly, and would have been an attack, a fight, and all happening there and then. It would not be a break-in to her own house, after dark, and an attack in her bedroom by someone who left no trace.'

'And came prepared,' Mercy added. 'And I found no one who suggested her affairs were more than flirtations. From what I heard of Graves, I commend her restraint. I would've gone a lot further!'

'You would have left him,' Blackwell said.

'If it had been he who had been killed, I would have understood it,' Mercy replied ruefully. She looked across at Daniel. 'I'm sorry, I know nothing of use.' She looked momentarily crushed, and Daniel realised how very much she wanted to repay the debt she owed him for saving Blackwell.

He forced himself to smile at her, but it felt artificial. 'There'll be other times.' He leaned back in the chair and looked again at Blackwell. 'I wish I could believe Graves killed her. It would be so much easier. I could let him hang with an easy conscience. I would have done all I could.' He took a deep breath. 'But I don't. I hear the pain in him now, I see the fear in his eyes, his anger, too. He's desperate not only to save his life, but he sees this all as urgent and unanswerable. He believes it's worth fighting, because it wasn't fair.'

Mercy rolled her eyes. 'You are too soft-hearted for your own good. Defending someone in the law doesn't mean you have to believe they're innocent!'

'But you said yourself, you couldn't find any enemy that hated her with that kind of intensity, that — '

'Not among her acquaintances,' Mercy interrupted him. 'I can quite easily believe that her husband could have. If she mocked him, rejected him, made fun of him . . . any abilities he might have — he's a proud man, by all accounts.' She made a little grimace of disgust. 'Yes? He could well have lashed out at her. You described him as arrogant, condescending . . . '

'Yes, to me, after he had been convicted, and was very afraid,' Daniel answered. 'He would hate me because I've seen him defeated and, whether he likes it or not, he's depended on me to save him. That would scald his pride like acid!'

'And if he failed in the bedroom, and his wife laughed at him, do you not think that would burn his pride even more than acid?' Mercy asked. 'He would never forget it. And I dare say she would never let him, and he knew that. He would lash out, maybe kill her in one blow.'

'But why the burning?' Daniel persisted.

'Take the smile off her face,' Mercy answered with a shrug, as if the answer were self-evident.

'All this may well be true, but it doesn't answer your problem.' Blackwell leaned forward a little. 'You must find who gave Graves the information for his book. And more than anything, you have to save the reputations of people you love. Cover their weaknesses, if they had them, with the privacy we all need. But first of all, make sure that none of your father's men did this.' There was no lift of question in his voice. It was a statement of fact.

Daniel drew a breath to argue, and knew it instantly from Blackwell's face that he understood and, more than that, he saw the gentleness in him. Perhaps he loved Mercy the same way, with the same absence of judgement or condemnation.

'We've got just over two weeks,' he said.

'Then we'd better get on with it.' Mercy poured more tea, as if she were free to start again. 'What do you need to know?'

Daniel thought for a moment. 'Where did Graves get his information and how reliable is it? Did anyone in Special Branch betray Narraway, or my father, and if so, who was it? I don't think why matters now, and even whether or not it was deliberate, or just carelessness: trusting the wrong man, drunken misjudgement, a confidence to a lover. We need to find out just who, so no one else will be implicated.'

Blackwell was making notes in what looked to be a script of his own invention. 'Would your father do that anyway?' Blackwell asked.

'Yes. But he doesn't have access to Graves. I do.' He winced as he said it. The thought of going back to Graves and trying to begin, or indeed ask him for information, was enough to chill him inside, in spite of the hot tea and the two bacon sandwiches.

Blackwell gave him a bleak, sympathetic smile, more a grimace, and poised his pencil for the next item.

'That'll do to start with. Kitteridge is

continuing to search for anything useful in the law,' Daniel said.

'There won't be anything in the law.' Blackwell dismissed it. 'Use him for something that matters, for heaven sake, he's not a fool.' He looked at Daniel, meeting his eyes. 'Don't need to tell him about your father. He'll know anyway — the whole world will — if you fail! Bite the bullet!'

Daniel heard the faint contempt in Blackwell's voice. He was about to fight back, then he realised he had nothing to fight with.

'You're standing in your own light,' Blackwell said. 'Get Kitteridge to help. fford Croft is in no position to complain. He got you into this. And you don't need to tell him so. He'll know.'

Daniel acquiesced silently.

'And there's one other thing,' Blackwell added. 'You need to find out how they burned her. Dropping a match on her might make a hole in her clothes, but not much more. Even if there was a fire in the grate, a hot coal would dig deep in the flesh, but it wouldn't have burned her face. Did someone come prepared? Or know where to find the means? We need to dig her up and get an expert to tell us what was used. Can this woman of yours, fford Croft's daughter, do that?'

'We'll never get permission to exhume the body!' Daniel said in disbelief. Please God, Blackwell was not suggesting they do so anyhow. 'Roman, we can't go grave-robbing! Apart from anything else, the evidence wouldn't stand up in court — that is, if we're even out of prison

224

ourselves and allowed to offer it!'

Blackwell pressed his hand over his eyes. 'Please, Daniel, couldn't we have a little sense? We'll get an exhumation order.'

'They'll never give one. The case is closed, as far as they're concerned. They had their evidence. The police surgeon looked at the body — or someone did.'

'Someone?' Blackwell's eyebrows shot up.

'I don't know. I wasn't there until the end of the trial. But they won't give us an order.'

'Would this Miriam of yours do it if we can get the body up, legally?'

'It won't happen . . . '

Blackwell slammed his hand down on the table. 'Would she?'

'Yes. I suppose so.'

'Fine. Then leave the exhumation order with me. I'll get one.'

'Not a forgery!'

Blackwell looked indignant for a moment then he gave a bright smile. 'No, not a forgery. It's got to be a real one, so I'll get a real one. Just go on with what you are doing. I'll let you know when I have it.'

'A real one,' Daniel insisted. He knew Blackwell's forgery skills.

'Of course, a real one! There's more than one way to skin a cat.'

'Disgusting!' Daniel's imagination ran riot.

'Not a real cat, you fool,' Blackwell sighed. 'When are you going to learn to speak English like an ordinary person?'

Mercy put her hand on Blackwell's arm.

'Enough,' she said gently. 'The poor boy's in a miserable situation. They're after his father. Just get on with it and speak to whoever you have to.' She turned to Daniel. 'And you get yourself ready to go back to Graves. And mind how you watch yourself! When you've got a rat cornered, that's when he'll bite anybody, starting with you.'

'I know,' Daniel agreed. 'Thank you for the bacon sandwiches.'

Mercy smiled. 'There are times when it's the only thing that works.'

14

Daniel left Blackwell's house, and went straight to the chambers in Lincoln's Inn. He spoke briefly with fford Croft. Apart from the courtesy of reporting in to him, he wanted to do it when he had something to say, rather than when he was sent for.

fford Croft was sitting behind his desk reading papers. He looked up as Impney announced Daniel, hope in his face. It faded rapidly.

'Good morning, sir.' Daniel stood in front of him.

fford Croft let the papers fall on the embossed leather surface of his desk. 'Good morning. Is it, Mr Pitt? Have you anything else to report?'

'Yes, sir. But I was wondering if Mr Kitteridge had discovered anything that would be usable. If not, I might ask his assistance.'

'With what?' fford Croft sat upright, shifting his considerable weight uncomfortably in the chair.

'That depends upon what I discover in the next few days, sir. I'm hoping Miss fford Croft will assist me with an autopsy.' Daniel replied.

fford Croft looked startled. 'Autopsy? On whom?'

'With the law's permission, of course, upon Mrs Graves — '

'For God's sake, boy! She's already decently dead and buried, poor soul. If you're hoping

Kitteridge can get you permission to dig her up, after the police have already done a post-mortem, you're doomed to total failure.'

'No, I'm not going to ask him for that,' Daniel replied, keeping his voice as level as he could. 'But, sir, have you wondered why her face burned so deep?'

'No — no, I haven't. Can it possibly matter now? What have you found? Do you really have some hope Graves is not guilty after all?' He put his head down and raked through his hair, making it even wilder than before. 'God in heaven, boy! That's the last thing you need! Was it something to do with Special Branch after all?' He met Daniel's eyes reluctantly, his own filled with pity. 'Do I need to take you off this case? I haven't anyone else free, or I would never have put you in court in the first place. You're not fit for that yet, and you're not fit to do this. But I've no one else. I'm sorry . . . '

'No, you don't need to take me off, sir,' Daniel said quickly. 'And I don't know whether Graves is guilty or not. He could be innocent. And you owe him the best chance of proving that.'

fford Croft's eyes were round. 'Oh! And that's your job, is it? And blame your own father, or someone under his command? In the eyes of the public, it comes to the same thing. I'm not going to let you do that!'

'Then let me find the truth. I'm not afraid that my father is behind it!' That was not entirely true. The sick fear still churned in his stomach that somehow, even in mistaken duty, Pitt would be drawn into it, if only to turn the other way, to disprove evidence of collusion. 'I'm not!' he reiterated, not moving his eyes from fford Croft's.

'What are you looking for?' fford Croft said slowly. 'What do you think there is to find?'

'Miriam says we should find what inflammatory material caused Ebony to burn like that,' Daniel replied. 'If it was something that Graves could not have had in the house then it was brought in by an outsider. How did they get in? Who let them in? A servant, or Ebony herself? Why the disfigurement? It's extreme. It would take a lot of extra time and care — time he could have used to escape. Sir, there's something here that we don't understand. The prosecution never offered an answer. We might find one — if we don't give up.'

'We didn't cover this at trial,' fford Croft pointed out. 'Was Kitteridge that negligent?'

'No, sir. We had no other reasonable suspect then. And we tried to find one among their social friends who disliked Ebony Graves enough, but she was actually well liked, if a little . . . over-enthusiastic. And she had had no affairs that we could uncover.'

fford Croft held up his hand. 'All right! Then if you get permission, which I very much doubt, I shall ask Miriam to perform the autopsy for you. You'll not get any reputable surgeon to do it! She'll not contradict the police surgeon, for a start!'

'I'm sorry to ask, sir. Will Miss fford Croft get into any . . . trouble . . . for it?'

fford Croft's eyebrows shot up. 'Trouble?

Miriam? She's even better at getting into trouble than you are! I will ask her — I have no intention of forcing her. But she has no standing or position to lose. And she is damn good at it!'

'Thank you, sir.' Daniel gave a brief smile, then excused himself and went out, intending to look for Kitteridge. And he must have time to prepare himself as thoroughly as possible before going back to face Graves again.

Daniel found Kitteridge despondent, and only half-attentive to the solid, leather-bound book he was reading. He looked up at Daniel. 'If you're hoping for something, I don't have it,' he warned.

'How about lunch?' Daniel asked.

'Can't afford the time. I'll get Impney to fetch me a sandwich. I think there's damn little point in this. There's no chance on earth that I'll find a precedent here. If you've got to eat, go — '

'I've got to see Graves this afternoon,' Daniel cut across him. He was determined to find the source who supplied the information to Graves linking Thomas Pitt to the Portuguese incident. He was not ready to share any of this with Kitteridge. 'And I want to talk to you first. I'm very polite about lunch. I'll make it an official request, if you like? I'm not in a position to make it an order, or I would.'

'No, you're not,' Kitteridge agreed. 'But perhaps I can oblige you. This whole thing is a waste of time. And personally, I am happy for the bastard to hang.' He pushed his chair back and stood up. 'The usual place?'

They walked in the brisk wind along to the public house, went in and ordered ploughman's lunches: a big crusty piece of bread with pickles, cheese, and a glass of ale.

'Well, what have you got that's worth disturbing me for?' Kitteridge asked hopefully, when they had found themselves seats.

'I think Graves really could be innocent, at least of killing Ebony,' Daniel replied.

Kitteridge froze in amazement, his bread halfway to his mouth. 'But guilty of what then? You aren't making a lot of sense. This is no time for fairy stories, Pitt. Their lordships of the court of appeal take a very dim view of it. No sense of humour at all. I should have warned you.'

'There's nothing funny about this,' Daniel answered him. 'Did you even look at Graves' notes for his next book?'

'Not closely. I glanced at it, and what I saw was rather unpleasant. It concerned a chap called Narraway, who's dead now. And it was pretty scurrilous, but famous men, especially powerful ones, do get grubby things said about them. Was someone else involved?'

'His wife. And probably loads of other people. Do you know who he was?'

'Not exactly.' Kitteridge frowned. 'Why?'

'Head of Special Branch.'

'Oh God!' He stared at Daniel, aghast, as suddenly the reality of this came to him. 'So, we could be looking at treason? Stupid sod. Are you saying he was to be judicially silenced? Only they got poor Ebony instead?'

'I don't know. He could have been framed for killing Ebony. In which case, it worked — so far.'

Kitteridge looked profoundly troubled. 'Why

didn't he tell us? It would have been a credible defence. What's the matter with the man?'

'I don't know,' Daniel said unhappily. 'I've read bits of it, but mostly his notes. If he's selling it by the word, he'll make a fortune! Who's his publisher?'

Kitteridge shrugged. 'I don't know. He's keeping that very close to his chest. I had no reason to think it mattered before, so I didn't chase it down. Not his usual publisher, is all I know. I can look further. It's got to be more use than what I'm doing at the moment.' His eyes narrowed and he looked at Daniel more closely. 'There's something else, isn't there?'

Daniel was torn. He did not want to tell anyone at all, but he could not handle this alone. What if he betrayed his father by telling people who would in turn tell others? His father had trusted him with secrets, never thinking he would repeat them. Certain, in fact, that he never would. And believing Daniel would trust him, as he had all his life.

But on the other hand, what if Pitt were destroyed by this because Daniel was too proud, and too afraid, to trust anyone who perhaps could really help?

'Pitt!' Kitteridge said sharply. 'We can't fight in the dark. What's the matter with you, man?'

What should he say? Daniel couldn't decide. He could not see clearly enough. 'I'm not sure what Graves wants . . . ' he began.

'Well, he doesn't want to hang, I'm bloody sure of that!' Kitteridge said tartly. 'Start there, and move on.'

'Which means he really thinks Special Branch could be behind Ebony's murder,' Daniel reasoned.

'Why should they care enough to go to those lengths to protect the reputation of their leader in the past?' Kitteridge continued. Then his voice dropped a little and was suddenly gentler. 'Or is it worse than that? Is he saying your father engineered it? Is it covering up something he was involved in, too? Is that what's got you pulling your hair out?'

Daniel did not need to admit it. The understanding was in Kitteridge's face, and surprisingly without judgement.

'Personal, or Special Branch business?' Kitteridge asked.

'Special Branch business. To do with a Portuguese political dissident of some sort, apparently very well connected.' There was no point in telling less than the truth now. 'Killed his wife in a fit of rage, and then panicked. Asked my father to get him out of the country. He did, I think because the man knew too much about Special Branch . . . and knew too much to stand trial over here.'

Kitteridge nodded, and then seemed to stop himself before asking anything further, as if understanding that Daniel didn't know any more. 'I understand about the political unrest all over Europe. I suppose your father's got to care about that, when the dissidents land up in London. Damn Graves!'

'Do you think he's got anything to do with politics?' Daniel asked doubtfully.

'Not a thing,' Kitteridge replied. 'He's all about money.'

'I think he's genuinely frightened now,' Daniel said. 'I . . . I wish I didn't, but I honestly think he might not be guilty.'

'You think it was Special Branch? Really?'

'No!'

'Then we'd better prove who it was,' Kitteridge said earnestly.

'Can I tell Graves you cannot find any cause for appeal?'

'Certainly. Looking is a total waste of time. I'd rather try and help you. Save the Empire, what?'

Daniel stiffened, then saw Kitteridge's face and realised he was teasing him, and also very seriously offering to help. 'Yes, please,' he accepted. 'Find the bloody publisher.'

★   ★   ★

Daniel went back to the prison and, after the briefest of questioning by the guard, was again permitted to see Graves alone. As they locked the door behind him, he sat down in the chair at the other side of the warped table, and looked at Graves. Daniel had the sudden, awful feeling that he had a glimpse of the corpse he could so soon become.

Hope flared for a second in Graves' eyes, then he looked at Daniel, and it died again.

Daniel wished that he could have brought better news. He even felt guilty that there was not much pity inside him.

'What do you want?' Graves asked. His voice

was strained, as if lack of use had left his throat dry.

'I have looked further into the possibility that someone else is creating evidence against you, as you suggested . . . ' Daniel began.

Suddenly Graves' body was rigid. 'Who? Who is it? What proof do you have?'

'I don't have proof who it is,' Daniel answered levelly. 'But I believe you that it is possible. The reasons are powerful enough to be believable. I will be able to prove more when I know where you got your information for the book on Lord Narraway. I imagine you kept the sources for all, because it might be necessary to consult them again? And you must have been aware that there were those who would try to stop you — up to and including causing your disgrace, and death.'

'A believer,' Graves said sarcastically. 'I'd applaud you — if I weren't in chains!'

Daniel ignored his tone. 'Why didn't you mention it earlier? It would have given us more time.'

'Because I didn't kill her! I thought you had enough skill to get me off before the court,' Graves said accusingly.

'That was nearly a week ago,' Daniel snapped.

'I thought Kitteridge would find some legal loophole. Has fford Croft got up off his arse and done anything? He owes me, and he's going to walk away and let me hang!' The hatred was so deep in him, he all but choked on it. 'You've still got two weeks left.' His look at Daniel was torn between loathing for his mention of having to beg, and the conviction that he was in the right.

Daniel disliked him even more, were it possible. He also believed him more. It was a ragged, powerful feeling inside him.

Was it worth wasting time answering? Probably not.

'Where did you get your information?' He went back to the original question. 'Papers? Letters? Face-to-face interviews? Confessions? You think someone betrayed you? Who?'

'Start with your own father!' Graves snarled. He looked straight into Daniel's eyes and, for a moment, all that was there was hatred.

'I did,' Daniel replied. It was almost the truth. In his own mind, he had refused to believe his father had a part in this. But that was an act, and they both knew it. Graves would have expected Pitt to order a junior to do the deed, never that Pitt would have done it himself. He was morally guilty, not stupid.

'You can't be as big a fool as you act,' Graves retorted. 'Look at his right-hand man. Whom would he trust enough with his dirty work? Someone who wouldn't betray him. Someone who couldn't afford to! With the secrets he knows, there must be a good few of those.'

'A lot of secrets,' Daniel agreed. 'Why not some of those people who have actually got evidence stacked up against them, not just a note in a book somewhere?'

Graves faltered for a moment, the absolute certainty drained out of his eyes.

Daniel realised his own failure to get names from Graves would jeopardise any chance of saving him, and of saving Pitt as well. Innuendo would not do much harm in the court of law, but it certainly would in the area of public opinion. If Pitt lost the confidence of the Home Office, he could not do his job.

'Give me your chief sources,' Daniel said. 'Give me the ones you will ruin.'

Graves hesitated and then slowly listed half a dozen names to Daniel, who wrote them down. They were all public figures. The damage would be enormous.

'It is just word of mouth — where is there proof?' he asked.

Graves sneered at him. 'So, you can go and destroy it? There's proof. What will you do? Sell it back to them? Give it to your father? Or use it yourself to steal my book?'

Daniel allowed his disgust into his voice. 'There'll be no book if you're dead. I want to find the one who killed your wife, you fool. Whoever did that to her deserves to — ' He bit off the end of the sentence. He faced Graves squarely. 'Names!'

'You'll give them to your father, and do you imagine he's going to go through them and give you the killer? He'll probably give you some men all right, but are you sure that it'll be the right ones? God! You're such a child!'

'Do you care, as long as you are not hanged?' Daniel made it sound like a new question.

For a moment, Graves' face was blank.

'I thought not,' Daniel said sourly.

'So, you imagine you'll question them? And they'll tell you?' Graves asked in disbelief.

'I'd leave that to Kitteridge. He's pretty good

at it. I'm going to dig up Ebony's body and do another medical examination, only this time more thoroughly.'

Graves looked aghast. 'You're what?'

'Going to exhume her.'

'For God's sake, why? What is it going to prove, that you don't already know?'

'Why burn her?'

'I didn't do it!' Graves raised his voice harshly. It was almost a shout. 'I didn't bloody well kill her!'

'How did they burn her like that?' Daniel went on. 'It takes a lot of heat to burn flesh.'

Graves' face went white, and his eyes hollow. 'What are you saying?'

Daniel leaned forward a bit. 'If they used something they brought with them, and not from the house, it would indicate premeditation. They are saying you quarrelled and lost your temper. But if what was used was something in the house already, that could have been on the spur of the moment.'

Graves was smiling, very slightly. 'Like who? The maid and her lover?'

'Most likely,' Daniel agreed.

'Then go and find who's trying to get the hangman to murder me!' Graves shouted. 'Do your job! Is it really your job to let them hang me?' A look of terror filled his face, and he jerked forward until the manacles stopped him, wrenching his arms. 'Or is that your job? To get the evidence banned and then let them hang me? They're good at covering up murder — ask your father! I'll wager he won't tell you. Ask him

238

about Amalia dos Santos! What did they do to her? How did he cover that up? Who helped him? He didn't do all that on his own.'

'Who put you up to this?' Daniel demanded. 'Tell me, or I really will let you hang.'

'Of course you will! That's what it's all about, isn't it? Your father to frame me, and you to make sure I hang!'

'I'm trying to get you off, you stupid sod! But I can't if I don't know all of it.' And then a sudden idea struck him. 'You haven't even sold the book yet, have you?'

'I have! I've got . . . offers . . . ' Slowly Graves sat back on the wooden chair. 'Is that what you want? You want to know who's publishing it? Well, I won't tell you.'

'Yes, you will, or I'm walking out of here. I'll suddenly find myself too busy to see you again. Too busy looking for your publisher — in your best interests, of course . . . '

He could see Graves thinking. Would he lie? There would be some record of any money paid in advance. Who would publish an exposé like that?

Then suddenly he realised. 'Someone who's on that list! Of course! And the price isn't money, is it? You don't need money, with the inheritance you've just come into. It's silence that this person needs. Your silence. He'll ruin everybody else if he has to, to buy his own safety! And destroy Narraway's reputation, and my father's, at the same time!'

Graves was white and his chest was heaving. There was a sweat of terror on his face, and

239

showing wet on his neck and chest, where Daniel could see his skin. 'God help me, I didn't kill her!' His voice was almost strangled. 'But you're going to be guilty of my death. You'll wear that for the rest of your life. Connive at murder, just like your father!'

Daniel looked at him with sudden chill. 'You are in the wrong place to be abusing me. I'm the only thing between you and the rope. You want me on your side. And *you* are calling *me* stupid?'

Graves looked as if he had been struck, and a dull tide of colour swept up his face. His eyes burned with hatred. 'You're going to let me hang?'

Daniel leaned forward over the table. 'Someone hated you enough to kill your wife, burn her face off and get you hanged for it. Please God, there aren't many people with that potential for hatred around! Concentrate. We've got to find who it is.'

'You? And who else? fford Croft? Kitteridge?'

'If my father still has Narraway's list of people, I'll let him do it,' Daniel replied. 'He'll know just how dangerous any of them really are. If there actually is such a list, we should make it work for us, shouldn't we?'

Graves was seething with anger, but he was trapped, and he knew it.

'Yes.'

15

Daniel went straight from the prison back to Lincoln's Inn, and then, a little after six, to his parents' home on Keppel Street. He wanted to give his father a copy of the names Graves had given to him, and it was best to do this away from his father's office. Daniel was still deeply afraid that someone in Special Branch had leaked the information to Graves, and flattered, bribed or threatened him into using it in the most damaging way, not only to inflict harm on Special Branch now, but to cast shadows over most of its past as well. He could only imagine what that reputation for corruption and black-mail would do to its ability to function at home, never mind abroad.

But most of all, he had to ask his father for the full story of Luz dos Santos. How much was Graves only guessing, and how much did he know? At some level, it would hardly matter. The damage of suggestion would be enough. And his father could not explain it publicly. Rightly or wrongly, he would be disgraced, perhaps even worse.

Daniel sat across from his father in his study, and reached over the desk with the list of people whom Graves had mentioned as sources for the book in his hand.

Pitt took it from him, looked at the names, and thanked him.

Daniel waited for something more.

'Who I expected,' Pitt said. 'One or two I didn't. It's time to see if I can find any corroborative evidence. I wouldn't damn anyone on Graves' words alone.' He smiled bleakly. 'But it casts a shadow, and that may well be all they expect of it. Thank you, Daniel.'

'I don't think Graves killed his wife,' Daniel said. It came out sounding like an excuse, and he had not intended that. 'I can't . . . let him hang just because he's a swine.' He wanted Pitt to understand. 'I wish he were guilty!'

'Letting him hang because he's a swine is roughly the same as killing him yourself,' Pitt answered. 'I dare say he felt like that about his wife. It's not an excuse.'

'Actually, she sounds rather nice,' Daniel answered. 'I think I would've liked her. She was far better than he. Interested, funny, brave, according to her children.'

'How old are they?'

'Why?'

'A lot of children view their parents uncritically for a time, and at others find them totally boring,' Pitt said a trifle ruefully.

'Oh . . . ' Then Daniel saw the wry smile and felt himself flush. 'We all take a little while to grow up. They are sixteen and nineteen. The girl is the elder, and takes care of her brother. He's in a wheelchair, and looks terribly frail.'

'Don't let pity slant your vision,' Pitt told him gently. 'It's only part of the truth.'

'They need their mother,' Daniel replied, as if he were defending them against some charge.

'She's only a girl, and has a heavy responsibility, now that her mother's gone, not least for poor Arthur.'

'I'm sorry. We take our health for granted. But don't let your pity rule you.' Now there was humour in his face. 'I've liked some people who have killed, a lot more than I liked their victims. Find all the mitigating facts you can, but do not lose the truth. Listen to me, Daniel! Most of any case has right on both sides. It's your job to find as much of it as you can, not to weigh it, and not to hide it.'

'Did you ever hide it?' Daniel asked, and his disbelief was plainer in his voice than he meant it to be, but the murder of the Portuguese woman was crowding his mind.

Pitt stared at him very steadily. 'Yes. I'm part of the country's defence against those who would spread terror and anarchy. You are not. Your part is to defend individuals against wrongful accusation, and to mitigate their punishment when their convictions are correct, in fact at least, if not in cause.'

'Yes, I know,' Daniel agreed. 'And I don't think that it was her husband. Which is a shame. I very much would have liked it to have been. He's a dangerous and vicious man. He loves the power to destroy, and he's hellbent on using it. Starting with Narraway and Vespasia, and going on to you, and then Special Branch in general.'

They stared at each other steadily.

Daniel knew that this was the moment. If he let it slip away, he might never have it again.

'What exactly happened about the Portuguese

murder? Graves is not going to let that go. Explain it to me, so I'm not fighting in the dark.'

Pitt was silent.

'I need to know! I'm a lawyer; you made me one. Trust me not to betray your confidence!'

'Is that what it is?' Pitt said wearily. 'I don't think Graves really knows anything about it, but I suppose on the chance that he does, I need to tell you.'

'You need to know if you've got a traitor in Special Branch, Father! And if you have, you have to find him.'

'I will. Believe me, I will. What do you want to know about the murder of Amalia dos Santos?'

Daniel swallowed. 'All of it. Then I won't fall into any traps.'

Pitt leaned back in his chair and looked at Daniel as he spoke. 'Luz dos Santos was giving me extremely valuable information about agitators and anarchists in London, and plans for insurrections here and around Europe. I disliked the man, but as an informant he was irreplaceable. He telephoned me late in the evening, almost hysterical, saying that he had been quarrelling with his wife and had lost his temper and struggled with her, and that she was dead. He asked for my immediate help, with a reminder of how much I needed him.'

His voice became a little more strained. 'I went to his apartment and found a dreadful scene . . . ' He stopped, breathing deeply as if to steady himself.

Daniel would have loved to have stopped him. He nearly did. Then he realised he would only have to make him begin again. That might be even more difficult.

'There was broken glass and porcelain all over the place. Amalia was at the bottom of the curving staircase, lying so crookedly her neck had to be broken. And there was blood all over her face, her arms and legs. To me, it was obvious that he had killed her,' Pitt continued even more quietly, his voice hoarse. 'I said so. He agreed that he had. Then he reminded me that he knew the names, descriptions, and whereabouts of at least half a dozen British agents in Lisbon. He listed them off, and I knew he was right. He said he would betray them to the revolutionaries if I didn't help him. They would all be murdered. I knew he was speaking the truth. He already set that in motion before he called me. Unless he rescinded it, it would happen. I knew he would do it. Amalia was dead and I couldn't help her, but I could save our men in Portugal. I didn't send them, but I knew the men who had.' He looked at Daniel. 'It was a bad choice, but the alternative was far worse. I called Tellman — you remember him?'

'Yes, of course.' Daniel had known Tellman ever since he had first become Pitt's sergeant, when Daniel was a child. He was now superintendent at Bow Street. 'You could trust him.'

'Together, we tidied up,' Pitt went on. 'We made it look as if poor Amalia had been drunk, and tripped and fallen down the stairs. When the police came, they accepted our word for it.'

'What happened to dos Santos?'

'We — we gave him safe passage back to Lisbon.'

Pitt's eyes were so steady on Daniel's face, he knew it was not a lie, but not the whole truth either. 'So, he got away with it? He killed Amalia, and you got him safely home.'

Pitt looked uncomfortable, but he did not avoid Daniel's gaze. 'Well — not exactly. Not safely. Most of the way there. There was a delay. Enough to get our men out of Lisbon.'

'You . . . '

'He met with an accident,' Pitt said flatly, and the look in his eyes was enough to warn Daniel not to go further.

Daniel said, 'Thank you . . . I think.'

Pitt reached across and put his hand gently on Daniel's arm. 'It's an ugly business,' he said, 'and I wish you didn't have to know. But this is an undeclared war, and there are some enemies who do so much damage that we have to stop them.'

Daniel had a new understanding of the weight his father carried, and why he had to make bad decisions sometimes: because the alternative would have been even worse. Better in his hands than the hands of someone who liked to use such power. For a moment, he was choked with emotion.

Pitt broke into the silence. 'You have to save him if he's innocent, but you know that already,' he said softly. 'Justice is not yours to deny. And if you do, you will regret it as long as you live. However a revolting creature he is, you've lost yourself if you decide to let him hang. In a sense, he'll have won . . . '

'I'm not going to! If I can stop it. You don't think I would, really?'

'No. But any mistake I may have made does not give you justification to do the same.'

Daniel smiled ruefully, to break the tension, which was growing unbearable. 'Don't worry, I'll make different ones.'

Pitt smiled also; there was anxiety, and an immeasurable tenderness in it. 'That will restrict you quite a lot. Go on, get on with it. Good luck.'

'Thank you.' And before it could tip over into any more emotion, Daniel went out of the room into the hall.

★ ★ ★

Daniel spent most of the next day in pursuits that earned him nothing further.

It was not until mid-morning of the following day — a fortnight before Graves was due to be hanged — that Impney knocked on the door and told him, with some misgivings, that a Mr Roman Blackwell had an urgent message to deliver.

'Thank you,' Daniel replied. 'Send him in, please.'

'Would you like tea, sir?' Impney barely raised his eyebrows.

'No . . . at least not yet. I may have to go out immediately.'

'Yes, sir.'

Impney withdrew, and barely a moment later

Roman Blackwell came in, practically glowing with a sense of achievement. 'Midnight,' he said simply.

'What?'

Blackwell closed the door behind him, then came back towards the desk. 'Midnight,' he repeated. 'That's the hour at which they disinter bodies.'

'I knew that — ' Daniel began, then stopped himself. 'Are you . . . are you saying you have permission?' He found himself holding his breath.

'Yes.' Blackwell reached into his jacket pocket and pulled out a piece of paper with a flourish. 'Duly signed and delivered. Permission to exhume the body of one Ebony Jane Graves.' He put it down on the desk in front of Daniel.

Daniel looked at it, then at Blackwell. 'Is it a forgery?'

Blackwell was affronted. 'Certainly not! It's a perfectly genuine order, signed by the judge whose name appears on it. Would I send you to a graveyard at midnight, to dig up a corpse, without genuine papers? Apart from that, to go to all that trouble of cutting it open, or whatever you're going to do to it, without proper justification?'

Daniel thought he would, if he could get away with it, but it was not the time to say so.

'How did you manage to do it?' he asked instead.

'Am I your client?' Blackwell asked, eyes wide.

'You mean if we get into trouble for this, would I defend you?'

'No, I do not!' Blackwell was indignant. 'I mean,

is anything I tell you privileged information?'

'It can be . . . '

'You don't want to know. Your father's career depends on solving this matter . . . '

'Is he involved? My father?'

'No!'

'Then why . . . Blackwell! What have you done?'

'I'm looking after you. That's all you have to know. Shut up, and get Miss fford Croft to do the job! She's not mentioned in this, and neither are you. If there's any risk at all, it's mine. Now stop wasting time and get hold of her.' Blackwell's face was suddenly devoid of all humour. 'Midnight tonight. They're going to hang the bastard, and when they do, you want your conscience to rest easy. Heaven only knows why. I don't know what you're looking for, but I suppose you do?'

Daniel's mind raced over the possibilities, and any other answer that fitted the facts. Was it worth it? What had Blackwell done? He had no answers.

Blackwell stared at him.

Daniel stood up. 'All right, thank you, Roman. Don't tell me any more.'

'I wasn't going to. You're a good man, and quite clever at times, but you don't know when to keep your mouth shut,' Blackwell replied.

Daniel gave him a withering look, but he did not bother to respond to the jibe. 'Thank you,' he said instead. 'Are you coming to the exhumation?'

'I'm taking Mother to the theatre. It's going to be a cold and a windy night,' Blackwell replied.

Daniel gave the exhumation order to fford Croft, who had far more weight of authority to see it attended to immediately. It was possible an innocent man might hang because of unexamined evidence.

'Don't wait for this.' fford Croft stood up from his desk, waving the paper in his hand. 'I'll get the information to the necessary people. The grave will be opened at midnight tonight. You go and tell Miriam. Here, I'll write the address for you. You will find her, no doubt, working on something in the library, but it can wait. Now hurry up and go, for heaven's sake, don't stand there waiting.' And he pushed past Daniel with an urgent enthusiasm.

Daniel turned and followed after him.

★　★　★

The butler showed him in, as if he had been expecting him, and took him straight to the door of the library. 'Miss Miriam, the gentleman your father mentioned is here for you. Would you like to have some luncheon in the dining room?'

Daniel found Miriam exactly where her father said she would be, curled up with a book in the huge library in his house.

'Oh?' She looked up with a smile. 'Not yet, Membury. We may not have time, thank you. Hello, Mr Pitt.' She rose to her feet. 'So, you have an exhumation order? That's brilliant! How on earth did you do it?' Her face was alight with interest. She was dressed in a plain white blouse and a dark skirt. Her wild auburn hair was so loosely tied back that half the pins had fallen out of it and were put back in anywhere, regardless of effectiveness.

He had thought beforehand how he was going to answer her. 'I asked the help of a friend who knows the right people to ask,' he said casually.

She looked at him very carefully. 'Oh, yes? They are judges, I hope?'

'Certainly, they are!' He was very glad that he had asked Blackwell. He did not like being even slightly misleading to Miriam. She was willing to help where probably no other doctor would have, considering the case, not to mention the urgency. And he had liked her on the journey they had made together just a few days ago to see the site of Ebony's death.

'Then we will arrange for the grave to be — '

'Mr fford Croft is organising it already. Do you need to arrange a place to . . . a laboratory, I mean . . . ?' He did not know what she would need. He had never had occasion to attend an autopsy.

She smiled. 'No, thank you. I have my own laboratory, and it is fully equipped. We just need a van in which we can carry the coffin, and the body, from the graveyard. I will need a little assistance with lifting the body, and that kind of thing. Are you good for it? She might be too heavy for just two of us. And you can assist at the autopsy, passing me instruments, and so on. Do you think your stomach will stand it?' She looked at him with amusement, but it was not unkind.

He knew she was trying to steer a course between not using him, on the one hand, and taking for granted that he could hold down his dinner when faced with the sight and, above all, the smell, of a two-month-old corpse.

He was not at all sure he could do that, but the embarrassment of vomiting, or even fainting, was not as bad as that of refusing even to try. 'Yes, of course,' he said. He nearly added, 'I'll try,' but changed his mind.

'Good. Then you may pick me up here, at half-past eleven tonight. I have some preparations to make, and I dare say you have also.' She smiled. 'Wear something warm, apart from a greatcoat. Graveyards are always cold at midnight, and standing around is not particularly pleasant. Not like a brisk walk. And it will be cold in the laboratory too. Believe me, it is better that way. And, Mr Pitt . . . thank you for including me in this task. The least we can do is find that there is nothing to discover, as a certainty, not just a guess.' She rose to her feet. 'Perhaps you'd better make it a quarter past eleven. There will not be much traffic, but I always find it is better to build in a quarter of an hour for unforeseen events.'

He went out into the hallway where Membury was waiting. 'Thank you, Miss fford Croft,' Daniel said. 'Until a quarter past eleven.'

★ ★ ★

At exactly a quarter past eleven he knocked on the fford Crofts' front door, and it was opened

252

immediately by Membury. Miriam was standing just behind him, wearing a plain, dark overcoat, and a shawl over her head. Apart from the hall light on her bright hair, she could have been somebody's housemaid out keeping an illicit appointment. Daniel was glad he also had dressed in his oldest, most casual clothes. He felt he looked disrespectful, but how could one be respectful digging up a corpse, and then cutting her open?

Miriam came outside, thanked Membury briefly, and said, 'Good evening.'

He led her to where the horse-drawn van he had hired was parked, helped her up beside the driver, and shortly after they set off.

It was no time to make light conversation. They rode through the fair, moonlit night in silence. It was not cold, but there was a rising wind and it blew in the leaves of those streets that were lined with trees.

They reached the graveyard without delay, and therefore were early. It was ten minutes before they saw anyone else arrive, and Daniel was happy they had paid the driver for the extra time so they could wait in the van, rather than stand outside in the wind. The gravediggers arrived, accompanied by the sexton. Daniel showed them the order again, and the sexton read it by the lantern light. Then, as he put it in his pocket, he gave the signal to the gravediggers to begin.

Daniel stood beside Miriam, then suddenly realised he was to the leeward of her, and the wind was strengthening, and moving shreds of cloud across the moon. He moved down to the other side of her, so he was sheltering her. The wind rattled the branches of the ancient trees at the far edge of the graveyard, and rustled the dense yews. They were dark, impenetrable. Why did they so often plant yew trees in graveyards? They were poisonous. They crowded together, like silent ornaments to death. The earth underneath them was black and seemed always to be damp.

Half a dozen lanterns were hung on poles that swayed in the wind, and the lights danced over the ground. It was mostly bare. There was not room enough between the graves for much to grow.

The gravediggers started to dig, carefully piling the earth so they could put it back again afterwards. They moved rhythmically, used to working the spade.

The process seemed to go on for ever, the spades getting only fractionally deeper every few minutes. No one spoke.

Then there was a sudden, sharp gust of wind and one of the lamps fell to the ground with a crash of glass on metal. Both gravediggers were standing in the hole they had created. The sexton was on the far side of the pit. Daniel was the closest, and he took a long dozen steps and bent over. The flame was out, and he could smell the acrid sharpness of oil.

'You need to go inside to light that,' the sexton told him. 'Take the one over to it, or they'll both go out. I'm telling you.'

Daniel took both lamps and walked over between the gravestones until he reached the church doorway, and the carved arch that decorated it. He put the lamps on the ground, took the cover off the lighted one, and very carefully lit the other from its flame. He covered them again and set out back. From a distance, they looked a spectral group, only the heads of the gravediggers now visible. Miriam seemed out of place, with the wind blowing her skirts and the ends of her shawl. The sexton was indistinguishable, like one of the carved stone figures signifying grief. Daniel made his way back to them just as the gravediggers stopped and asked for ropes.

It was backbreaking, lifting the coffin out of the earth. Even with Daniel and the sexton both helping, it took them several minutes to get it up and manoeuvre it onto the waiting handcart. Daniel was warmed through, except for his hands, by the time they were finished and were trudging through the gravestones back to the van by the roadside. The coffin was loaded on, and there was just room for Daniel to sit on the end, backwards, while Miriam sat up in front and the driver finally persuaded the horse to move. It seemed to have been asleep on its feet, impervious to the activities of men.

When they reached the fford Croft house, Miriam opened the back, tradesmen's entrance for them, and Daniel and the driver, with a deal of effort, set the coffin down by the door.

'I'll go and get the butler and the footman,' Miriam said quietly. 'No doubt you could use a hot cup of tea?' she said to the driver. 'And a piece of cake?'

'Yes, ma'am, that I could,' he agreed.

'Then wait here,' she ordered, and opened the back door with a key.

The driver looked at Daniel, as if he were about to ask for an explanation, then he thought better of it. Perhaps he did not really want to know.

Membury and the footman appeared and helped take the coffin into the house and down the back stairs to the cellar.

Miriam made tea in the deserted kitchen for the driver and Daniel and herself, and served it with thick slices of Madeira cake.

By three o'clock, the driver had departed with an extra reward for his civility. Membury and the footman were long returned to their own beds, and Miriam had informed Daniel that the spare room was made up for him, because he was expected to report to the kitchen at 6a.m., and by half-past six to be ready to perform the autopsy.

★　★　★

He had breakfast in the kitchen. It still felt like the middle of the night, although it was only about five weeks before the longest day of the year; it was full sunlight and the dew was already gone from the herbs in the small beds he noticed outside the back door. He ate hungrily, knowing it would waken him up sufficiently to pay attention. He had finished his third slice of toast with sharp Seville orange marmalade before it occurred to him that, considering the job he was about to assist with, he might have been better with an empty stomach. Too late now to cancel!

At half-past six on the dot, Miriam appeared at the cellar door and said, 'Good morning,' brightly. 'Don't worry, Membury and the footman helped me with the coffin. It's open. We can remove her and begin.' She did not bother with any polite questions as to how he had slept, or how he felt. She was ready to begin, and she expected him to be also.

Determined to live up to his promises, Daniel followed her inside. The cellar must have been half the size of the ground floor of the house. It was perfectly arranged to be an autopsy room, with large tables, running water, and plenty of space to put a coffin. Other doors led off into further rooms. He presumed it was for analysis, experiments, and maybe even ice boxes to store a body afterwards, until it could be buried.

All kinds of instruments lay neatly put out on trays. He would find out what they did if he had to. Some of them were obvious in their purpose: several Bunsen burners, scales of various degrees of refinement, calipers, magnifying glasses of different sizes.

'Come in.' Miriam guided him to where a coffin stood on a trestle, the size and height of the table near it. The lid was open away from the table, so it would be easier to move her body.

Daniel took a deep breath, and looked down at Ebony Graves.

She seemed small, with her face so charred he had no idea what she had been like in life. Most of her hair was gone. He could not have told, from what was left, even what colour it had been. Her jaw must be broken; it hung at an odd angle. The left side of her skull above her ear was terribly misshapen.

He looked at the eyes, then looked again. They were not there. She had no eyes. Just deep hollows where they had been. And now that he looked again, her nose was gone, too. Was this what happened to you, when you were burned?

Miriam touched his elbow.

Gently, they lifted the body out of the coffin, Daniel taking her head, Miriam her feet, and laid her down on the table.

'Now that you are behaving like a detective, forget the woman she was; the spirit has gone. Where to is a matter of belief. Cling on to whatever seems to you good.'

'Her hair . . . ' he began. 'Her eyes and . . . what happened? She looks so — small!'

'That's what we're going to find out,' she answered gently. 'You are going to write down everything I can deduce, without touching her. Pick up the pad there, and the pencil, ready to begin. It doesn't have to be neat, only legible.'

Just as well, Daniel thought silently. He would have trouble holding the pen steady.

Miriam told him the height she measured, with a note that she was not lying straight, so she was probably taller alive. Then she described her clothes, her boots. She touched one of them lightly. 'It looks . . . too small. It isn't on properly. I wonder why. Very fashionable. Expensive. A pair of boots like these would cost several guineas.'

'Could she have worn a smaller size out of vanity?' Daniel asked.

'Don't look very beautiful if your face is creased up in pain.' She gave a little gesture of pity. 'It's not much too small. I wonder if the leather tightened? Or the foot swelled? I'll have to think more of that when I see her feet, and look at the burns.'

She worked upwards on the body for a few moments in silence. 'Dress is too short,' she observed. 'Not much. But she didn't seem from her wardrobe to be the sort of woman that skimped on her appearance. And she certainly wouldn't have had hand-me-downs.'

For a little while, she said nothing more, and Daniel had time to look at the body on the table. The frizzled and burned hair made it easy to see where the blow to the side of the skull had been. It was also easy to see the flesh of the neck, which was burned to the bone in some places. In other areas, he could see the flesh coming away from the bone, burned deeply.

She had once been beautiful, according to the accounts of her. He stared at her and was overwhelmed by the reality of death. The mess of torn and burned clothes, charred flesh, face and hair destroyed, only a few months ago had been a woman. Now she looked pathetic, so alone, without dignity or meaning. Was death always like this, so . . . real? So complete?

And how unusual that she had been buried in the clothes she was wearing when she died. Maybe it was a favourite dress, but that seemed unlikely as it didn't even fit very well.

Miriam became aware of his stillness and looked up. 'Do you want to go away for a little while?' she asked.

He shook his head. 'She barely looks like a person at all. She's . . . anonymous! She hasn't even . . . a face?'

'I know,' Miriam said quietly. 'She doesn't need one now. But we have to find who destroyed this one, how, and eventually why. I've learned what I can from her clothes, although what it means I don't know yet.'

'What? What did you learn?' He wanted to know, he had to, and yet he was afraid. Death was more visceral, more intensely real than merely speaking of it would ever convey.

'I cut a little of the clothes free. She looks older than I thought. Older than I expected. And her hands, too. But many women show their age in ways you would expect, even when they take care with their faces, and hair of course. Her hair is . . . destroyed.' For a few moments, she regarded the face and neck very closely.

Daniel marvelled how she could do it dispassionately, as if this were not all that was left of a woman who had been intensely alive less than three months ago. Who had laughed at jokes, loved her children, fought for causes she believed in. Now she wasn't even recognisable!

The contrast with the living, breathing Miriam was strong. Standing only fifteen or twenty inches away from Ebony's face, or where it would have been, her own skin was perfect, her auburn hair shining with colour, so soft it tickled her and irritated, until she pushed it aside.

Then she moved down a little and looked at the edge where the burned skin met the skin still whole. 'Pass me the glass,' she requested, gesturing toward the magnifying lens.

Daniel handed it to her.

She took it and looked at the charred skin, and the whole skin, just reddened a little.

Daniel found himself holding his breath.

Finally, she continued. 'There was something added to make her burn. You can see where it dripped, and on her clothes, the fire has scorched places, and left it somewhat close to whole. I wonder what it was. And here.' She pointed to pile of charred black bone where Ebony's nose would have been.

Daniel tried, but he could not see anything recognisable. He looked up at Miriam, confused.

'This lump.' Miriam picked up black, charred pieces with her forceps. 'That's fabric, burned badly. Used to feed the fire, I imagine. I found a small piece of oiled silk near her bosom. Caught in the folds of her dress.'

'What . . . ?' Daniel began.

'Oiled silk is highly flammable,' she said grimly. 'It's great stuff. Waterproof, light, bends or sews evenly. But it burns like a beacon fire. Pour a little more oil on cotton, or something light, and you have a fire that would burn flesh.'

Daniel swallowed. 'What sort of oil?'

'Fat, lard, even butter, I suppose. Didn't you say the son painted?'

'Yes.'

'Well, the linseed oil that artists use would be perfect!'

'You don't think Arthur . . . ?' Daniel shook his head violently.

'No, I don't. But somebody else could have.' She straightened up. 'Come. Sit down here, away from what's left of her.'

He did not argue. He felt a little queasy, and was glad she did not remark on it. He sat down on a chair opposite the one in front of her desk.

'Isn't that what you want to know?' she asked. 'What burned her? At a well-educated guess, I'd say highly flammable oiled silk, and a bit of lightweight cotton or muslin, and the whole lot doused with linseed oil. Lights quickly, hot, and burns very well if there was cotton to feed it. Quite enough to burn her face. And . . . ' She hesitated. 'I'm sorry to say this, but I can't even say for sure that this is Ebony. With all the burns . . . plus the boots and dress don't fit. Maybe it isn't her.'

'But her family — her daughter identified her!'

'Before or after this was done to her?' Miriam asked. Her face was white, and her lips moved stiffly at the horror of the thought.

'Oh God!' Daniel stared at her. 'What have we fallen into? What is this?'

She put her hands over his. 'We've still got a few days left. We must find out.'

16

Daniel stayed a little longer, helping Miriam lift the body, although it was not very heavy. He watched while she took samples from various parts of the intestines, lungs, and other regions. She spoke very little, except to dictate the notes to him on everything she discovered. He wrote it down exactly as she said, once or twice asking her how to spell certain long words, names of chemicals, or little-known anatomical terms.

She seemed to learn little that was unexpected until they very carefully laid the body on a machine that Daniel had never seen before, and could not work out its purpose.

'X-ray,' she said proudly. 'Father gave me that for Christmas and birthday combined.' Her face lit with pleasure and suddenly it was easy to imagine her opening an enormous parcel with a bow on the top on Christmas morning, and discovering this strange monstrosity.

She was already explaining to him, with pride, what it could do and he had not been listening

'Daniel!

'I'm sorry . . . '

'It can see through flesh and make pictures of the bones beneath. Or it can find anything solid, or metal we may have eaten, and trace it anywhere through our digestive system. It can find bullets, or broken-off pieces of a knife, for example.'

'Is that what it's used for?' He was surprised. How often could they need such a thing?

'Not in the hospitals,' she dismissed the idea. 'But we may find something useful in her bones. For example, an old break, or an abnormality.'

He did not reply, but watched her as she put one part of the body, and then another, in front of the machine. It was rather like a camera, but fastened to the table with clamps from which two metal rods of about an inch in diameter held it at a height of two feet above the table's surface. The table itself was long enough for an adult man to lie upon.

The machine itself consisted of several distinct parts. The first was an eye piece, like a funnel, through which the operator looked. It was attached to a complicated box with projecting lenses and dials. In front of that was another, larger box made of something transparent. Inside it was more machinery, smaller and circular; attached to it was a large frame, as if to hold another part. It was all focused downward, less than a foot away from the body Miriam was examining.

Then suddenly she stiffened, and stopped completely. 'Look!' she ordered him. 'Look at this!' She stepped back for him to see through the focus.

He moved closer to her and looked down at the fuzzy black-and-white image. It was little shadows, blotches. It took a moment or two for him to realise what it was. 'It's a foot!' he exclaimed in amazement at the complexity of it. He turned to her. 'Are all those separate bones?'

She smiled. 'Yes! Marvellous, isn't it? You can

see a skeleton, and it's hard to realise it is mere fragments of a person. And of course, we hardly ever know who. At first, in medical school, we were given the names, but they're not real. It's . . . better now to think of them being what's left of someone.'

He looked at it again. 'How do you know if you're seeing something normal, or not? What's that — that smudge there? It's blurred.' He peered closer.

'That is what I was looking at. It's a lot whiter than the rest of the bone, and a bit wider. See?'

'Yes. What is it?'

'It's an old break, well healed. There are more of them.'

'She has lots of broken bones? An accident?' He winced at the thought of bones snapped, jagged. He had only broken a bone once, playing football, but it had hurt appallingly. His arm had healed in about six weeks, but it still ached now and then.

'I don't know,' she said gravely. 'A different bone and I would say probably an accident, a certain fracture of the wrist. You can put your hand out to save yourself when you're falling. But some bones, fingers, forearm, toes . . . '

'You mean deliberate? You think he hit her? Hard enough to break bones?' A hatred boiled up inside him towards Graves. If he had been there, he would have lashed out and hit him back. Is that what Graves had done when he couldn't control Ebony? Then he remembered what Mrs Warlaby had told him and knew it was the truth.

'Probably. But the interesting thing is this . . . '
Miriam pointed out the whitest part of the bone.

'Why?' he asked. 'What does it mean?'

'That's where it healed.'

'Why is it interesting?'

'Look at it through the magnifying glass.' She
passed it to him and Daniel peered at the
pictures. Enlarged, it was still not clear to him.
'The thickness of it, the density. And the other
bones as well,' she prompted.

'They don't look so dense. At least, they don't
to me. What am I missing?' He turned to her.
Her eyes were shining, and there was a faint
flush in her cheeks.

'You're looking at a bone that was broken a
long time ago,' she said quietly, but there was a
tension in her voice. 'Probably over twenty years,
at least. And the bones in general are losing
mass. They are more brittle than when they were
broken, not as dense.'

'An illness? Is that why they broke? Then the
illness was cured!' he exclaimed.

Her face was bleak for just an instant, and then
it cleared again. 'No, there is no cure for it . . .
better diet, perhaps. More exercise. It delays it,
but doesn't cure it.' A shadow of humour crossed
her eyes. 'The bones were broken more than
twenty years ago, at least. More like twenty-five.
The less density is because she is older. People's
bones do become less dense as they grow older.
That is why when old people fall, they so often
break bones, where younger people don't. Children's bones are far less fragile. Sometimes they
bend instead of breaking. Women tend to lose

bone strength more than men. This woman is a lot older than Ebony claimed to be. About ten years, I'd say.'

'Why would she do that?' he asked. 'How could she get away with it? Ten years? That's an awful lot . . . '

She turned away.

'Wouldn't people know?' he asked. 'Do you think it has anything to do with her death? That Graves found out . . . ?'

'Do you think it's such a sin?' she asked, looking not at him, but at the X-ray again. 'She had children. She can't have been that old.'

He looked at Miriam, bent over the magnifying glass again. He remembered what fford Croft had said about her studies, her intelligence, and that the authorities had not recognised her achievements, or given her degrees, even though she had passed all the examinations.

Nobody cared how old a man was in marriage, but a woman had to be young enough to bear healthy children, to be acceptable as a bride. That meant probably his own age, or less. Ebony had lied for a good reason. 'But she was funny, charming, brave and clever, according to what Mercy Blackwell told me,' he said aloud. 'And beautiful, in her own way. Why should Graves care?'

'I don't think it had anything to do with it,' she replied. Her loss of composure had been so slight perhaps he had only imagined it, because he had made an insensitive remark.

'What then?' he said. He was lost.

'Remember the clothes, and the boots in particular?'

'Yes.'

'Those boots don't fit her very well.'

'What are you suggesting?' There was only one idea on the edge of his mind, growing clearer all the time. He took a deep breath. 'This isn't Ebony Graves!'

Miriam looked at him, her eyes bright again, clear. She nodded. 'Exactly. Which raises many questions. Who is she? And where is Ebony? Is she alive, or dead? And why did Sarah say it was her mother? Did she think it was? Did she ever really look at that terribly disfigured corpse enough to know who it was? And why was it dressed in Ebony's clothes, and Ebony's boots, which don't fit her?'

'And who killed her?' Daniel added. 'And why? 'Why?' may answer all the rest.'

'I think we had better go back to Graves' house and ask a few more very probing questions.' Miriam stood up straight and stared at Daniel. 'Come with me. You must need these answers as much as I do. Graves might be telling the truth when he says he did not kill Ebony. But he may have killed somebody else.'

'We'll go on the early train tomorrow,' he said.

'Why not now?' she asked impatiently. 'There's no time to waste!'

'I've got something else to do this afternoon.'

She appeared startled. 'Oh.'

Daniel realised how rude he had sounded. 'Forgive me, I'm taking you for granted. It's a rather delicate matter I need to attend to, and

I'm not looking forward to it.'

Miriam smiled in sudden sympathy. 'I'm sorry.'

'Do we need to bring any of this with us?' He gestured towards her equipment.

'No. But I need to pack this woman, whoever she is, in the ice chamber, and make sure I have all my notes. Now that we're not leaving until morning, I can take my time.'

'I'm going back to the office to report to Kitteridge and your father.'

★ ★ ★

'What?' Marcus fford Croft's face filled with amazement and complete incredulity. 'I hope this is not your idea of humour, Pitt?' He blinked and shook his head, as if to clear it of delusions.

'No, sir,' Daniel said soberly. 'Miss fford Croft found evidence — '

'Miriam . . . ' fford Croft ran his hands through his hair and left it standing on end. 'God have mercy! Have you told Kitteridge? I suppose you haven't.'

'I thought I should tell you first, sir.'

'Yes, so you should. Well, you'd better go and tell him now!'

'Thank you, sir.' Daniel left immediately and went to look for Kitteridge. He found him in the library.

'You look flustered,' he observed, looking at Daniel curiously.

Daniel took a deep breath. 'The body isn't Ebony,' he said bluntly. 'We don't know who it is.'

Kitteridge did not know whether to laugh or lose his temper. He decided to laugh. 'God help us!' he said with sincerity. 'We are going to need it.'

*   *   *

The next morning, he met Miriam at the railway station. He thought he might have difficulty finding her because he had not arranged a particular place. Before Daniel had returned to chambers with the news, they had taken a long time to store the body properly, finish all the notes, and wash and put away every instrument that had been used or possibly contaminated. Even washing the floor of the pieces of burned hair and skin had been a large task. She would not leave it until the room was ready for the next autopsy she might perform. Probably it would be a tidy-up job, some detail left out of an earlier example of somebody else's work. Perhaps something to prepare for an anatomy lecture at one of the universities. She did not complain, but Daniel saw in her face that she felt wounded only to be given low-level jobs.

He should have agreed a place to meet with her. He had been too tired, and overwhelmed. He thought now that under the central clock in the station would be a good place. Most people looked at the clock, at some time or other. He would have to hope the same thought would occur to her. He had been there less than five minutes, watching businessmen stride by with their rolled-up umbrellas in one hand, and newspapers in the other. Even though it was a bright May morning, most of them were wearing grey or black and, of course, pinstripes. Would he get to look like that, in ten or fifteen years? It was like a uniform, and there were certainly ranks: the commanders and the junior managers, corporals! And foot soldiers, except that they did not keep step and they were dressed in a variety of browns and greys.

Was the law going to be like that? The crusade to save someone, like Blackwell — or more like Graves, whom you wanted to see condemned with a sigh of relief. But mostly it would be petty burglaries, squabbles over mistakes, and the occasional grievous bodily harm.

'Daniel?'

He turned and saw Miriam walking quickly across the platform. She was wearing a beautifully tailored suit of dark grey, with a crisp white blouse. It had just a touch of lace at the collar. Perhaps a hat was necessary, but he preferred her bright hair without it. He nearly said so, but realised it was far too personal a remark to make to a woman he barely knew.

'Good morning, Miss fford Croft,' he said, snapping to attention. 'We have fifteen minutes. I don't think it's enough time to get a cup of tea.'

'I had breakfast this morning, thank you. Didn't you? And for goodness' sake, call me Miriam.'

'Yes.' He hesitated. 'Miriam. I had breakfast. Mrs Portiscale is trying to fatten me up. They might give us luncheon in the servants' hall. It was very good indeed when I was there before.

271

And you hear a lot by listening to their conversation.' He fell in step beside her as they made their way onto the platform they needed. The train was already there, and ready to board. 'Although I'm not at all sure they'll invite us this time.'

'Who have you decided to give this news to first?' she asked, putting her Gladstone bag in the rack above the seat before he could reach up and do it for her. They had agreed to be prepared in case an overnight stay was necessary. He put his beside it, then waited for her to choose a seat next to the window, and facing the engine.

'Sarah should be told first in respect for her being the elder child. Falthorne, the butler, is head of the household in all but name, but he would think it out of order for me to tell anyone other than Sarah first,' he replied. If he had learned anything at all about Falthorne, it was his love of order. Daniel had learned from his mother that when life is in chaos, there is a certain comfort in order. Things don't get lost, moved, or forgotten. One still needs to eat, to sleep, to have laundry done. The rhythm of housework, busy hands, can hold the world together when it seems to be falling apart. There had been a murder in the house — believed to be Arthur and Sarah's mother. Their father was due to be hanged for murder less than a fortnight from now. Then Sarah and Arthur would be alone. The house would have to be sold, and the servants scattered to find whatever new positions they could. The shadow of the scandal would follow them.

Daniel saw from Miriam's expression that she understood as much.

He determined to speak on something else on the journey.

'Where did you study?' he asked.

'Cambridge,' she answered with a smile. 'My professor said I had an insufficiency of humility and an overabundance of opinions. I admit, if I possessed any of the genius my school mistress had believed of me, it was for fending off inconvenient questions. It was more than all the rest of the students put together.'

He smiled. 'I think I knew him.'

'I haven't even told you his name.' Then she realised his humour and laughed. 'I guess he gets around.'

'Did you enjoy it? There's a lot in Cambridge, other than a few tediously pompous professors.'

'Oh, yes. It's a lovely city. I loved exploring it. And I belonged to the amateur theatrical society.' She stopped and stared at him ruefully. 'Ridiculous, isn't it! Not at all a suitable thing for a chemist to do.'

'But perfectly suitable for human beings,' he said with certainty. 'Which is more important. If you cut out anything other than mathematics, you may know everything about how the world is made, but you've missed the purpose of it all. That's the difference between the wise man and the fool. It's not counting stars, or knowing what they're made of, it's actually seeing them, and caring.'

'Are you sure you're right to follow the law?'

She looked at him earnestly.

'No. Not really. Sometimes I am. When I got Blackwell off, I was thrilled. Graves, I'm not so sure about. The exactness of the law says I must pay attention only to whether he is innocent or guilty of this count. I won't punish him for this, if he's only guilty of wanting to ruin most of the people I love, and turning Special Branch on its head.'

Her face reflected all his emotions. Now it was anxiety. 'So, what are you going to do?'

'I wish I were certain,' he answered. 'Just find out whose body it really is. If Graves killed her, whoever she is, I'd be perfectly happy to see him hanged, except that it may take a while because he'll have to be tried for that person's death, if Ebony is still alive. Maybe long enough to finish this damn book and publish it. I don't know what I can do about that. Blackwell may have some idea.'

'And your father?'

'I wish he didn't have to know.'

★   ★   ★

Daniel wished that questioning Sarah Graves could be avoided, but since it could not, he would rather do it himself than trust anyone else not to hurt her more than was absolutely unavoidable. Her mother was dead, so far as she knew, and it seemed inevitable that her father would be also. Her brother was brave and sensitive, and totally dependent on her.

Daniel chose to do it in the sitting room. It

was not as formal as the withdrawing room, and as far as possible from the room in which she believed her mother had been killed. But whether it was Ebony, or not, certainly someone had been killed there, and almost worse than that, disfigured.

Miriam sat quietly, almost in the corner, and he knew she would not speak unless she judged it necessary.

He stood as Sarah came into the room. He could see by the way she held her head, and her stiff, straight shoulders, that she was afraid. The pallor of her face could have been grief, or emotional exhaustion. She barely glanced at Miriam.

'Please sit down, Miss Graves.' He gestured towards the chair opposite the one on which he had been sitting. 'Miss fford Croft is here as a chaperone, so you do not need to have any of your own staff here, in case you wish to say something that you would rather keep private from them.'

She hesitated a moment, as if she might refuse. Then she obeyed, holding her hands in her lap, back still perfectly straight. No doubt she could walk with a book balanced on her head, and not let it fall. It was the classic exercise for a young lady's deportment. He could remember Jemima doing it, under protest. But this was so far from anything Jemima had had to endure. How easy their lives were, compared to this!

Would it be kinder to be blunt? Not to stretch out the things he had to ask her, increasing her fear? How could he know the best approach? He knew nothing of her, except her obvious circumstances, and the fact that she sat opposite him and refused to avoid his glance.

He should not even be thinking of her feelings. He should be more practical, and perhaps show more courage. He should be looking for the most effective way to get her to tell him the truth.

'Miss Graves, we looked at the body of your mother.'

Her eyes widened. 'How? She is . . . buried!'

'We dug her up . . . I'm sorry. She is not in her body any more. She is at peace, whole again . . . I think.'

For a moment, confusion was clear in her face. 'You . . . think? Are you not sure of your own beliefs, Mr Pitt? Or are you questioning whether she was good enough . . . to go to any kind of heaven?' Then there was nothing left in her eyes but anger.

He was taken aback. 'No, Miss Graves. I am questioning whether the body was that of your mother.'

Sarah glanced at Miriam. 'You dug up the wrong body?' She did not need to say more; accusation was complete.

'No!' he swallowed. 'No, we got the right grave, it was quite clearly marked.'

'Thank you.'

He had to start again. But he was more determined. He had a new respect for her, even though it impeded his attempts to discover the truth. 'The body was that of a woman who had died from a head injury, and her face and upper body had been burned, enough to disfigure her. I am not sure that it was your mother.'

'I . . . ' Sarah began, then stopped.

'Yes?'

'Didn't Mr Falthorne identify her, and in my mother's bedroom? Dressed in her clothes, who else could it be?'

'You were going to say that you did not see her?' he asked. She must have been protecting Falthorne when she claimed to have identified the body. He would have respected her less had she not done so.

'He . . . was saving me from that.' She found it difficult to say.

Was that the thought that disturbed, or was she reluctant to lay the blame on Falthorne for what might have been a profound mistake? Or was Daniel chasing a ridiculous fantasy, and she did not dare to say so to him?

But the evidence suggested it was not Ebony Graves.

'I don't know,' he answered her question. 'Who else would call upon her? And it was not in her bedroom, it was her boudoir — a natural place to entertain a woman who knew her well. More private, a little more comfortable than the withdrawing room.'

She stiffened again. It was only the smallest of movements, but the last vestige of colour drained from her face. He looked at her hands; her knuckles were white. He was glad that Miriam was present, in case Sarah actually fainted.

He leaned forward a very little. 'Miss Graves, if it was not your mother, and you keep silent and allow your father to be hanged for having killed her, you will be guilty of his death. I cannot believe you wish that, whatever the truth of the matter. Apart from the morality of it, who then will look after Arthur?'

She stared at him with something close to hatred, but she did not answer.

'Who was she, and how did she die?'

She clenched her jaw tight, as though to prevent herself from letting the words course their way out of her mouth.

'Did your father kill her?' he persisted.

She closed her eyes and tipped her head a little downwards. Was that a denial?

'Are you prepared to let him hang?' he said again.

It was as if he had struck her.

He wanted to reach out and touch her. He even started to, and then realised how inappropriate it was. He barely knew her. And yet his pity for her was overwhelming.

'Who was she?' he repeated.

Her eyes filled with tears.

'Miss Graves, who was she?'

'I'm not Miss Graves, I think.' There was the edge of a smile on her lips, a bitter, self-mocking smile.

What did she mean? He was totally confused.

She saw his look and spoke almost gently. 'Oh, Russell Graves is my father. I wish he were not. The woman on the carpet was Winifred Graves. His first wife. Or so she said. I believe her.'

'What?'

Sarah shook her head. 'He has recently

inherited a title, of all things, and the money and estate that go with it. Isn't that absurd?' The contempt in her voice was scorching. 'Winifred found out about it, from wherever she lives. I don't know. She came to tell us that he never divorced her, so she is still entitled to a wife's share of his good fortune. We are illegitimate, Arthur and I. And my mother has no marriage. So, she is a bigamous wife.'

He understood what that meant. He could see the injustice of it, and the disaster of it in her face. She had no rights, no position, and if Graves so chose, no home and no money.

But Graves also would be disgraced. Bigamy was a crime, punishable by imprisonment. He had cause to have killed her — Winifred. But so did Ebony — and Sarah, for that matter. Arthur had cause, but not the ability. Daniel thought for a fleeting moment he could have hit Winifred, in Ebony's cause. A moment's rage at the intolerable loss not so much to herself as to her children. The injustice of it would scald anyone.

'Who killed Winifred?' he said, recalling himself to the present. It could still have been Graves. Would Sarah lie? It would be so easy. 'Was it your father?'

Would she tell him the truth? He might never know. Would she let Graves hang anyway?

Her eyes filled with tears and she shook her head. It was so minute a gesture, had he not been watching her so closely he would have missed it. She swayed a little. Miriam stood up, came silently over to Sarah, and put her arms round her, almost as if she were holding her up.

'Who did?' she said in almost a whisper.

Sarah leaned into her. 'It was accidental,' she said with her voice wavering. 'She lunged at my mother, who defended herself, and Winifred slipped on the hearth and hit her head. If you know so much, you probably know that it was only one blow.' The tears slipped down her cheeks, but her eyes were challenging again. She intended to fight both of them all the way, protecting her mother, and her brother.

'Did your father know?' Daniel said. He would not ask if Arthur did. She would lie to protect him anyway, and Daniel would look the other way.

'No.'

It was just one word, but that was all it needed. Graves was innocent after all — at least of murder. It sat with the ease of truth in Daniel's mind, but with the pain of intolerable injustice.

'Then I can't let him hang for it,' he said miserably.

'And neither can you,' Miriam said as if it were a certainty. 'It would weigh on you for the rest of your life.'

Sarah jerked her head up and glared at Daniel. 'I can't let him come back here, either, and beat her again, or Arthur! And what would they do to my mother? I can't prove it was an accident! They wouldn't believe me, even if I swore to it on a stack of Bibles. We are illegitimate, Arthur and I. If we were out on the street, who would look after him? Who would pay for his medicine? I won't let you do that, just because my father is

. . . is a bigamist and . . . ' She bent her head onto Miriam's shoulder and sobbed quietly, trying to choke back her anger and despair, and at last, failing. Miriam tightened her arms around her and let her weep.

What could Daniel do? And he must do something! He must find Ebony, tell the truth to someone. Marcus fford Croft? They could not hang Russell Graves. He was not guilty of murdering Ebony. But dear God, he was guilty of much else! This was not justice.

Blackwell? Could he help?

But he would not use the law. Daniel knew him well enough to be certain of that.

Kitteridge? He would use the law — and it would be useless.

Miriam might be the only one. She might use science, and somehow or other prove the truth that Ebony was not guilty, though not perhaps totally innocent either. He looked at her now, holding Sarah in her arms. He was as sure as he could be of anything that she would do all she could, regardless of the law, and of the risks.

But as Ottershaw, the fingerprint expert, had said, the jury will seek for ways to return the verdict they want! One that appealed to their sense of justice. Perhaps Daniel could prove that Winifred's death had been an accident? The burning was another thing. But Winifred had been dead when it happened. Ebony had grasped the chance to escape, ignore Winifred's existence, and hope that Graves would hang for it — or perhaps she had not thought that far? But then Sarah and Arthur would be left with their father's name, or his money. Not ideal — but survival, at least!

'Sarah,' he said quietly.

She turned and looked at him.

'Take us to your mother, and we will put this right.' He was making wild promises he wished to keep for her, although had no idea if he could. 'You must do this, for Arthur's sake, as well as your own. He was no way at fault, but he will not survive alone. Don't leave him. It will take a lot of courage, but to run away will make it worse.' He hesitated a moment, then plunged even further. 'I will have to save your father from the gallows, but I will see him in prison for bigamy.' Please heaven she had told him the truth, or he might well be in deep trouble himself.

Slowly, she raised her head and looked at him. 'I will,' she said almost immediately. 'I will take you to her.'

17

When they were left alone, Miriam turned to Daniel, her face white and unshed tears in her eyes. She straightened her shoulders and deliberately made an effort to keep the emotion from her face.

'We have an hour at most to make up our minds,' Miriam said.

She seemed to include herself in the problem, and he was relieved he would not have to ask her.

'We . . . I . . . have no choice — ' he began.

'We always have a choice,' she interrupted him. 'At some point . . . '

'We don't have one here,' he contradicted her, but quietly. It was an admission, not a victory. 'Only in how we do it. We have to know if this woman is Ebony, or not. We know the dead woman is not her. You proved that.'

She winced so slightly that he barely saw it, but it cut him because he saw the pain behind it, and he knew he was not meant to. For the first time, she looked away from him.

'Science is safe,' she said very quietly. 'Perhaps not to the intellect. It can force you to look at all sorts of things you might not wish to. That can destroy your grandiose ideas of who mankind is. It can confuse us as much as enlighten, sometimes. But it does not touch the heart . . . That's a silly expression — you don't feel with your heart! What do you feel with? Your imagination? Where are your emotions? Everywhere! You see someone's pain, and it doesn't leave any part of you untouched.'

'I know. The law is safe, when it stays on paper. It seems elegant and quite refined. When actually it is about as delicate as a sledgehammer at times. And as soon as you fix one part, you break another. But we still can't let Graves hang if Ebony is alive. If I could think of a way to untangle this legally, and not leave Sarah with the weight of guilt for it, believe me, I would!'

She met his eyes again, but it was a second or two before she spoke. 'You would . . . wouldn't you!' She said it with surprise.

'It's academic. You can't unknow anything.'

'What if it isn't provable whether it is Ebony or not?' she asked.

He smiled. 'It's provable,' he said with certainty. 'Her children will look like her, not overtly, but in little ways, gestures, tone of voice, an understanding before the sentence is finished. Arthur's colouring, the way Sarah holds her head. But quite apart from that, she will not be able to hide her feelings for them.'

A shadow passed over Miriam's face, almost too slight to see, and yet it left its mark in her eyes. 'You are close to your mother?'

He was surprised. 'Yes. If you saw us together, you would know. I am built like my father, but my colouring is hers, and . . . I don't know exactly, but little things. My sister, Jemima, is more like her. The way she walks, certain gestures, things that make her laugh . . . ' He

284

stopped because he saw that the pleasure, the longing he felt when he spoke of the likenesses in his family was not echoed in Miriam's face. He knew that the subject had touched a wound.

'I hardly remember my mother,' Miriam said. 'She died when I was very young. And we don't have any pictures of her. I don't look much like my father, so I suppose I must look like her. The only things I know about her are that she had red hair, and that my father loved her very much. He couldn't bear the idea of marrying again, even to provide me with a mother. And that's a miserable thing to do to a woman — marry her without loving her, in order for her to look after your child!'

There were so many things Daniel knew about his mother, he could not think of them all at once. There had never been a day in his life from which she had been completely absent, within memory, or effect, something learned from her, something she had given him, a joke shared, even a quality to rebel against! What could he say large enough to be of any meaning?

Miriam must have seen his difficulty. She smiled. 'Then you will recognise Ebony, even if I don't. Everything hangs on that. Can we persuade her to give herself up? If I had been treated as she had, I might be very afraid to come back. If we save Graves — and we have to — can we save her, too?' Her face shadowed. 'And there is the question of the book as well. What can we promise her, honestly?'

His mind leaped ahead. 'I'm not sure. Even if Graves hanged, that wouldn't stop it being published. We have to discredit him. At least show his stories are not true. There's too much to do . . . '

She gave a tight little smile. 'Then we had better hurry and get this part of it over with. Really, we have no choice in this.' She stopped. She closed her eyes for a moment in intense concentration. 'If this is really Ebony we're going to meet, then we have to save Graves.' She shook her head slowly, as if denying something to herself. 'What if Sarah is wrong, and Ebony did kill Winifred on purpose? How do we protect her and not betray Sarah's trust? And she does trust us, or she wouldn't take us to Ebony — '

'We left her no choice,' Daniel interrupted her.

She stared at him. 'That's not enough. She could simply have refused. If she has to choose between her father hanging or her mother, she'll choose her father. She hates him, and she's afraid of him, not only for herself, but for Arthur, too — and, if it comes to that, for Falthorne, who's been loyal to her ever since she was born. We have to be careful, Daniel — and very clever.'

'I know,' he acknowledged. 'I hate it! But we have to save him, or at any rate, save Sarah from the horror of deliberately having let him hang for a crime we all know he did not commit. There will be no coming back from that.'

Miriam frowned. 'There's always a way back, I think. But it might be a very hard one.'

'I want to put Graves somewhere where there is no way back!' he said, the anger burning hot inside him. 'And there's no time to wait.'

She held out her hand. 'I know . . . I know.' As she started towards the door, they heard footsteps in the hallway outside.

He went forward and together they found Sarah was waiting for them, already dressed in her outdoor clothes.

'I am ready,' she said a little uncertainly.

'Have we far to walk?' Miriam asked.

'Perhaps a mile, or a little more,' Sarah replied, glancing at Miriam's feet to see if her boots were up to such use. She apparently decided that they were. 'Please will you follow me?'

They went out of the front door and walked in the bright May noon down the street and through the main shopping area of the large village. London was expanding rapidly until it was almost seamless. Nevertheless, there was a distinct centre with shops, churches, and a few very handsome residences, and offices of various sorts. Sarah nodded to several people, but did not stop to speak. Her situation was almost uniquely uncomfortable.

At the far side of the village, the streets led to open land, farm buildings, a few pigs and goats in fields, and here and there, cows. Sarah walked more slowly; she seemed uncertain. Had she lost her way, or was she about to change her mind about leading them to Ebony?

Miriam shot a quick glance at Daniel, and then moved forward to catch up with Sarah and linked her arm with hers. It looked loosely held, but Daniel had a feeling it was tighter than it appeared.

Sarah was dragging her feet.

She stopped outside an old wooden gate, took a deep breath, then pushed it open. Miriam followed immediately after her, and Daniel caught up with them. They walked across the grass and towards the front door of a cottage, and a woman in a plain brown dress opened the door and came out onto the step. She looked hard at Sarah, then shifted her gaze to Daniel, then to Miriam.

'It's all right, Mrs Wilson,' Sarah said quietly. 'They are friends, and have come to help. Where is my mother?'

Mrs Wilson turned and looked into the passage behind her. Slowly, another figure emerged. It was a woman of medium height and very slender build. She looked tired and frightened, and her skin was very pale. Daniel knew who it must be because of her jet-black hair and eyes so dark they seemed to be hollows in her head. Even though their colouring was so different, there were echoes of Sarah in the bones of her face, the shape of her mouth, even the delicacy of her hands. And the recognition between them no one could have missed.

'Mother, they worked out that you are alive, and these people are here to help you . . . help us. We don't have a choice any more.' Sarah's voice was strained as if her throat were parched.

Daniel could feel her fear as if it were his own.

Miriam stepped forward. 'Ebony.' She could not now call her Mrs Graves! 'There is only one way forward for any of us. You cannot let him hang. Sarah cannot. It would haunt her the rest

288

of her life, even if she got away with it. Don't make her do this.'

Daniel looked from Ebony to Sarah and saw the desperation in Sarah's face. Then he looked at Ebony again, as her shoulders sagged and all the will drained out of her.

Sarah saw it, too. 'Don't . . . ' she began, and then stopped.

Ebony turned to Daniel. 'What do you want me to do?' It was a question, not a surrender. She was not yet giving him anything.

Again, it was Miriam who answered. 'Let us go inside, if Mrs Wilson will be gracious enough? I'm a doctor. I may be able to prove the ill use you have been subject to, and Sarah also.'

'Broken bones heal in time,' Ebony said bitterly. 'They ache in the cold and wet, but you can't see that. And anyway, a man may beat his wife. It's not against the law. Or his child. That's not illegal either.'

'But you are not his wife,' Miriam pointed out.

Ebony flinched. 'I thought I was,' she said bitterly.

'He can go to prison for bigamy,' Daniel spoke for the first time. 'As much as seven years. A lot can happen in that time. And Winifred will not be his heir. I don't know what may be said, but for now we must stop his being hanged. That must be done now, or the rope will be around your neck, and Sarah's, for the rest of your lives. Arthur's too, if he knew about it.' He had a sudden thought. 'And Falthorne's, if he helped you. He did, didn't he? Can you let this weigh on his soul for the rest of his life? And it will!'

Ebony put up her hands to cover her face. Her shoulders were rigid, but she did not weep. Perhaps she was exhausted beyond even that. She looked cornered, and too tired to fight any more. But neither would she yield.

'Mr Graves is still in prison,' Daniel told her softly 'You can safely come home. Miriam will take you to a machine that she has that can show pictures, through your skin, to tell if the bones were broken, and prove you were beaten. Scars, too. It can even prove they happened over a period of time.'

Ebony put her hands down and stared at him in disbelief.

'There is a lot we can do,' he hurried on. 'But it has to be done carefully, and quickly. It is not too late to appeal, and if Mr Graves is executed we will all be guilty of his murder.'

'We have to go back to him?' She spoke in low, grating voice; it was all she could do not to refuse.

'No. Back to the house, your house. He's in prison, and I will do everything possible to see that he is charged and found guilty of bigamy. But you will have to answer for not coming forward and saying you were alive.' He drew a deep breath and let it out slowly. This was appallingly difficult to say, but it was necessary. To put it off would be dishonest, and lose her trust irrevocably.

'And you'll have to testify as to who Winifred was, and how she died,' he went on. 'And that you deliberately disfigured her so she would be mistaken for you ... knowing that Russell

Graves could very well be hanged for it.'

'Will they send me to prison? What about Sarah and Arthur? They knew nothing about it at all!'

Daniel would have known from the timbre of her voice, the fear in her eyes that she was lying. He did not need Sarah's admission. He preferred not to know about Arthur.

'Ebony, Sarah helped you — '

'No! Sarah knew nothing about it!' Her voice was shrill and she shook her head vigorously.

'You used silk, and linseed oil, from Arthur's paint supplies — '

She looked at Sarah, and then forced herself to look at Daniel again. 'No!'

'Yes, you did,' Miriam insisted. Her voice was steady and calm. Ebony would not have heard the pain in it, but Daniel did. 'She was dead. You didn't hurt her. You just disguised her as yourself. You put your clothes on her. And her clothes in your wardrobe. It was a way for you to escape at last.'

'Sarah didn't . . . '

'I know,' Daniel took over again. 'You did that all by yourself. Or were you going to tell me that Mr Falthorne helped you?'

The struggle in her face was obvious. It was painful to watch.

'I can help you, but I have to know the truth.' Was he making more rash promises he was not able to keep? 'Ebony, if you lie the court will know it! Do you want to be hanged for killing Winifred?'

'I didn't kill her!' Her voice was desperate

now. 'She came at me, screaming, clawing. I pushed her away. She was trying to get at my face, my eyes. I pushed her and she fell backwards over her own skirts and hit her head on the hearthstone. I swear!'

'Then help me prove it! For Sarah and Arthur's sake, if not your own!' Daniel begged. But he wanted her freed as well, and Graves proved a liar and totally discredited, and imprisoned long enough to break him. 'Please!'

She stared at him, searching his eyes, looking for hope, belief that she could trust him. She couldn't believe, but she was tired of fighting, and there was no one else to turn to. 'All right. But Sarah had nothing to do with it! You've got to prove that!'

Daniel glanced at Miriam, but she shook her head, just a fraction, as he had known she would.

He did not tell Ebony that it was not true, and he knew it. One problem at a time. There was no other, better answer.

Miriam held out her hand. Wearily, too exhausted to fight any more, Ebony took it.

18

It was now little over a week before Russell Graves would hang, if they did not launch an appeal against his conviction, which, since Ebony was not dead, would not be difficult to substantiate.

Miriam had taken the X-rays of both Ebony and Sarah, and was satisfied that they were clear and accurate.

'See,' Miriam said in her laboratory in the cellar, as she pointed to the X-ray machine's pictures of Ebony. 'The bones here have been broken also, and here, and here, in the wrist.'

'Could it have been an accident?' Daniel hoped profoundly that it could not.

'Hardly one accident,' Miriam murmured. 'See how they are differently shaded? This one on the wrist is plain? The other one is duller white, and this one is the whitest of all, that means it is older. It was healed a long time ago. I would estimate it is sixteen or seventeen years old. There are others there, in the left leg, and another in the right foot. And three ribs. There are no two made at the same time. And nobody has that many accidents.'

'We can't prove he caused them, can we?' Daniel held only the faintest hope, but it was worth asking. 'Someone must know!'

'The lady's maid probably does. Except he would have got rid of her. I'll wager you that she has had a series of maids.'

'Wouldn't she want to keep them, to look after her? She must have wanted someone to trust,' he insisted.

She rolled her eyes, in momentary exasperation. 'Daniel, for heaven's sake, she wouldn't hire the servants! He would! And he'd get rid of a maid who knew too much, whether she was brave or rash enough to say so or not.'

Daniel had a sudden, searing impression of Ebony's loneliness. What a façade she must have kept from society, from her friends, the people beside whom she fought for the same issues she cared about, and even from her servants.

How many of them knew anyway, and were too tactful to let her see? Or too afraid? He felt almost overwhelmed with his revulsion for the man! 'We have to prove it. We can't let him go back to that again. And Sarah — '

'I wish we could let him hang,' Miriam said seriously, the light completely gone from her face. 'But we can't.' She looked at him intently. 'What are you going to do, Daniel?'

'I cannot leave it any longer before telling Kitteridge, whose case this is. And I have to tell Mr fford Croft when I am certain I know what proof I have of anything. But . . . ' He stopped. He wanted to tell her more about the biography, which was always on his mind. He struggled for a way to tell her without admitting that there was some strong element of truth in the accusations about his father — at least about the things that Narraway had known about vulnerable people, people who had made mistakes somewhere, and thus had given a lifetime as hostages to fortune. His father had said there was such a file. One could not work in Special Branch without learning some people's secrets, at least. It was judgement, a balancing act, weighing one person's happiness against perhaps someone else's life.

Were all Narraway's judgements right? Were anybody's?

Daniel did not want to be in a position to judge anyone, least of all those he cared for, and had never before questioned. Were most people like that? See kindly those you loved, and less kindly anyone you disliked? That was unfair. It was unkind, and impractical. And it was not the law. The very essence of justice was that it was impartial. How often was affection wrong?

In practical terms, what damage could Graves' book do to Special Branch and its ability to hold the power it needed in order to perform its functions? Could he possibly report it from his father's point of view, no matter how much he might wish to? Somebody had told him that a good portion of wisdom was humility; he could not remember who.

He would see his father, and speak to him. Warn him, if nothing else. But before that, he must see Kitteridge. He owed him that much.

★　★　★

He found Kitteridge in the law library, where Impney had said he would be. He recognised Kitteridge's awkward figure as soon as he

295

entered the reading room. He was bent over a huge table and he appeared uncomfortable, because his elbows stuck out and his jacket puckered at the shoulders. He was deep in concentration. Daniel had reached him and his shadow lay across the page before Kitteridge looked up.

'What do you want?' he whispered. 'I've got the publisher for you, but nothing more.' His face looked tired and disappointed, rather than angry. He was senior in position, as well as age; it was his duty to lead the way.

'I have something,' Daniel said.

'Oh, yes?' Kitteridge rubbed his eyes. 'What?' He was trying to be polite, but there was no interest in his voice.

'Come and have a cup of tea,' Daniel suggested. 'And I'll tell you.'

Kitteridge looked weary. 'We haven't time for cups of tea. There are only eight and a half days left to get the appeal in! Can't you count?'

'It will be enough, if you listen to me and help,' Daniel said urgently. He did not mean to crow. He needed Kitteridge's help if he were to trap Graves without letting his book be published, and that was far more important to him than anything Kitteridge was pursuing.

Kitteridge stood up awkwardly; his legs had been too long to fold easily underneath the stool.

They walked out of the reading room in silence, along the hallway, out of the double doors and into the street. Kitteridge was not prepared to listen until they had reached the tea room and had sat down.

'What is it?' he said at last.

'Graves isn't guilty of killing Ebony,' Daniel insisted. 'It's beyond any doubt at all — because Ebony isn't dead.'

Kitteridge's face tightened. 'I'm not in the mood for humour, Pitt. They're going to hang Graves, unless we find a way to take this to appeal.'

'Ebony isn't dead,' Daniel repeated. 'The dead woman was Winifred Graves, his first wife — well, *only* wife, as it happens. Graves was a bigamist. She found out about the inheritance and came to cash in on it — '

'Damn!' Kitteridge said savagely. 'Then who killed her? Ebony? I can't entirely blame her! God damn him!'

'It was an accident,' Daniel said earnestly. 'And I think we can prove it. By the way, her X-rays show that she was pretty consistently beaten over twenty years. Scars, too. And I want to put him in prison for bigamy.'

'An accident? We'll have to work hard to prove that. Ebony had every reason to kill this woman.' Kitteridge's face was twisted in an odd expression of pity. He believed it, and it hurt him.

Daniel liked him the better for it. 'It won't be easy,' he admitted. 'But we have to try. Much as we might like to, we can't hang him for killing a woman we know is alive.'

'It would be deeply embarrassing for him when his first wife showed up. I don't suppose there's any chance he killed *her*, is there?' Kitteridge asked hopefully.

'No, unfortunately not. He'd have dealt with it before now, and made sure Ebony paid for it, or someone else other than himself. Got rid of the body, probably. It's about the only sensible thing.'

'But there was a body, we know, so Ebony didn't do that?' Kitteridge said.

'That's why it was burned,' Daniel pointed out. 'To pass it off as her.'

'And have Graves hang. Nice.' From Kitteridge's face, it was impossible to know how much the last was said sarcastically, and how much bitterly. 'Why are you telling me now?'

'Because I need your help.'

'Marcus will probably take this case himself. He was pretty outstanding in his day. One last hurrah, and all that,' Kitteridge said.

'Possibly,' Daniel agreed. 'With your assistance. Anyway, let us just get him to see that Graves is charged with bigamy, for the family's sake. Once his first wife's existence is established, they're pretty well ruined anyway. But there's something else I must do, and it's even more important to me than . . . '

Kitteridge was about to protest, but he saw something in Daniel's face, perhaps in his eyes. 'But?'

'This book he's writing,' Daniel said quietly. 'I told you it's an exposé of several people, but mostly two people I care about, even if they're dead now, and of course, my father, who is very much alive.'

'You mentioned Lord Narraway and his wife . . . '

'Lady Vespasia Cumming-Gould — '

'Lady Vespasia Narraway,' Kitteridge corrected.

'Most of my life I knew her as Lady Vespasia Cumming-Gould.'

Kitteridge's eyes widened. 'You knew her? Really?'

'Yes, my parents knew her very well. I've got to find a way from stopping this book from coming out before we reveal that Graves is innocent, at least of killing Ebony. Guilty of bigamy isn't enough.'

'Any idea how you're going to do it?' Kitteridge went on.

'Not really . . . only vaguely . . . there isn't long.'

'That's an understatement.'

'What would you like me to do?' asked Daniel, a little more tartly than he intended.

'Don't tell fford Croft just yet. I mean . . . wait until tomorrow. Late tomorrow.'

Daniel would have said later than that, but it was unfair to ask that of Kitteridge. It was his job, too, and he did not owe Pitt anything, either Daniel or his father.

Kitteridge stared at him.

Daniel looked back. 'Sorry,' he apologised. 'I suppose I want you to look up all the details of his first marriage. All I know is that it was over twenty years ago, within a hundred miles of here, and her name was Winifred Carter. It would look idiotic if it turns out to have been invalidated, or even annulled.'

'Or even non-existent,' Kitteridge pointed out.

'Don't worry. It's not so very hard. It would help if I knew either the date or the place, but I'll find it. To know the parish would be too easy. It's just a matter of swotting up the books. Unless it wasn't the first marriage after all and he was a bigamist twice over!' He saw Daniel's expression. 'Winifred is not such a common name. Just be glad it's not Mary or Elizabeth. We've still got a week — roughly. Although that's cutting it very fine indeed.'

'Too fine!'

'Then get out of here and start seeing Special Branch, or whatever.' Kitteridge gave a twisted smile, both wry and warm. 'By the way, the publisher's name is on your desk.'

Daniel acknowledged his gratitude with an answering smile, and went out.

Daniel caught a cab and directed the driver to Lisson Grove. He would stop a block or two short of his father's offices at Special Branch. It was a habit to conceal the address so ingrained in him he did it without thought. If Pitt were not in, he would wait for him. At least he had been there often enough he would not have to explain who he was, or for that matter, why he was there. They knew enough not to ask him questions.

In the cab, he sat back and thought about exactly what he would tell his father, whom he would visit, and what it would be better if he did not know. By the time he was there, he was certain.

When he was inside, he explained to his father's deputy his need to see Pitt. It was a further ten minutes before the junior Home

Office minister left Pitt's room and Daniel was called in.

'I'm sorry, Father, but it's very urgent, and it is Special Branch business,' he said again before he sat down.

Pitt smiled with bleak amusement, but his face was grave. 'I assumed as much,' he responded. 'You have insufficient evidence to persuade Graves not to publish. The fact that the man was hanged will make it so much more appealing. I foresaw that.'

'No,' Daniel shook his head. 'But at least I know no one from Special Branch killed Mrs Graves . . . '

'Are you certain, or do you hope?' Clearly Pitt was not yet assured.

'Positive. She isn't dead.'

Pitt frowned. 'Her skull was cracked and her face and upper body disfigured by fire, and she's not dead?' His disbelief was too heavy for even the faintest smile.

'No — it wasn't Mrs Graves. At least it was . . . the first Mrs Graves, not the current one.'

'Daniel?'

'I know! Let me tell you.' He went on to give Pitt the briefest account he could that covered the facts. 'But I'll get him for bigamy. Seven years, if possible. I would keep him there for twenty, if the law allowed it.'

'But it would still sell the book, probably even more copies,' Pitt said quietly.

'Yes,' Daniel said miserably. 'I've got very few days left to discredit him enough to stop publication. I wish I could bring it to you accomplished, I don't know where to begin, or how to do it in time. I don't know where Graves got much of his information from, or how to find out in time.' He drew in a deep breath and then let it out again. He hated this.

Pitt waited. And it seemed he was not going to help. He must know what Daniel was going to say!

'Did you do anything?' Daniel asked instead. 'You said you were going to.'

'I found out as much as I can,' Pitt replied. His face was utterly without the light of humour. 'He appears to be a man who keeps his promises when it suits him, but always keeps his threats. But if you were asking, did I find a weapon against him, no I didn't. I didn't even find the one you did! Have you proof?' It was asked softly, not even a shred of implied criticism.

Daniel wondered why. Was Pitt too gentle with him because he was his father? Did Daniel not have to meet the same standard as anyone else?

'I've got Kitteridge looking,' he replied, trying to keep the emotion out of his tone. 'All we know about her is her name, Winifred Carter, and that she married Graves well over twenty years ago. And I suppose, less than forty. That's a very wide window. That much is proved, and we shouldn't take anything for granted, and certainly not trust Graves over anything. What I was going to say was, have you any information in your secret papers — Narraway's secret papers — that can help?' He felt himself blush that he could say such a thing. A week ago, he wouldn't even have imagined it. Perhaps his integrity was perfect, only so long as he didn't have to use it?

'I don't believe Narraway ever used his knowledge to save himself. And whether he did or not is irrelevant to whether I would. What do you suggest? That I threaten to ruin people if they don't help me suppress the book?'

Daniel was hurt. 'No! Of course not. But some of them might be in it. If they knew, they might have the power to suppress the book for their own sakes. Graves must make specific charges, or it will be too vague to be worth anything as an exposé. He'll ruin specific people for specific . . . weaknesses, failings, even crimes not prosecuted, ones on which the statute of limitations has not run out. Things that are not crimes, just scandals or tragedies. They'll have to pay for old griefs all over again, innocent or guilty. He's . . . ' Daniel would not use the word he was thinking of in front of his father.

Now, Pitt smiled twistedly, but there was humour in it. 'I agree,' he said quietly. 'And in a way, he would be fulfilling exactly what he says of us.'

'So, we do nothing!' Daniel could not keep his anger hidden.

'No. You have only a few days left. You must use them well — '

'Aren't you going to do anything?' Daniel cut across him.

'When you give me the facts, I will, if there's anything I can do.'

'They were your friends! I can remember them sitting in the kitchen at home, half the night — '

'You were in bed.'

303

Daniel was unabashed. 'I wasn't! You thought I was, and Jemima, but we sat on the stairs and listened.'

'Did you, indeed?'

'Yes, we did. But that isn't the point. You worked the cases together, you and Mama and Narraway and Aunt Vespasia. Gracie was there for the early ones, too. You fought the same battles, and even if you thought were going to lose, you never gave up. That's what friendship is about — winning or losing together because you believe in the same causes. You can't sit back now and let them be ruined by this . . . this . . . this guttersnipe! You — '

'I won't,' Pitt interrupted him. 'But if I let Graves drive me to use the very weapon he is accusing Narraway of using, then he has won.'

'And Aunt Vespasia? Are you going to let him call her no better than a whore?' Daniel demanded.

A faint blush stained Pitt's cheeks. 'And if I react with anger like yours, what do you suppose he will think, and no doubt will say?'

For a moment, Daniel did not understand, then it came in a flood, and he, too, felt the blood in his cheeks. 'That you, too . . . ' He could not bring himself to say the words, not of his own father. Thoughts were one thing, words another. He swallowed hard, almost a gulp. 'Then we must find someone who really did use such a weapon, and is not ashamed of it. Someone powerful, who would crucify Graves for making it public,' he began.

'Not quite,' Pitt argued.

'Why not? If you don't, then I will!'

'Not crucify Graves. With any luck, you will send him to prison for bigamy. It will be far more effective to crucify the publisher.'

Daniel shut his eyes. 'Of course! How could I have been so . . . stupid?'

'You're a beginner at this,' Pitt said gently. 'Find the people who cared about Vespasia, or who could not afford to have their parents' frailties exposed. And find all the people whom he said Narraway blackmailed, and we'll see which charges are the most useful to us. Preferably, those that are false: the possibility of law suits may make the publishers change their mind very quickly.'

'Wouldn't they check anyway?' Daniel said reasonably. 'I imagine they would have to look true, or be half true, for Graves to get away with it. Many famous people have weaknesses. He wouldn't put in those he knew who could prove themselves innocent.'

'Some of the charges may be true,' Pitt agreed. 'You need a few that are untrue, or which may spread further and wider than the intended target, and the publishers will thank you. They have interests, too. Read the manuscript, and tell me. We haven't long. So, move quickly, but carefully. We cannot afford mistakes.'

Daniel stood up slowly. He was relieved, he was determined, but most of all he was filled with respect for his father, even admiration. It was like sweet wine, almost a little heady. 'Yes, Father — I will!'

19

Daniel went back to his lodgings and asked Mrs Portiscale if he could have sandwiches and a pot of tea in his room. He assured her that he was perfectly well, just had a mountain of work to get through.

And he had. When he took the manuscript out of its box, there were over four hundred pages of it. He put it down carefully on the bedside table. It was roughly formed notes, rather than narrative. If he dropped it, it might take him the rest of the night to put it back in order. It was a daunting task. Exactly what was he looking for? Names of important people who might still care about Vespasia, or Narraway: people whose reputations could be injured.

He went over to the cupboard that served him as an office, and took out a block of note paper and three sharp pencils, then he sat down to begin.

It was eleven o'clock and his eyes ached from reading the print, his head throbbed and his muscles were tight where he had clenched his hand to hold the pencil, but he had found no names.

He realised reluctantly that he was progressing very slowly indeed. Bluntly, he was taking too long. He marked the page he had been reading, put the whole lot back in its box, put the box in a Gladstone bag and went downstairs with it. He would be days discovering anything at this rate. He must get help.

He slipped out of the front door. Quietly closing it, he walked to the end of the street, carrying the manuscript in the heavy bag, and stopped a taxi. He gave the driver Blackwell's address, and sat back. If neither Blackwell nor Mercy were in, he would have to leave them a note, asking for their urgent help, and travel all the way back again.

He rang the doorbell, and after several minutes, and several more rings of the bell, Blackwell himself opened the door, rather cautiously.

'I need help,' Daniel said. 'This is more than I can manage on my own. And I'm not sure Kitteridge could do this anyway, even if he had the time.'

'Then you'd better come inside,' Blackwell answered, blinking a little owlishly. 'Pay the driver first, or we'll never get rid of him. Anyway, only a fool stiffs a taxi driver; you'd be bound to meet him again one day, when you really need him.'

'Thank you,' Daniel said with profound feeling. He put the Gladstone bag on the doorstep, turned on his heel, and walked back to the road to pay the driver. When he returned, Blackwell had taken the bag inside and stood by the door in his nightshirt, looking rumpled and curious.

Daniel went in and shut the door. The hallway was barely lit, but it was warm and smelled faintly of furniture wax. 'Nothing is as we thought,' he began. 'For a start, the body isn't Ebony Graves.'

Blackwell turned to face him. 'What? Who says so? Who is it?'

'Miss fford Croft. It's too long a story for just now. But that isn't why I've come. I've got Graves' manuscript here and have to read it, find the accusations we can prove are not true, and do that — prove it — and find the people who will be prepared to fight to defend — '

'Stop!' Blackwell held up his hand. 'Just tell me what to look for. I don't need to know why. It's important, that's all that matters. Now tell me, what are we looking for exactly?'

For a moment, Daniel hesitated. He was afraid of what he would find. Not that it might be true, but that it could not be proved untrue. Often accusations stay in the mind, even after the apparent facts have been shown to be false. He had learned that with juries. Some people think that the police cannot be wrong. Why would they have accused a man if they had no proof? Charges gave credibility, just as print can. Blackmailers know that. Politicians know it. It can become a high and murderous art with some men, as it had with Robespierre in the French Revolution.

Blackwell was waiting, hands held out.

Was Daniel betraying Pitt to exposure for a weakness real or fancied? Should he find it himself, so that he could protect it properly, without anyone else knowing?

Blackwell was still waiting.

There wasn't time. He must believe Blackwell

could be trusted; Blackwell had believed in him! But he had had no chance, no alternative.

But then, neither had Daniel now.

He put the manuscript in Blackwell's hands.

'I'm looking for any accusation against Narraway, or against Lady Vespasia Cumming-Gould, later Lady Narraway, that we can prove is not true. Ideally, if we can find them, with proof that they are untrue, we can, by implication, invalidate all the accusations. Or at least show that to level them would prove ruinous to anyone who did so. That should be enough to persuade the publishers that it would definitely be against their interests to bring out Graves' book.'

Daniel could see before he had finished speaking that Blackwell understood. 'We must stick to the truth,' he ended, smiling to soften the effect of his words, 'because we may well have to prove what we say.'

Blackwell's face broke into a wide smile. 'Of course. When you're playing for high stakes, and against a man who has much to lose, always stick to the truth.'

Daniel let out his breath with a sigh. 'Thank you. Can we get a start now? Please!'

'Of course! No time to waste. I understand. No whisky, but a cup of tea would be nice.'

'Make it later. Let me show you the manuscript, and the notes I have made so far.'

'I wasn't going to make the tea myself,' Blackwell said with eyes wide. 'Is there some reason why we should not get Mercy in to help us? She probably knows more about the indiscretions of society than both of us together.

309

Not that I suppose you know anything anyway. Too young, and too innocent. You are as clean as a baby just out of the bath.'

Daniel did not waste time protesting that. 'If she doesn't mind, I'd be . . . '

Blackwell had already turned to leave. 'I'll tell her,' he said at the doorway. 'Start reading.'

Daniel got out the papers, made himself comfortable in one of the armchairs, and resumed his reading where he had left off. He begrudged admitting it, even to himself, but Graves was an engaging writer. He was not likeable in the least, but he knew how to draw out the curiosity of the reader and build suspense so that you turned the page. Each section led satisfactorily into the next. He was fascinated, in spite of himself.

It was about twenty minutes later that the door opened and Mercy Blackwell came in. Her hair was piled loosely instead of coiled, but it was still elegant, perhaps more so because it was natural rather than artifice. She was wearing a robe of deep violet purple, but no particular shape.

'So, we are hunting,' she said, as if it were something she did regularly and found no disturbance being got up out of bed to take part. There was no mention of it being in the middle of the night. 'Show me where.' She sat down as Daniel scrambled to his feet out of the most basic manners.

'Are you sure?' he said, and immediately felt foolish. There was no accepted way in which to conduct themselves in such circumstances.

She did not bother to answer him.

'Start here, if you please.' He gave her a pile of pages. 'We are looking for — '

'Yes, I know. Roman told me,' she interrupted him. 'Scandals concerning certain people, and particularly those that can be disproved. First, we must find every reference to their name, then see what stories can be given the lie. It might be a good idea to see other people that are condemned, even obliquely. You never know who might be a useful ally. Shall I write down their names, and the page numbers on which they are mentioned? It looks as if we have a long list, and a short time.' She gave him a dazzling smile, then went immediately to Daniel's notes.

Blackwell himself came in ten minutes later with a pot of tea on a tray, with mugs, a jug of milk, and a plate with several slices of rich fruitcake. He said nothing to interrupt either Mercy or Daniel. He poured the tea, and then as each took a mug and cake, he joined them in their labours.

Daniel was intensely grateful to them for this, but he did not know how to say so, more than he already had, and there was no time or effort to waste on trying.

It was easy reading, most of the time, but Daniel made notes of the names mentioned in connection with anyone he knew, or knew about. He gradually began to realise how much was innuendo: inference rather than fact. It drew the reader in like quicksand. First a little extra temptation to that area, a little suggestion of scandal, or illicit romance, the odd joke or two,

311

and then he found himself turning the pages more and more rapidly in contemplation of a name turning up again, more interestingly.

Twice he caught himself racing to find another reference to a woman cleverly described, not literally, but only by the effect she had on certain men. People were fascinated by her laughter. No matter how often she laughed, they turned towards her. She moved with a grace that made others look awkward. Men straightened their shoulders and stood more elegantly when she was present. Daniel turned page after page to see who she was. He had to read further to know, forgetting to note all the names as he went.

He forced himself to go back and be more diligent. He hated doing it, but Graves knew the weaknesses of human nature, and how to mask ugliness as ordinary frailty, how to make observation seem like familiarity rather than intrusion.

Daniel looked across at Blackwell. He, too, was bent over his pages, and his hand was writing notes almost automatically. Was that also how he saw it? Weaknesses, that in compassion should be covered rather than exposed? Daniel had seen both humour and compassion in him, but did not know him well enough to know what aroused one more than the other in a frailty observed.

How did his father deal with weaknesses in others, vulnerabilities? He knew the answer to that. He had overheard enough discussions of cases to know that he rarely exposed them if he could avoid it, and when he did, it hurt him.

Was that what Graves considered weakness in Daniel, too?

It was a deeper question than he had thought at first. What was weakness? Where was the line between weakness and compassion? A judgement call? The division where it exposed only yourself, and the place where others were hurt? There was a judgement call too, most of the time. It looked as if, to Graves, it was where danger to yourself met profitability. What was the risk to him? Of course, there was also the pleasure in malice and revenge. It did not always come at a price. Was, for him, the judgement call the weighing of price against pleasure?

Another hour went by. To Daniel, words were beginning to waiver on the page. He rubbed his eyes, found that they still blurred.

'Enough,' Mercy said quietly, watching him. 'Go to bed and we will wake refreshed, or at least better than we are now, and I will make us breakfast. Bacon and eggs, toast and marmalade, hot tea.' She stood up slowly, as if her back were stiff. She moved her shoulders a little.

Daniel rose to help her, but he was too late.

'You are asleep,' she told him briskly. 'Go to bed. Top of the stairs, first door to the right. Bathroom is next after that. Don't argue with me. I haven't time for it. Or the strength. Good night.'

'Good night, Mercy,' he said obediently. 'Thank you.'

'You saved Roman's life. What did you expect me to do?' she replied. 'Go to bed!'

★ ★ ★

313

Daniel slept soundly, although he had not expected to, and woke up to find the room full of sunlight, and Mercy standing beside his bed, fully dressed and her hair wound up like usual, the white streak blazing.

'Breakfast in fifteen minutes,' she said. 'I expect you at the table, washed and shaved, and dressed of course. Then we will continue to work.' She did not wait to see if he was going to answer.

They worked the rest of the morning and all afternoon. No one mentioned that the last day was fast approaching on which they could hope to get their appeal before a judge in time to get a stay of execution. No one needed to say that they did not want to let Graves be hanged.

Daniel felt that they had to have a plan ready for the next morning. That was going to mean a hard day followed by a hard night.

In the middle of the afternoon, he reached the end of his pile, and Blackwell reached the end of his ten minutes later.

Mercy looked up. 'Well?' she asked.

Daniel felt defensive. The book was principally about Victor Narraway, with major digressions about people he had known, and letters that were personal and had little to do with his career. But it was cruel. There was more than one interpretation of most events, and Graves had always chosen the one that fitted his own estimate of Narraway as greedy, vain, and in the end always self-serving. So many stories that he had found skirted the edge of slander, but never tipped over. Daniel felt as if all the defence somehow made more of the fault rather than less. If there were nothing wrong, why would anyone leap to offer an excuse? It drew more attention to the lapse and made most people consider it in the light of the assumption that it required defending.

'Clever,' Mercy said quietly. 'But not infallible, I think.'

'Do you?' Daniel heard his own voice sounding absurdly hopeful. 'Not infallible?'

'There is this story here.' Mercy held up a sheet of paper and pushed a strand of hair out of her eyes. 'Page one hundred and sixty-eight. It concerns Dorothy Devoke. Graves says Narraway was having an affair with her. Used her to gain very personal information about her husband, Richard Devoke. Forced him into supporting Narraway in some venture or another, and when it turned out badly — Devoke lost a fortune — it transpired that Narraway did not put any of his own money into it. Dorothy was furious and caused a very ugly scene at Claridge's, of all places. Devoke left the Government and retired to the country. Narraway prospered.'

Daniel had reached the place where Graves referred back to it. 'It sounds bad . . . '

'That is because of the language used,' Mercy explained. 'Put in other words, it sounds different. It's all supposition. And I know a lot about Dorothy Devoke. I could make as good a case for the opposite view . . . which is that Narraway warned him not to invest, and he did, out of perversity.'

315

'But does it help us?' Daniel insisted. Doubt was not enough. Especially if Richard Devoke had been so upset about the losses that he had given up his position in the Government.

Mercy smiled patiently. 'You're missing the point, my dear. Robert Devoke, Richard's son, is a very powerful man now. Discreetly, of course, but he has the ear of some very important people. He knows the truth behind this, and if he has temporarily forgotten, I for one would be happy to remind him. Narraway actually helped him. I happen to know that because I — ' She stopped abruptly. 'I just know.'

Daniel did not wish either to probe her personal life, or hear things he would rather not know.

'Richard Devoke would be happy to have his revenge. If this book comes out, he'll be . . . embarrassed. It is an affair he would prefer we all forgot. I would be happy to warn him that this book repeats it, in the worst possible light. He will be happy to make the publishers wish they had not given it house room.'

'Good!' Daniel allowed himself some relief. 'Page . . . ?'

'One sixty-eight to one ninety,' she answered. She handed him the twenty-three pages.

'Thank you.' He attached them together, and when he looked up, she had resumed reading again.

Daniel glanced across at Blackwell, but Blackwell was deep in concentration and unaware of Daniel, or of his mother. There was a deep frown on his face, and his mouth was

316

turned down at the corners, as if he found something he was reading to be more and more distasteful.

Ideas raced through Daniel's mind. Was Blackwell discovering a truth that he knew would distress Daniel profoundly, but that sooner or later he would have to hear? Daniel liked Blackwell. In his own way, he was honest. He would be deliberately vague about facts, but never about his own kind of morality. And he could not bear unkindness, arrogance, or hypocrisy. He could not afford to be judged, and in turn he judged others gently.

Looking again at his face as he read, Daniel was certain that Blackwell had found one of the sins he despised.

But Daniel could not afford to sit watching Blackwell, and wondering what arguments he might be seeing, and if it would hurt Daniel to know it. He was no use to his father, or his memories of Narraway and Vespasia, if he could not face the darkness as well as the light. Everyone made mistakes, even those you loved the most. Friends did not require you to be perfect, and to live up to their dreams of you. To do so was unfair, juvenile, and in itself deeply unkind. He had made a few mistakes of his own. He would prefer that those who loved him did not know. You carried these things alone, if you are permitted to. Sometimes they were public. It was tempting to lie, find excuses, but in the end it only increased the burden.

How was he going to find out about Narraway? The whole book was based on this trivia. There were bound to be failures as well as successes, otherwise he would never have attempted anything that stretched his knowledge or judgement, his abilities, or his honesty. What kind of a man is that? The question that bothered him now was not that Narraway had made mistakes, it was whether he had blamed others for them or acknowledged them himself.

He bent back to his own reading again.

He found Narraway's occasional mistakes, but Graves had found them through Narraway's own admission. He had added to them generously, crediting other events to those errors. Daniel thought that, with care, those could be proved false, or at least questionable. But he also realised explaining them away, no matter how successfully, looked like making excuses. Narraway would emerge as unlikeable, self-justifying. Graves had called him a weasel in the night. The image remained in the mind.

Certainly, it was not enough to make any publisher afraid to bring out the book.

He bent to look further.

Ten minutes' later, it was Mercy who interrupted him. 'I found a story about Lady Vespasia that I know is not true,' she said with triumph in her voice. 'And what is rather more to the point, Lord Shadox is still alive and has a large family, who among them own a number of houses of finance, and could call in a great many loans, if they wish to. They might make life most uncomfortable for the publishers, if they felt insulted, either for Lady Vespasia or on their own behalf. Page two hundred and five.'

She passed him the papers. 'If this were true, the current Lord Shadox would lose his part of the title, and with it his home in Northumberland, which I happen to know he is extremely fond of. Oh dear, what a mistake. Hot temper, too.' She smiled even more widely. 'Very hot! He won't like this, it's grubby.' She looked up at Daniel. 'Victor Narraway seems to have been quite a character, in his time. There are some of these events that could be embarrassing to a good few. Graves gives the true beginnings of them, and then allows his own imagination to complete them. He is clever, but I think he has outwitted himself here. The suggestions are scandalous. He all but says Narraway covered them up for payment. Which, whether it is true or not, leaves the reader believing them. That is a very serious error.'

'You can't prove it, though,' Daniel argued. 'We can't try it in court.'

Her eyebrows rose. 'For goodness' sake! We want to stop this long before it gets into any court! You have to go to the publisher and point out the people who will fight! And what they will do to protect themselves. This is what the publisher has to fear. Lawsuits! A fortune in damages. Put him right out of business — and onto the street!'

Blackwell looked up for the first time in nearly an hour. 'And I have a charge against your father that I can prove is made from spite. I think the person concerned would deeply regret having this issue raised again. He was proved wrong — in fact, he made the charge to hide a particularly nasty piece of behaviour. This book takes his point of view, but a little investigation will show not only that he was wrong then, but there are other things connected to that which are not criminal, but are deeply embarrassing. The publishers would make new and very dangerous enemies.' He smiled. 'It will show your father as very charitable in his judgements, perhaps at a glance naïve, but on further reading of it, he gathered many favours as a result. Not always for himself, but for the service. He was either naïve, or very astute indeed. I've not made up my mind which.' He gave a rather wistful smile. 'If I were his enemy, I wouldn't take the chance that it was the latter. I think we can make sure the publishers see it that way, too. It could unravel to become very close to treason — if we played it that way. Mr Graves is not as clever as he thinks.' His smile grew even wider. 'But we have a lot to do! We must lay our plans carefully. And tomorrow we must move. Much as I personally would like to see Graves swing, I know you cannot do that.'

'I would love to!' Daniel said fervently. 'But I would regret it later.'

'You would regret it immediately,' Blackwell corrected him. 'You're like your father.'

Daniel was not sure for a moment whether that pleased him or not. Then he thought about it again, and was absolutely certain that it did.

20

'Yes, sir.' Daniel stood in Marcus fford Croft's office on the last full day they had in which to appeal Russell Graves' case. 'I know we've cut it a little fine. There were many aspects to the case.' He saw the look on fford Croft's face. Should he say that he had kept Kitteridge informed? That was a cheap shot. fford Croft might see it as an attempt to shift the blame.

'I wanted to make sure the book would not be published. It would do a great deal of damage, not only to my father, and thus Special Branch in general, but also to a great many other people, sir . . . '

fford Croft sat stone-faced. He did not like being outmanoeuvred, especially by one of his own most junior men. 'And you did not think to tell me about all this?'

Daniel raised his chin a little higher. 'Yes, sir, I did. But I went to Mr Kitteridge for legal advice, because if it went wrong I thought it better, and fairer, that you should be able to deny any knowledge of it.' He met fford Croft's eyes with some trepidation. 'You told me you promised Mr Graves your best effort to acquit him, sir. He will be acquitted, beyond any doubt at all, of murdering his wife. You will have kept your word.'

'And publishing the book?' fford Croft's eyebrows went up.

'I don't know if you promised my father, or Special Branch, any sort of consideration, but if you did, you will have kept your word in that, too.'

'You're impudent, sir,' fford Croft said a little stiffly.

'I'm sorry, sir. I'm very new at these complicated problems.' Daniel kept his appearance innocent with some difficulty. He could not afford to have fford Croft think him sarcastic.

fford Croft's face very slowly relaxed, and a smile curved his lips more and more. 'Nonsense,' he said. 'You are a born conniver. One day you will make an excellent lawyer. Although I imagine you will always like the wrong cases. Don't lead Kitteridge astray, even if he wants to go! Do you understand me?'

'Yes, sir.' Relief eased throughout Daniel's aching nerves. 'I think Mr Kitteridge will always go with the law.'

'And you won't?' fford Croft raised his hand. 'No, don't tell me, I will affect ignorance as long as I can. So, the publisher will decide against publishing Graves' beastly book? Are you sure?'

'I hope so, sir. We managed to get several people whose families were implicated in it, to explain their extreme displeasure at the idea, and make it plain that these feelings might result in some very ... costly outcomes for the publishers, should they so slander their parents, or whoever it was who was mentioned. A certain peer of the realm still carries fond memories of Lady Vespasia. Any further reference to certain people's frailties, when it was quite unnecessary, would be similarly treated. This book would awaken a lot of . . . nasty recollections, which should be let go of.'

'And how did you find that out, young man?'

'A lot of detailed study, sir.' Daniel kept his face perfectly straight.

'And a lot of help from that scoundrel Blackwell, no doubt,' fford Croft said wryly.

'A little,' Daniel admitted.

Marcus grunted. 'Be careful who you trust, Daniel. You are very young and a good deal too idealistic.'

'Yes, sir.'

Marcus slapped his hand on the desk. 'Don't 'Yes, sir' me, dammit! I know there is no use warning you. I tried warning your father, and he went his own way. But while you work for fford Croft and Gibson, you'll do as I tell you. If you don't, you'd better be careful I don't catch you.'

'Yes, sir.'

'Yes, Sir, what? You'll be careful?'

Daniel smiled sweetly. 'Yes, sir.' He stood a little straighter. 'But we have a lot more to do, sir. Ebony Graves is to be charged later this morning. I have promised to represent her, sir, and I trust the charges will be withdrawn against Graves. With your permission, sir, Mr Kitteridge will be in court also, to be certain there is no error.'

'I will be in court myself,' fford Croft answered him. 'This is a spectacle worth seeing. I dare say Miriam will, too. She will not forgive me if I leave her out of it. We will be there at eleven o'clock. Now get all your information in order and don't disgrace us by making an ass of yourself, when you are this close to winning!'

'No, sir, thank you.' Daniel turned to leave, with a sigh of relief. Then a new burst of energy as he thought just how much there still was to prepare.

Daniel left fford Croft's office and almost bumped into Blackwell, and his chest tightened until he could hardly breathe.

Blackwell's face broke into a slow smile.

'Tell me, tell me,' Daniel demanded.

'I went to see a certain publisher,' Blackwell said, 'and managed to persuade him that publishing a particular biography would be against his interests. Very much against them, indeed. It would make him a remarkable number of enemies in very powerful places. I'm happy to say I scared him out of his wits!' His face was transformed by a dazzling smile. 'Serve the bastard right!'

Daniel was almost too choked to speak. He took Roman's hand and shook it. 'Thank you! Thank you, Blackwell.'

★　★　★

The hearing of the appeal of Russell Graves against the sentence of death in the murder of his wife, Ebony Graves, began at eleven o'clock exactly. Kitteridge appeared for Russell Graves, who sat in the court looking ashen. He seemed at least ten years older than the last time Daniel had seen him.

It was not an appeal as to a matter of error in

the law, but that was how it seemed at the outset.

Kitteridge looked nervous, although he could hardly fail.

'My lord, Russell Graves has been found guilty of murdering his wife, Ebony Graves. To prove that it is incorrect in law, I would like to call one witness, if it pleases your lordships.'

There was a moment of total silence, then one of the three judges of appeal nodded very gravely. 'You had better be certain of your facts, beyond a doubt, Mr Kitteridge. Who is your witness, and how are they relevant to this case?'

'My witness is Mrs Ebony Graves, my lord,' Kitteridge said perfectly steadily.

There was a moment of blank disbelief, then gasps; someone cried out in denial. There were shouts and the sound of movement as several journalists shot to their feet and stumbled out, making for the street. Daniel turned to look back and up at the dock. Graves was paralysed with shock. He was leaning forward, as if he could not believe what Kitteridge was saying.

At last the presiding judge leaned forward. 'I will not tolerate levity in this extremely serious matter, Mr Kitteridge. Be warned, should you fail, your client is due to be hanged very soon. And you will be severely punished if this is done in anything but the best good faith.'

'My lord, my witness is Mrs Ebony Graves, or was so, to the best of my knowledge and belief, until earlier this year,' Kitteridge replied.

The judge's temper was clearly frayed. 'I don't know what you mean. You had better proceed, but if you are acting in anything but the best possible faith, not only will your client pay for it with his life, you will pay for it with your career.'

'Yes, my lord. I call Ebony Graves to the stand.'

There was utter silence as Ebony appeared. She was dressed in dark grey, even though it was a bright May morning. She looked sober, but not bowed. She walked with her head high and her black hair gleaming in the courtroom lights. Her expression was composed, and at a glance you would have thought she was without nerves. But Daniel could see the stiffness of her shoulders, and the hand nearest to him was clenched, knuckles white.

She took the witness stand and was asked to swear to her name.

'You are Ebony Graves?' Kitteridge asked.

'No,' she said very quietly. 'I thought I was, but I discovered at the beginning of March this year that I am not. Our marriage was bigamous, all twenty years of it. And therefore, both my children are illegitimate. I am still Ebony Cumberford, as I was born.' She was having difficulty controlling her emotions, and it showed in her face and a very slight unsteadiness in her voice.

'But until then, you thought you were Ebony. Graves?' Kitteridge asked.

'Yes.'

'There was no one else by that name, to your knowledge?'

'No.'

'How did you discover this situation that you are in? Do I call you Miss Cumberford?'

'I suppose you do. I have no other name — now.'

'How did you discover your situation?' Kitteridge repeated.

'A woman came to visit me, at my home — or I believed it was my home. She introduced herself as Winifred Graves. Only when she was inside, upstairs.'

'Upstairs?' Kitteridge interrupted.

'Yes, sir. I have a private sitting room upstairs, for family guests. It is less formal.'

'I see. Please go on.'

'At first I assumed she must be my sister-in-law. My husband had not spoken of his family; I knew that he had a sister.' She drew a deep, shaky breath. 'Only when we had been speaking some little while, and I had mentioned to her my two children, Sarah and Arthur, did she laugh and say it was a pity for them.'

'What was she referring to?'

'It was then she told me Graves was her married name. She was not my sister-in-law, she was my husband's first and only wife. He had married her nearly thirty years ago, and the marriage had never been dissolved. She was still Mrs Russell Graves. And now that he had inherited a title, and considerable lands and money, she had decided to take her share of it — which, as far as I was concerned, was all of it. I, and my children, would be out in the street.'

'I'm sorry,' Kitteridge said with deep feeling. He waited a moment before continuing.

Daniel knew Kitteridge was tense. Not only did he want to win this case, as he wanted to win all cases, but his sympathies were very much with Ebony. Graves had been his client, and he had seen enough of him to dislike him heartily. She was, technically speaking, not his client: he sought her information in order to clear Graves.

'That must have been a dreadful shock to you,' Kitteridge resumed. 'What did you do?'

'I argued with her,' Ebony replied. 'I don't remember exactly what I said. I told her I had two children, and the result would be to make them illegitimate. I have not the means to care for them without my . . . as I thought, husband. I appealed to her mercy . . . ' She stopped. The memory was clearly humiliating.

Kitteridge did not help her.

Daniel felt his body knotting tightly. He knew why Kitteridge was silent, but he also knew that had he intervened, it would have been wrong. Did the judge see her distress, and know that she had tried, and failed?

'She laughed at me,' Ebony said, lifting her head and staring straight back at Kitteridge. 'She said she had had her years of being beaten and humiliated by him, and she was owed what she would get out of it now. Either she would tell everyone she was his legal wife, and she could prove it — I never doubted her — or he could pay her off every month for her silence and I could stay . . . and be abused by him, and pretend I didn't know the truth: I was a kept woman, a mistress and not a wife. And — and my children had no claims on him for inheritance — or help of any sort. I . . . ' She stopped.

'Is that important to you — inheritance — Mrs . . . Miss Cumberford?'

'Yes. It is. My son, Arthur, is an invalid. He is confined to a wheelchair. His life depends upon regular medical attention. There is a treatment that might ultimately restore him to something like normality, but it is expensive. Without my husband's providing for us, we would have no way of survival, let alone medical care. My daughter, Sarah, would have no prospect of a good marriage if she . . . she was known to be illegitimate.'

'Not in your own society, perhaps,' Kitteridge agreed. 'But she might find a man who loved her for herself . . . ' His voice trailed off. That was irrelevant at this point, and he realised it. 'Did you kill her, Mrs . . . Miss Cumberford?'

Her face was white. 'Yes . . . I suppose I did. I did not mean to. She was very unkind in her language. She called me a whore, an adventuress, and my children bastards. I called her a few things in return. I don't remember what, but it was equally unpleasant. She lashed out and struck me. I staggered backwards, and when I regained my balance, I slapped her back, open handed, across her face. She lost her balance and fell sideways. She struck her head on the hearth, and did not move again. I realised she was not breathing, and bleeding from her head.'

'She was dead?'

'Yes.'

'But not burned?'

Her voice was barely audible. 'No.'

'Did you seek help? Call a maid, or the butler?'

She stiffened. 'No.'

That was a lie, and Daniel could see it in her face, in the rigidity of her body. Did the judges see it as clearly as he did? Had Kitteridge meant to do that? Or was he unbelievably clumsy? Or worse than that, was he going to betray her by implicating Sarah, or Falthorne? He would have to! Anyone who defended her would have to. She could not have done it alone. But how far was he going to go? What more was necessary to prove that Graves was innocent?

'Your husband did not help you in any way — I'm sorry, I mean Mr Graves — did not help you?'

She looked surprised. 'No, of course not! If he had, he'd have known I was not dead, and would never have tolerated being accused of having killed me, let alone come within days of being hanged.'

Kitteridge looked thoughtful. 'But Winifred Graves was as much a threat to him as to you, surely?'

She looked blank. 'She could not make him illegitimate, or rob him of his means to live.'

Kitteridge tried to suppress a twisted smile, and did not entirely succeed. 'No. And I presume his parting from Winifred Graves was not against his will, to put it mildly. But his marriage to you was bigamous, although you did not know it. Bigamy is a crime.'

'I didn't know!' she protested.

'Not for you, Miss Cumberford, for the person committing it, Russell Graves. It might have remained a secret if Winifred had not presented herself at your home.'

She struggled with temptation. It was visible in her face.

The judge leaned forward and was about to speak, when she finally answered.

'He did not know anything about it. It was I who . . . who damaged her face so she would not be recognised. I dressed her in some of my clothes, and set fire to her, and — '

Kitteridge did not allow her to finish. 'How did you that, Miss Cumberford? It must have taken great nerve, and strength.'

'I suppose so.'

Kitteridge had to make the judge believe him. Daniel had seen his reluctance before the hearing began.

'You dressed her in your clothes, and then put her back where she fell, so it would still look like the accident it was. How did you make her clothes and flesh burn? Clothes I can see, but flesh?'

Ebony looked so pale now that Daniel was afraid she might faint. He knew that Kitteridge noted it, too, and he felt a sharp pity for him. Not something he had thought he would ever do.

'I . . . I took some of my son's art supplies,' Ebony continued in hoarse voice. 'Linseed oil and some oiled silk that I had. It is waterproof, you know. I knew they would burn. I put down some old cotton sheet, soaked in the oil, and the silk, and set fire to them.'

'I see. And you did all this alone?'

'Yes.'

'Think hard, Miss Cumberford. Not only

Russell Graves' life depends on this, but your own does also. I want to believe you, but I find it hard. Winifred was a larger woman than you are, even if not by much, and a dead weight. You managed to strip her of her own clothes and dress her in yours, then lay her back in exactly the same position, without any help at all? Please . . . tell me the truth. Are you sure Mr Graves did not help you?'

'I am certain! Do you think he would be prepared to hang, rather than admit that I was still alive, and he had had a part in making Winifred look like me? He does not love me enough to die for me! He does not love me at all. I don't think he ever did. Or he wouldn't have beaten me . . . '

'Then who helped you?'

She stood silent.

'Was it Falthorne, your butler?'

'No! Do you think I would — ' She stopped abruptly.

'Trust him? Yes, I do. But I do not think you would allow him to be blamed for something he did not do. I believe it was your daughter, Sarah, who knew how Russell Graves had beaten you, because he beat her also. I think the two of you saw your chance to escape from him, and you took it. I don't think you thought further than that. I don't think you foresaw Russell Graves being hanged for murdering you, or what would happen to Arthur and Sarah after that, the guilt that might hurt the rest of their lives. I think you have come forward now precisely to prevent that, no matter the cost to you. But you would have borne it all, and chance she could not help you, as absurd as that seems. I cannot blame you, Miss Cumberford, but neither can I believe you.'

She did not answer him.

He turned to the judge. 'My lord, that is all the evidence I have to offer the court that Russell Graves is not guilty of having murdered Ebony Cumberford, whom the court believed to be Ebony Graves.'

'Thank you, Mr Kitteridge, it is not necessary for us to retire to consider our verdict. Quite clearly, Miss Cumberford, or Mrs Graves, is alive and well. The verdict of guilty against Russell Graves is reversed. Appropriate action will be taken to that effect.'

'Thank you, my lord.'

'However, that is hardly the end of the matter. Charges must be made against Miss Cumberford. I think circumstances do not require that Miss Sarah . . . Cumberford . . . be charged as an accessory to the desecrating of Mrs Winifred Graves' body. There is no proof that she did any more than assist her mother in the most tragic circumstances. No doubt she was shocked and frightened. She came forward before it was too late.'

'Thank you, my lord,' Kitteridge said fervently.

'However, Ebony Cumberford will be taken into custody and held for trial on the defacement of a corpse, with the intention to portray an accident as a crime, and allow her common-law husband to be tried and sentenced for a crime that did not exist. This court is adjourned.'

Daniel waited for what he knew was

inevitable. Ebony was arrested and charged. It was more lenient than he had feared it might be. Sarah was free, but she was so concerned for her mother that her own escape hardly registered with her. She looked at Daniel with terror in her eyes — and guilt.

'You had no alternative,' he said to her as they stood in the hallway outside the courtroom. 'If you had left it any longer, the charge would have been murder.'

'But what will happen to her? What will happen to us? Arthur . . . and me? We have nowhere to go, and I can't look after him by myself.'

'You will not be by yourself.'

'We're not staying with him!' Her fear was so intense she was almost paralysed by it.

'He is not going home,' Daniel assured her. 'He's being arrested for bigamy. He won't dare touch you now, and you will have plenty of time to work out what to do next. Anything can happen — in seven years.'

'Everyone will know we are . . . not legitimate. We have no money or . . . '

'First we must think of defending your mother. For tonight, you can go home and be safe.'

'Will you defend her? We can't pay you . . . '

'Let me have one of Arthur's paintings. That will be payment enough. Not his favourite — another one.'

'He'll be happy.' Suddenly a smile broke through. 'They are beautiful, aren't they?'

Before he could answer her that they were,

they were joined by Marcus fford Croft and Kitteridge.

'Thank you, Mr Kitteridge,' Sarah said with the utmost sincerity. 'I know you defended my father the best way possible. Mr fford Croft, I am very grateful. I imagine my father will settle what he owes you. Perhaps you will defend him for bigamy. That is not up to me. But . . . but can Mr Pitt be permitted to defend my mother? I'm sure she would ask him to, if she were allowed.'

'I will not defend your father,' fford Croft replied. 'I have discharged my duty to him, and I think it very likely he would prefer his defence to rest with someone else . . . who . . . who can wholeheartedly represent him. My firm would gladly represent your mother. Mr Kitteridge is my best litigator, and he is at your mother's disposal. I will send him to her as soon as it is possible. We must get the matter concluded as satisfactorily as we can.'

Daniel knew it was intrusive, and perhaps he was asking for something he had no right to, but the case was not over yet. Not only must Ebony be defended, but it must be done in such a way that the final blow must go to Russell Graves' reputation. The trial must accomplish his ruin, so that when he was tried for bigamy he would receive the maximum sentence, and he would no longer be believed in the repetition of his lies about anyone else, particularly about Sir Thomas Pitt. If Kitteridge failed to save Ebony, the legal charge against her was grave and the evidence powerful. Graves himself might well be permitted to testify. He would be desperate for vengeance. This judge had been gentle with her. He could not rely on another being so.

'Sir, may I take this case? Please . . . ' Daniel glanced at Kitteridge and knew he understood. He did not wish to offend him. He found, to his surprise, that he actually cared about his feelings. But Kitteridge relied on the law, which was against Ebony. This was a case where the jury must be made to care for Ebony and seek reasons to acquit her, or at least find a way to lessen the charge.

Marcus looked startled.

'Mr Kitteridge would . . . assist me . . . and make sure I honour the law, sir,' Daniel pleaded.

Kitteridge's eyes widened. The thought of being assistant to anyone was abrasive, to say the least, but to Daniel Pitt, who was a total beginner, clearly appalled him.

Marcus looked from one to the other of them. 'Kitteridge?' he said hesitantly.

'This once!' Kitteridge granted with obvious difficulty. 'It will never happen again!'

'Thank you,' Daniel said very soberly.

Marcus nodded, and turned to walk away.

'I'll even second you, if it's possible,' Kitteridge said under his breath.

21

Sitting at his desk almost a week later, facing the reality of the trial, Daniel did not feel nearly so certain of himself. He should have been less arrogant, and let Kitteridge do it. What had made him think that he knew better? Trials were about law, not emotion, and certainly not justice. His professor at university had told him often enough, 'You go to court for the law, not for justice.'

It was too late now. He would be facing a lawyer named Grisewood, an agreeable-faced, fleshy man of roughly forty, whom nobody seemed to know much about. He was not a Londoner, but came from somewhere in the Midlands, and was beginning to make a name for himself.

Kitteridge interrupted his thoughts. 'I've got all the witnesses you asked for.'

'Oh, thank you . . . ' Daniel did not want to ask Kitteridge's advice, but he was overwhelmed with the idea of what he had asked for, and been given. 'Can you think of anyone I've missed?'

Kitteridge raised his eyebrows. 'If I had, I'd have told you. Do you think I want to see you shot down? I think Graves is a total bastard, and I'd see him hanged with pleasure, if I thought it was even remotely legal, but it isn't. You can't hang a man for being a swine.'

Daniel said nothing. He didn't really want to

hang Graves. If he imagined it, the reality of it, a gallows, a rope, the drop beneath, and a person's life gone in minutes — where there had been a human being alive, thinking, feeling, and there was now just a corpse — it was horrifying. What if you had made a mistake anywhere? At any point along the line? Even if you hadn't, that kind of judgement was too big to make. And yet he had been willing enough to think of it.

Perhaps he thought too much. It could make a person impotent to act. Sarah and Arthur were both relying on him to act. And he had given his word. Why? Because he couldn't bear to see them so afraid. He wanted them to feel safe. Now he must make good his promise.

'Pitt?' Kitteridge said firmly.

'What?' Daniel looked at him.

'Don't underestimate Grisewood,' he warned. 'He's known for letting his opponent think he's won, and then pulling something extra out of his back pocket.'

'Thank you. I'll watch.'

'I don't like playing second chair to anyone,' Kitteridge went on. 'Let alone somebody as green as you are, I admit. But if I can't make a good job of it, then I can't make a good job of first chair either! And believe it or not, I want to win this one nearly as much as you do.'

'I do believe it,' Daniel smiled at him suddenly. 'You like Sarah!' It was not a question. He had seen Kitteridge watching her, and seen the faint blush on his cheeks when she spoke to him.

'I'm sorry for her,' Kitteridge said, then

immediately went back to his own desk and buried himself with papers.

Daniel did not comment, but he found himself liking Kitteridge more these days than he expected to.

★ ★ ★

The trial began two days later. All the formalities were gone through, and Grisewood rose to open his case. He looked uncomfortable in his wig and gown, as if they had been made for somebody else who was an elegant shape. And yet he seemed confident enough. He strode out into the body of the court, bowed to the judge, and faced the jury.

'Gentlemen, you are about to hear an extraordinary story about an ambitious woman, beautiful, clever, but of poor background, and ruthless self-control. I ask you not to look at her, not look at her tears or her smiles, not at the broken bones she claims to have suffered, nor those of her daughter, but at what I shall prove to you she had done to her.

'My learned friend, for the defence, will tell you that this whole story is a series of huge accidents, with no thought of malice, only fear. No thought of material gain, only preservation for her children. No intended violence, or deceit, only circumstances beyond her control.'

He shook his head slowly. 'I will show you a story of cunning, deceit, and ruthlessness, ending in violence, which has never been far from the heart of it.'

Daniel turned to Kitteridge. 'What the hell is he talking about?'

Kitteridge looked puzzled. 'No idea.'

'The defence will try to tell you it was a sudden and unforeseen accident, gentlemen. I will show you that it was heartless and cold-blooded murder.'

It was Kitteridge who shot to his feet, while Daniel was still sitting up in shock. 'My lord, the accused is charged with disfiguring a corpse, not murder! Perhaps our learned friend is in the wrong courtroom? I understand he's not from around here.'

There was a murmur of laughter around the gallery.

Grisewood smiled, all teeth and no charm. 'The law is no different in London from the rest of England, my lord. When you plan the death of any human being, and then bring it to pass, and run from the scene, that is murder, even in London.' He looked at Kitteridge. 'The charge has been amended. I did not apprise you of that. Perhaps you have not looked at your papers recently.' He looked at Daniel. 'Or your young friend has not — if he is indeed leading this case.'

With a flash of memory that was like a cold hand on his flesh, Daniel remembered Impney coming in with an envelope, still sealed, and putting it on his desk. It was handwritten, and he had taken it for a personal letter, possibly as Grisewood had intended. There was no point in arguing the issue now. It would cost time and give him nothing.

He rose to his feet quickly. 'My lord, I did receive a handwritten note yesterday, which I'm afraid I did not open. I took it for personal correspondence. It makes no difference. The plea is still *not guilty*, as I will prove, in time.'

'Very well, Mr Pitt. Do you require extra time, or are you prepared to proceed?'

'I am prepared to proceed, my lord. The truth has not changed, nor has the evidence that proves it.'

'Then you may address the jury, but please be brief.'

'Thank you, my lord.' Daniel turned to face the jurors. He had their total attention, and he thought he saw, in one or two, some trace of sympathy as well.

'Gentlemen, this is a story of many emotions, as my learned friend has said. It starts with love on the one side, and deceit on the other. It goes forward to tolerance, and then abuse, and in shame, with a lifetime of betrayal and violence, but not by the perpetrators he suggests. It ends in terror, misjudgement, and then redemption. I shall prove it to you step by step.'

There was a murmur in the gallery, and the whisper of silk as people moved positions. No one spoke.

Grisewood called his first witness — Falthorne.

Daniel watched the butler, formally dressed in a dark suit and looking extremely ill at ease as he climbed the steps to the witness stand. He swore to tell the truth, the whole truth, and nothing else.

He gave his name, and his position in the home of Russell Graves.

'And did you hold that position on the night Mrs Graves disappeared?' Grisewood asked.

'Yes, sir.'

'In fact, you have held it for some twenty years, is that not so?'

'Yes, sir.' Falthorne was uncomfortable, and it was also clear that he disliked Grisewood. It might not have been apparent to everyone, but Daniel had had several encounters with him, and all but the first time, when there was great stress upon them, he had observed his manner, and he both liked and respected the man. He knew by the inflection of his voice, the rigid arms at his side, how deeply he despised Grisewood.

'So, it was quite natural that when Mrs Graves found herself in a desperate situation, one with which she could not contend alone, she would ask your help, in the certainty that she would get it?' Grisewood asked.

'I hope so, sir.'

Grisewood treated Falthorne as an unwilling witness. Daniel wondered if he would say so openly. Did the jurors see the tension between them? They would judge it as loyalty, or obstruction, according to where their sympathies lay. Perhaps that would offer Daniel the chance to further expose the household dynamics?

Grisewood smiled. 'Did she, in fact, turn to you when she found herself with the dead body of her victim, and no satisfactory explanation, indeed no legal one?'

Daniel stood up. 'Objection, my lord. It has

not been established that there was no legal explanation. In fact, we intend to show that there's a perfectly legal explanation, and that the woman attacked Mrs Graves and, in so doing, slipped and fell.'

Grisewood was immediate. 'It is not legal to burn a dead body until it is unrecognisable, my lord, even in London! No one can imagine that it is . . . if they can imagine any such thing at all!'

'That has not been established either, my lord,' Daniel replied. 'My learned friend asked if Mrs Graves called the butler when she had a dead body . . . that is all.'

'You are correct, Mr Pitt. Keep your questions in order, Mr Grisewood. You asked the witness if Mrs Graves called the butler when she found herself with a dead body. Mr Falthorne, you may answer.'

'Yes, my lord,' Falthorne said unhappily. 'She did. She was extremely distressed, and told me — '

'Yes, that will do, Mr Falthorne,' Grisewood cut him off. 'Did you see the body of Mrs Graves — the real Mrs Graves?'

'I saw the body of a middle-aged woman. I had no idea at all, at the time, who she was,' Falthorne replied punctiliously. He had years of training, of conducting himself, as required, and keeping his own emotions in check. Grisewood would not easily catch him off balance.

'What you now know to have been the body of Mrs Graves,' Grisewood said irritably. But he knew better than to be seen to bully a servant on the witness stand. 'Was she burned in any way?

What injuries did she have? Would you describe what you saw, please.'

'I saw the body of a woman of middle years lying on the floor, with her head by the edge of the hearthstone, and a considerable amount of blood on the hearthstone, and on the carpet beside her.'

'Did you ascertain that she was dead?'

'Yes, sir.'

'How?'

'She had no pulse, and she was not breathing. The wound on her head appeared to be quite deep, but I did not touch it.'

'Did Miss Cumberford make any request of you regarding the body?'

'Not at that time, sir.'

'Then later? Don't make me pull teeth! Did she later ask you to assist her in disguising the body with her own clothes, to make it seem as if it were she who had been murdered?'

'No, sir, murder was never mentioned. She told me what happened, that the woman was indeed Mrs Graves, her husband's first, and, as it turned out, only wife — '

'I did not ask you to discuss the testimony that — ' Grisewood interrupted.

'I beg your pardon, sir. I thought that was exactly what you did ask.'

The judge almost hid his smile, but not enough that Daniel missed it, and no doubt the jury did not, either.

'Mr Grisewood,' the judge began. 'You must either make your questions more specific, excluding what you wish Mr Falthorne to omit, or put up with his fuller answers. I do not see the point of your objection. If he does not answer that on your examination, Mr Pitt will hardly fail to ask him on cross-examination. Make yourself clearer, sir.'

Grisewood flushed with annoyance, but he was obliged to obey. 'Yes, my lord. Mr Falthorne, let me be plain. Was the body, as you saw it the last time, in any way burned?'

'No, sir.'

'So, the burning, the disfiguring of her face and the upper body, happened to her after she was dead.'

'It must have, sir.'

'Did you have any part in it?'

'No, sir.'

'Did any of the servants?'

This time Falthorne was caught. Daniel knew it. He would be as loyal as he could to Ebony, but he would not allow any of the other servants to take the blame for something he was sure they had not done. The conflict was clear in his face, probably to the whole court, but certainly to anyone who knew him.

'Mr Falthorne?' Grisewood prompted.

'No, sir.'

'So, we may conclude it was not conceivably an accident, or part of her death, and none of the other servants was responsible. Was there anyone else in the house, apart from Miss Cumberford, and her daughter, Sarah, and her son, Arthur?'

'No, sir.'

'Thank you, Mr Falthorne, that is all.' He turned to Daniel. 'Your witness, Mr Pitt.'

Daniel rose to his feet. Grisewood had left the door open, just an inch, for Daniel to push, if he dared. Did he? Was it a trap? The sweat trickled down his body, and his hands were clammy. Everyone was staring at him, waiting for him to begin. He had had no time to prepare for this change to the charge. The first judge had believed Ebony; clearly the prosecutor for the case did not.

Daniel must take the chance. 'Mr Falthorne, we must deduce from your testimony so far that only Mrs Graves, as she believed herself to be, and possibly her daughter, Sarah, were responsible for disfiguring the body of Winifred Graves.'

Falthorne looked at him as if he had betrayed his trust. 'Yes, sir.'

'Not Arthur Graves — or whatever his name now is?'

'No, sir. He is confined to a wheelchair.'

'It seems an extraordinary thing to do, without reason by Mrs . . . may I refer to her as Ebony? The situation is confusing. Can you think of any reason whatever why Ebony, with the help of Sarah, should change Winifred's clothes, and dress her sufficiently that she could pass for Ebony? If she had left the body alone, it would have been clear enough that she had slipped and fallen, injuring herself fatally. Why did Ebony not do that? Why on earth disappear?'

Falthorne hesitated.

Before Grisewood could object, Daniel spoke again. 'Mr Falthorne, if you are afraid of someone, it is your duty to tell the court.'

A glimmer of understanding shone for a

moment on Falthorne's face.

'My lord?' Daniel appealed to the judge.

'You must answer the question, Mr Falthorne, if you can.'

Falthorne straightened up. 'Yes, my lord. I believe that . . . I can only think of her as Mrs Graves . . . was afraid of Mr Graves, sir. He had treated her with considerable violence on many occasions — '

'Objection!' Grisewood was on his feet, his face twisted with anger.

Daniel interrupted. 'My lord, my learned friend opened the door by asking — '

'Yes, yes. Indeed, he did. You may answer, Mr Falthorne, if it is of your own knowledge, and not hearsay.'

'Thank you, my lord,' Falthorne replied. He looked back at Daniel, his expression completely altered. 'I dislike speaking of it, sir, but most of the servants were aware that Mr Graves, on many occasions, over the years, beat Mrs Graves, and even Miss Sarah. And, at least, to our knowledge, he even beat Mr Arthur, when he was young, before he became an invalid confined to a wheelchair.'

'As butler, how did you become aware of this while carrying out your duty, Mr Falthorne?'

'I was frequently upstairs, sir, because I attended Mr Arthur. His mother was able to do everything for him when he was a child, but at a certain age it was no longer appropriate. I was aware of what occurred because I was frequently close to . . . close enough to hear.' His emotion almost overcame him, and he suppressed it with difficulty. 'And certain injuries are impossible to hide. The lady's maid confided in me, in extreme distress, the first time Mr Graves actually beat Mrs Graves so hard he broke bones in her shoulder and her arm.'

'The first time? There were others?' Daniel did not even try to keep the emotion from his voice.

'Yes, sir. I am not exactly sure. Five or six, I think. And Miss Sarah, also. Only one that I'm sure of with a broken bone.'

'So, you understood Ebony's desire for him to consider her dead, and not pursue her?'

'Yes, sir.'

'You do not deny helping her, at least insofar as you did not enlighten anyone in the police that she was alive, and therefore that Mr Graves could not be guilty of having murdered her?'

'No, sir. I am prepared to be judged on that account. I knew you were defending him, sir, and I believed that you would be successful in saving Mr Graves from the gallows.'

'Thank you,' Daniel said slowly. 'You had greater trust in me than I had in myself. That is all the questions that I have for you.'

Grisewood rose to his feet, looked at the jury, saw their faces, and sat down again.

Falthorne was excused.

The police who had been called to the scene at the time of Winifred's death came to the stand and testified at some length to all the circumstances. Grisewood made much of the state of the body, and the fact that Sarah had identified it as that of her mother.

There was nothing for Daniel to do but wait

silently and not make more of it than was already there. He did seem as if he were about to press further, but Kitteridge shook his head.

The evidence took until the final adjournment.

'All right so far,' Kitteridge said to Daniel as they left the court and went outside, into the summer day. The street was loud with the sound of traffic, both horse-drawn and automotive. They were getting accustomed to the smell of fumes, as their parents had with the smell of horse dung.

Daniel said nothing. He was full of doubts. He had not foreseen them changing the charge, and he felt that he should have.

After a few steps, he spoke. 'I should have known that Graves wasn't finished,' he said bitterly.

'We all should have,' Kitteridge admitted. 'But we have to work with how it is. Getting that information from Falthorne was good. Now what are we going to do to build on it? Grisewood will call the police surgeon first thing tomorrow morning. He'll give the jury all the most disgusting details about Winifred. For what it's worth, I don't think there's any point in fighting him. We've got Miriam. Do you honestly think they'll take notice of her? She's got no recognised qualifications.'

'I know that.' Daniel already felt himself getting defensive. And the police surgeon, Grisewood, and probably the judge also would give her a far harder time than Kitteridge did. 'She'll bring only the evidence she can show them. I know her word won't serve anything, even though she knows more than all of them put together.'

Kitteridge smiled lopsidedly. 'Don't let your temper show, Pitt. Righteous indignation has its place, and this isn't it. Listen to me — I know what I'm talking about.'

Daniel did not argue. They had been over this before. His indignation wouldn't help at all. But the jury's might. He wanted the jury to feel for Ebony, and Sarah. And for Arthur, too, if it helped. 'We've got to prepare for tomorrow,' he said instead. 'Feel like an early supper at the Boar's Head, before we begin in earnest?'

'Good idea,' Kitteridge agreed immediately.

*　*　*

The following morning, Grisewood called the police surgeon, as expected. He was a sympathetic figure and gave the facts as he had observed them, precisely as Grisewood asked. He described the disfiguring in detail, but without ascribing any emotion.

When it was Daniel's turn to question him, he rose to his feet, determined to treat the man with a respect the jury would see.

'Good morning, Dr French. You have given us a very detailed, yet completely understandable picture of what must have happened to the body of Winifred Graves. May I ask you one or two further questions?'

'Of course,' French replied. He was at least forty years older than Daniel, and his lean, silver-haired look was a distinguished one that the jury would not forget. 'What do you wish to know?'

'You believed it was the body of Ebony Graves, because you were told it was. Is that correct?'

'Yes, I was informed that the daughter, Miss Sarah Graves, had identified it as her mother. The butler also confirmed that, and the lady's maid identified the clothes.'

'There was nothing of the body itself that confirmed that to you?'

'I was not acquainted with Mrs Graves, or Miss Cumberford, as I believe she is more correctly known.'

'Actually, the woman you examined was Mrs Winifred Graves. Ebony Cumberford is alive and well.'

The moment he had said it, Daniel regretted it. He did not want to antagonise the doctor.

French stiffened. 'I was told who she was, and had no reason to question it. It was the body of a woman of perhaps sixty or so, and she had died from a severe blow to the back of the head. The damage to her face, neck, and shoulders was inflicted after death. That is all I testify to.'

'No one doubts you, Dr French. Can you tell me what caused the burning? More than extreme heat, of course.'

Several expressions crossed French's face, finally a degree of interest. 'No. I was asked to ascertain whether it was before or after death, and whether it could be accidental. It could not.'

'Does flesh burn easily?'

'It blisters easily. It does not ignite. Anyone who has burned themselves is painfully aware of that. If you are asking me how the burning happened, I do not know. I was only required to say that it was not caused by falling into the fire, or by coming in contact with burning logs, or a domestic iron for clothes.'

'Or some other, more deliberate act?'

'If you say so, sir. I cannot see how that serves your client.'

'It serves only to prove that she is telling the truth. Thank you. Oh, before you go! Did you find any evidence on the body of broken bones? Or scars from having been beaten?'

'If I had, young man, I would have reported it, as a matter of course. There were old scars, well healed, which could have been caused in any number of ways. They are all at least twenty years old.'

'Dating from the time of her marriage to Mr Graves?'

'Apparently.' A flash of interest crossed French's face, then died.

'Thank you, sir. That is all I have to ask you.'

French inclined his head in a slight bow, and left the stand.

Grisewood's final witness was Graves himself. The man who climbed the witness stand was outwardly very different from the one who had sat in the dock only a short while ago. At that time, he had been angry, frightened and exhausted, alternating between hope and fear. Today, staying temporarily in London, he stood upright, dressed in an expensive and well-tailored suit, freshly pressed white shirt, and his hair was expertly cut. It altered the whole aspect of his face and his entire bearing.

Grisewood treated him with almost deferential respect. 'After your recent ordeal, I'm sorry you have to experience this new distress. However, I have to ask you to relive the whole story of your marriage, your difficulties with Ebony Cumberford, and the facts that have brought you to this tragic place.'

Daniel felt a chill of apprehension. He glanced at Kitteridge and saw him shift in his seat, as if he too feared something as yet unknown.

'You were married to Winifred Graves when you first met Ebony Cumberford, were you not?'

'Yes. However, we were living apart,' Graves answered.

'Did you tell Miss Cumberford that you were married?'

'Of course.'

'You were attracted to each other?'

'Yes, at that time she was a very attractive woman.'

Daniel studied Graves' face. He did not seem in the least nervous. No one looking at him would see any tremor of fear, only a weariness at having his private grief examined yet again in front of strangers. Perhaps the jurors would sympathise with him.

'And did you go through some form of marriage?' Grisewood continued.

'We had a ceremony. It was not a marriage. I was already married, as Ebony well knew. She was prepared to accept me, and the life I could offer her, in those circumstances. I admit, at first I was not willing to get involved in . . . a deceit. But she insisted, even after I had told her of the disadvantages. She said she would move to a place where Winifred was not known, and would not find us. I agreed, if that was what she wanted. She was . . . ' He bit his lips, as if momentarily embarrassed. 'She was a beautiful woman then, and very . . . skilled in the arts of persuasion.'

'Are you saying she seduced you, Mr Graves?' Grisewood asked with as much innocence as he could contrive.

'I suppose I am,' Graves agreed.

'So, you lived together for twenty years, and no one suspected?'

'As far as I know, no one did.'

'What changed, Mr Graves?'

'I inherited a title, quite unexpectedly. It was not a direct ancestor, but someone on my mother's side of the family. There were two deaths in a row, and the title passed laterally to me. With a considerable amount of both land and money.'

'And Ebony was aware of this?'

'Of course. I would not have kept such a thing secret from her.'

'How did that change things? Why on earth would she want to run away from such good fortune? Was there some threat that your marriage arrangements would be exposed?'

'None at all. But somehow or another Winifred found out, and she arrived to claim her place as my wife. She had fallen on harder times

— and saw I was a famous man, about to have a title and even more wealth. I was worth much more to her, and she felt she had a right to her place.'

'To be exact, to Ebony's place,' Grisewood countered with a smile.

'Yes.'

'Did you tell her she could not return now?'

'I didn't see her. She approached Ebony. I don't know exactly what transpired, except that Winifred is dead, and Ebony is alive. I don't know if she ever intended to tell me, but things went badly wrong, and she ran away to escape the results of her actions. I did not know at the time, obviously. I was in danger, quite wrongly, of being hanged for having killed Ebony, who is clearly alive. I never actually saw Winifred, and I certainly did not kill her. From the evidence of Falthorne, who used to be my butler, you know more than I did until now.'

Beside Daniel, Kitteridge let out his breath. 'The bastard!' he said bitterly.

Grisewood gave a slight bow, very slight, but it was a gesture the jury would not miss. It was as if Grisewood were acknowledging Graves as a gentleman, an equal for whom he had been able to perform a service.

Kitteridge nudged Daniel. 'Do you want me to do this?'

'No!' Daniel took a breath. 'No, thank you.'

'Then don't make me wish I had,' Kitteridge said with a smile. 'Nail the swine!'

Daniel rose to his feet. 'I don't need to introduce myself to you, Mr Graves. We know each other quite well. Mr Kitteridge had the responsibility of mounting the appeal after you were convicted of murder, and we found the proof that you were, in fact, not guilty. I dare say you remember me?'

There was a rustle of movement, and definitely of interest, around the room. The jury stared at Daniel with renewed attention, and even respect.

'Indeed.' Graves knew enough to be polite, whatever his actual emotion.

'As you say, you did not know what happened in that bedroom, or that the body was that of your first wife — in fact, your only actual wife. I believe you. What I find more open to question is that the 'arrangement' you reached with Ebony Cumberford was with her agreement, even more than your own. She says otherwise. In fact, she has a certificate of marriage which she believed to be valid.' Daniel turned to the judge. 'I submit it into evidence, my lord.'

It was duly passed up, and the judge regarded it. 'If it is not, then it is a remarkably good forgery,' he said unhappily.

'Mrs . . . I mean . . . Miss Cumberford will swear that she believed it to be real, my lord,' Daniel told him. Then he turned back to Graves. 'Have you seen this document before?'

'No,' Graves said vehemently. 'I always told Ebony that I was married, and not free to marry her. She was perfectly happy to live 'in sin', as they say. Until Winifred turned up and threatened to resume her place at my side, and accept her share of the inheritance.' His face was perfectly calm, as if he could see nothing more than unimportant pretence in the matter.

'And what would have happened to Ebony, in that case?'

'She would have been exposed as a kept woman, I imagine.' Graves smiled very slightly. 'She had a certain laxity in morals, but I think that would have caused her considerable discomfort. The loss of position in society, at least.'

'And the loss of a roof over her head, food on her table?' Daniel added.

'Yes, I imagine so.'

'And even more, the illegitimacy of the children, *your* children,' Daniel went on. 'Sarah would find herself a bastard, with little hope of making a fortunate marriage. But rather more than that, Arthur would be without a name, without the medical attention he needs, if he is to survive. That would have been devastating to all of them, would it not? You made no provision for them, did you?' It was barely a question.

'I would have!' Graves said angrily, temper sharpening his voice.

'But as of today, you have not!' Daniel pointed out. 'You have had plenty of time. You have given them no comfort or assurance at all.' He glanced only momentarily at the jury, but he saw the anger and the pity in their faces, and something that looked like disgust. 'As far as they are aware,' he continued, 'you are determined to put their mother in prison, and leave them illegitimate and abandoned. Perhaps that has not fully sunk into their consciousness — they are too hurt and sorry for their mother — but it will. Sarah, at least, is terrified that Arthur will die, and she will be unable to save him.'

Daniel looked at the jury and saw several of them in deep anger and distress at the situation.

Grisewood must have seen it too, because he rose to his feet. 'My lord, I know Mr Pitt is young and inexperienced, but this is all an appeal to the emotions. It has nothing to do with the facts that Miss Cumberford coldly and deliberately murdered Mrs Winifred Graves. That is what we are here to try.'

'Indeed, Mr Pitt,' the judge said gravely. 'Mr Grisewood is correct. You will please address the facts relevant to that. You have only succeeded so far in making Mr Grisewood's case for him. Miss Cumberford had excellent motive for wishing Mrs Graves to disappear, as she almost succeeded in accomplishing that.'

'Yes, my lord. I apologise to the court. I only wanted to establish Miss Cumberford's character, and the honesty, or otherwise, of Mr Graves, the chief witness against her.'

'Your point is taken, Mr Pitt. Have you any other questions for Mr Graves?'

'Yes, my lord, a few.'

'Then proceed, but see that they are relevant.'

'Yes, my lord. Mr Graves, you have suggested that your butler, Mr Falthorne, is telling lies, rather than the truth, when he says you beat both your wife and your daughter regularly, causing them serious injury. Is he, in fact, lying? If we were to ask the lady's maid the same questions, would she have different answers? And apparently Mrs Winifred Graves had several scars dating from the time she was married to you.'

'She was a clumsy woman!' Graves said darkly.

'And was Ebony clumsy, too, and Sarah?' He allowed the sarcasm he felt to be heard in his voice.

'Occasionally,' Graves replied, but there was a flush in his face and a sharp, brittle edge to his voice.

'Are you clumsy also?' Daniel asked. 'Have you had broken bones?'

Grisewood rose again. 'My lord, this is impertinent, intrusive, and ridiculous.'

'It is not entirely irrelevant,' the judge replied. 'And I do not find it ridiculous. I would like to hear the answer.'

'No, I am not clumsy,' Graves said irritably.

'Never broken a bone?' Daniel raised his eyebrows. 'Be careful to be exact, Mr Graves. We have science these days that can tell if a person has any broken bones, even before they are dead. Bones heal, but they look different from bones that have not been broken.'

'No, I have never broken my bones, and no science will find that I have,' Graves answered tartly. 'What has this to do with the fact that Ebony killed Winifred and tried to get me hanged for killing her?'

'Oh, quite a lot,' Daniel said with a tiny smile. 'But we will come to that later. Thank you, my lord, that is all I have for this witness.'

Grisewood stood up and had Graves restate his total innocence, and add some details of his suffering as a result of having been wrongly accused of murdering Ebony.

Daniel addressed the judge. 'I am quite aware of all that, my lord. In case Mr Graves has forgotten, it was I who worked night and day to prove his innocence.'

'Indeed, Mr Pitt knows it most of all,' Grisewood said with a wide smile. 'The prosecution rests, my lord.'

22

Daniel began his defence immediately after an early luncheon recess. He had spent the time with Kitteridge, turning over and over in his mind the possibilities. Should he present as much evidence as possible? Or should he not risk boring the jury, or giving Grisewood too much testimony to challenge? Grisewood would certainly do all he could to destroy Miriam. He would try everything to discredit her skills or make a mockery of her in the courtroom.

'Are you sure I should expose her to that?' he kept asking Kitteridge. 'He'll try to make her look ridiculous. He'll use every prejudice possible.'

'For heaven's sake, Pitt! She's a grown woman! Do you appreciate your mother fussing over you to protect you from life?'

'No, of course not, but that's different!'

'Yes, it is! She's your mother. It's her job. You are not Miriam's parent. In fact, she's almost old enough to be yours.'

'No, she isn't!' Daniel replied hotly.

'She's about two or three years short. She's got Marcus treating her as if she's made of porcelain, she doesn't need you too!'

But Daniel was not convinced. All his witnesses were women, and he felt as if he were missing something vital. But which men could he call? Falthorne had already testified, so had

Graves, the police, and the police surgeon.

'Believe in yourself!' Kitteridge said. 'If you don't, the jury will sense it and you'll lose them. Bite the bullet, Pitt! Get on with it.'

And so Daniel began by calling Ebony Cumberford.

'I apologise if I should slip and call you Ebony Graves,' he began. 'But the majority of the time I have known of you, it was by that name.'

She smiled ruefully. 'I thought of myself by that name,' she told him. 'I will take no offence.'

'Thank you.' He then led her through her first meeting with Russell Graves, from her point of view. She insisted she had known nothing of Winifred's existence. Graves appeared to be single, and behaved as if he were. He had courted her; she mentioned certain places and events they had attended together. He asked her to marry him, and she had accepted.

In time, they had moved to their present address in the outskirts of London. Sarah had been born, and then Arthur. In none of that time had Graves made any mention of an earlier marriage.

She knew nothing of the inheritance involving a title and estate. She had learned of it only when Winifred arrived and demanded to see her.

'That must have been a tremendous shock to you,' Daniel observed.

'Small, compared to the news that she was Russell's legitimate wife, and I was a bigamist, and my children had no standing at all,' she replied, her voice a little shaky.

'But you believed it?'

'She had her marriage lines with her. I could hardly refute it.'

'You believed her that there had been no divorce?'

'Russell told me he had never married before. If there had been a divorce, he would have said so, surely. Yes, I believed her. She had come to reclaim her place, now that there was a title and money. If she were divorced, then she would have no claim. There would be no point in her coming.'

'What did she expect you to do?'

'I don't know. I was so horrified I called her a liar and said I would fight her . . . that . . . that was when she lunged at me and I stepped back, and she slipped. I . . . she . . . she slapped me, and I slapped her back. I think she was so surprised, she stepped away and turned her ankle, and fell sideways.' Her voice was shaking. 'She struck her head on the corner of the hearthstone . . . and . . . she didn't move. Not at all. I stood for a moment, expecting her to rise, but she didn't. She didn't move . . . even to . . . breathe. I bent over her, and that's when I realised she wasn't breathing.'

'You knew that?' Daniel asked.

'I do now. Then I thought . . . I thought she was merely insensible. I stood up and I called for Sarah, my daughter. I knew she was in her own room.'

'Why?'

'I thought she could help me lift her up, maybe put her on the bed, and . . . revive her. I told her to bring smelling salts. They're very sharp. If you faint . . . '

'And did she?'

'Yes, she brought the salts . . . but as soon as she kneeled by the woman and touched her, she realised she was dead. I told her what had happened . . . ' Ebony looked desperate. She had at first refused to involve Sarah at all, but Daniel had told her she would not be believed if she said she had managed to lift the body without any help at all. And to implicate her lady's maid was not only untrue, it was monstrously unfair. And above all, would not be believed. Sarah herself would not allow it.

'And did Sarah help you to change the clothes on the dead woman to those you were wearing? And the boots also?' Daniel prompted.

Grisewood might have objected that Daniel was leading the witness, but he had nothing to gain from it, and sat instead with a half-smile on his face, almost a sneer of disbelief.

'Yes,' Ebony admitted reluctantly.

'When the clothes were changed, you placed her back where she had originally fallen?'

'Yes.'

'You dressed in other clothes, leaving hers in your wardrobe, and then you left the house?'

'Yes.' Ebony's voice was growing fainter as she relived the horror.

'Allowing Sarah to identify the body as yours?'

'Yes.'

'Why? Why did you do that, Miss Cumberford? Why not simply report the death, that she had attacked you, and slipped and fallen?'

'It would have come out who she was . . . and

therefore that I was . . . that my children were illegitimate.'

'Is that all?'

She stared at him with anger in her face, and utter misery. 'No. I was afraid of being beaten again. I was tired of it, and frightened. It hurts when your bones are broken, it hurts appallingly. I . . . I couldn't take it another time.' She did not add that Sarah had persuaded her to, although Sarah had told Daniel that herself. Ebony refused to compromise Sarah any more than she had to.

'The last time you were beaten was just recently, was it not?'

She closed her eyes, as if she could not bear to see the expression of pity and revulsion on people's faces. 'Yes.'

'Did he injure you?'

Grisewood stood up slowly. 'My lord, this is all very heartbreaking, I'm sure, but it is completely unprovable. Even if Miss Cumberford could embarrass us all by showing bruises, there is no proof where she got them, or how. She could have slipped and fallen downstairs.' He shrugged exaggeratedly.

The judge looked at Daniel. This was the moment he had been angling for. He must word it exactly. This chance would not come twice.

'My lord, I understand this is hard to believe, and the whole of Miss Cumberford's story is in the balance, as my learned friend suggests.' Grisewood had not gone so far as to say anything on it — but Daniel had.

'Well, Mr Pitt?' the judge asked.

'I call Miss fford Croft to the stand, my lord.'

'Miss fford Croft?' Grisewood's eyebrows shot up. 'In what capacity?'

Daniel turned to the judge, as if it were he who had asked. 'She has sat the degree examinations at Cambridge in medicine, and in chemistry, my lord. I think that expertise will become apparent.'

'Oh, really!' Grisewood was filled with derision.

The judge looked up at him with dislike, then turned back to Daniel again. 'Is she related to Marcus fford Croft, by any chance?'

'Yes, my lord, she is his daughter.'

'Very well. But you will have to allow Mr Grisewood to cross-examine her when you are finished.' He made it almost a question, giving Daniel time to withdraw if he thought it too much for Miriam. He actually thought Miriam would take him to pieces if he did that!

Miriam was duly sworn and prepared to face Daniel. She was dressed in a deep wine-coloured suit, very plain but so well-tailored it managed to look businesslike and yet very feminine at the same time. She was not as slender as Daniel had remembered, and rather more gracefully curved. Her bright hair was coiled very fashionably. She looked fragile, compared with the sturdiness of Grisewood. Daniel was suddenly afraid for her. Perhaps this was a mistake? He was not willing to sacrifice Miriam, no matter how angry she might be, in order to save Ebony. There had to be another way.

'Mr Pitt?' The judge brought him sharply back to the present.

'Miss fford Croft, would you tell his lordship,

and the court, what expertise you have to give evidence before this court? What have you studied, where, and for how long?' Did his voice sound as shaky and defensive as he felt?

'I studied medicine for some six years, and chemistry for five. At Cambridge, my lord. I passed all my exams with honours.'

'So, you have degrees in both medicine and chemistry?' Daniel prompted.

'No, sir.' She kept the anger from her face, but she could not hide the grief. 'As may be apparent, I am a woman.'

'I see,' said Daniel. 'Or actually I don't see, but I have checked with the university and I know it is true. Thank you, Miss fford Croft.' He turned towards the judge. 'With his lordship's permission, I will now question you regarding your knowledge in this particular case.'

'Proceed.' The judge nodded his head fractionally.

'Yes, my lord.' There was no help for it now, no way except ahead. 'Miss fford Croft, the police surgeon examined the body by the fireplace, and accepted Miss Graves' identification of it as Ebony Graves. In the course of my attempts to defend Mr Graves on the charge of having murdered his wife, did you have cause to examine that body yourself? And if so, what conclusions did you reach?'

Grisewood rose to his feet, and the judge ordered him to sit down before he could raise his objection. 'I will tell the jury to ignore it, if it is irrelevant, Mr Grisewood,' he said sharply. 'Let us hear it first.'

'What did you find, Miss fford Croft?' Daniel asked. He was nervous now, and it was reflected in his voice. He could hear it himself.

'That the burns had been made after death, using linseed oil and oiled silk, and some such thing to ignite, as a safety match, or possibly a taper from the fire,' Miriam replied. 'And a certain amount of cotton had been used to carry the heat and provide fuel. I also X-rayed the bones, and discovered that they had four old, well-healed breaks in them. Three in the hand and arms, one in the ankle.'

'How did you know they were long-healed?' he asked.

'When a bone is healing, the body puts new calcium on the breach, rather as we would put cement on a piece of broken china. It thickens with time, and I have X-rays here that perhaps I will be allowed to show the jury?' She turned to the judge. 'If I may, my lord?' She held up a very large photographic print. He put out his hand.

She deliberately left the witness stand and walked gracefully across the floor of the court, and offered him the photograph, although actually it was shadowy black and white, allowing the light through it — a negative rather than a print.

'Thank you.' He took it and looked at it.

'That is a hand,' she offered. 'It's rather beautiful, is it not? You can see the structure and how many bones there are in it. A most perfect instrument, strong, easily manipulated, delicate, agile and fit for an infinity of purposes.'

The judge smiled. 'You are very enthusiastic in

368

your art, Dr . . . Miss fford Croft.'

'Not *my* art, my lord. God's, or whoever you believe created us. I merely explain.'

She handed him another picture.

He looked at it, then at her. 'What's this? This is not a hand.'

'No, my lord. It is a clavicle, a collarbone, if you like. And this leading off here,' she pointed, 'is a shoulder blade, and you can see the spine behind it.'

'And these white marks?' he asked, frowning at her.

'Here and here?' She looked at him. 'They are places where the bones have been broken. And here. This one was some time ago, it is now healed. This one was more recent. That, I should judge, was less than a year ago.'

He looked startled. 'Good God, what happened to her?'

'I believe she was systematically beaten and abused, my lord.'

'What on earth kind of life did she lead? No wonder she sought to relieve it by making claims on Mr Graves!'

Miriam cleared her throat. 'These are not pictures of Winifred Graves' bones, my lord. These are pictures of the right shoulder and arm of Miss Cumberford — Mrs Graves, as she believed she was, until Winifred turned up. That is when Ebony took the chance to escape, even at such cost to her reputation, her wellbeing, and the temporary loss of her children.'

The judge stared at her, for a moment wordless.

'If I may offer an opinion, my lord,' Miriam continued before the judge could speak. 'I do not think that these shoulders of Miss Cumberford would have had the physical strength to fight Winifred. There are many other injuries, both to fingers and toes, in addition to two broken ribs, a broken ulna — the lower arm — and a broken fibula in the left leg. All of them are healed, but over a space of approximately twenty years.'

'Good God!' exclaimed the judge. 'And do you swear to this, Miss fford Croft?'

'Yes, my lord, but if you have any doubt they can be X-rayed again. The results will be the same.'

'I recall breaking my heel once, when I was a young man. The pain was extraordinary. This woman must have suffered . . . beyond my imagination.'

'Yes, my lord. And been very afraid. I found two broken ribs in Miss Sarah, also. I did not examine Mr Arthur.'

'Show these images to the jury,' said the judge. 'If they have any questions, answer as best you can.'

Daniel remained standing, swinging between hope and despair, while the jury examined the X-rays with fascination. Each, at one time or another, looked across at Graves, then at the white-faced figure of Ebony.

Grisewood started to make some protest, but then thought better of it.

Daniel wondered what it would be, and how he would contain it. Would Graves say he was not responsible? It was preposterous that some other man was systematically beating his first wife, and then his second wife, and then his daughter, and he had not known of it.

Miriam left the X-rays with the jury and returned to the witness stand. The judge offered Grisewood the chance to cross-examine Miriam but he had no questions for her.

The jury stared at her, but in admiration and delight at the complicated and beautiful pictures of bones. Daniel saw at least two of the jurors hold up their own hands and gaze at them, as if marvelling at their beauty, as if they could imagine what existed beneath the ordinary flesh.

The judge requested summations, and they were both brief. Grisewood concentrated on the broken law and the fact that Ebony had acted a lie. But for Daniel, she would have allowed her husband to be hanged.

Daniel rose to his feet. He still had all to win — or lose. He looked at Graves, at the sweat on his face. He must beat him! Not only for Ebony, but for Sarah and Arthur, and for the family of servants. Most of all to him, he must discredit him for his own father's sake, and Narraway, and Aunt Vespasia. And of course, for Kitteridge — and for himself.

'Gentlemen of the jury, which of you has children?' He saw most of them nod. Some smiled. 'When they were young, you would do anything to protect them. When they became older, did you love them any less? If a man threatened your daughter, would you not leap to defend her, and perhaps think afterwards?' Daniel spoke softly, although his voice carried in the silence. 'And her mother? Have you ever tried to tear a child from its mother? Have you not seen a woman labour all day to care for her child, sit up all night to nurse them when they are sick, defend them when they are criticised, rightly or even wrongly? Have you not seen her go without food, and taking her portion to her child? Of course, you have. So have I. As children, we would not survive if our parents did not defend us when we were too small and too weak to defend ourselves. Even a grown man in terror or despair, in unbearable pain, will think of his mother.'

He had said enough and he knew it.

'Ebony Cumberford knew of the beatings, indeed she took most of them herself. But on the day Winifred turned up, and made a lie of Ebony's marriage, the safety of her children, and the future of Sarah's chance at a decent marriage — and more importantly, of Arthur's continued medical treatment without which he couldn't survive — good manners, common sense, consequences to herself vanished. She was a mother defending her children — in Arthur's case, a crippled child who could not possibly defend himself.' He looked at the face of each juror in turn.

'Winifred died trying to attack Ebony,' he continued. 'It was an accident. She fell back on the hearthstone. No one could have attacked her from behind at that angle. She fell down on the stone; it could not have been raised up to strike her. Certainly, Ebony took advantage of the situation and disfigured her and redressed her, so she would be taken for Ebony. And yes, although she did not foresee it at the time, it would not be perceived as the accident it was, but as murder. And Russell Graves was charged with it, and found guilty.' He shook his head. 'Ebony did not plan that. All she planned was to escape the beatings before he finally went too far and killed her. Or one of her children. If she were dead, then who would care for Sarah and Arthur?' Falthorne would do what he could. But Russell Graves could get rid of him with a word, and he would! Then who would look after Arthur? He is in a wheelchair, helpless to care for himself, and Sarah has not the strength to do it alone. Yes, Ebony was wrong. But which of you would do less? She is guilty of having disfigured a dead body. She is not guilty of murder. She came forward before her tormentor was hanged. She let him suffer — perhaps he was even as afraid for a few days as she was most of her life with him. But she did not let him die. I ask you to find her not guilty, certainly of killing Winifred Graves or of knowingly committing bigamy by marrying Russell Graves, only of damaging a corpse, and defending her children with all of her strength.'

The jury retired.

Daniel paced the floor in the hallway outside the courtroom. He could not bring himself to leave, even for a cup of tea or a glass of ale. Kitteridge waited with him. Seemingly, he cared just as much.

'She's damn good, Miriam,' was all Kitteridge said.

'Yes,' Daniel agreed, his throat too tight to say more.

Time seemed to stretch endlessly, but actually it was only just over half an hour when they were called back into the courtroom.

They wouldn't hang her, would they? They couldn't!

Daniel could scarcely breathe.

The foreman rose to his feet. He looked nervous.

'Have you reached a verdict?' the judge enquired.

'We have, my lord.'

'How find you?'

'With respect, my lord, we find the accused not guilty.' Daniel was almost numb with amazement, relief, joy. The first thing he was aware of was Kitteridge hugging him. He immediately hugged him back, and found his eyes were full of tears. It was seconds before he even saw Marcus and, behind him, his father and mother, smiling.

Epilogue

The second Sunday after the trial ended, Mercy Blackwell gave an afternoon tea party. Daniel was one of the first to arrive. The only two other people already present were Marcus fford Croft, looking faintly uncomfortable, and Miriam, who was sitting beside an unnecessarily large fire, for midsummer, and smiling.

'Come in, Daniel! Come in,' Blackwell invited expansively. 'We are celebrating!'

Daniel felt a stir of anxiety. What had Blackwell been up to? 'Really? What, in particular?' The instant he said it, he regretted asking. He would probably be much happier not to know.

'Everything.' Blackwell smiled. 'Graves has been sentenced to seven years for bigamy. I think the judge took a dislike to him. Very natural, after Miss fford Croft's exposure of his wretched character. We shall take great delight in missing him, for a long time. But fortunately, since he is not dead, we do not need to be anxious as to who inherits his property, particularly his house.'

'Houses,' Mercy corrected him. 'Tea, Daniel?'

'Thank you,' he accepted.

She poured him a cup, and cut a large slice of Madeira cake and put it on a plate for him. It was one of his favourites. She did not need to ask.

Daniel turned to Marcus fford Croft. 'Will

Ebony be able to live there? She is not his wife, nor does she wish to be.'

'No, but Arthur is his son,' Marcus fford Croft replied. 'And he is more than willing that his mother and sister should live with him. And, of course, the full family staff. We are expecting them any minute. The purple chair should be comfortable for Arthur.'

'How will he . . . ?' Daniel began.

'Don't fuss!' Blackwell waved away the question. 'Falthorne will carry him. It's good he should see the outside world, for a change.'

'And when Graves comes out?'

'For heaven's sake! We've got at least six years to settle that. Maybe all seven. Anything could happen. We'll have to see that it does.'

There was a knock on the door and Blackwell went to open it. He came back triumphantly, leading Falthorne, who was carrying Arthur in his arms, followed by Ebony Graves and, behind her, Sarah.

Greetings were exchanged and Arthur settled comfortably and was provided with a nearby small table, and hot tea and slices of cake, and a tray of jam tarts.

Daniel went over to speak to Miriam, who seemed to be absorbed in watching the fire burn. Did she feel so alone here, away from her work and both its fascination and its safety? He could think of a dozen things he wanted to say to her, yet none of them came to his lips.

'Is the Madeira cake good?' she said with a wry smile. 'Mercy made it especially for you.'

He looked at her plate and saw that she had

none. 'I'm sorry! How inconsiderate of me. Take mine.' He offered it to her. 'I'll get some more.'

'No, thank you. I've already had a jam tart. They are my weakness.'

'Would you like another?' Now that they had nothing to talk about, he had lost his ease in speaking to her. It had seemed so effortless before.

'Later, perhaps,' she answered. 'Sarah looks a lot better, doesn't she?'

He turned to look, and found Sarah looking back at him, her face filled with gratitude. Arthur, too, turned towards him and smiled, then gazed back at the room and the multitude of pictures, ornaments, and mementoes that filled it.

Kitteridge was the last to arrive. He came in as angular as usual, seeming all legs and elbows and wearing a most flamboyant necktie. Mercy made him welcome and offered him tea and fruitcake, which he accepted warmly, and narrowly missed spilling it over Sarah. He apologised profusely, and she assured him that it was perfectly all right. It was not his fault at all.

A slight flush spread up Kitteridge's cheeks.

Daniel looked away, conscious of staring. It seemed the only thing left to worry about was Graves' manuscript, but that mattered more to him than he dared tell anyone else. They all looked so relieved, he felt selfish to darken the party with his own fears.

Miriam reached forward and gave the fire another dig with the poker, and it seemed to gain new energy.

'Are you cold?' he said incredulously.

'Oh, no, thank you.' She hesitated a moment. 'Are you still worried about the manuscript, Daniel?'

'Yes . . . ' he admitted.

She gave a sweet, gentle smile. 'Don't be,' she said, and gave the fire another sharp prod. 'It will never see the light of day, I promise you.'

'How can you be so sure?' he pressed.

'Daniel, would you reach into the coal scuttle?'

He lifted the lid and his fingers touched a thin pile of paper. He pulled out the last pages of the manuscript. With a flood of relief, he passed them to her. And silently, she fed them to the fire.

ANGELS IN THE GLOOM
AT SOME DISPUTED BARRICADE
WE SHALL NOT SLEEP

THE WILLIAM MONK SERIES:
A SUDDEN FEARFUL DEATH
THE FACE OF A STRANGER
SINS OF THE WOLF
WHITED SEPULCHRES
THE TWISTED ROOT
DEATH OF A STRANGER
THE SHIFTING TIDE
DARK ASSASSIN
EXECUTION DOCK
ACCEPTABLE LOSS
A SUNLESS SEA
AN ECHO OF MURDER